Christmas at Miss Moonshine's Emporium

A festive story anthology from
nine northern romance authors

Mary Jayne Baker • Sophie Claire • Jacqui Cooper
Helena Fairfax • Kate Field • Melinda Hammond
Marie Laval • Helen Pollard • Angela Wren

Published by OPS Publishing

ISBN 978-0-99303-562-3

Cover design and typesetting by Oliphant Author Services
(cover illustrations © Shutterstock)
Edited by Helena Fairfax
Printed and bound by Kindle Direct Publishing

CONTENTS

The Ghost in the Machine

By Mary Jayne Baker

Chapter 1

'Penny in the old man's hat, love? I mean, er, darlin'?'

Scarlett peered at the busker who'd accosted her. His belly was stout with pillow, his cheeks rosy with facepaint. Tucked under his chin, above the pocket watch arranged on a chain across his green velvet waistcoat, was a fiddle.

'I'm sorry?' Scarlett said.

The Mr Bumble lookalike – who, now she examined him, was sporting a peppering of teen pimples around his stuck-on muttonchop whiskers – pointed at a sign announcing he was collecting for a local charity.

'Penny,' the lad said. 'Well, allowing for inflation and everything, so maybe a quid. All for a good cause, like.' He paused. 'Er, lor' love a duck, guv'nor, and no mistake.'

Scarlett laughed at the cod cockney delivered in a broad Yorkshire accent. 'Good effort, kid. All right, here.' She threw a pound into a battered top hat at the boy's feet and he struck up a tuneless wail on his violin.

It was a fortnight before Christmas. Geese were getting fat, wallets thin, and the little town of Haven Bridge was bustling with bustles, crammed with crinolines and packed with pantaloons as visitors descended on the place for its annual

Dickensian Christmas Festival. Scarlett Greenwood was the intrepid *Yorkshire Enquirer* reporter who'd been assigned the unenviable job of writing the whole ghastly business up for her paper.

Not that there were many of them picking out short straws these days. Scarlett was one of only a handful of staff correspondents still left at the *Enquirer*.

It hadn't always been that way. At thirty-two, Scarlett was too young to have worked during the newspaper's Golden Age, but she did remember when staff numbers had been treble what they were now. Over the years she'd watched the *Enquirer* downsize, get sold to new owners and downsize again. One by one old colleagues had disappeared, until only a skeleton staff remained.

Scarlett's grandad had been the *Enquirer*'s editor way back when. He shook his head when she visited him at the hospice to tell him about the latest batch of lay-offs.

'It's the damn internet,' he grunted. 'No one wants the news a day after it's happened. They want it at their fingertips, as it's occurring. It's all Twitter and clickbait and citizen journalism now. Scarlett, your kids' kids won't even know what a newspaper is.' He paused to cough into a handkerchief. 'Dying breed, that's us, lass.'

Scarlett knew it was true, but what could she do? This was all she'd ever wanted to do, and she'd cling on until the bitter end.

And if this was the end, it certainly was bitter, she thought, as she grimaced at a market stall selling a horrific array of stuffed animals.

'So these are… interesting,' she said to the stallholder, trying not to meet the creepy glass gaze of a morose-looking stoat. 'Do you, um, do them yourself?'

The woman in the frilled bonnet nodded eagerly. 'Yes, it's

a fascinating hobby. Might you be interested in my classes on ethical taxidermy?'

Pickle your own roadkill, fun for all the family. Lovely.

'I'm afraid I'm only in town for a few days,' Scarlett said. 'Could I get a pic? For the *Enquirer*?'

Norman Bates's terrifying sister agreed and Scarlett took the photo before moving on to the next stall.

This one was more palatable. It was covered with handmade items – paperweights, fans, jewellery – intricately painted with swirling floral patterns. Scarlett picked up a brooch in deep peacock blue and watched rainbows dance in the embedded stones.

'These are gorgeous,' she muttered.

The woman behind the stall beamed at her. 'Thanks, I make them myself. Can I interest you? Perfect Christmas gift.'

Scarlett couldn't think who on her sparse present list would appreciate a brooch, but it was a pretty thing. She nodded and fumbled in her handbag for some cash.

'Not from round here?' the woman said as she bagged up the brooch.

Scarlett smiled. 'Shows, does it?'

'Just a vibe I'm getting. I'm Callie, by the way.'

'Scarlett.'

'So are you in town for the festival, Scarlett?' Callie asked, handing over the paper bag.

'Yes, although it's work, not pleasure. I'm writing it up for the *Enquirer*.'

'And do I sense you're not keen?'

Scarlett glanced down the packed street, bulging with market stalls selling everything from Christmas wreathes to home-brewed ale. The air was stifling, oppressively scented with cloves and roasted chestnuts. She took a deep breath through her mouth, trying to absorb some oxygen molecules that weren't cinnamon-flavoured.

'Nothing personal. I'm just not big on crowds,' she told Callie. 'Hey, do you know any good pubs? I need somewhere to eat tonight.'

'The Packhorse does nice meals.' Callie pulled a face. 'Be sure to go before half-seven though, or you'll be subjected to the delights of karaoke night. No out-of-towner deserves that.'

'Uh-huh.' Scarlett was only half listening. Her gaze had settled on an old building a little way down the street. An arch wreathed with festive red and white flowers led to a courtyard area, with a flickering chandelier in the window casting sinister shadows onto the cobbles.

'Eerie-looking place,' she said. 'What is it, a shop?'

'Yeah, Miss Moonshine's. It used to be a church, in the dim and distant past.'

'How come it's open?' Every other shop in town was closed for the festival, their owners out selling their wares on stalls.

'Oh, Miss Moonshine's is always open,' Callie said. 'Or it's never open. Ask anyone in Haven Bridge and you'll get a different story.'

Scarlett frowned. 'I don't understand.'

'No. No one does, really.' Callie smiled as she started arranging necklaces on a stand. 'Sorry if I sound like I'm talking in riddles. Miss Moonshine's is a bit of a local enigma.'

'Looks like your standard unloved tat shop to me.'

'That's what I thought the first time I saw it. Still, it's thanks to Miss Moonshine that I met Richard, my fiancé. I'm not the only one with a story like that to tell either.' She looked up. 'I'd think twice about going in if I were you. It might just change your life.'

Scarlett laughed. 'Well now I have to, don't I? Otherwise I'll look as superstitious as you, and I rather pride myself on being a bitter, jaded old cynic.'

Callie shrugged. 'Don't say I didn't warn you.'

Simultaneously intrigued and irritated for allowing herself to get reeled in by what was obviously some local fairy story concocted to impress the tourists, Scarlett pushed her way through the crowd of fake Victorians to the shop.

It was an odd little place. The front window was packed with such an assortment of mismatched items that it looked more like someone's attic clear-out than a shop. Art deco lamps, china teapots, phrenology heads, old barometers…

Still, there was something enticing about it. It seemed to make everything else – even the sounds and smells of the busy Dickensian market – disappear into the background.

A bell jangled over the door as Scarlett entered. She squinted into the gloom, waiting for her eyesight to adjust.

'Hiya. Can I help you?'

The deep tones that greeted her didn't quite match Scarlett's idea of the shop's proprietor. She blinked at the figure in front of her, trying to bring it into focus.

It was a figure worth bringing into focus, she discovered when her eyes had caught up. Tall, broad, with warm brown eyes and a head of scruffy jet-black hair. A Santa hat sat jauntily on the man's head.

'So you're the mysterious Miss Moonshine,' Scarlett said. 'You know, you're not at all what I was expecting.'

He laughed. 'No, just the Saturday boy. Miss Moonshine's my aunt. Were you looking for something specific?'

Was she? For the life of her, Scarlett couldn't think why she'd decided to come in. She was supposed to be outside, talking to stallholders and getting photos for Owen, her editor – not sneezing in the inch-thick dust of decades' worth of unsellable junk. Damn it, she never could resist a mystery.

'No, just browsing,' she said.

'Fill your boots. Although word of warning, we're closing soon. If you want to buy anything, better make it quick.'

So much for Callie's 'always open, never open' daftness. It was amazing how Chinese whispers could evolve into the stuff of legend in these little towns.

Scarlett wandered among the shelves, examining the mismatched items. Some were really stunning, she thought, as she delicately touched her fingertips to an ornate ebony music box. Others deserved to perish in petrol and flames. She shuddered at a marionette with a Chucky-like expression of joyful homicide twinkling from its painted pupils.

Scarlett cursed as she almost tripped over a stuffed dog, curled in a sleeping position on the floor.

'Good God, what a gremlin,' she said, bending to examine it. 'It's not from that ethical taxidermy woman, is it?'

'No, it's an old family heirloom,' the shop assistant told her. 'Go ahead, feel it. You'll be amazed how lifelike it is.'

Scarlett placed a tentative finger on the thing's fur, then yelped as its eyes shot open and it bared its little teeth to her.

The man laughed. 'Sorry, I couldn't help myself. This is Nappy – short for Napoleon, not because he's permanently asleep. Say hi, Nappy.'

Napoleon glared at her before going back to sleep.

'That was a dirty trick,' Scarlett said.

He grinned. 'Made you smile though, didn't I?'

'No.'

'Yeah? Then why's your mouth twitching like that?'

Scarlett gave in and let herself smile. 'All right, don't get smug. Aren't you a bit old for a Saturday boy?'

He shrugged. 'It's only temporary. This time next year, Rodders, I'll be a millionaire. I'm working on a guaranteed bestseller.'

'You're a writer?'

'I try to be. How about you?'

'Journalist. I'm reporting on the festival for the *Enquirer*.'

The man raised his eyebrows. 'Wow. A writer who actually earns money. Any tips?'

'Yeah. Don't get into it for the money.'

He held out a hand. 'Lucas Pickering.'

'Scarlett Greenwood,' she said, shaking it. 'Don't.'

'Don't what?'

'There's a *Gone With the Wind* gag heading my way, I can see it in your eyes. Trust me, I've heard them all and I resent my parents accordingly.'

'No, I like it. Exotic.'

She laughed. 'Well, I think the "Greenwood" rather takes the shine off.'

'That's a proper local surname, you know. Haven't got Haven Bridge connections, have you?'

'Not that I know of. I'm a Leeds girl.'

Scarlett's gaze fell on something in one corner and she approached it to take a closer look.

'Lucas, this is beautiful,' she murmured.

'Isn't it?' Lucas's voice, too, had sunk to a reverent whisper. 'I've been begging my aunt to let me buy that for years, but she won't part with it. She just keeps it in the shop for atmosphere, she says.'

Scarlett ran her fingers along the old typewriter. It was in remarkable condition for something that must be at least eighty. Each glass key was polished to a factory shine, with the word *WOODSTOCK* and the company logo – a majestic eagle with wings outstretched – picked out in gilt above the carriage.

'Not that I could really afford to buy it,' Lucas said. 'A Woody in this condition must be worth a fair bit. But since I was a kid, I've loved the old thing. I used to imagine all the stuff that might've been typed on it. Stories, poems, letters. Their echoes trapped inside, like –'

'– like ghosts,' Scarlett murmured.

He looked at her, frowning. 'Er, yeah.'

She shook her head to dislodge the fog that had filled it and turned to smile at him. 'You really are a writer, aren't you?'

'The king of purple prose, that's me.'

'Lucas?' a voice called. 'Have you turned the sign, my love?'

'Not yet, Aunty. I'm serving someone,' he called back.

'Well, please tell her to hurry up. I'm going to be late.'

'So did you want to buy anything?' Lucas asked Scarlett with an apologetic smile. 'Sorry, but we were supposed to close ten minutes ago.'

'Oh. No, I –'

She was interrupted by Napoleon, galloping across the floor and yapping frantically.

'Aww. Did someone miss his mummy?' crooned the old lady who'd appeared at the foot of the stairs. She picked up the little chihuahua and he snuggled contentedly into her arms.

Scarlett tried not to stare, but she couldn't help it. This had to be the oddest-looking individual she'd ever seen. Certainly the one with the weirdest fashion sense.

Miss Moonshine had a shock of white hair, fluffed beehive-like on top of her head like an elderly Dusty Springfield tribute act. She was dressed in a long, black-fringed dress that would have suited the widowed dowager in an Agatha Christie, complete with string of pearls. And on her feet, a pair of massive Doc Marten boots.

How old was she? If someone had told Scarlett the woman was sixty, she wouldn't have been surprised. If someone had told her she was nearly a hundred, Scarlett still wouldn't have been surprised.

'Miss Moonshine, I take it?'

The old lady glanced up from fussing Napoleon. Her mouth twitched.

'So you're here,' she said softly.

Scarlett blinked. 'Er, yes. I appear to be.'

There was silence while Miss Moonshine looked her up and down.

'Look, could we make this quick, dear?' she said eventually. 'I've got a poker game to get to.'

'You play poker?'

'Oh no, I never play.' Miss Moonshine's hazel eyes glinted. 'I win.'

Scarlett regarded her for a moment. 'Huh. I believe you.'

She followed Miss Moonshine's gaze to her own fingers, still resting on the typewriter.

'Oh.' She jerked her hand away. 'Sorry. I didn't mean to touch it, I just… sorry.'

'You wish to buy my Woodstock, do you?'

'No. I mean, I know it's not for sale, your nephew told me. And I doubt I could afford it if it was.' Scarlett turned to look at it, feeling a strange thrill. When her grandad had been a junior reporter, newsrooms would have been filled with rows of machines like this, clacking away as journalists rushed to file their copy before deadline. 'It's a lovely item though.'

'Isn't it? It's been with me ever so long now.' Miss Moonshine cast a fond glance at the typewriter. 'Well, my dear, I'm afraid we really must close up. Do come again.'

Chapter 2

'Oh, Scarlett,' Gloria said, when Scarlett got back to her lodgings that evening. 'Your package arrived.'

With her wife Christine, Gloria ran the Old Smithy B&B, where Scarlett was booked in for the duration of her stay in Haven Bridge.

Scarlett frowned. 'Package?'

'Yes, we put it in your room. It was a bit heavy, but me and Chris managed it between us.'

'But I'm not expecting any package.'

'Well someone left it in the porch, addressed to you. We assumed it must be from your newspaper.'

Full of curiosity, Scarlett galloped upstairs, Gloria following. She unlocked her room and headed to the parcel on the desk. But she could guess what was inside, even as she tore off the brown paper.

'Oh, how lovely,' Gloria cooed from the doorway. 'A typewriter. My grandad had one like that. Where did it come from?'

'Moonshine,' Scarlett muttered.

'Pardon?'

'Miss Moonshine. The old lady who owns that manky shop in town. I was there earlier and…' Scarlett shook her head. 'She told me it wasn't for sale.'

'Ah well, she's a funny old stick. She'd say that just because it isn't for sale doesn't mean it isn't for you.'

'Don't you start. I've had enough fairytales today to last a lifetime.' Scarlett drew her fingers over the black glass keys, experiencing that same urge to touch the thing as she had in the shop. 'How did she get it here?'

'I don't know, love. No one knocked. It just appeared.'

'But how did she *know* to get it here? I never told her where I was staying. I never even told her my name.'

'Well, our Miss Moonshine has a way of –'

'Yes, I know, Miss Moonshine has a way of knowing stuff and changing lives and so on. But here in the world of things that are actually possible, how did she know?' Scarlett frowned. 'That writer bloke, Lucas. He could've told her my name. I don't suppose it's hard to find out where someone's staying in a small town like this.'

'Why should Miss Moonshine want to give you a type-writer?'

'No idea. It must be worth good money.' Scarlett tore her gaze from the Woodstock. 'Sorry if I was abrupt just now, Gloria. It's been a long day.'

'No offence taken, pet.'

The landlady turned to go.

'Gloria?' Scarlett said, before she could disappear.

'Yes?'

'This is going to sound like an odd question, but... do you mind if I ask how you and Christine met?'

She turned back, smiling. 'Ah, now there's a tale.'

'Go on.'

'Well, Chris had bought herself this lucky charm bracelet. Only as soon as she put it on, it brought her nothing but bad luck. First she lost her housekey. Then she missed the bus to her sister's to pick up the spare. And when she tried walking there, she ended up spraining her ankle.' Gloria laughed. 'And her final piece of bad luck was that the only person around to offer a supportive shoulder was me. That was fifteen years ago and she's still stuck with me.'

'Do you know where she got the bracelet?'

'From the emporium, of course. Miss Moonshine's, I mean.'

'I had a feeling you might say that.' Scarlett summoned a smile. 'Thanks, Gloria. That's a sweet story.'

When Gloria had gone, Scarlett examined her new typewriter. Once she'd located a serial number, she took out her phone to Google it.

This Woodstock was a 1922 model, she established. How could something not far off its centenary look as new as this? It was uncanny.

Scarlett found herself remembering what Lucas had said earlier. All the stories it had told, their echoes trapped inside, like shadows… like ghosts. Shuddering, she grabbed a towel and covered the thing up.

She almost leapt out of the window when her phone burst into melody.

'Owen,' she said, patting her heart. 'What's up?'

'Just checking up on you, out there in yokel land,' her editor said. 'Did they wheel out the wicker man yet?'

'Funny.'

'You OK, Scar? You sound a bit wobbly.'

'Do you have to call me Scar, Owen? It makes me sound like a women's prison inmate.'

'I know, it suits you. So what's up?'

'Nothing.' Scarlett sank onto the bed and rested her head on her palm. 'Ugh, I need to get out of this place. It's sending me strange.'

'You were already strange.'

'Well, stranger then.'

'How the Dickens are you getting on?' He laughed at his own joke. 'You see what I did there?'

'You rang me just to crack that, didn't you?'

'No, I rang to remind you I need a thousand words of copy and at least eight decent photos by end of play tomorrow. So how's the festival?'

'Tacky as hell.' She grimaced. 'This morning I got attacked by the Ghost of Christmas Yet to Come.'

'Attacked?'

'Well, sort of. The guy in the costume was struggling with his stilts and careered into me. Honestly, you don't know fear until you've had an eight-foot skeleton in a hooded robe bearing down on you with a sharpened scythe.'

He laughed. 'See? And you thought this job wouldn't be fun.'

'Did you have to send me, Owen? You know I hate these naff costumed events.'

'I sent you for your own good, darling.'

Scarlett frowned. 'You what?'

'What're you doing for Christmas this year, Scar?'

'Dunno. Drinking Bailey's until I fall down, probably.'

'You haven't booked a single day off. I bet you'd come into the office on Christmas Day if I let you, wouldn't you?'

'Maybe. Why, are you going to?'

'Scarlett, you work too hard. Relax a bit, eh? Treat this weekend as a holiday. You never know, you might get a taste for the things.'

'Hmm. My idea of a holiday tends to involve a lot more mojitos and a lot fewer street urchins.'

'Just take a bit of downtime while you're away. I don't want you burning out.'

Scarlett laughed. 'Says the man who rang to remind me I've got a deadline tomorrow.'

'Oh, you'll pump out the fluff piece in no time. Why don't you do it tonight? Then you can take tomorrow off to enjoy the festival.'

'Enjoy the festival. Now that is funny.'

Scarlett's gaze wandered the room as they talked. For some reason, it always came back to the towel-covered typewriter. Something had been nagging at her ever since the afternoon: her reporter's Spidey sense tingling.

'Owen. Suppose I could actually get you a decent story while I was here?' she said.

'About what?'

'Kind of a local legend. There's… this shop.'

'Right. This isn't exactly blowing me away, Scarlett.'

'It would if you were here. The whole town's steeped in this thing. There's an old lady and she matchmakes for the people who buy stuff from her tatty shop.' She glanced at the typewriter again. 'The locals seem convinced there's a touch of magic about her.'

'What, like a witch?'

'Or a fairy godmother.'

Owen laughed. 'OK, now I know you need a holiday. We're the *Yorkshire Enquirer*, Scar, not the *National Enquirer*. When did you start believing in all that rubbish?'

'Don't be daft, of course I don't believe it. But don't you think it could be a good little quirk piece for Christmas? The magic matchmaker and her mysterious shop? It definitely got my story nose twitching – you were the one who taught me never to ignore that.'

She could practically hear him shaking his head. 'Never thought I'd see the day Scarlett Greenwood started believing in magic.'

'I told you, I just –'

There was a faint click, and the room was plunged into darkness.

'That's weird,' Scarlett muttered.

'What is?'

'The lights just went out. One of the old dears who runs the place must've tripped a fuse. Better go, Owen.'

'OK, talk later. And try to relax, will you?' He hung up.

There was a knock at the door. Scarlett opened it to Gloria's wife Christine, who was clutching a candle stub in a Wee Willie Winkie-style holder. It was probably the most authentically Dickensian thing she'd seen all day.

'You OK?' Christine asked, putting it down on the desk.

'I'm fine,' Scarlett said. 'What's going on, Christine? Do you need to borrow money for the meter?'

The landlady laughed. 'No, it's a power cut, I'm afraid. We get them quite often in this part of town.'

'How long do they normally last?'

'Minutes sometimes, hours others. We've got used to keeping a stock of candles in.'

Scarlett sighed. 'Well, nothing to be done, I suppose. Thanks for the candle.'

'You're welcome, love.' She cast a glance at the towel-shrouded Woodstock, throwing flickering shadow-shapes across the desk in the candlelight. 'It's a bit creepy, that thing, isn't it?'

'You're telling me,' Scarlett muttered as Christine disappeared.

Ugh, she was being ridiculous. It was only a typewriter. Why was she letting this Moonshine nonsense get under her skin?

She went to the desk and jerked the towel away to reveal the Woodstock in all its glory, the candle flame dancing in the polished black enamel.

'There,' Scarlett said. 'I'm not afraid of you. See? You're just cogs and bolts and – and sprockets, whatever a sprocket is. And OK, so I'm talking to a typewriter, but it's been a long day and I'm really quite tired so… look, just shut up, all right?'

Scarlett was filled again with an instinctive compulsion to touch the thing, like a mother bonding with a newborn. She pressed her index finger to one of the metal strikers and pushed until an L was imprinted on her skin.

When she drew it away, it was shining black.

'Ink,' she muttered. 'Huh. She put a fresh ribbon in. Just what is your game, Miss Moonshine?'

She wiped her finger and went to sit on the bed with her laptop, preparing to type her festival notes up into a feature. But when she tapped the power button, nothing happened.

Dead battery. Typical. And no power to charge it up. Muttering under her breath, she left the room and groped her way downstairs.

She found Gloria and Christine in the lounge, organising a game of Snakes and Ladders for the other guests. A couple of kids looked rather thrilled at the idea of a board-game night by candlelight. Scarlett smiled, remembering the excitement of a power cut when she was little herself.

'Are you here to join us, Scarlett?' Christine asked. 'The more the merrier.'

'Er, no. I was just wondering, is there a café with power sockets in town? My laptop's dead and I've got an article to write.'

Gloria shook her head. 'The only places open at this time of night will be the pubs.'

'Do they have sockets for customers?'

'I don't think so. Sorry.'

She sighed. This wasn't the city, was it? Of course they didn't.

'OK, thanks,' she said.

'Anything else we can do for you?'

Scarlett paused, looking down at her smudged finger. Inky fingers had been the telltale sign of her trade, once upon a time.

Damn it, she was still a reporter, wasn't she? And a reporter always got her story. Or was that Mounties?

Well, they never missed a deadline anyway. Not if they worked for the *Enquirer*.

'There is one thing,' she said. 'Have you got any paper?'

*

'Right,' she said, feeding a sheet of A4 into the Woodstock. 'We'll have no more magical thinking, Greenwood. It's a machine, that's all. You just need to churn out a thousand words of crowd-pleasing fluff you can scan in later, then you can go out for food.'

Half an hour later, when Gloria and Christine called up to see if she needed a fresh candle, Scarlett was resting her face on the desk and groaning softly.

Gloria frowned. 'Are you OK, Scarlett?'

'No. I'm in pain.' She held up her hands. 'Look at that, fingers like raw pork sausages. How did reporters cope in the old days? These keys are *evil*.'

'Did you write your article?' Christine asked.

Wordlessly Scarlett yanked the paper out of the machine and handed it to her.

'"All work and no play makes Scarlett a dull girl. All work and no play makes Scarlett a dull girl. All work and…" Oh dear,' Christine said. 'Gone the full Jack Torrance, have we? Glory, we must remember to hide the firewood axe.'

'If Miss Moonshine gave me this thing for a bit of magical inspiration, she should ask for her money back,' Scarlett mumbled. 'She'll need it when I send her the medical bill for my mangled sausage fingers.'

Gloria smiled. 'Look, why don't you go out for a bit? Buy yourself a nice meal at one of the pubs. Maybe inspiration will strike over a Yorkshire pudding and a glass of wine.'

'You know what? That sounds amazing.' Scarlett roused herself and stood up to grab her jacket.

Chapter 3

Scarlett breathed a deep sigh as she sauntered through the narrow streets. A low rumble in her stomach reminded her she hadn't eaten since breakfast – the constant smell of roasting chestnuts had killed her appetite for lunch – but ravenous as she was, she didn't want to waste the crisp winter evening.

Haven Bridge nights weren't like the nights of the city, which shone even brighter than the day. Night-time here was pocketed and patched, stitched with light. The houseboats on the canal cast shimmering spears of illumination into the water, and the black silhouettes of hills and mill chimneys hemmed the town in like a little self-contained universe.

What was that pub Callie had recommended? The Packhorse? Scarlett looked up the address on her phone and headed in the direction of the river.

As much as she wasn't the world's biggest Christmas fan,

she had to admit she loved a proper old-fashioned pub in the wintertime. There was nothing like a blazing fire, oak beams strung with fairy lights and the tempting aroma of home-cooked food when outside was cold and bleak. She knew as soon as she laid eyes on it that The Packhorse was her sort of cosy country pub.

But Scarlett was destined to be disappointed in her desire for a quiet night. As soon as she entered, she was hit by a wave of noise. It would've been a bit of a stretch to call it singing.

Ugh, karaoke night. She'd totally forgotten Callie's warning.

Well, it was too late to find anywhere else now. Most places would stop serving food soon, if they hadn't already. She'd just have to grin and bear it.

The bleach-blond mullet king behind the mike, sixty-four if he was a day and looking like the lovechild of Pat Sharp and Pat Butcher, thrust his hips to the beat like a randy human metronome as he murdered Rod Stewart's 'Do Ya Think I'm Sexy?'. Scarlett claimed herself a table out of sight. She could still hear him, unfortunately, but at least she wouldn't have to put up with an eyeful of pelvis while she ate.

'Roast beef sandwich, please, and a glass of merlot,' she said to the waitress who came to take her order. She'd decided a sandwich was best, so if the next performer was as bad as this one she could grab it and go.

As it turned out though, the next singer was actually quite good. His version of 'Never Gonna Give You Up' was very easy on the ear. So much so, in fact, that Scarlett abandoned her tea to peep round the bar and get a look at him.

As soon as she'd caught a glimpse, she jerked out of sight. The scruffy black hair and Santa hat were all too familiar.

Lucas. Scarlett started wolfing down what was left of her sandwich, keen to get out before he spotted her.

She was just swallowing the last of her wine when he appeared and pulled up a chair opposite.

'You shouldn't eat so fast,' he said.

'And you shouldn't make personal comments about people's eating habits.'

He blinked. 'OK. Sorry. Just a joke.'

'What're you doing here?'

'I work here.'

'As what, a club singer?'

He laughed. 'Barman. I finished my shift an hour ago, but I always stick around for karaoke night.'

'Is there anywhere in this town you don't work?'

'Hey. We skint artistes need to eat, you know. Do I sense you're not very pleased to see me?'

'Hmm.' Scarlett nodded at his Santa hat. 'Don't you ever take that thing off?'

'Well, the family usually stage an intervention if I keep it on past Easter.'

'Couldn't you get a top hat or something?'

He shook his head. 'My aunt never lets us join in with the Dickens Festival. She says old Charlie would pitch a fit if he saw how they're mangling his work.'

'Knew him well, did she?'

'You know, it wouldn't surprise me,' he said. 'So, how's my Woody?'

She raised an eyebrow.

'OK, I could have phrased that better,' he conceded, laughing. 'Not a sleazy chat-up, I promise. It just slipped out.'

'This isn't getting any better, Lucas.'

'Come on, how is it? Did you use it yet?'

'What's it to you?'

'Look, did I upset you or something? You've gone all prickly.' He took a sip of his pint. 'It was the singing, wasn't it? I scare off too many women that way.'

She relaxed slightly. 'No. Sorry. It's… look, Lucas, I feel like

I'm drowning in the Twilight Zone here. Why did your aunt send me a typewriter?'

He shrugged. 'Who knows why she does anything? I'd just go with it if I were you, it's easier.'

'She said it wasn't for sale.'

'And she was right, wasn't she? You didn't pay for it.'

Scarlett shook her head. 'You are one weird family. Are you magic too, or just her?'

He smiled. 'You've been listening to gossip.'

'Hard to avoid it.'

'Well, I like to think I'm pretty magic,' he said. 'Although we're not really family. Miss Moonshine's an honorary aunty – old friend of my mum and dad's. I'm her godson.'

'Let me guess. She introduced them to each other.'

'Good guess,' he said, smiling. 'She did, yes.'

'She must have a lot of godchildren,' Scarlett muttered.

'You're right, she has. But I'm her favourite.'

'So what's with the karaoke?'

'Just a way of letting off steam,' he said, shrugging. 'You ever try it? It's great for stress relief.'

'Me, are you kidding?'

'Come on, it's fun. How about a duet? "Don't Go Breaking My Heart", I'll let you be Elton?'

She laughed. 'Sorry, it's a pass on humiliating myself in front of a roomful of strangers. But kudos for managing to rickroll a whole pub.'

'Now that's better. I could almost believe you liked me.' He drained the last of his pint. 'And I'm out of beer, which means I'm going to the bar and you're going to let me buy you a drink.'

'You should let me buy you one. You're the impoverished author.'

'True, and you just stole my favourite typewriter. But since you were so nice about my rickrolling, I'm going to insist.'

As she watched him walk away, Santa hat bouncing merrily, she found she was smiling. In the city Scarlett always felt she was wound about as tight as she'd go, but Lucas's laid-back attitude to life seemed to have a calming effect on her.

'So what do you like to do other than work?' he asked when he got back with their drinks.

'I don't really.'

'What, no hobbies?'

She shrugged, taking a sip of her wine. 'I'm lucky, I actually enjoy my job. Not everyone gets to have that.'

'Well yeah, but there're other things in life. I mean, I love what I do as well but I don't just write.'

'I noticed,' she said, smiling. 'But you're still not getting me to sing.'

He laughed. 'Any exciting plans for Christmas then?'

'Not really. My parents always go away somewhere hot, so I just tend to mooch around my flat.'

'Seriously, on Christmas Day? Scarlett, that's the saddest thing I ever heard.'

'OK, well now I feel pathetic.'

'And it's just you? No boyfriend or girlfriend, flatmate, anything like that?'

'No,' she said, wondering if that was a sneaky attempt to find out if she was attached. 'Just me.'

'I mean it, you're breaking my heart here. Don't you have family you could go to?'

'I used to spend it with my grandad before he went into hospice care. Other than that, there's just my sister, and she's got her own family. I don't fancy sitting there like the ghost at the feast.'

'What about friends?'

'There's Owen, I suppose – my editor. Not sure how his boyfriend would feel if I turned up on the doorstep demanding

Christmas dinner.' She frowned. 'He actually is kind of my best friend. Never thought about it before.'

'Your best friend's your boss?'

'Yeah. Sad, I know.'

'I guess you hate this time of year then.'

She shrugged. 'More indifference than hatred. I'm used to my own company.'

'Not at Christmas though.' The look of disbelief in Lucas's eyes made her smile.

'Even at Christmas. It's just another day.' She finished her wine. 'Anyway, thanks for the drink.'

He looked up as she stood to leave. 'You sure I can't tempt you to a duet? "Fairytale of New York", I'll let you be Shane McGowan? Actually, there is a resemblance.'

She laughed. 'Enticing, but no. I need my bed.'

'All right, here.' He plucked the Santa hat off his head and handed it to her. 'Present to get you in the festive mood.'

'Oh. Um, thanks.' She stuffed it into her handbag and left.

*

In her bed at the re-electrified Old Smithy, Scarlett glanced at the sheet of typescript in the Woodstock, reminding her over and over that *all work and no play makes Scarlett a dull girl*.

Perhaps she did need a holiday. It had to be stress that was sending her imagination into overdrive.

She winced when she remembered the nonsensical feature on Miss Moonshine she'd pitched to Owen earlier. How ridiculous must she have sounded? No wonder he thought she was losing her touch. And very possibly her marbles.

A picture appeared in her mind of Lucas's smiling face as they'd chatted at the pub. She couldn't help but envy his carefree, unhurried way of living. Maybe she'd take a holiday here in Haven Bridge, see if it would rub off. As hostile as she'd been to coming, the place was starting to feel oddly like home.

She flicked off the bedside lamp and fell into a dreamless sleep. Glinting in a chink of light from a lamp-post outside, the eagle on the Woodstock seemed to smile.

Chapter 4

'And how are we today?' Gloria asked when Scarlett appeared in the dining room next morning.

'Ugh, don't ask.' She massaged her temples. 'Two wines at the pub and I feel like death. Aches and pains, headache… I must be getting old.'

'Well, I'm sure it's nothing one of Chris's fry-ups won't fix.' Gloria ushered her into a seat.

'That does sound good. But I'd love a coffee first.'

'Right you are.'

Gloria bustled away, emerging from the kitchen minutes later with a steaming cafetière. Scarlett's nostrils twitched at the welcome aroma of fresh coffee.

'You know, love, you really shouldn't work so late,' Gloria said as she poured her a cup. 'I'm not surprised you're tired, up till all hours on that ancient contraption. I wonder you didn't use your laptop once the lecky was back on.'

Scarlett frowned. 'Sorry, what?'

'Christine said she could still hear you clacking away when she came to bed at midnight. Anyway, I'm glad you got your article done.'

'What? But I –' Scarlett pushed the coffee away, feeling suddenly nauseous. 'You know, I'm actually not all that hungry. Never mind the fry-up, I'll grab a bacon butty off one of the stalls.'

She hurried from the room, Gloria staring after her.

*

Scarlett fought her way through the Dickensian throng to Miss Moonshine's shop.

'Closed,' she muttered when she got there. 'Of course it is. Open when you don't want it, closed when you need it. It's a wonder the place makes any money.'

She headed to the stall where the woman she'd met yesterday, Callie, was selling her craft pieces.

'Hi again,' Callie said. 'Something up?'

'Miss Moonshine – will she be open today?'

'Who knows? She's a law unto herself, that woman. Why, were you looking for her?'

'Not her.' Scarlett patted the back pocket of her jeans. 'I thought Lucas might be working. Do you know where I could find him?'

She pointed in the direction of St John's Church. 'You could try the graveyard. He's often in there at the weekends.'

'Really? How come?'

'He makes rubbings of the gravestones. Says the inscriptions give him story inspiration.'

'Oh. Right. Thanks, I'll take a look.'

Callie was right. When Scarlett reached the churchyard, she found Lucas examining an ornate monument near the church door.

'Scarlett, come read this,' he said without looking round.

Scarlett joined him and examined the inscription engraved onto a stone scroll borne aloft by winged cherubs.

EMILY SHAW, 1905–1924
I love thee with a love I seemed to lose
With my lost saints. I love thee with the breath,
Smiles, tears, of all my life; and, if God choose,
I shall but love thee better after death.

'Elizabeth Barrett Browning,' Lucas said. 'Poor lass, she was only a kid – Emily, I mean. I'd love to tell her story.'

'It sounds like someone loved her a lot.'

'Someone did.' He turned to face her. 'And that's the big mystery I'm trying to get to the bottom of.'

'What is?' Scarlett asked, interested in spite of the mystery she needed to solve herself.

'That's just it. I don't know.' He nodded to a nearby bench and they took a seat. 'All I've been able to find out is that Emily Shaw was a working-class girl who died from pregnancy complications. Unmarried.'

'Working-class?' Scarlett looked at the elaborate monument with its scroll and cherubs. 'But that's the fanciest grave in here.'

'Exactly. Emily's family worked in the textile mills. They could never have afforded a memorial like that.'

'A wealthy lover, do you think?'

'I did, yes. But I've investigated every option for well-off squires around here and I can't find evidence any of them would even have met Emily, let alone be willing to compromise their position by drawing attention to an affair with a mill girl.' He frowned at the frost-encrusted grass for a moment, then looked up. 'But sorry, I'm rambling. Are you OK? You look knackered.'

'Mmm. Apparently I had a late one last night after the pub.'

'How do you mean, apparently?'

She looked at him. 'Lucas, I can trust you, can't I? I mean, if I tell you something completely insane, you won't think I'm… well, completely insane?'

'Try me.'

Scarlett reached into her back pocket and handed him a sheet of paper covered in type. 'Here, read this. Read it aloud, I haven't absorbed it yet.'

'"Dearest",' he began. '"I'm sorry. I ought to have tried harder. If you were here to make things right, I'd do everything to convince you to have me. Oh, why did you have to be so stubborn? I *loved* you! You, not duty or honour or any of the hateful words you threw in my face the last time I was ever to see you. And now there's nothing left for me, except memories. Choosy, chancy, temperamental memory, but darling, believe me – I will remember you, fully and completely and every day for the rest of my life. Your William". Lucas looked up. 'What is this, Scarlett? Did you write it?'

'So I understand.'

He shook his head. 'I'm not getting this. Explain.'

'Right. OK.' She took a deep breath. 'Lucas, have you ever heard of a James Bond novel called *Take Over*?'

He blinked. 'All right, rather abrupt change of subject but I'll go with it. No I haven't. Who was in the film?'

'No one. I mean, it wasn't one. Ian Fleming wrote it six years after his death.'

Lucas nodded. 'He was always a high achiever.'

'Seriously. Apparently his spirit dictated the whole thing to an anonymous woman. I've been reading about it online. Automatic writing, they call it – writing while in a trance. I mean, it was nonsense, obviously. The book was dreadful, nothing like Fleming's style. But I'm not sure this woman didn't believe she could really do it.'

'What are you getting at, Scarlett?'

'Lucas, I wrote that,' she said, pointing to the paper in his hand. 'Me. No one crept into my room. The Woody's not the typewriter equivalent of a player piano, tapping out masterpieces while mortals sleep. I wrote it, and I woke up exhausted, fingers like watermelons, with absolutely no memory of ever pressing a key.'

He stared at her. 'So you're saying… you wrote it in your *sleep*?'

'I must have done.'

'And William – the name doesn't mean anything to you?'

She shook her head. 'Not a thing. I don't know any Williams.'

Lucas steepled his fingers and rested his chin on them. He was silent for so long, Scarlett wondered if he'd dozed off.

'Well, Scarlett, that's quite a story,' he said at last.

She slumped back against the bench. 'You don't believe me.'

'No, I do, honestly! I mean, I believe you wrote it. It's just… look, don't take this the wrong way, but did I get the impression you take your job pretty seriously?'

'And?'

'So is there any chance you might've been, you know… overdoing it?' He held up his hands when she scowled at him. 'Well, sleepwalking can be a symptom of stress, can't it? Why not sleeptyping?'

'And what about William?'

'A dream figment, I suppose. The mind can play some odd tricks.'

'But you were the one who – What about story echoes, the ghosts of words?'

'You're right, I'm sorry. I planted the idea and your subconscious seized on it. I know what it's like, I've been there myself when I've been sleep-deprived. But Scarlett, if you're really claiming the Woody pulled an *Exorcist* on you…' He gave her arm a pat. 'Maybe you need some rest, eh?'

'God, I should've known you wouldn't get it.' She snatched William's letter off him. 'I don't know why I ever confided in you, except –' To her disgust, she found herself choking on a sob – 'except I thought you might understand. Forget it, OK? Just forget everything.'

Jumping up, she stormed off.

*

'What's up, Scarlett?' Christine said when Scarlett trudged into the Old Smithy that afternoon.

She'd spent the day wandering the woods, hoping some fresh air might calm her troubled mind. But after hours of walking, her brain was still in a whirl.

'Nothing.' Scarlett held a palm to her head. 'Christine, I'm sorry, but I'm going to check out a day early. I need to go home.'

'Are you OK, love? You don't look well.'

'I'll be fine once I get out of this place. Could you book me a taxi?'

'What, you're leaving right this minute?'

'No, but I need to drop something off before I go.'

In her room, Scarlett heaved the Woodstock onto the bed and glared at it.

'Right, you. I'm sending you back to whatever demon dimension you came from and I'm drawing a line under all this. Magic or no magic, I won't be played with. Hear me?'

The eagle on the paper rest looked a little hurt.

Scarlett sank down next to it. It felt like there was a tornado in her head, thoughts and feelings swirling up a tempest.

Now she'd had time to calm down, she did feel guilty about yelling at Lucas. She wasn't even sure why she'd been angry. He'd only said exactly what she'd been telling herself – that the William letter was the product of an overwrought brain badly in need of rest.

Had she secretly hoped there might be magic at work? That Lucas or his aunt might have the key to unlocking this mystery – who William was, and who he'd been writing to? The part of her that was pure reporter was knotted with frustration that it had been presented with a question to which no one seemed to have an answer.

There was a knock at the front door, and a second later Christine's voice sailed up the stairs.

'Scarlett! Door for you.'

The taxi already? That was quick.

'Can you send him up?' Scarlett called back. There was no way she could get the Woody downstairs on her own. If the driver wanted to earn his tip, he was going to have to lend a hand.

A second later, a tousled head appeared round her door.

'Lucas,' she said. 'What're you doing here?'

'I came to apologise. And to tell you something.'

'I'm the one who should apologise.' She sighed. 'You were right. I've been working too hard, that's the only explanation. I don't know why I was angry, except... wounded pride, I suppose, seeing you giving me that oh-no-she's-cracking-up look.'

'Scarlett, that's just it, you didn't –'

'Anyway, I'll be OK when I get home. I've overdosed on Dickens or something. Some quality sleep and everything will go back to normal.'

'Scarlett.' He sat down on the bed, facing her. 'Can you stop jabbering and listen? I'm trying to tell you you were right.' He took a deep breath. 'I know who William was.'

If Scarlett hadn't been sitting down, she'd probably have fallen down.

'What?' she whispered. 'You mean he was someone? A real person?'

Lucas nodded. 'He was apprentice stonemason here, back in the twenties.'

'You can't possibly know that.'

'I can and I do. It clicked into place about half an hour after you walked off. I've been in the library all morning getting the facts together.'

'What facts? What click? Lucas, tell me what's going on.'

'Here. Give me the letter.'

She handed it over.

'"Choosy, chancy, temperamental memory",' he read. 'Does that sound familiar?'

She shook her head.

'Well, it does to me. Elizabeth Barrett Browning.'

Scarlett stared at him. 'Emily Shaw.'

'Emily Shaw. Sweetheart of twenty-year-old William Greenwood, who went on to become a master stonemason and sculptor of some of the finest gravestones in Haven Bridge.' He glanced at the letter. 'He promised to remember her every day of his life, and he used all his skill to make sure no one else would forget her either. Emily's lover wasn't a wealthy man, Scarlett – he was a craftsman.'

'Greenwood… did you say Greenwood?'

'Mmm, I noticed that. Like I said, it's a common local name, but… well, the coincidences do seem to be piling up. Do you know anything about your family tree?'

'No, but I know someone who does. My grandad. He's become addicted to Ancestry.co.uk since he's been in the hospice.'

She tapped out a text.

Hiya Gramps. You know anything about a William Greenwood, Haven Bridge stonemason? Wondered if he was a relative. PS love you x

'Hey.' Lucas put a gentle hand on her arm. 'Do you mind if I ask what's wrong? With your grandad, I mean?'

Scarlett blinked on a tear. 'Lung cancer. He was a heavy smoker his whole life. It caught him up in the end.'

'You're close?'

'Very. He was the one who inspired me to become a journalist.'

'I'm sorry.' Lucas's dark eyes filled with sympathy. 'That must be tough.'

'Yeah. I suppose it's why I gave up on doing Christmas properly. It just wasn't the same without Gramps.'

'Come here.' He pulled her into a tight hug.

'Thanks,' she whispered, feeling tension leave her body in the safety of his embrace.

'Look. Scarlett.' He held her back to look into her face. 'Sorry if I'm crossing a line here, but I wondered… OK, so how would you feel about spending Christmas night here in Haven Bridge?'

She blinked. 'You mean with you?'

'Yeah. I hate to think of you on your own.'

'Oh.' She looked away. 'I don't need a pity date, Lucas. But thanks for your charity.'

He reached out to turn her face back towards him. 'No charity involved. Just a jumbo tin of Quality Streets to dispose of and an earnest desire for your company. Think about it, OK?'

Lucas's fingers were still resting on her cheek. His gaze held hers, his parted lips beginning to inch closer. Scarlett's eyes had started to close when the buzzing of her phone crashed rudely into the moment.

She turned away to scan the screen.

'I don't believe it,' she muttered.

'What?'

'William Greenwood. He is a relative. A great-great-uncle.'

Lucas shook his head. 'Bizarre,' he muttered. 'What do you think it means?'

Scarlett scowled. 'It means, Lucas, that someone's playing games with us.' There was a knock at the door as her taxi arrived. 'And I've got a pretty good idea who it is.'

Chapter 5

Scarlett didn't bother checking the sign to see if Miss Moonshine's was open. She just barged in, the Woodstock grasped precariously in her arms, and plonked it down on the counter.

'All right, Glinda the Good, get out here,' she called.

A curtain behind the mahogany counter billowed, and Miss Moonshine appeared. 'Scarlett Greenwood. Is there a problem with your typewriter?'

'Yes, there's a problem.' Scarlett nodded to the Woodstock. 'That thing's haunted.'

Miss Moonshine's lips twitched. 'Now, don't tell me a sensible young lady like you believes in ghosts.'

'I didn't believe in anything before today. Now I'm quite willing to put my faith in ghosts, goblins, fairies and any assortment of enchanted woodland creatures. Although I think hypnotism is still my favourite theory.' She glared at the old lady, whose crinkled face – while barely changing its expression – seemed alight with amusement. 'Come on, how do you do it?'

'Do what, dear?'

'Everyone who enters this shop leaves with something. And every one of them winds up meeting their true love or whatever.'

'Oh, no. Not everyone. Some of them, yes.'

'So, how do you do it?'

'I don't. Things that are meant to be are meant to be.' There was the briefest flicker of a smile. 'You may think that occasionally, very occasionally, I give a little helping hand. I couldn't possibly comment.'

'Why did you send me the typewriter? Because it'd been my uncle's?'

'The typewriter chose you, Scarlett. And you chose it.' She held up a hand as Scarlett opened her mouth to protest. 'Yes you did. The Woodstock had a story to tell you and somewhere inside your head, you knew you needed to hear it.'

'William and Emily's story, you mean?'

'That's right.' Miss Moonshine sighed. 'Poor girl. You know, he wasn't the baby's father.'

'How would you know?'

She carried on as if she hadn't heard. 'Yes, the father was a boy from the mill, and she wouldn't be the first girl young Jim Emery got into trouble back then either. But it was William who loved her. They'd been friends since childhood.'

'Yet she wouldn't marry him.'

'No. She was proud, despite her situation. She believed William proposed only to save her reputation, and she told him if he didn't want her for love, she wouldn't take him. They argued and that was the last he ever saw of her. A month later, she left us.'

'But he did want her for love. Didn't he tell her?'

'He was an awkward, shy boy. A dreamer, nose always stuck in a book. He was good with words when they were written down but rather a fumbler with his speech.' She gazed mournfully at the typewriter. 'Poor Will. I tried my best for him.'

'She'd still have died though. They'd have had a month together and then he'd have lost her.'

'Some might say a month's happiness is better than a lifetime of sleepwalking.' Miss Moonshine looked at her keenly, and Scarlett felt her cheeks growing hot.

'Why did I need to hear the story?' she asked.

'To remind you life is short, and chances at happiness few. To help you find your place.'

'My place... You mean in Haven Bridge?'

'I mean in life, dear.' The hazel eyes twinkled. 'And perhaps the Woodstock knew that there are two people around here who can't resist a mystery. Did you make any plans for Christmas?'

'Lucas,' Scarlett muttered. She laughed, pushing her fingers into her hair. 'I don't believe it. You set this whole thing up just to force us together, didn't you?'

'Now, now, don't be angry.'

'Don't be angry? You manipulate me, torment me with…
with other people's tragedies, then you tell me not to be angry?
What's in all this for you, Miss Moonshine? What even *are* you?'

'Someone who hates to see emptiness where there ought to
be joy.' Miss Moonshine turned away to rearrange some of her
stock. 'Why don't you go for a little walk in the woods, my dear?
You'll feel so much better for some air.'

'I will. I will go for a walk. And after that, I'm going to ring
my editor and talk at him until he lets me write a feature about
the meddling matchmaker of Haven Bridge. Pretty hard to
keep your poker face on after that, wouldn't you say?'

Miss Moonshine smiled. 'We shall see.'

*

Scarlett strode out of the shop and headed not for the woods
but the canal. She definitely needed a walk to clear her head,
but she'd be blowed if she was going to take orders from Miss
Moonshine.

Just where did that woman get off? Treating human beings
like rats in a maze. Forcing her and Lucas together without so
much as a by your leave. Well, if she thought Scarlett would
be pushed around the board as easily as that, she could think
again.

She bloody would write the feature. Her nose for a story
hadn't completely atrophied, and she knew readers would lap
up a piece on Miss Moonshine. She'd talk Owen round and
get it into the Christmas supplement. Let Miss Moonshine try
using her Paul Daniels Magic Set mind games on people after
that.

She tapped out a text to Owen, asking him to call her as
soon as he was free.

Scarlett was so wrapped up in her thoughts, she almost
walked into a man crouching on the towpath, topping up the

paint on some narrowboat calligraphy that read *The Caf on the Canal – home of The Book Defacers' Club.*

'Whoops. Sorry.'

The man smiled. 'Don't worry about it. I've met some great girls that way.'

A hatch on the side of the boat opened and a head popped out. It was Callie, the woman from the market.

'Sweetheart, do you want a cuppa before I head back to the stall?' she asked the man. 'Oh. Hi, Scarlett.'

'Hi again.'

'This is Richard, my fiancé. Rich, do you want a drink or what?'

'No, I'm good.' He put down his brush. 'I wouldn't mind a kiss though.'

He approached the hatch and planted a soft kiss on her lips. Callie smiled for a moment before flicking him away with a tea-towel.

'Give up, you daft sod. There's people watching.'

'I know. Don't care.'

He leaned forward to kiss her again. Scarlett discreetly left love's young dream to themselves and carried on with her walk.

They were another Moonshine pair, weren't they? And Gloria and Christine at the B&B, still blissfully happy after years together. Lucas's mum and dad, and the parents of Miss Moonshine's numerous other godchildren. Hell, she must've set up half the town.

'Not again,' she muttered as she approached a bench under an arched bridge.

Lucas. Wherever she went in this town, there he seemed to be.

'So the Woody's back where it belongs then?' he said when she joined him.

'Yes. What're you doing here, Lucas?'

He nodded to the notebook on his lap. 'Writing. It's a good spot for it. Although obviously you need a few layers on at this time of year.'

'Do you write here often?'

'Yeah, pretty often.'

'And your aunt – she knows that?'

'Well, yes.'

Go for a walk in the woods… Had Miss Moonshine known Scarlett would rebel and head straight for the canal and Lucas?

'So what're you writing?' Scarlett asked.

'I'm making some notes on our friends Emily and William. I pitched a short story based on them to a magazine editor pal earlier and he bit my hand off.'

'That's great news. Well done, Lucas.'

'Thanks. Not much money, but every little helps. Good thing too, since I just got laid off.'

Scarlett frowned. 'What, from the pub?'

'No, the shop. My aunty called to tell me I didn't need her any more.'

'You mean she doesn't need you any more.'

'Yeah, she got a bit muddled, I think.' He glanced at her. 'Do you mind me exploiting your relatives for fiction?'

She laughed. 'Actually I'm quite flattered. Not that I even knew I had said relative until this afternoon.'

'So then, Miss Greenwood,' he said, smiling. 'You're one of us. I had a feeling you belonged here.'

'I kind of did too.'

He put his notebook on the ground and turned to face her. 'Look, Scarlett, I'm sorry if I got ahead of myself when I asked you over for Christmas. I know we just met yesterday, but… well, you must've worked out that I like you. I mean in a more than just friends sort of way. And if I've misread the signals, feel free to give me a slap, but I did think maybe –' He took off his beanie and rubbed awkward fingers through his hair. 'You know.'

She looked at him, feeling her body fill with that calm he always seemed to produce in her. He really did have the most gorgeous dark eyes...

'Lucas... don't you get the feeling this has all been kind of arranged for us?' she said at last.

'All I know is, this feels right.' He took her hand in both of his. 'Arranged or not, I'd be a fool to ignore it.'

'I just hate the idea the universe is playing chess with us.'

'Who cares if it is, if we're winning?' He stroked soft fingertips over her cheekbone. 'We don't get many chances to be happy, Scarlett,' he said quietly. 'I hope you don't mind if with my own free, unguided will, I have a go at grabbing this one.'

He leaned forward and pressed his lips gently against hers.

'Now did that feel arranged?' he murmured when he drew back.

'No. No, it felt...' She smiled as he drew her into his arms. 'You know, I'm not sure. I think you'd better do it again.'

'Don't mind if I do.' He brought his mouth back to meet hers, his fingers burrowing into her hair while they kissed.

'Hey,' he whispered when they broke apart. 'Are you still in town tonight?'

'I told my landladies I was going home, but I'm booked in until tomorrow. Why?'

'They're having a singalong night at Haven Bridge Picture House. *Muppet Christmas Carol*. Would you go with me?'

She raised an eyebrow. 'Muppets?'

'Of course. You have to have muppets at Christmas, it's the law.'

'And I bet you know all the songs by heart, don't you?'

'How well you know me,' he said, grinning. 'So pictures and pub – is it a date?'

She smiled. 'Well, I do owe you a drink.'

'Exactly. And I can tell you're far too much of a lady to welch on your round.' He pressed her fingers to his lips. 'Come on, Scarlett,' he whispered. 'Come sing with me.'

For a second time, their tender moment was interrupted by Scarlett's phone.

Lucas glared at it. 'You know, I've a mind to chuck that thing in the canal.'

'Sorry,' she said with an apologetic grimace. 'It's my boss. I'd better take it.'

'OK, Scar, where the hell is my copy?' Owen demanded when she picked up.

'Ugh, that.' She put a hand over the receiver. 'What time's the film, Lucas?'

'Eight.'

'That should be long enough.' She uncovered the microphone. 'I'll have it to you by seven, Owen.'

'Hmm. Cutting it fine but OK. What was the text for?'

She hesitated, looking at Lucas as he curled a strand of her hair around one finger.

'I just… wondered if I could book some time off,' she said at last.

'Well, wonders never cease. When?'

'Can I take a week around Christmastime? I thought I might come back here for a proper holiday. I've kind of fallen in love with the place.'

He laughed. 'OK, who are you and what've you done with Scarlett Greenwood?'

'Can I?'

'Course you can, darling. I'm glad you're finally taking a rest break. Anything else?'

'No. No, that's everything. And… happy Christmas, eh?'

When she'd hung up, Lucas gave her a squeeze. 'That's the spirit.'

She reached into her bag for the Santa hat he'd given her and placed it on her head.

'So, how do I look?'

'Like all my least appropriate Mrs Claus fantasies made flesh.' He stood up and offered her his arm. 'Come on then. You've got a feature to write before we're allowed to go have fun.'

It really wasn't so bad being a chess piece when Miss Moonshine was in charge, Scarlett reflected as she leant comfortably against him. Because when it came to arranging things just how they were meant to be, Miss Moonshine never played. She won.

Mary Jayne Baker is a novelist from Bingley, West Yorkshire. Since her debut in 2016 she has published six romantic comedies, and she also writes humorous emotional romances with a family focus under the name Lisa Swift. Her novel *A Bicycle Made for Two* – set in Yorkshire against the backdrop of the 2014 Tour de France – was a finalist for the Romantic Novelists' Association's Romantic Comedy Novel of the Year Award 2019.

maryjaynebaker.co.uk

The Boy Next Door

By Helen Pollard

Wednesday 1st December 1982

17 years old today! This time next year, I will be a child no more – everything will be legal, and I will no longer need to bat my eyelashes at every barman in town to get my hands on a lager and lime. I have, of course, been entitled to have sex for a year already, not that anyone's offering... although apparently, Paul told Diane at school today that Robbie fancies me! Jackie's upset because she fancies him. Not sure how I feel. Robbie is a hunk, but Jackie thinks Will might ask me out soon, and since I've been pining after him ever since we worked backstage together for the school Summer Concert – those arm muscles, and all those sexy smiles he sent my way! – I don't want to give up on him just yet.

The Christmas tree's up in the school hall. That thing looks mangier every year they drag it out. Wish they'd get a real one.

Assembly for the lower sixth to encourage us to apply to university next year. Crikey. I thought all I had to worry about was A levels.

Off to the pub with Jackie and Diane to celebrate – my birthday, that is, not impending life decisions. No doubt Mum'll give me a ten-minute lecture about underage drinking (again), but it'll be worth it.

Thursday 2nd December 1982

Celebrated too much, so I felt too iffy at school to concentrate. Picked loose plaster off the walls in History, in between snores and the thought of French to follow. Boredom relieved by Jackie's hopeless lusting after Robbie at Badminton Club after school. He is fit! But despite what Diane said yesterday, he didn't show any sign he fancies me.

Jackie came back to mine for tea. She's taken to calling Mum 'Jan' instead of Mrs Burrows. I know she's my best mate, but even so! She says it's because we're older, which is the reason I gave to Mum. She also says that since Mum was only a proper Mrs for a few months until Dad scarpered before I was born, and she's been divorced for donkey's years, it didn't seem appropriate anymore. Cheeky mare! Didn't tell Mum that. Mum kept her married name all these years for respectability's sake. She doesn't need my mates' opinions.

Jackie's landed herself a Saturday job at the sweet shop in Haven Bridge from now until Christmas. I could do with some extra money myself. I wish Mum hadn't made me give up the tills at the minimarket before my O levels, because they haven't had any vacancies since. Mum says education's more important than money, but a bit extra wouldn't go amiss.

Watched Top of the Pops *(my favourite) and* Only Fools and Horses *(Mum's favourite), so no arguing over the telly tonight, at least.*

I'm determined to see writing this diary through to the end of the year, but only because I promised Gran when she gave it to me last Christmas. 'This is the best time of your life, Lizzie,' she said. 'In years to come, you'll look back and enjoy remembering it all.' Huh. Why I'd want to look back in thirty years' time and remember a bunch of homework and what I watched on the telly, I have no idea. Hope she doesn't buy me another one this year.

As she hurried along the frosty pavement, Jan heard the familiar ping of the bell from Miss Moonshine's Emporium and glanced over at the old stone building set back from the road, vibrant red and white flowers adorning the archway over the short stone path to the door.

Miss Moonshine waved. 'Jan. Have you got a minute?'

'Of course.' Jan usually loved chatting to Miss Moonshine, but she had curtains to finish for Mrs Stubbs' sitting room and a trendy but tricky Roman blind to start for Mrs Naylor's bathroom. That was the trouble with working from home. Sometimes she didn't have as much work as she'd like, and sometimes she was snowed under, like now. Everyone had suddenly decided that something needed sprucing up before Christmas – new curtains or blinds or bedspreads for guests coming – which meant Jan's small dining room would look like a midden for the next few weeks. Still, she shouldn't complain. Her skills with her sewing machine had kept a roof over her and Lizzie's heads all these years, once Ed had left her high and dry and pregnant after their 'shotgun wedding'. His grudging monthly cheques in the post were a pittance.

She hurried up to where Miss Moonshine waited in the emporium doorway.

Clutching her purple mohair cardigan around her, her grey bun loosening with the wind, Miss Moonshine shivered. 'Goodness, it's cold! I'm glad I caught you, Jan. Would it be all right if I offer Lizzie a Saturday job for the next few weeks? I get so busy in the run-up to Christmas, then I like to have a good clear-out in January.'

'That would be perfect. Lizzie was saying only yesterday that it'd be nice to have extra money for Christmas.'

Miss Moonshine's hazel eyes twinkled. 'She won't mind spending her Saturdays with an old lady?'

'You're hardly old! And Lizzie used to love rooting around in the emporium. She'll enjoy it. Thank you.'

As she continued on her way home, her scarf pulled tight, Jan smiled. Extra money for Lizzie at Christmastime – solved.

Lizzie out of the house for half the weekend, leaving only half the time for her to mope around the house and argue about everything – solved.

Jan sighed. She and Lizzie were as close as any mother and daughter could be, but lately? Not so much. Lizzie was almost grown up. At her age, Jan had already left school, got a job and was dating Ed. And look how that had turned out! Jan only hoped there would be more for Lizzie.

Friday 3rd December 1982

Sixth form sponsored walk today – the brainchild of Mr Howell, our new and overeager Deputy Head. Upside – no classes. Downside – stupid time of year. I was frozen, and my feet are killing me.

As I was hobbling home from the bus stop, old Miss Moonshine rushed out and offered me a Saturday job, starting tomorrow! It's only for a few weeks, but I'm chuffed. Haven't been in the Emporium for a while, but I loved it when I was a kid. Mum's always popping in there to keep an eye out for something interesting fabric-wise, but she enjoys having a natter with Miss Moonshine, too. Mum doesn't have many friends her own age. She says it's because she's been too busy working and looking after me all these years. But I'm old enough to look after myself now!

Watched Crackerjack whilst soaking my feet in some disgusting mustard stuff that Gran brought over. 'It works wonders, Lizzie,' she said. Now my feet hurt and *stink.*

Saturday 4th December 1982

My first Saturday at Miss Moonshine's. Wasn't sure what I was doing at first, but she said to just get reacquainted with the stock. Ha! With all the stuff she sells in there, that would take forever. She had me hanging paper chains in the windows, but we were soon too busy with Christmas shoppers, so I was run off my feet tidying up after everyone and working out the fancy, old-fashioned till. I'm knackered, but eight quid richer. And it was fun to chat to Napoleon, her chihuahua. She even asked me to walk him at lunchtime. He's so small, I was worried he'd get stepped on!

Bob from next door came to watch Shōgun with us – 'for a bit of company', Mum said. He's been coming around more and more lately with some excuse or other, ever since his wife ran off with the TV repair man in the summer. Jackie said she heard his wife left him because he was 'firing blanks'. For some reason, I felt the need to defend him. I told her that's nobody's business but his. Jackie looked put out, but honestly, that's information I don't need when I have to speak to the poor bloke several times a week! Besides, it was good riddance when his wife left, if you ask me. At least now we don't have to listen to them arguing with each other all the time. These old walls don't half carry sound.

Sunday 5th December 1982

Gran came for Sunday dinner as usual, so we watched Hi-de-Hi (her favourite). After Gran left, I told Mum our crowd want to go camping next summer, and we had a humungous row. When I pointed out I'm 17 now, she said, 'Older doesn't mean wiser, Lizzie.' Mum doesn't like that it'll be a mixed crowd, even though I told her nothing's going on (unless Will asks me out, ha ha). But she kept harping on about the dangers and being unreasonable, so I ended up saying just because she got pregnant with me at 17 and was a single parent by 18 didn't mean I would be as stupid as she was – at which point, she burst into tears. I felt awful and said sorry a zillion times, but Mum said I was right and she only wants me to have opportunities and not end up in the same boat.

Jackie phoned to say her parents aren't happy either. This bloomin' camping trip'll never get off the ground (no pun intended) at this rate.

As Jan entered the emporium, she did her usual quick scan of the place, from the gifts to the books to the antique china. Most especially, she was always on the lookout for fabrics, ribbons, vintage buttons and lace.

'Hello, Jan.' Miss Moonshine stood at the counter, unravelling tinsel from an old box.

Jan didn't put her own Christmas decorations up too early – her house was tiny, and crowded enough already – but she liked to see the shops in Haven Bridge gearing up for the festive season. She smiled at Miss Moonshine, who was embracing the trend for legwarmers over drainpipe jeans and pixie boots. And why not? It must get draughty with people trooping in and out all the time.

'Morning, Miss Moonshine. Crumbs – almost Christmas already? I can't believe it'll be 1983 soon!'

Miss Moonshine gave her an enigmatic smile. 'Time flies, doesn't it? Will it be the usual at your house on Christmas Day? Just you, Lizzie and your mother?'

'I suppose so.' They were hardly the traditional family unit, what with Ed never having shown any interest in Lizzie, and Jan's own father passing away when Lizzie was still little. Unexpectedly, the idea of Bob sitting at home all alone next door on Christmas Day popped into Jan's head. Did he have family to go to? She pushed the extra worry away. Bob wasn't her problem, surely?

'What can I do for you?' Miss Moonshine asked.

'I wanted to check whether Lizzie got on all right on Saturday?' Jan reached out to stroke Napoleon, peacefully napping in his basket. He opened one eye, acknowledged her presence, then settled his chin back on his paws.

Miss Moonshine beamed. 'She was marvellous. Nervous at first, but she soon came into her own. No standing around – she busied herself with tidying, and she picked up the till quickly enough. We'll get along famously.'

'Hmmph. Better than her and me nowadays, then,' Jan muttered.

Miss Moonshine's brow furrowed. 'But you two have always been like twins.' She turned to switch on her kettle. 'Anything wrong?'

'Oh, not in the grand scheme of things.' Jan sighed. 'I suppose I've got off lightly so far, but Lizzie's growing up. This bond we have can't last forever.'

Miss Moonshine pushed a mug of steaming tea across the counter. 'Nonsense. That bond will last a lifetime, Jan Burrows. It will stretch and sometimes feel fragile, but it will always be there.'

Jan took the tea gratefully, warming her hands on the vintage china. 'I hope so. But everything's coming so thick and fast now. Her seventeenth birthday. Drinking, which they all do. She doesn't go mad, but I worry. And boys. The other day, she was on the phone chatting about someone. That's nothing new, she's had boyfriends before, but she doesn't confide in me like she used to. Her friends want to go camping in the summer, too, a whole gang of them. We had a dreadful row and said some awful things to each other. And school have been on at them about university already! She's only just started the sixth form.' When Miss Moonshine raised an eyebrow, Jan said defensively, 'If Lizzie wants to go, then I want her to. She's bright. She could do it. I never had that opportunity. But…'

'You're entering a new phase in your lives,' Miss Moonshine said kindly.

'Yes.' Jan sighed. 'I can cope with little squabbles and putting my foot down and Lizzie not liking it, but the idea of her leaving takes some getting used to.'

'I know, dear. But that bond between you? Don't pull it too tight. You don't want it to snap.'

Monday 6th December 1982

Handed in my Geography essay. I never want to see that thing again. Helped Jackie with her tuck shop duty at morning break because she had a headache – not surprised, surrounded by greedy first- and second-formers. Extra-long choir practice for the music evening on Friday, so I got out of General Studies. Skiving with permission! Great invention!

Back at school for Senior Prizegiving this evening. It was supposed to last an hour, but the speeches alone took 45 minutes. Never been so bored. Diane came all dolled up and walked onto the stage like the Queen of Sheba, all for a Best O Levels Certificate. Anyone would think she'd won a Nobel prize.

Stayed up till 1am to finish reading Salem's Lot. *Terrifying! Not a good idea on a school night.*

Tuesday 7th December 1982

Everyone was depressed today after the bombing in Ballykelly last night. I told Mum I don't really understand what's going on in Northern Ireland. She said, 'I thought you were doing A level History?' so I pointed out that the Corn Laws from 1815 to 1846 aren't particularly useful in this instance and have a tendency to send you to sleep. 'Ask Bob when he comes to fix the toilet flush,' she suggested. So I did. It turns out Bob's surprisingly knowledgeable on Northern Ireland. And he's good at fixing toilets – but since he's a plumber, I'd expect him to be.

Mum and Bob have really got into the swing of doing swapsies lately. Bob comes to change a light bulb; Mum hems his new trousers. Bob mends the latch on our gate; Mum takes him a pot of 'leftover' casserole (leftover, my foot – she made enough for six people). It's like some medieval barter system. When I told Jackie, she said she wondered what Mum would do for Bob if he did something major like decorate the stairs and landing. Ugh. That girl has a dirty mind.

Wednesday 8th December 1982

Got up at 6am to finish my History essay, but it turned out it didn't need to be in till next Wednesday! Couldn't believe it! At least it's out of the way now. I need to get everything done before the French trip to Boulogne next week – all 48 hours of it. Still, 48 hours of excitement is better than none.

Jackie told everyone about Robbie fancying me. Then Will asked me to go out with him tomorrow! Jackie said it's because he heard about Robbie, but Diane told me that Jackie persuaded Will, to save Robbie for herself.

Two years since John Lennon was shot, so we listened to his greatest hits LP at Diane's house after school as a memorial. Made sure I was home in time to watch Dallas, *though.*

Jan's mind was on Christmas shopping, and Miss Moonshine's Emporium was the obvious place to go for stocking fillers. Dainty soaps for her mother, Jan was thinking. Something unusual for Lizzie (although none of those pungent incense sticks Lizzie had become so fond of. They got right up her nose). She'd spotted bath salts in pretty jars last time, so they would do for her aunts in Lancashire. With any luck, she could get her mother to deliver those, since she herself had no fondness for the aunts. The feeling was mutual. They didn't approve of a niece with 'loose morals'. The only thing that had saved her from being officially an outcast was that Ed had at least had the decency to marry her before running off.

As Jan jingled through the door, she saw a bright blue budgie hopping about in a cage near the counter, Napoleon watching cautiously from his basket.

'I see you've met Billy,' Miss Moonshine said, coming through from the back.

The corners of Jan's mouth turned down. 'It seems such a shame, keeping him locked up like that.'

'I know. I wouldn't have one myself, but a friend asked me to look after him for a few days while she visits her daughter. Don't you worry – he's perfectly happy.'

'How do we know he wouldn't be happier if he had his freedom?' Jan replied tartly.

'I'm sure if he was in his cage the whole time, he'd be most unhappy, but Billy has the best of both worlds. He's warm and fed and watered and has company while he's in his cage, but he's allowed out, too.' Miss Moonshine reached for the cage door. 'Flip the sign to "Closed" and put the latch on, will you, dear? We wouldn't want to lose him.'

Jan did as she was asked, and Billy was freed. He perched on the threshold of his cage, then he was off, flitting from the top of the china cabinet to the bookshelf to the curtain rail across the changing room at the back. Jan hoped he wouldn't make a mess on any of Miss Moonshine's goods, especially the lovely vintage clothing.

Napoleon leapt out of his basket and scuttled around the shop in the general direction of the budgie as it explored and perched and explored again, yapping his disapproval but making no effort to jump up and try to catch it – an endeavour in which his short legs would be a distinct disadvantage. The spectacle made Jan chuckle, despite herself.

'I let Billy out before I open and again after I lock up,' Miss Moonshine told her. 'He enjoys being out and about, but he likes knowing he has a cosy cage to come back to, where he'll be looked after. And he always does come back.' She chirruped, and Billy flew to her hand, calmly allowing her to place him back inside his cage, where he set to work on his cuttlefish.

Jan burst out laughing. 'Well, really, Miss Moonshine, you've outdone yourself this time!'

Miss Moonshine's face was a picture of innocence. 'What do you mean, dear?'

'Billy the bloomin' Budgie. It's all a bit obvious, isn't it?'

'Obvious?'

'All this talk about keeping things cooped up, making them unhappy if they're over-protected. Giving them enough freedom so they'll enjoy it but still want to come back to their own home for comfort and support.' She shook her head. 'About as subtle as a Carry On film!'

Miss Moonshine gave her a sheepish smile. 'The old ones are the good ones, I always say. Stocking fillers, is it?'

Jan wasn't sure whether to laugh or cry at Miss Moonshine's meddling. And how on earth did she know she was after stocking fillers?

Thursday 9th December 1982

Diane's going skiing in February. They go to Spain every summer, too. All we ever get is a week in Gran's caravan at Bridlington. This year, we had to jack it in after four days. There are only so many card games you can play whilst trapped in a sardine tin with the rain pounding down on the roof before you go stark raving bonkers. Can't say I fancy it again this summer, what with not getting on too well with Mum. We'd probably kill each other – which is why I want to go camping instead.

Talking of killing each other, I told Jackie that if she doesn't stop humming 'Rio' by Duran Duran, I'll throttle her. You can have too much of a good thing.

Badminton Club after school. Robbie was there, looking as fit as ever. Sigh... and oops, because it was my first date with Will tonight. Told Mum I was going to Jackie's, because I couldn't face the Spanish Inquisition. We stayed in Haven Bridge, since it's a school night – chatted in the pub, then walked along the canal. When we got back to my house, he kissed me. Put it this way – I won't be spending my Saturday money on mistletoe unless things improve.

Friday 10th December 1982

Monthly library duty at lunchtime. Boring. But it got me away from Jackie and Diane, who spent the entire day trying to grill me about my date with Will. After waiting all these weeks for him to ask me out, I didn't want to admit what a damp squib it was.

The bus was noisy on the way home and gave me a headache, but no doubt revision for next week's end-of-term tests will have a dulling effect on the brain over the weekend.

Cheered myself up by watching The Munsters. *Mum said, 'Aren't you a bit old for that?' then suddenly looked all teary and said it didn't matter; there was no need for me to grow up too fast. She's been weird like that, lately.*

Back to school, this time for the Music Evening. Feels like we're never away from the blinkin' place! Bob drove us. I told Jackie it was because he feels sorry for us not having a car, but she thinks he and Mum fancy each other. 'Can't see what your mum sees in him,' she said. 'Talk about boring!' I told her he's not, really. I agree he looks boring – brown hair, brown eyes, brown corduroys, brown jumper (yawn) – but he's quite chatty, and he doesn't treat me like a kid. Unlike Mum.

On the drive home, Bob was very complimentary about our choir's Christmas medley, which was overly kind of him, although even I thought we were a damned sight more tuneful than the woodwind group's attempt at 'God Rest Ye Merry Gentlemen'.

'Bob. Are you doing anything on Christmas Day?' Jan asked as she steadied the stepladder while her neighbour changed the bulb in her outside light.

As usual, her neighbour on her other side, Mrs Knox, had pulled back her net curtains to watch proceedings. The woman never even tried to be subtle about it.

Bob finished screwing the casing back on the light before turning to look at her with something like resignation on his face. 'Well, no. Not what with… Well. After everything that's happened this year.'

'No family for you to go and annoy?' Jan asked him.

'Ha. I thought about going to my sister's, but my parents are going this year and staying over, so I'd be one too many, space-wise. She said I'm welcome, of course, but I think not. I don't want to…' He hesitated. 'I don't want to be fussed over.'

He clambered back down the ladder. Jan could imagine his family treading on eggshells, trying not to mention his unfaithful wife, then overcompensating by smothering him in too much seasonal bonhomie.

Bob stumbled on the bottom step, so he landed a little too close to Jan. Practically nose to nose, in fact. Gosh, he has lovely eyes, Jan thought, surprised by the unbidden thought. She took a hasty step back.

'Well. All done,' Bob said awkwardly.

'Thank you, Bob. I really appreciate it.'

'No problem. That's what neighbours are for.' He smiled.

Gosh, he has a lovely smile, too. Jan's eyes widened. Jan Burrows, what is wrong with you today? 'Yes. Of course. And if you need me to do anything for you in return, you'll let me know?'

There was a long pause before Bob nodded. 'Yes. Thanks. See you.'

As he stepped over the fence between their houses, reaching back for her to hand him his stepladder, Jan was already mulling over what he'd said. Bob was going to be alone on Christmas day. That just wasn't right, was it?

Saturday 11th December 1982

Busy again at the Emporium. It's unbelievable how much mess people can make when they're 'just browsing'. But we sold loads, too. Miss Moonshine asked if I was planning on going to university, and I said I probably would, but I'm not sure what to study. History, maybe.

Thought Will might ask me out again, but he's at his grandparents' all weekend.

Bob's become a regular fixture at our house for watching Shōgun. *Mind you, he might as well be – the walls are so thin in these terraces, you can hear what your neighbours are watching anyway. He got bonus points for bringing us fish and chips for supper.*

I decided to test out Jackie's theory by sitting in the armchair so that Bob and Mum had the sofa to themselves, but they behaved impeccably. Then, as he was leaving, out of the blue Mum asked him if he wanted to join us on Christmas Day. Wasn't expecting that!!

Sunday 12th December 1982

The Greenham Common women were on the news again. Thousands of them joined hands to make a human protest chain around the missile base. 9 miles! Gran said they do right and she'd join them if she were younger. Mum said she wouldn't last two minutes without proper toilets and Coronation Street.

Will finally rang and asked me out again – tonight! Unfortunately, Gran was still here when he called for me, so no doubt she'll have an opinion to express. As will Mum. Also unfortunately, it was no better than last time, although he varied the rubbish kissing with a clumsy grope.

'Good morning. Anything in particular today?' Miss Moonshine asked Jan, her eyes bright. Her sweater was on the bright side, too, with its diamond shapes of bright orange and electric blue – an interesting combination and certainly eye-catching.

'Morning. Well. You see, I – er – I invited Bob to join us on Christmas Day, because I don't like the idea of him being on his own, and now that he'll be with us, I'm thinking I ought to give him a present,' Jan babbled.

Miss Moonshine smiled at this news. 'Anything in mind?'

'No. My mind's a blank.'

'I see. Well, what do you want to say with the gift?'

Jan thought for a moment. 'I want to say that he's welcome at ours for Christmas. And I want to say thank you for all the things he's done for us.' She hesitated. 'But I don't want it to be any old gift. I want…' She stopped, unable to find the right words.

'Something special? Perhaps something you've taken time and trouble over?'

'Yes. That's exactly it.' Jan let out a sigh of relief. Miss Moonshine was so good at capturing your thoughts for you.

'How much work have you got on at the moment?'

'One job to finish, then nothing that can't be put off till the New Year. It's too late for any more panic jobs now. Why?'

'I was glancing through this.' Miss Moonshine pointed to a book lying open on the counter next to Napoleon's basket. She showed Jan the cover – a crafting manual – then leafed through to the right page. 'Don't you think this is an interesting idea? It's made from old ties, would you believe?'

Jan studied the double-page spread of a patchwork quilt, masculine in design and colour. 'Old ties?'

Miss Moonshine led Jan to her vintage clothing section at the back of the shop and kicked a large cardboard box full of them, forlornly tumbled together. 'Nobody seems to want them second-hand, and I get so many – clear-outs when someone's passed on, or unwanted presents.' She lifted out a particularly hideous brown and orange tie, and they both shuddered then laughed.

'But would Bob want a bedspread?' Jan wondered aloud.

'Do you know what kind he has at the moment?'

'Of course not! I've never been in his bedroom.'

Miss Moonshine's mouth twitched. 'I see. Still, it might be nice. Something of his own, not connected to his wife?'

Jan thought about what she'd seen of Bob's house, which was only the living room and kitchen. It was all rather feminine, despite his wife taking the ornaments and pictures with her. Jan had offered to run him up some new living room curtains to replace the floral ones when she got a decent gap in her workload, but that wouldn't be till the spring.

As though she could read Jan's mind, Miss Moonshine went on, 'This would be nice and masculine for him, wouldn't it? Unique, made by you with him in mind.'

Jan eyed the box of ties, then went back to the book. 'It could look spectacular, if the colours were co-ordinated. But it'd take ages to hand stitch all these pieces. Although...' Jan closed her eyes, her skilled mind playing with the design. 'Maybe I could do most of it on the machine, if I adapt the pattern. Instead of cutting the ties into pieces, I could use the whole tie, with the narrow ends in the middle and the wide ends radiating outwards. I have some navy fabric that would do for the backing.' She sighed. 'Even so, I don't know if I could get it done in time.' Opening her eyes again, she scanned Miss Moonshine's selection of men's goods on display – cufflinks, leather wallets, badger-hair shaving brushes, ashtrays that Bob had no use for. But the quilt was lodged in her brain now. She wanted to do something special for the man who had been so kind and such good company over the past few months; the man whose morning and evening routine she already knew off by heart through the thin walls, his next-door presence comforting when Lizzie was out and Jan was home alone. 'How much per tie?'

'For you, twenty pence each. Or you can take two boxes – I have another upstairs – for a fiver.'

'Done!' Jan clasped Miss Moonshine's hand. 'Oh dear. What have I let myself in for?'

Monday 13th December 1982

French test was a killer. Mr Llewellyn striding around the classroom with that sadistic smile of his didn't help. The multi-choice questions were more multi-guess on my part. When it was over, he went through arrangements for the Boulogne trip later this week – again. How complicated can a day trip be?

Jackie lent me The Thorn Birds. *She loved it, so I'll give it a go over Christmas.*

Gran's verdict on Will: 'He looks very sweet, but isn't he a bit short?' I pointed out that at least he's taller than me, and six-footers don't grow on trees.

Mum's verdict on Will? She hasn't said a word. I think she's sulking that I didn't tell her about him before.

Avoided revision by watching Happy Days *and* Quincy. *Wouldn't mind being a forensic pathologist, although the fact that I'm not doing science A levels might not help. Or the fact that I faint at the sight of blood.*

Tuesday 14th December 1982

Literally made up half of my Geography essay in the test today. Then, in History, Mr Whitall made Jackie and me sit apart like three-year-olds, all because I said Starsky was more attractive than Hutch, but Jackie thinks the opposite. Half the class got involved, and it all got a bit heated. It's not my fault I picked such a controversial topic, is it?

No word from Will, and I couldn't get Robbie out of my mind all day. Diane didn't help by telling me to imagine him all hot and sweaty at Badminton Club, taking his shirt off!

School Christmas Fair from 6-8pm. I was knackered, so I could have done without running the hook-a-duck stall, plagued by noisy children. Bonus, though – Mr Llewellyn agreed to go in the stocks to be pelted with wet sponges, shaving foam pies, you name it. There was a very long queue! Jackie and I both got him square in the mush. That'll teach him to set tests before Christmas.

Wednesday 15th December 1982
Wrote 8 sides of A4 in the History test. Diane wrote 9. She has to do everything better.

According to Will's mate Simon, Will's thinking of chucking me because I'm a rubbish kisser. Absolute cheek!

Finally. Rucksack packed. Off to Boulogne tonight!!

Jan handed her mother a cuppa. Her parent had a habit of popping round unannounced, something Jan had long since given up trying to discourage.

'I've decided to buy Lizzie a new Christmas tree,' Jan said, in an effort to steer the conversation away from Bob, having already caused consternation by admitting she had invited him for Christmas Day. Her mother was never shy of poking her nose into her daughter's and granddaughter's affairs.

'What on earth do you need a new tree for?'

Jan winced. Their current tree was originally Jan's parents', donated to Jan after Lizzie was born. Painfully artificial and only three feet high, it had to be placed on a table to be seen, and its fronds had seen better days. Lizzie had complained throughout her teenage years about how pathetic it was.

'The old one never bothered Lizzie when she was a child,' Jan said tactfully. 'But kids are easily pleased. Almost-adults, less so.'

'Hmmph. And how do you expect to drag a big Christmas tree back here?'

It seemed Jan's Bob-avoiding ploy was backfiring already. 'Bob offered to fetch it from the DIY store outside town,' she admitted. 'We're keeping it a secret from Lizzie. He'll bring it on Saturday and set it up while she's working at Miss Moonshine's.'

Her mother's eyes narrowed. 'Bob seems to do an awful lot around here nowadays. Anything going on that you haven't told me about?'

'Not at all!' Jan denied hotly. 'He's a good neighbour, that's all.'

'Yes, well. Bob's a nice enough bloke. You could do worse. Heaven knows, you have done worse. Ed was neither use nor ornament. Running off like that. Ignoring the fact he has a daughter.'

'He sends cheques, Mum. And it wasn't his fault. Not really. He was too young.'

'And you weren't?'

Jan sighed. She could do without another ride on the Ed merry-go-round. 'Mother, can we leave Ed alone for once?'

'With pleasure. As for Bob? As I said, he's nice and you could do worse.'

Jan bristled. 'I'm sure I could, but I'm not looking to do better or worse. I have enough on already.'

'Well, it's a shame, if you ask me. But in that case, be careful, Jan. Accepting too many favours can lead to a man expecting more, you know.'

'I do plenty to pay him back,' Jan snapped, rolling her eyes when her mother raised a badly-pencilled eyebrow. 'And I don't mean that sort of favour!'

Her mother sniffed. 'It wouldn't bother me. A woman of your age shouldn't be celibate. All I'm saying is, think about how much you want to be beholden to him.'

Jan did think about it afterwards. She knew her mother would like to see her settled with a decent bloke. But it wasn't like that with Bob… Was it? What if, as her mother suggested, Bob did expect 'more'?

Jan thought about Bob's kind manner, his gentle smile,

his broad shoulders as he set about his DIY tasks; the way he chatted with Lizzie without getting her back up – no mean feat these days. The more she thought about it, the more Jan realised she didn't have too many qualms about 'something more'.

But that was a moot point. She had a household to run and a daughter to finish raising to adulthood. She certainly didn't have the time or energy to worry about that sort of thing.

Friday 17th December 1982

Back from the sixth form day trip to Boulogne. I say day trip, but it was actually a one-day-and-two-nights-of-no-sleep trip. The coach set off from school at 10pm on Wednesday and drove through the night to Dover – no, we couldn't sleep, duh – then we got the early morning ferry over to Boulogne to be let loose for the day. Or so we thought, until Mr Llewellyn handed out a long set of instructions of places we had to find and questions we were supposed to stop random French people on the street to ask, whether we wanted to trouver le bureau de poste or not. And what were our illustrious teachers doing? Jackie overheard Mr Llewellyn telling the others about a great little bistro he knew, so we reckon they were in there all day, necking wine.

Bought a leather handbag at a street market for Mum's Christmas present. Hers is getting a bit battered. Hope she'll like it, because it used up most of my Saturday money.

Back on the evening ferry, then the coach. Supposed to arrive at school at 1am, but it was after 2am. Bob had offered to pick me up, so I felt terrible for him. And we were told we had to attend school! We were half-dead all day. Poor Bob probably was, too.

'Where do you want it?' Bob asked as he battled his way through the door with a six-foot-long cardboard box.

'In the lounge,' Jan told him. 'I'm hoping it'll fit in the corner. Fingers crossed, eh?'

'Lizzie'll love it.' Bob pulled a penknife from his pocket and knelt to tackle the box and its fastenings.

'Hope so. I should've done it a few years ago, but I was worried about spending money on something that only appears for a couple of weeks a year.'

'So why now?' He began to slot the pieces together.

'It's coming home to me that Lizzie might only spend a few more Christmases here with me. I want to make them special for her. I bought new decorations, too. We don't have enough for such a big tree.'

Bob rose, lifting the tree vertical, and shot her a sympathetic look. 'It's nearly two years till Lizzie goes away – if she does. And she'll be home every Christmas. Every holiday, in fact, bringing all her dirty washing with her. You won't lose her, Jan. You two are like this.' He held up two fingers, tightly entwined. 'I envy you that. It's not something I'll ever experience.'

Jan was immediately contrite. 'Oh, Bob, I'm so sorry. Here I am, wallowing in my own misery, while you...'

'Just because I've got miseries doesn't mean you're not entitled to your own. All I'm saying is, appreciate what you've had, what you've got now, and what you can still have in the future.' He gave her a quick, tentative hug. 'Don't worry about me. I've known for a while that I can't have kids. I'm resigned to it.'

Already flustered from putting her foot in it and from the all-too-brief sensation of Bob's arms around her, Jan babbled, 'You could – I mean, if you were to start dating–' She stopped abruptly. She realised how upset she was at the idea of Bob dating someone, and she had to force herself to finish her sentence. 'Maybe you'll find someone who has kids?'

'Maybe. But I'm nearly forty, Jan. I'm not sure I could take on a whole brood of little kids now. I would like to be with someone, though. For companionship and what have you.' He flushed. 'If that someone happens to have a kid, then I wouldn't mind.' Clearing his throat, he busied himself with carrying the tree to the corner.

It dominated the small lounge, but as Jan stood admiring it, she knew it was worth it. She couldn't wait to see the look on Lizzie's face when she came home.

*

'So, did she love–' Bob began as he came through the door that evening, stopping when he saw Jan sitting on the sofa, surrounded by unopened boxes of Christmas decorations, her face blotched with tears. Perching next to her, he gave her shoulder a squeeze. 'I'm guessing the answer is "no"?'

'I'd tell you, if I knew,' Jan sniffled. 'When Lizzie came home, she looked almost impressed. Then she had some sort of panic and demanded to know where the old one was. When I told her I'd thrown it away, she went mad. She raced out to the back yard, saw it sticking out of the bin, burst into tears and ran up to her room.' Jan looked up into Bob's sympathetic face and burst into tears herself. 'I can't get anything right.'

'You do your best, Jan.' He patted her knee. 'Do you think she'll mind if I go up?'

Jan shrugged. 'You're welcome. I daren't.'

'Don't be silly. Come with me.' Bob pulled her off the sofa, and Jan allowed herself to be dragged upstairs, her small hand dwarfed in his large one.

When there was no answer to his knock, Bob cautiously opened Lizzie's door an inch. 'Can we come in?'

Hearing a 'S'pose', he opened it wider, exposing a mess of teenage rubbish across all surfaces, the small room dominated by Lizzie's prized Harrison Ford poster on the wall.

Lizzie sat cross-legged on the bed, her face tear-streaked. Her eyes narrowed when she saw Jan. 'What are *you* crying for?'

Bob picked his way across the book-strewn floor to perch on the end of the bed. 'Your Mum's upset because you're upset, Lizzie, but she doesn't know why you are. She thought you'd wanted a new tree for ages.'

Lizzie sniffed. 'I did. But then I remembered all the Christmases we had with the little one, and it seemed awful to throw it out, and when I saw it in the bin...' She burst into renewed tears, making Jan start all over again.

Poor Bob, a distant part of Jan's brain thought. Two females in tears. What a good man he is. And what a stupid woman his wife was to have left him.

Reaching for the tissues on Lizzie's bedside table, Bob passed them a handful each, stood and said, 'It seems to me that what you two need to do is embrace the new whilst cherishing the old. Follow me, ladies.'

Saturday 18th December 1982

At work, I showed Miss Moonshine the handbag I bought in France for Mum. She thinks Mum will love it. Then she asked whether I'm buying anything for Bob. I told her it hadn't occurred to me. 'It might be a nice gesture, dear,' she said in that way she has – kindly, but hinting that you should follow her advice. 'I gather he'll be at your house on Christmas Day. Your mother's making something for him.' So that's why Mum's been at her sewing machine all hours, even though it's nearly Christmas. I told Miss M that I wouldn't know where to start, so she said, 'He often browses the history books upstairs.' I remembered how patiently Bob explained about Northern Ireland to me. It's good that we both like history – gives us something to talk about, especially since he's at our house so often. Wonder what he knows about the bloomin' Corn Laws?

Made a total fool of myself in front of Bob this evening, though, all because Mum threw away the old Christmas tree. Goodness knows what he thought, surrounded by two weeping women – I managed to make Mum cry, too – especially since he'd fetched the new one and set it all up. But he was brilliant. He went out to the yard, got the old one out of the bin, made some repairs and set it up in the corner of my bedroom. Then he climbed into the attic and dragged all my childhood deccies down, so Mum and I could decorate it while he made us some mulled cider – very fancy. Then we opened the new deccies that Mum had bought, and all three of us decorated the new tree in the lounge. It looks lovely, and I can still enjoy the old one in my room.

I like Bob. I hope Mum likes him, too, because if he can sort out two hysterical women without running for the hills, he's worth a second look, if you ask me.

And all this in time for the last episode of Shōgun. I thought Bob sat a bit closer to Mum on the sofa, but it might have been my imagination. The pair of them could do with a bit of imagination!

Sunday 19th December 1982

Blimey, Mum can be so dim. Gran didn't come for dinner today because she has a cold, so there was Bob, trying to persuade her to go for an afternoon walk, obviously meaning just the two of them, and Mum was all 'What about Lizzie?' and Bob was all 'We wouldn't want to keep Lizzie from her homework. I'm sure she has lots to do.' Yeah, right, the last weekend before Christmas? I had to pretend I was desperate to watch some rubbish black-and-white film on the telly, just so she'd go. Honestly! Why can't she see the way Bob looks at her? He goes all doe-eyed. Jackie said he's only after one thing because his wife left him and he isn't getting 'it' any more. I laid into her for that, because Bob isn't like that. I think he really cares about Mum. Jackie said I'm getting soppy in my old age.

Robbie was on my mind all day (when isn't he?!) Got fed up of waiting for Will to call – I've barely seen him all week, *what with the French trip – so I phoned him. He said he'd been meaning to speak to me (yeah, I bet) because he doesn't think we're 'compatible'. Damn right! I told him he was the crap kisser and rang off.*

Monday 20th December

A chemistry teacher was knocked out by a plastic waste paper basket balanced on top of a door by a fifth year and had to be carried out by ambulance men! A whole-school emergency assembly was called, and our drippy headmaster came out of hiding long enough to tell us he wanted no more end-of-term 'high jinks' or 'horseplay'. What century was he born in?

Found out I got 81% in the French test. Shock of the year! Diane got 82%. One of these days…

Turns out Will's idea of us not being compatible is for him to be compatible with someone else. He asked Diane out! She's welcome to him.

Tuesday 21st December 1982

Choir sang at the school's annual old people's Christmas party this afternoon. Upside – got out of French, merci. *Downside – had to serve the old dears with tea and biscuits afterwards and be nice.*

School's finished for the holidays! Yippee!

'Everything alright, Jan?' Miss Moonshine asked as she pushed a cup of tea across the counter to her. Tiny, glittery Christmas baubles dangled from Miss Moonshine's ears, and she wore a halo of gold tinsel around her head. Not to leave Napoleon out, she had tied a large red ribbon around the rim of his basket, finished in an elaborate bow. He looked unimpressed by the addition.

'Ah, I don't know, Miss Moonshine. Some days, it all gets on top of me. Bringing up a child on my own, working all hours to pay the bills whilst trying to find time for Lizzie. Other days, I tell myself how lucky I am to have such a wonderful daughter, a roof over our heads, a mother who's supportive – if opinionated. A skill that enables me to work from home.'

'Today's not one of those days?'

'Alas, no. Today, it looks like I'm in for a spot of self-pity.' Jan brushed a hand over a pale blue vintage ball gown hanging to one side of the counter, its long folds smooth under her touch. 'When I was little, I dreamed of dresses like this. I thought I'd be like Cinderella, you know? And I did think I'd found my Prince Charming. But then he ran away, and look where I am now – still in metaphorical rags, waiting for an invitation to the ball.'

Miss Moonshine gave her a speculative look. 'When did you last go out on a date, Jan Burrows?'

'Let me see.' Jan wrinkled her nose in concentration. 'That would be… Jack from the butcher's. Maybe three or four years ago?'

'It's five years since the butcher's shop changed hands, Jan, so that means it's over five years since you last had a date.'

'But it's so difficult, Miss Moonshine! When Lizzie was little, I wasn't interested. I was still smarting from being left holding the baby – literally. I couldn't afford babysitters. Mum and Dad were already doing so much for us, and Dad wasn't well. As Lizzie got older, I tried a few times, but nobody floated my boat. And I knew that if I got serious about someone, it would affect Lizzie. Once she hit her teens, it seemed like more trouble than it was worth. I've had enough on, keeping us from throttling each other, never mind adding some fella into the equation.' Jan shrugged, resigned. 'I work from home. It's not easy to meet people. And it's a small town. We haven't had bucketloads of eligible men in Haven Bridge over the years, and those there were got snapped up pretty sharpish by women without a child in tow.'

Miss Moonshine nodded her understanding. 'But Lizzie's almost grown up now. She'll be off to university soon.'

'Don't remind me.'

'Jan, you've devoted all these years to your daughter, but now it's time to get a life for yourself. You're still a young woman.' When Jan made a scoffing noise, Miss Moonshine insisted, 'You are, Jan – unlike some of us. How old are you?'

'Thirty-five.'

'That's nothing! You still have time to build something new for yourself. To have a relationship with someone who cares about you – and Lizzie.'

'Oh? And where am I going to find this Prince Charming?'

Miss Moonshine gave Jan a long look. 'Never heard of "the boy next door"?'

Jan frowned. 'Bob's just a neighbour and friend. He does me a good turn, I do him one.'

'Friends can become something more,' Miss Moonshine pointed out. 'Perhaps it's time to open your mind to a few possibilities.'

Jan made a huffing noise. 'I daren't put my poor, tired mind under any more pressure for quite a while yet, I'm afraid. I have enough trouble, paying the bills and keeping my daughter on the straight and narrow. Maybe one day…'

But her sigh as she sipped her tea was a wistful one.

Wednesday 22nd December 1982

Went ice-skating in Bradford with Jackie and Diane. Had an ace time, but the boots rubbed the skin off my heels, and my legs ache like mad. Diane's family got a video player! We went around there afterwards to watch Private Benjamin. *Gran says too much telly rots your mind, so I doubt she'll approve of videos.*

When I got home, Jackie phoned to say she hadn't wanted to tell me in front of the others, but Robbie has told her he won't ask me out because I went out with Will instead of waiting for him. Gutted! I had no idea he would actually ask me out, and I'd been waiting for Will for ages, but then it was rubbish anyway. And now I fancy Robbie – I bet he isn't a rubbish kisser – but he doesn't want me!

Mum caught the brunt of it, but she was good about it in a mum sort of way. Poor Bob came round and nearly scarpered, but Mum went to make us all a cup of tea, leaving the poor man with me. He was good about it, too – I would say 'in a dad kind of way', but how would I know? My own dad has always been what they refer to as an 'absent parent'.

'All boys are idiots at that age, Lizzie, love,' Bob said. 'There's no rush. Especially if you're going to university. Better not to get too involved at this stage, eh? You don't want to end up...' 'Like mum?' I said, but he shook his head and said, 'I was going to say, "tied down too young".' I couldn't help myself. 'But Bob,' I said, 'Mum doing everything so young means she'll be free sooner, doesn't it? Free from me. Free to start dating again.' Bob looked a bit startled. Tee hee. 'Aye, that's true,' he mumbled. I didn't have the heart to push it any further. Besides, I was too busy wallowing in my own misery. And we missed Coronation Street.

Thursday 23rd December 1982

Oh, my giddy aunt, as Gran would say. (Who was this aunt, and why was she giddy?) Got home from tea at Jackie's house to find Bob and Mum discoing their way around the living room to Top of the Pops *on the telly! And then, when he left, he stopped at the gate and burst into a rendition of that song that's at No. 1, 'Save Your Love'. There he was, serenading her like Renato, with Mum standing at the top of the steps like Renée at her bedroom window, giggling. Mrs Knox next door looked gobsmacked through her net curtains. I can't blame her. Bob can't sing for toffee. What on earth has come over those two? They're acting like teenagers!*

Christmas Eve 1982

Mum and I had a lovely day, just the two of us. Telly over a milky coffee – Charlie Brown's Christmas, *then* Tarzan and the Leopard Woman. *Mum says Gran still has a crush on Johnny Weissmuller. To be fair to Gran, I can see why. Then we walked around Haven Bridge together, looking in the shops and admiring all the decorations and the real tree in the square. It was great to have Mum to myself. She's been so busy lately.*

In the afternoon, we made mince pies, like when I was little. It made me feel a bit sad, even though I was happy. I think Mum felt the same way. She put her floury hands on my face and said, 'You'll always be my little girl, Lizzie. But you have your own life to live, and you should take every chance you get, love.' Then we both had a little cry.

In the evening, Bob drove us to a posh hotel outside town and bought us cocktails. Not had one before, but I quite liked it (especially since he was paying, ha ha).

Christmas Day 1982

Happy Christmas!

Mum loved her handbag, thank goodness. Gran was pleased with the scarf I bought her from Miss Moonshine's, and Bob says he can't wait to start his book on the history of medicine through the ages. Gran flicked through it and said it looked on the gory side and she'd stick with her historical romances, thank you very much.

I got a good haul this year: book tokens, the latest Madness *LP, a blue jumper that Mum knitted without me knowing – cosy. Oh, and lip gloss from Jackie. Gran had crocheted a blanket for my room, so I told her it would come in handy when I go*

to university (where I will definitely not be taking it. Imagine!)
No diary for next year, though. I'm a bit disappointed, after all.
Maybe it would be a laugh to read it when I'm old and grey.

Best of all was the bed-cover Mum made for Bob. It's so clever!
All those ties in every shade of grey and blue, spreading out in
a pointy circle from the middle. Bob looked all choked up, and
Gran winked at me when he gave Mum a thank-you hug.

Yummy Christmas dinner, followed by the Top of The Pops
special. Gran insisted on watching the Queen's speech, then we
went for a walk to work off dinner before evening telly. Get this:
Bob had his arm around Mum throughout The Two Ronnies!
And when he left, he kissed her, right there in the doorway. Only
a quick one, but on the lips, not her cheek. I don't know who was
more surprised – him, Mum, or Gran and me. Happy Christmas,
indeed!

Jan woke early on Boxing Day with a great deal on her mind
– but for once, her head wasn't filled with what needed to be
done today, what she might cook for lunch, what sewing jobs
she would have to start on in the New Year. For once, she wasn't
worrying about her and Lizzie getting along, or even about
Lizzie going off to university.

Jan's head was filled with Bob. With the way his arm had
felt across her shoulders as they watched television the night
before – heavy and comforting. With the booming sound of
his laughter at *The Two Ronnies* and his smile when he turned
to her to see if she found it as funny as he did. With the way
his lips had felt on hers – a light brush that would have only
been classed as a peck if it had landed on her cheek. What
would have happened if they hadn't had an audience? Filling
the kettle, Jan giggled nervously as she realised how much she
wanted to find that out.

With her stomach fluttering as if she was Lizzie's age – she hadn't felt like this in such a long time – Jan washed and dressed as she drank her tea, taking an extra minute with her hair, an extra minute for mascara. Seriously decadent for morning time.

Through the walls, she could hear Bob moving about. He was up already. Good. Lizzie would sleep in for at least a couple more hours yet.

Jan slipped on her shoes. As she passed the fridge, out of habit she opened it and peered inside to see what leftovers they had, looking for an excuse to pop next door, as she always did.

After a moment, she closed it again. What was it that Miss Moonshine had said? 'Perhaps it's time to open your mind to a few possibilities.'

When Jan left her house and knocked at the-boy-next-door's, she was standing there empty-handed. She didn't need an excuse to see Bob any more.

As a child, Helen Pollard had a vivid imagination fuelled by her love of reading, so she started to create her own stories in a notebook. She still prefers fictional worlds to real life, believes characterisation is the key to a successful book, and enjoys infusing her writing with humour and heart. Helen is a member of the Romantic Novelists' Association and the Society of Authors.

amazon.co.uk/Helen-Pollard/e/B00O2E0BRC/

My True Love Gave to Me

By Sophie Claire

13th December

Jason waved as he crossed the yard, but Mandy didn't wave back and he felt a shot of disappointment. He told himself not to be irrational. They had a date tonight, but it was dark out here and she couldn't see him, not when the lights were on inside her mum's terraced house. She was sitting at the kitchen table in deep conversation with someone – her sister? – and stroking her fingers through her liquorice-black hair, a sharp frown pulling her brows together. She looked beautiful but worried, and it made him want to wrap his arms around her.

As he approached the back door, a cat scooted out from the shadows and rubbed itself against his leg. He put his briefcase down. 'Good evening, Elton,' he murmured, and bent to scratch the cat's chin.

'…I don't know what to do, Lola. He's going to be here any minute and I don't want to hurt him, but I can't carry on as things are.'

Jason stilled.

A spidery sensation tiptoed down his spine and he squeezed the bouquet in his hand. He'd bought the flowers to make peace after their argument yesterday. Mandy had mentioned wanting to expand her beauty salon and hire three new members of staff, so Jason, having expertise in that kind of thing, had offered to go through her books with her. But he'd taken one look at her accounts and warned her she couldn't afford it.

She hadn't taken the news well, yet he still couldn't understand how she'd ended up in tears, sobbing that he didn't have faith in her. He'd only been trying to help, and of course he had faith in her. He just didn't want her to end up bankrupt.

Elton rubbed against his leg, but Jason's attention was focused on the conversation happening on the other side of the door and the words he'd just heard. *I can't carry on as things are.* He couldn't imagine a world without Mandy. She was the sun in his sky, the North in his compass; she was everything. He stepped closer to the door to listen. Eavesdroppers never heard any good of themselves, he knew, but he was too afraid to knock now.

'He doesn't make you happy?' asked Lola.

Silence followed. Jason's shoulders dropped. Elton stared up at him, his eyes green beacons in the dark.

'He's so down about everything. And I mean everything – not just the salon business. I suggested we go away for the New Year, but he's saving for a car. I asked if he wanted me to buy him a watch for Christmas, but he said it would be a waste of money, because the one he has is perfectly fine. It's driving me mad, Lo. It's like being with the Grinch.'

Her sister's laughter tinkled like bells and Jason had to close his eyes against the dart of pain that shot through him. The Grinch? Was that really how she saw him?

Lola's voice cut through his thoughts. 'Are you sure you're not still sulking about your argument? He's an accountant, Mands. He knows what he's talking about, and if he says it's risky to expand too fast, perhaps he has a point. You do sometimes get carried away when you have an idea.'

The scrape of a chair against the tiled floor made Jason jump back.

But she didn't come to the door. The sound of running water told him she was at the sink. 'You always say that and it's so unfair.'

'It's true! You're a dreamer. Me and Mum took care of the practical stuff so you never had to. It must be a big adjustment for you to suddenly be running the salon single-handedly.'

He heard a sigh. 'It is hard. It was much easier when Mum ran the business side of things and I just did the treatments.'

'So maybe you should think this over before you do anything hasty? I think you and Jason are good together. You balance each other out. Like yin and yang, that kind of thing.'

Mandy's reply took a little while coming. 'Maybe. Or maybe I'm fed up of being with someone whose glass is always half empty.'

Jason's pulse hammered in his ears as a long silence followed. He squeezed the flowers so hard the rose thorns dug into his palm.

'So what are you going to do?' asked Lola.

'I'm not sure. Perhaps it would be good for us to have some time apart.'

'Oh Mands, are you sure? I mean, it's nearly Christmas. And is a break really what you want anyway? Anyone can see how much he adores you.'

'If he does he's never said it.'

Her words made him flush and he tugged at his shirt collar, suddenly feeling hot despite the chilly December air.

Love was such a nebulous concept. He loved being with Mandy, he loved her bubbly character and caring nature – but he could never say those three words unless he was one hundred percent certain of his feelings. He was a man of his word. And perhaps he also wanted to be sure she would reciprocate. Hadn't he always worried Mandy was out of his league? By the sounds of this conversation, he was right.

'To tell you the truth, Lo, I'm not sure how he feels about me.'

'Really?'

'We've never discussed anything like that.'

'How long have you two been together?'

'Nearly three months.'

'That's not very long –'

'But you're right. I can't break up with him just before Christmas. He's got no family left since his mum died.'

'Well, that gives you twelve days to think about it. And whatever you decide in the end, you'll be sure you've made the right decision.'

14th December

Jason stood outside Miss Moonshine's Emporium hopping from one foot to the other and blowing on his hands. It was zero degrees, but the wind chill factor meant it felt more like minus five. As soon as the glossy black door swung open, he scooted inside and was grateful to see a fire burning in the grate.

Mind you, what that would cost to keep burning all day, he dreaded to think.

'You're very keen. You like shopping, then, do you?' asked the white-haired shopkeeper. Miss Moonshine, he presumed. The tiniest dog he'd ever seen followed at her heels.

He shook his head. 'I hate shopping. But I have to get a Christmas present for my girlfriend and it needs to be something she'll love.'

After what he'd heard last night, he had to get this right. He thought guiltily of how he hadn't told Mandy he'd overheard her conversation with Lola. He'd given her the flowers and they'd made up, but he knew the next twelve days were crucial. He tried to ignore the drumming in his chest. There would be no second chances.

'Were you looking for anything in particular, dear?'

'Yes, I thought a mirror for her dressing table. Hers is cracked, you see.' It was something she'd use every day and perhaps she'd be reminded of him as she did her hair and make-up. 'It needs to be a pretty one, though. Mandy likes beautiful things.'

The old lady, who had been peering at him curiously, adjusted the shoulder of her tartan dress – or was it a blanket? He honestly couldn't tell, but it looked a little strange along with the knee-high argyle socks.

'Well, I'll leave you to browse. Shout if you need any help, dear. Come along, Napoleon,' she said to the dog. When it ignored her, she muttered, 'Suit yourself,' and vanished through a curtained doorway.

The dog tilted its head and looked at Jason, then trotted over to a basket, circled on the spot three times, and curled up.

Jason did a lap of the shop, then stopped and looked around helplessly. There were several mirrors, but how was he to know which Mandy would like best? The one with the gilt-edged scroll pattern? The whitewashed wooden one? Or the plain black frame which, frankly, was his favourite? But this wasn't about him or his tastes.

'What do you think?' he asked the little dog. 'Should I go for the most expensive? Or text Lola and ask for her advice?'

The dog looked at him with only the faintest interest.

'No, that would be like admitting defeat. I have to do this myself. I have to get this right.'

The dog yawned.

'I'm boring you, aren't I? Mandy too. That's the trouble. I bring her down, she said. I can't help being cautious. It's just who I am.' He sighed. 'But I don't want to lose her. What should I do, Napoleon?'

At the sound of its name, the dog's ears pricked up.

'Can a man change?' Jason asked. 'Or should I accept that

I'm just not the man for her?'

The blue curtain rustled and Miss Moonshine glided back in, nodding approvingly.

Jason stepped back, horrified. 'Did you hear all that?'

'Hear what, dear?'

That was a relief. 'Nothing. I was just talking gibberish to your dog.'

'He's a good listener, is Napoleon.' She cast the dog a fond look before turning back to address Jason. 'Deaf as a post, of course.'

'Oh.'

She opened a drawer and pulled out a slim silver case. 'Now, here's what you need, dear. I get the feeling you're going to be a little slow on the uptake, so this should speed things up a bit.'

She handed him the case. He turned it over in his hands. It bore a hallmark – sterling silver, possibly? – and when he opened it up it looked like an old-fashioned cigarette case with a mirror inside.

He frowned, puzzled by her choice. 'But that's too small for a dressing table.'

'It's not for your girlfriend, dear. It's for you.'

'Me?'

'Yes. You might find it helps.'

'But I don't need a cigarette case. I don't smoke. Never have. Filthy habit. Not to mention expensive.'

'It was originally a cigarette case, but it could be used for…' she waved a hand vaguely, '… something else. And look. There's a mirror inside.'

'I think you've misunderstood. It's my girlfriend who needs a mirror. Not me.'

The shopkeeper cast him a beady look. 'Look closer at it.'

Her tone made him feel like he was back in school again, so he did as he was told. He ran his fingers over the embossed pattern of a bee and studied the initials engraved below: HKW. This case was a piece of history. In bygone times it might have belonged to an aristocrat, perhaps, or a rich merchant.

'His name was Hugh Knightly-Winterson,' said Miss Moonshine, as if she could read his mind. 'He was ever so charming – with a taste for adventure.'

A picture formed in Jason's mind of a suave, successful man with a waistcoat and an easy smile.

Still, he didn't understand why the white-haired lady thought he'd want it. 'I'm afraid I'm none the wiser,' he said.

'Isn't it beautiful?' she asked pointedly.

He looked at the case again, confused. 'Perhaps,' he said slowly, 'but I don't think aesthetics alone justify an expensive purchase. Nor any purchase, for that matter.'

Her eyes narrowed. 'Young man, what were you worried about when you arrived here?'

'Mandy...' he began warily. His cheeks fired up with heat. How much had she heard exactly? 'We had an argu–'

'Don't tell me!' She held up her hand, and a ruby ring the size of a paperweight gleamed in the morning light. 'I don't need to know the details. This might help, that's all. Give you a new perspective.'

He looked down at the open case again, and his reflection frowned back at him. A new perspective?

He's so pessimistic, Mandy had said. What kind of man did she want him to be? She was fun and beautiful, she lit up a room with her laughter and smiles. She didn't want a dull accountant like him. She deserved someone exciting, someone who would shower her with affection and compliments. He practised a smile. Yes, someone like that.

Bells jangled as the door opened and a hiker came in, stamping her boots and rubbing her hands against the cold.

Jason snapped the case shut. Since when did he pay any

attention to such irrational thoughts and feelings? The old lady was trying to con him into buying a cigarette case he didn't need. He shook his head. 'I don't think–'

'If you don't want it, that's fine with me.' With a turn of her heel and a dramatic toss of her head, she began to walk away.

Panic flooded through him. 'No – wait!'

She stopped.

He cleared his throat, unsure why he'd felt such panic or why the case felt so warm in his hands, so… reassuring. He didn't know what she meant about a new perspective, but he had the strongest sense he needed to find out.

'How much is it?' he asked.

Miss Moonshine named her price. He blinked.

'Are you sure? That seems, ah–' He coughed, and had to force the words out because they didn't come naturally. 'It seems very cheap.'

'Good value, my dear. Everything in here is good value, especially if you take into account the life-changing potential.'

'Life-changing potential? I really would caution against making exaggerated claims you can't deliver.'

Her shrewd gaze held his. 'Who says I can't deliver? My, you are a sceptical young man, aren't you?'

'Realistic,' he corrected.

She smiled. 'We'll see. I'll wrap it up, shall I?'

'I haven't–'

'And what did you decide about the Christmas gift?' Tissue paper rustled and he stared. Her hands moved incredibly quickly and deftly for a lady of her age. She sealed the package with a gold sticker that read Miss Moonshine's Wonderful Emporium. Then she reached under the counter. 'I recommend this trinket box.'

She placed a small round box in front of him. It was studded with brightly coloured beads that caught the light and reminded him of the fairy lights strung all around Mandy's bedroom.

'You don't think the mirror is a good idea?'

'Not for her.'

'W-why for me?'

'You're an intelligent young man. I have no doubt you'll work it out for yourself in the end. You'll find the answers if you look hard enough.'

'Please tell me. I'm not very good at–'

'Your sweetheart will adore this,' she said firmly. 'It can be used for storing make-up or jewellery or even…' her eyes twinkled as she smiled, 'false eyelashes.'

He blinked. 'You've met Mandy, then?'

'Actually, I haven't had that pleasure.'

'So how do you know so much about her? Or me, for that matter?'

'Young man, there are some questions you should never ask a lady.'

He stared at her, awed by the air of mystery that surrounded her. Unnerved, too.

Yet there was nothing but warmth in the old lady's smile as she handed him the trinket box to examine. 'Well?'

'Mandy will love this,' he said weakly. 'Thank you.'

16th December

'What do you want to do tonight?' asked Mandy as she handed him a cup of tea. It was just what Jason needed after a long day at the office. He'd showered and changed as fast as he could, then rushed over to her place, anxious not to be late.

'Whatever you want,' he said carefully. What he really wanted was to stay in and watch television, but her conversation with Lola had made him nervous. It felt like he was on borrowed time and the clock was ticking until Christmas Day. Only nine days left.

'How about we go out for dinner?'

'In December?' He sucked in air. 'Restaurants inflate their prices at this time of year and it will be horribly busy with work parties. The staff will be overworked and the quality of service will be terrible.'

'But it's Christmas.'

'Exactly.'

Her smile faded a little. 'So you want to stay in all December?'

'Well, there'll be bargains in January.'

Too late, Jason glimpsed the disappointment in her eyes, and wished he could bite back his words.

He's so down about everything.

He cringed. This wasn't the man he wanted to be. His fingers gripped the cigarette case in his pocket and resolve washed through him.

He smiled at Mandy. 'Which restaurant were you thinking of?'

'Forget it. It doesn't matter.'

'No, you're right. It's Christmas.'

She peered at him, surprised. 'Well, I've heard that new place – The Colossus – is really special, but it's probably expensive.'

He'd heard about the place – and its prices. He tried to sound casual even as his heart sank at the thought of the bill. 'Let's go there, then.'

Mandy blinked. 'Are you sure?'

'Absolutely.' Jason pulled out the silver case which he had put to practical use as a business card holder. 'In fact, I was given one of their cards. I'll call now and book a table.'

Her eyes widened with delight and she clapped her hands together. 'Oh, how exciting! I've been wanting to go there for ages. Did you know they do a baklava and mince pie sundae? Wait a minute while I run upstairs and get my purse.'

Delight rippled through him to see her look so happy. He glanced down at the case, and saw the man in the mirror grinning back at him.

This was who he wanted to be. The man who could make Mandy smile.

*

Mandy looked around and sighed. 'I'm not sure I want a sundae after all. At this rate I'll be having it for breakfast.'

They'd finished their main courses fifty-three minutes ago, but no one had cleared their table. Jason tried to catch the attention of a waiter, but the guy rushed past, muttering for the third time that he'd be with them shortly. Jason was tempted to carry the plates to the kitchen himself.

'This was such a mistake. You were right,' Mandy said apologetically. 'The prices are extortionate, the poor staff are rushed off their feet, and the service has been terrible.'

'The entertainment is good, though,' he said dryly, as the male belly dancers spun and twirled in their silk outfits.

The music stopped and the entertainers began to move around the room, inviting customers to join them on the stage. A couple of men went up and were encouraged to strip to the waist. Jason watched in horror, suddenly feeling the urge to grab his coat and run.

Mandy turned back to Jason, eyes gleaming. 'Are you going to have a go?'

'No way.' Getting up in front of a roomful of strangers would be his worst nightmare, but to bare his belly and dance – he couldn't think of anything more humiliating. Painful memories of school P.E. lessons rushed to the front of his mind.

He tore his gaze away from the stage. 'Mands? Are you OK?'

She was rummaging desperately through her purse. 'It's my eyelash,' she explained. 'It's come loose. Damn! I don't have a mirror with me.'

Jason glanced around, looking for a sign for the ladies' toilet, then he remembered. 'I have one. Here.'

He opened the silver case and passed it to her. She fiddled with the lash until it was back in place, then turned the case over in her hands. 'Is this new? Where did you get it?'

'Miss Moonshine's.'

'It's nice. Really stylish. And I love the bee on the front.' She handed it back. 'It's not very you, though.'

He tried not to be offended by this. 'Why not?'

'Well, it's not practical or necessary.' She smiled at him from beneath her lashes. 'Not like the waste paper basket you bought me for our anniversary.'

Jason blushed. 'Not that again. You said you needed one!'

'I did. But we'd been going out a month. An anniversary is supposed to be about romance and seduction. Not–' she giggled, '–waste paper baskets!'

'I only wanted to help.' When she'd mentioned she needed one, he'd simply tried to fix the problem. But judging by the laughter which had exploded from her when she'd unwrapped it, she had interpreted it differently. Besides, she'd sprung the anniversary business on him. He knew about wedding anniversaries, but he'd had no idea you were supposed to mark a month of dating someone. What other milestones were there that he didn't know about? They were almost three months into their relationship now, and she hadn't mentioned it again, fortunately.

'I misjudged the situation, and you're never going to let me forget it, are you?'

Mandy grinned. 'Nope! Lola and I have never laughed so much.'

He absently fiddled with the case, flicking the catch open then shut. Was that how she saw him? A laughing stock who, when he did try to be romantic, got it hopelessly wrong? He glanced at his reflection. He looked so worried, so serious.

'So why did you buy it?' she asked, nodding at the case.

'Good question. I'm not sure, really. Miss Moonshine suggested it might come in useful. She was a bit scary, to be honest. I didn't dare contradict her.'

Mandy laughed. 'Yes, my sister had a run-in with her, but she sings her praises since Miss Moonshine gave her that angel stone. It gave Lola the courage to follow her dream and start a new life. She's never been happier.'

Jason fervently hoped the cigarette case wouldn't have the same effect on him. He was very happy with his life in Haven Bridge.

Mandy flicked her long hair back over one shoulder. 'I was so jealous when she went travelling round the world – especially when she was in Oz. Can you imagine anything more exciting?'

A short silence followed, then Jason cleared his throat. 'Actually, I was offered a job in Australia.'

'Were you?' Her eyes widened. 'You've never mentioned that before. Did you take it?'

'No. I turned it down.' He snapped the silver case shut.

'Turned it down? Why?'

'I decided it was too risky.'

'Risky – how? Money-wise?'

'No, it was well paid. But I didn't know the people, the place, and the thought of uprooting myself and going over there only to find I might not like it…'

Mandy stared at him. He felt his cheeks burn under her scrutiny, and the noise of the restaurant seemed to dim a little, as if everyone was leaning in to listen.

'But you might have loved it. It could have been the job of your dreams.'

'Better the devil you know, that's my motto.' He tried to sound casual but found he couldn't quite meet her eye. The silver case glinted in the light as he turned it over in his hand.

She bit her lip. 'Tell me, Jason, have you ever taken a risk?'

'In what?'

'In anything.'

He was quiet a moment while he considered this. He hated risk. He avoided it wherever possible. 'I prefer to make decisions based on facts and logic. I suppose I'm cautious by nature.'

'What about a tiny risk, like trying a new food, or a different route to work?' she asked. 'A more scenic road, for example.'

'Don't be silly,' he blurted. 'That wouldn't be fuel-efficient.'

He could tell this was the wrong answer because her brows pulled together and she quickly tried to hide her exasperation. His gaze dipped to the silver case and it suddenly felt warm in his hand. He pictured the original owner of the cigarette case: debonair, flash, generous. He wouldn't get hung up about the cost of fuel. 'I know it sounds dull,' he muttered, 'but I like to think I'm careful.'

It was a pitiful attempt to justify himself.

Mandy nodded but didn't speak. An awkward silence followed, and when the waiter suddenly materialised, Jason was relieved. He'd said all the wrong things. At this rate his relationship with Mandy wouldn't even last the evening, never mind until Christmas. His throat tightened.

'What can I get you both?' the waiter asked as he cleared their plates.

'Just the bill please,' Mandy said quickly.

Jason watched the waiter disappear, then realised Mandy was looking at him pensively.

'Is that why you became an accountant?' she asked. 'Because it's a safe job?'

He shook his head. 'Absolutely not. I know it's not exciting, but I love my job.'

'Do you? You don't find it… dull?'

He found it hard to put into words how reassuring he found the numbers, the columns, and how satisfying it was to help others. He shook his head. 'I like how logical, how methodical my work is, and it makes perfect sense to me. Unlike…' He looked at Mandy, thinking of how muddled her accounts had been when he'd first taken on her books. 'Well, some people.'

'It's OK. You can say it. I hate that stuff. All the columns and credits and debits. It's all gobbledygook to me.'

He smiled. 'But you're good with people. I'm not. Sometimes I find it so hard to know what to say and what not to say.'

Like his feelings for her. How could he communicate how intense they felt, how vivid? 'Mandy, I – I…'

She blinked at him.

Jason squeezed her hand as he tried to find the words – but his tongue knotted. He was out of his depth. She was glamorous and outgoing, whereas he was quiet and got more satisfaction from balancing a set of accounts than having a night out on–

'Your bill,' said the waiter, slapping it down on the table and making them both jump.

They sprang apart, as if they'd been caught doing far worse than holding hands.

Jason picked up the bill and reached for his wallet.

'I'll pay,' said Mandy. 'You didn't want to come and you were right. It was a waste of money.'

'No,' he said firmly. 'I'm glad we came. We had fun. Let's go halves like we always do. OK?'

She smiled and nodded.

As they stepped out into the night, Mandy turned to him. 'What were you going to say before?'

'When?'

'When the waiter interrupted.'

'Oh, I can't remember,' he lied. His cheeks burned in the darkness. 'It can't have been anything important.'

20th December

Jason switched his computer off, unplugged it, and went to fetch his coat.

His colleague, Isobel, looked at the clock and raised a brow. 'It's not like you to leave so early. What's going on?'

'I'm taking Mandy to the Christmas market in Manchester.'

She peered at him over her glasses. 'Really?'

He buttoned up his coat, then stopped. 'Why are you looking at me like that?'

Her mouth twisted in a pained expression. 'You don't like shopping or crowds, and the Christmas market is going to involve both.'

'It was Mandy's idea.' He sighed. He'd been on the verge of refusing to go when his fingers had brushed against the metal case in his pocket and he'd agreed instead. 'She loves Christmas. And we're going to drop by and see her sister, too. It's not the best timing, I know, but I'll come in early tomorrow to catch up with all this.' He pointed to his computer, visualising the accounts and spreadsheets waiting for his attention, all urgent and needing processing before Christmas.

Isobel took her glasses off. 'Jason, do you think maybe you're trying too hard? First that expensive restaurant, now this. You keep agreeing to do things you don't want to do, just to please her.'

'Yeah, well. I'm trying to be more fun, more exciting.'

She screwed up her nose. 'Why?'

'Because...' he only had five days left to prove himself, he thought. But he couldn't tell Isobel about that. Their conversations were usually about clients or balance sheets, not personal stuff. 'Just because.'

Isobel tutted. 'Did Mandy say something to make you feel that way? You shouldn't feel you have to be more fun or exciting. Is she the right woman for you if you can't be yourself with her?'

Jason shuffled his feet. He was determined to try. His world would have no colour without Mandy. He didn't want to lose her.

But he didn't expect Isobel to understand. She and Mandy had never met, but he suspected they wouldn't get on. They were chalk and cheese.

So he took the coward's way out. 'Better be off,' he mumbled, looking at his watch. 'Don't want to miss the train.'

*

'Be careful of pickpockets,' said Jason as the security man waved them through. The crowd sucked them in and bodies pressed themselves against him from every angle, prodding, jostling and standing on his toes. Jason tensed. Isobel was right. He hated crowds.

'Ooh, look at these miniature houses,' said Mandy, tugging his hand. 'Aren't they amazing?'

He cast a critical eye over the display. 'What would you do with those?'

She shrugged. 'Put them in your living room – or your bedroom. They'd look so cute lined up on the windowsill.'

He picked one up and examined it. He'd wondered if it might have a hidden function as a money box, but there was no secret cavity. It was simply a miniature house. Puzzled, he put it down. He didn't get it at all.

Meanwhile, Mandy had already moved on to the next stall. 'Rhubarb-flavoured gin!' She grinned. 'I could buy a bottle for Lola. She'll love it.'

'At that price? Can't you buy rhubarb in the supermarket and make your own?'

'Oh Jase, you're so funny.' She turned and squealed. 'Chocolate flavour! Now that I'm definitely having.'

She paid and, clutching the bottle, began to push her way through the crowd again. Jason followed.

'Keep tight hold of your handbag,' he warned.

'Stop worrying.'

'I'm just looking out for you.'

She sighed and threw him an exasperated look. 'I don't need looking after, Jase.'

He shrank back. 'I'm sorry. It's just so – so crowded.'

She stopped and peered at him curiously. 'Is that why you're tense?'

'You know I don't like crowds.'

'I didn't realise it affected you so much, though.' Her features suddenly brightened. 'Now I see why you've always avoided shopping with me. All those excuses you made that you were busy. Why didn't you tell me the truth? And why did you agree to come tonight?'

He swallowed. Because there were only five days left and he was petrified she was going to end it. He'd do anything in the hope she might change her mind. 'Because you wanted to,' he managed finally.

Her beautiful dark eyes widened, then she smiled. 'That's so sweet. Tell you what, why don't we leave the shopping and get something to eat instead?'

Half an hour later, Mandy wrapped her fingers around her little red mug and giggled as Jason finished eating his hot dog.

'What?' he asked.

'You've got tomato sauce on your face.'

'Where?' He reached into his pocket and produced a neatly folded tissue. He flicked open the silver case and looked in the mirror.

'You're always prepared for every eventuality, aren't you? I bet you were the model Boy Scout.'

'I was.' He wiped his chin. 'Better?'

She nodded, then reached up onto tiptoes and kissed the spot where the sauce had been.

He stilled. 'What was that for?'

'Do I need a reason? Can't I just kiss you on impulse?'

His cheeks flushed and he instinctively glanced around, wondering if anyone had seen.

Then again, did it matter if they had? He thought of the man in the mirror. He wouldn't be embarrassed or tongue-tied. He'd kiss her back.

Jason brushed the hair out of her eyes, still puzzling over what had prompted her to kiss him. Her nose and cheeks were red with cold beneath her woolly hat, but her smile was as bright as the lights strung around the wooden chalets. 'You really like the Christmas market, don't you?' he said fondly.

'I love it!' She closed her eyes and inhaled. The air was rich with the smell of cooked food and syrupy spiced wine. 'Don't you think it's wonderful, all the excitement and magic of Christmas? Just think how many nationalities there are here.' She gestured to the stalls around them. 'Holland, Spain, France. All sorts of exotic places.'

'They're probably from Huddersfield,' he said dryly.

Mandy gave him a playful thump on the arm. 'You know, I'm beginning to realise we're opposites, you and me.'

The back of his neck prickled with panic. 'We are. But perhaps we complement each other. Perhaps I can help you with the things you find difficult, and vice versa.'

'Like you tried to do when you looked at the salon's accounts last week?' she said and smiled. 'Which reminds, me – we need to talk about that. Properly, this time.'

He tensed. 'Are you sure? I don't want to make you cry again.'

She dipped her head. 'You were only trying to help and I took it the wrong way. But I would appreciate your advice, because I don't know what to do. We're so busy that our customers have to book months in advance to get an appointment.'

He glanced at her, worried about saying the wrong thing

again. 'You could employ one new person then see how it goes,' he said carefully. 'If business continues to grow, take on another in six months' time. Perhaps think about raising your prices, too. Just proceed cautiously, and that way your risks are minimised.'

She smiled, and he felt a rush of relief.

'Proceed cautiously,' she repeated. 'Were you always so sensible?'

'Actually, my nickname at school was Captain Sensible.'

A giggle escaped her lips. Damn. Why had he told her that?

She stroked his cheek affectionately, and the heat from her fingers permeated his skin.

'I'm sorry I got angry the other night. It had been a long day and I really liked the idea of having more people to help me.' She hung her head. 'I don't want the business to go down the drain after Mum worked so hard to establish it.'

He blinked with surprise. 'But it's not going down the drain. It's doing well.'

'You said it wasn't. You said I shouldn't take on new people.'

'I said it was a high-risk decision when you balance income versus costs.'

'Oh, Jason.' She winked. 'I love it when you talk dirty.'

He blushed and thought again about kissing her.

Instead, he looked at his watch. 'We need to be at your sister's place in thirteen minutes. We'd better make a move.'

She hooked her arm in his and they set off down another alley of stalls. Star-shaped paper lanterns glowed crimson and gold, and as they walked past, tinny Christmas carols butted up against each other, clashing discordantly. They paused a moment to listen to a school band squeezing out the tune of 'Little Donkey', and Mandy tossed a pound coin into their collection. When it finished, they moved on downhill towards the high street, where the crowd thinned a little.

Someone bumped into Mandy.

'My bag!' she shrieked, and began to run after the man.

Jason froze. It took him a moment before he realised what had happened, and by then the hooded figure had already disappeared. In her high-heeled boots Mandy hadn't got very far. Jason ran past her, but when he turned the corner the road was thick with people. He quickly scanned the scene, looking out for anyone running or clutching the colourful bag, but he saw neither.

He rushed back to Mandy. 'Did he hurt you?'

She shook her head, mute.

'Are you OK?'

'Yes, but – but my purse was in there. All that cash…' She had withdrawn a thick wad from the cash machine before they left Haven Bridge. Her brown eyes shone under the golden streetlight. 'That was everything I had saved for Christmas.'

'Don't worry about that.'

'But how will I buy Christmas presents now?'

'Mandy, I'll replace the cash.' He had more than enough put by. Perhaps there was an upside to being careful with his money. 'Come on, we need to phone the police and report it.'

*

He stayed with Mandy while she gave the police her statement, then he called her sister, explained what had happened, and bought her a new train ticket so they could get back to Haven Bridge. At Mandy's, he lit the fire in the lounge and poured her a chocolate-flavoured gin. Her hand shook as she took the glass.

'When does your mum get back from America?' he asked, taking a throw and draping it round her shoulders. Everyone had been thrilled when her mum had realised her dream of becoming a full-time singer and gone on tour with a tribute band, but at times like this he knew Mandy missed her.

'Not until tomorrow.' Her teeth were chattering. She looked so lost and vulnerable.

He glanced at his watch. He had a mountain of work to catch up with in the morning, but he didn't want to leave her here alone. 'Do you want me to stay the night?'

'Yes.' She smiled at him from beneath her lashes, the vulnerability suddenly gone, replaced with a devilishly flirtatious look. 'But not because of what happened.'

Heat rolled through him, and it wasn't just lust. It was so much more than that. It swelled in his chest, it made his lungs pound as if he'd been running. 'Yes, well, they say there's a big freeze coming tonight. Perhaps I can make myself useful and keep you warm in bed.'

The fire crackling was the only sound as Mandy looked up at him. 'Thank you for looking after me,' she said softly.

'I didn't, though, did I?' He shook his head. 'If I'd reacted faster, he wouldn't have got away. I should have chased him down and got your bag back.'

'Don't be silly. What if he'd had a knife? You could have been hurt. And you have looked after me, anyway.' Her eyes gleamed, reflecting the dancing flames. 'You're always there when I need you. I know I can depend on you, Jase, and that means a lot.'

He took her hand and squeezed it, because he couldn't speak. The look in her eyes made his throat tighten, and emotions bulldozed him. He was glad she saw him as dependable and someone she could lean on, but he wanted to be more. He wanted to be her hero, the man in the mirror who swept her off her feet. Not the cautious accountant with a ticking bomb poised to detonate and blow him out of her life on Christmas Day.

'Jase, there's something we need to talk about,' she whispered.

Dread plunged through him. He jumped up, stammering; 'I – I'll go and run you a hot bath, shall I? Let you relax for a while.'

She stood up too. 'Jase–'

'It'll warm you up.' He stepped back, bumping into the coffee table. 'You're still shaking.'

'Jase, it won't take–'

'I'll put the kettle on, too. You've had a shock. Perhaps gin wasn't the best idea. I'll make you a cup of tea. Sugary tea, that's what they recommend for shock.' He moved and she reached to stop him, but he snatched his arm away and fled the room. His feet pounded up the stairs.

In the bathroom, he pressed his back against the closed door and slid down. His legs shook, his pulse was a drumroll in his ears.

She wasn't going to wait until Christmas was over. She wanted to end it now. And he'd been so terrified, he'd run rather than let her speak.

He hung his head. What kind of coward was he?

A coward in love.

The realisation only made him feel worse.

A quiet thud caught his attention. The silver case had slipped out of his pocket onto the bathroom floor. He picked it up and flicked it open. His reflection stared forlornly at him. The man in the mirror would have caught the thief, James Bond style. He would have wrestled the guy to the ground and heroically turned him over to the police.

But Jason wasn't heroic or athletic. He wasn't even brave enough to tell Mandy he loved her. It was hopeless. He could never be the man she wanted him to be.

The case trembled in his hand. Had he been deluding himself that he could change?

A mirror couldn't change your life, no matter what Miss Moonshine said.

21st December

Jason had woken early, ready to go to work, but he'd glanced outside and quickly gone back to bed. No one would be going anywhere today, he'd told himself, trying to quash his guilt, and he'd make sure he caught up with all his emails.

But then he'd spent the next two hours watching Mandy sleep.

Now her alarm sounded and her eyes fluttered open. He brushed the hair back from her face. She was beautiful like this, her face naked, her velvety skin warm next to his.

As she got out of bed and went over to the window, he tried to hold the moment in his head, to commit it to memory. Whatever happened in future, he didn't want to forget how it had felt to hold her.

'It's snowed,' she cried. 'Jase, look! OMG, there's loads of it!'

'I know. I can't get to work.'

'Oh no.' Her hands flew to her face. 'I'll have to cancel all my clients.'

'Will that be a problem?'

She thought about it a moment. 'Nah. They'd probably have cancelled anyway. A lot of them have kids and the schools will be closed.' Her anxious look was replaced with an excited smile. 'I know! Why don't we go sledging?'

'Sledging?' He frowned. 'It's dangerous. You might get hurt. And after yesterday you should be taking it…' His words trailed off as disappointment pulled her dark brows together.

He thought of the silver case. What would the other man do?

'Do you have a sledge?'

She grinned and nodded. 'It's in the shed.'

Hope made her eyes sparkle like glittering baubles.

'Fine. We'll go sledging.'

*

'So where was your favourite place to sledge?' she asked as

they trudged away from town. Even in boots they were having difficulty. The snow had been swept into deep drifts, and patches of ice made even walking treacherous.

'Favourite place?'

'Growing up. Where did you go sledging?'

'I've never been.'

Mandy stopped and took his arm. 'What?'

He shrugged, uncomfortable because she was staring at him.

'Not even when you were a boy?'

'Especially not when I was a boy. Mum would never have allowed it.' He set off again, tucking the sledge under his arm. Shouts and squeals could be heard before the hill came into sight.

'Why not?'

'She was afraid I'd have an asthma attack. Or break my glasses.'

'You wore glasses?'

He nodded. Contacts were a lot easier. They climbed the hill and Jason's stomach sank as three children piled onto one sledge sped past them at breakneck speed. Why had he agreed to this? He'd never understood the appeal.

'Would it have been the end of the world if you had broken them?'

'Definitely. We couldn't afford new ones.'

'We weren't exactly rolling in money either, but Mum never let it stop us having fun.'

He tilted his head a fraction, wishing Mandy could have met his mum and seen for herself the warm, nurturing woman she had been. 'Mum had me late in life,' he explained quietly. 'For many years she and Dad thought they would never be able to have children. Perhaps that's why when I came along she was very protective.'

'Because she loved you.' Mandy smiled.

'Yes.'

They reached the top and he laid the sledge down. The hill looked impossibly steep from up here. 'So how do we do this? One by one, or together?'

'Together, of course. I don't want to miss your first time sledging. I'll go in front and you can steer.'

'Steer?' Icy fear slipped down his spine. 'How do I do that?'

Mandy sat on the sledge and demonstrated. 'Just lean your body left or right. Don't worry, it's not rocket science.'

But he was worried. He didn't want her to get hurt, and if she did, he certainly didn't want to be responsible.

He sat down behind her. She fitted snugly between his legs and he wrapped his arms around her. The sledge began to slide forwards, slowly at first.

'That's it,' she said, and leaned back. 'Now lift your feet up. Ahhh!'

Suddenly they were speeding down the hill, slicing past other sledges, racing past people who had fallen in the snow. The rush of wind on his face snatched his breath away. Blood fired through his veins. It was like flying, it was so fast and free and – and primal. Mandy's cries of delight matched his own, and they reached the bottom, breathless.

'Quick!' he said, glancing over his shoulder. 'Get out of the way before someone lands on top of us.'

He jumped up and pulled her with him to the side.

She was still laughing as she threw her arms around him. 'Oh, that was amazing! I'm sure I never went so fast with Lola. How was it for you, sledging virgin?'

He looked up at the hill they'd just descended. The cold air on his face, the adrenaline pumping through him. It had been exhilarating. And not so dangerous, after all. In fact, as long as you didn't sledge towards a tree or a lake, he reckoned the statistical probability of an accident happening was actually very low.

He grinned. 'I loved it.'

23rd December

'Jason?'

He smiled into the phone. 'Mandy.'

But his smile faded as his gaze fell on his desk calendar. Just two days left.

'I can't talk long, I've got a client waiting, but what are you doing tonight?'

'Erm…' He sat back in his chair, feeling more than a little smug. 'Celebrating with a beer that I've finished work.'

Isobel looked up from her computer and stuck her tongue out at him. He did the same, although he knew that once he'd put the phone down he'd be helping her finish her work, too.

'Oh, and wrapping presents for your mum and sister,' he remembered.

'Nothing important. Good.'

'Why?'

'A customer gave me a voucher for a dance class. It's tonight at eight o'clock.'

He shook his head and smiled. 'You know I don't do dancing.'

Isobel smirked as she got up and left the room. He heard her filling the kettle next door.

'Oh, Jase. Please?'

'No, I really don't–'

'The lessons cost thirty pounds and we've got the chance to go for free.'

'Even if they paid me, I don't want to be humiliated in public.'

Mandy giggled. 'Jase, I can't go alone. I need a partner.'

'Trust me, you don't want me. I'll stand on your toes or break your leg or something.'

'Don't be so dramatic. This isn't an extreme sport we're talking about, it's dancing. The jive, in fact.'

'You could ask your mum. She'd like that kind of thing.'

'She's got a gig.'

'Your sister?' he said desperately.

'She's not coming home until tomorrow. Jase, please…' He could picture her expression, her long lashes curving seductively. 'For me?'

Oh, how much he wanted to please her. But he couldn't dance.

He closed his eyes and resignation swept through him. What difference did it make if he made a complete fool of himself now? In two days it would be Christmas.

*

They hurried up the stone steps to the top floor. A couple of Mandy's clients had been late so she'd got behind schedule, and now it was apparent the class had begun without them. Everyone was clustered together, listening carefully to the teacher. Jason did a double take when he saw the small, white-haired figure in dainty silver heels.

'You didn't tell me Miss Moonshine was the teacher,' he whispered.

Mandy shrugged. 'I didn't know. I thought she rented the room out to a dance company.'

'You, young man,' said Miss Moonshine. 'Come up here and help me demonstrate.'

He looked behind him, ready to step aside. But there was no one behind him. His heart skipped a beat.

'Come along,' she said impatiently.

His palms broke out in sweat. This was going to be excruciating. Just like drama lessons at school when he used to stammer so badly he couldn't speak, and the whole class would fall about laughing.

Mandy nudged him and smiled encouragingly. He stepped forward and Miss Moonshine took his hand.

It turned out to be easier than he'd expected. In fact, it was quite logical. He kicked his legs, one two three, in time to the music; he turned, he mirrored Miss Moonshine's moves, slightly shocked by how gracefully the old lady moved. When it was over, he came back to Mandy, relieved he hadn't made a complete ass of himself.

They spent the rest of the lesson practising with their partners, and the old lady threaded her way round the room, giving them each pointers and words of encouragement.

'Keep your back straight and chin up,' she told him.

'I love your shoes, Miss Moonshine,' said Mandy. 'Where are they from?'

Miss Moonshine looked down. 'These old things? I can't even remember. It's a long time since we first danced the jive.'

'When was that? In the sixties?'

'Oh no, dear. The thirties.'

As she moved off, Mandy and Jason exchanged a smile. 'Did she say the thirties?'

'She must be getting confused.'

A curious sensation overtook Jason as they carried on practising the moves.

'You're really good at this,' said Mandy as they danced opposite each other.

'Thanks.' He beamed, amazed he could keep up and his limbs weren't getting tangled. It did help that the dance had structure, but still – he'd never expected to enjoy it so much.

By the time they'd finished learning the dance, he was quite out of breath, but when Miss Moonshine announced, 'This time we'll start at the beginning and go through the whole dance,' he couldn't wait to practise the full routine.

The music started. Out of the corner of his eye, Jason

noticed other couples glancing at them and he thought he saw Miss Moonshine nod in their direction, but it took his full concentration to remember the moves, so he focused on kicking his legs and wiggling his hips, and grinned as Mandy did the same – all in perfect time with him. The space around them seemed to grow wider as they span and jumped. One by one the other couples stopped to watch, but he barely noticed. Pleasure exploded in him and adrenaline pumped through every vein. This was incredible.

They finished the dance with a final flourish, the music stopped, and there was a heartbeat's silence before a cheer filled the room. Shocked, Jason realised everyone had been watching them, and clapping the loudest was Miss Moonshine. He glanced at Mandy, and she beamed at him. Never in a million years would he have predicted that he'd enjoy dancing or be any good at it. But the whole class was cheering, and not in mockery like at school, but with genuine admiration.

As the clapping died down, Miss Moonshine approached them. 'Well, I never! You two really do have something very special.'

'He's amazing, isn't he?' Mandy grinned.

Jason felt a surge of pleasure as their gazes met and held. He'd come here to please her, but discovered something he loved. He couldn't wait for the next lesson.

Miss Moonshine peered at him curiously. 'You've learned fast. Much faster than I expected.'

He blushed.

But it was only later that he wondered, had she been talking about the dancing – or something else?

25th December: Christmas Day

Jason watched nervously as Mandy tore the tissue paper off her gift. She held it up, and the jewel-encrusted trinket box gleamed and twinkled as it caught the light.

'Oh Jason, it's gorgeous.' She opened it and touched the satin lining. Her eyes shone as she kissed him. 'Thank you so much.'

'You're welcome.' He was glad she liked it. It might be the last gift he ever gave her. 'And thanks for my dancing shoes.'

He looked forward to using them, although after the euphoria of the class had worn off, he'd realised that one successful jive probably wasn't enough to save a relationship.

A timer sounded in the kitchen. Mandy's mum looked up. 'That's the nut roast. Lola, can you give me a hand with the gravy, love?'

'I'll get the beers,' said Lola's boyfriend, Scott. 'You having one, mate?'

Jason nodded. The three of them disappeared into the next room, leaving Mandy and Jason alone. He busied himself picking up the discarded wrapping paper, smoothing it all and folding it flat.

Mandy reached out to stop him. 'Leave it,' she said, and touched his hand.

'But if you fold it flat it takes less space in the–'

'Can you stop? Please. While it's just the two of us, there's something I need to talk to you about.'

He stilled. His mouth became dry, but he did as she asked and put the paper down.

'There's something I need to tell you, Jase.'

He pressed his palms together, steeling himself. 'Yes, I know.'

Her head jerked up. 'You know?'

He nodded, unable to bring himself to look at her. He felt like a condemned man finally facing his fate. His limbs were painfully heavy. 'This conversation is overdue. Go ahead. I'm listening.'

Mandy cleared her throat. 'Well, to start with, you haven't been your usual self lately and it – it's been worrying me.'

It was his turn to look up, startled. This wasn't what he'd expected her to say. 'How do you mean?'

'It's like you've been trying extra hard to please me. I know you weren't keen on going to the Christmas markets or sledging. And then the dance class…'

He sighed. 'It hasn't worked, then?'

'What hasn't worked?'

'I have a confession to make.' He rubbed a hand over his face. 'I overheard you talking to Lola. The day after we argued. I heard you saying you were thinking of breaking up with me.'

She frowned, then her mouth made a perfect circle as realisation dawned. Her eyes filled with regret. 'I'm so sorry you heard that. You must have been so hurt.'

'It's how you felt,' he said flatly. 'And in a way it was what I needed to hear because it made me realise how much–'

The words stuck. The room fell silent.

'How much?' she prompted.

Jason closed his eyes. She might laugh. She'd almost certainly pity him. He couldn't say it. 'Nothing.'

She looked disappointed.

He pulled the silver case out of his pocket. 'I was scared of losing you so I tried to change. I tried to be more like the man you want, the man you deserve.'

'But–' she started.

He held his hand up. He didn't often interrupt others, but he might as well finish his piece. 'I tried to be less cautious and more relaxed, more fun instead.' He gave a dry laugh and tossed the case onto the sofa. 'I know I didn't succeed, but I tried to change. For you.'

Silence filled the house. Even the kitchen was quiet, and he glanced at the door. The shadows of three pairs of feet told him Scott, Lola and her mum were listening too. He cringed. This was one Christmas he was never going to forget. But his humiliation seemed insignificant compared to the crushing of his heart.

'All because of what I said.' She shook her head. 'I feel so guilty.'

'It's OK, Mandy.' He got to his feet. 'I'll let myself out. Thank your mum for everything, will you?'

'No!' She jumped to her feet. 'Don't go.'

'I think it's for the best.'

'No, it's not,' she said fiercely, and took his hands in hers. 'It's sweet that you tried to change for me, but you didn't need to. That conversation you heard – I was angry and I didn't mean what I said.'

'I was a glass-half-empty person. It was all true.'

'No, it wasn't. That's what I've learned over the past few days.' She squeezed his fingers and he glanced down at her glittery gold nails. 'I love that you're cautious and careful and you plan for the future; I love that you're a good listener and you're calm in a crisis and always there when I need you. You don't get carried away in the excitement of an idea like I do, but you weigh up the pros and cons and consider it carefully. I love that you're clever and you can look at a page of numbers and instantly understand them, whereas I add up a column three times and get three different answers. And I know you don't like to talk about your feelings, but you need to know that I love you, Jason.'

He frowned. 'What – what did you just say?'

She grinned. 'I've been trying to tell you for the past week. I love you.'

His mouth worked, but no sound came out.

'When we had that argument about the salon I flew off the handle because I thought you didn't have faith in me. I was scared you didn't feel the same way about me.'

He stared at her, not following the logic of what she'd said, and not believing his ears. She loved him? Mandy loved him?

'So the question is,' she went on, 'how do you feel about me?'

'I – I…' The words stuck in his throat. He did love her. Why couldn't he say it?

'I knew it.' She dipped her head and her long hair fell over her face.

'Mands–'

'Forget it.' She held up her hand and his mouth snapped shut, defeated.

Silence followed, then the door opened and her mum came back in followed by Lola and Scott. Mandy picked up a piece of discarded wrapping paper and turned away.

Scott put a beer in his hand. 'Here you go, mate,' he said quietly.

'What's this?' asked Lola. She was holding the silver case.

'Oh – er – just something I picked up at Miss Moonshine's.' He couldn't take his eyes off Mandy. She looked hurt. Because of him.

'Really? What did she say when she gave it to you?'

He dragged his gaze away and tried to remember. 'She told me I needed to get a new perspective.'

'A new perspective? What do you think she meant?'

'I'm not sure.'

He'd thought she meant he had to change. Lighten up and try new things. But perhaps she'd meant something else…

'Excuse me a moment,' he murmured, and left the room.

Upstairs, instead of turning left for the bathroom, he tiptoed into Mandy's room. There, on her dressing table, was what he was looking for.

When he returned to the lounge, the television was on in the background and everyone was chatting loudly. He sat down beside Mandy. She threw him a weak smile.

He handed her the silver case and her brows pulled together in a quizzical look. 'Open it,' he said softly.

She unclipped the catch and the mirror caught the light as

she opened it. He watched her face as puzzlement gave way to surprise, then delight.

'Oh, Jase,' she whispered, grinning. 'Really?'

He smiled and nodded. Her eyes shone as she reached to kiss him.

'I'm not very good with words,' he said apologetically.

'Maybe not the spoken kind, but this…' she gazed at the mirror, 'it's beautiful. Can I keep it?'

He bit his lip. He'd become quite attached to the silver case. But, on reflection, perhaps it had fulfilled its purpose. 'Yes,' he said. 'It's yours.'

They both looked at the words written across the mirror in red lip pencil:

I love you, Mandy.
Always have, always will.
Jason.x

Writing the words had felt like a weight off his chest. It had felt… right.

'What are you two looking so pleased about?' asked Lola.

Mandy grinned, and she and Jason exchanged a knowing look. 'Nothing,' she said, and snapped the case shut. 'Jase just gave me the best Christmas present.'

He sent a silent message of gratitude to Miss Moonshine. The silver case had led him to try new things and be braver, all of which had been more satisfying than he'd expected. But having the courage to acknowledge how he felt about Mandy had been the most rewarding of all. And he couldn't have done that without the mirror.

Sophie Claire writes emotional stories set in England and in sunny Provence, where she spent her summers as a child.

Previously, she worked in marketing and proofreading

academic papers, but now she's delighted to spend her days dreaming up heartwarming contemporary romance stories set in beautiful places.

sophieclaire.co.uk

How to Save Christmas

By Kate Field

The road swung to the left, and there, at last, was the sight that Tabitha had been longing to see for the last few, dark miles. A farmhouse lay just across the fields, and the lights blazing from the windows lifted her spirits, which had begun to waver as she'd left behind the streets of Haven Bridge and plunged deeper into the countryside. She turned off the road as her headlights picked out a tatty sign for Broad View Farm, bumped along a narrow track, and finally pulled up with a sigh of relief on the gravel outside the front door.

She left the car, wrapping her scarf more tightly round her as the biting December wind tried to creep through the wool, and knocked on the front door. No answer. She checked the instructions on her phone again. She was in the right place, at the right time. There was supposed to be a warm welcome waiting for her. But she knocked three more times, and no one came to the door.

Lights shone from the two downstairs windows. Surely that meant someone was at home? Tabitha peered through the one on the left of the front door. It looked into a living room, a cosy place with a roaring open fire, squashy sofas and books abandoned on the coffee table. A large Christmas tree smothered in tinsel and baubles filled one corner of the room. There was no one inside. She crossed to the window on the right, cupped her hands round her face and pressed her nose to the glass.

She recoiled as she spotted a man, standing completely still, gazing right at her. She smiled and lifted her hand in a friendly wave, but he didn't react, and peering again, she realised that while he was facing the window, his gaze was focused inwards rather than outside. He didn't appear to like what he saw; deep frown lines scored his forehead and his shoulders hunched forwards, as if weighed down by an invisible burden.

Tabitha stood transfixed, and then, as she was wondering whether she dared bang on the glass and disturb him, a child ran into the room – a girl of about six, her face full of laughter. The transformation was instant; the man switched on like the lights on a Christmas tree, sparkling with life as he scooped the girl into his arms. He was younger than Tabitha had initially thought, perhaps mid-thirties like herself, not bad looking when he smiled with such tangible love softening his features...

Tabitha drew back, waited a moment, then knocked on the front door again. This time, the door opened, and the man she'd seen in the kitchen stared out at her in silence.

'Hello! I'm Tabitha Grey... I've rented the Chicken House for Christmas. Are you Rob?'

He nodded, but a look of dismay passed over his face.

'Oh, bol –' He stopped as the sound of skipping feet behind him announced the arrival of the little girl, who grasped his hand and stared at Tabitha curiously. 'Is that today? I thought you were arriving tomorrow. I was going to light the fire...' He sighed, pulled down two coats from the pegs behind the door, and bundled the girl into one and himself into the other. 'It's across the yard. I'll show you the way.'

He grabbed a large torch from the hall table and led the way round the side of the house, over a cobbled courtyard, through a gate, and down a short path until the beam of his torch lit a small, stone building. He pushed open the door and flicked on the light. Tabitha followed him in and looked round quickly, her worries rushing away. The welcome might not have been as warm as the website had claimed, but this place was exactly as advertised. The door opened into an open-plan, rectangular room, with a log burner and sofas at one end, and a compact kitchen with a breakfast bar and two stools at the other. A steep flight of stairs presumably led up to the bedroom and bathroom. It was perfect. Except…

'There are no Christmas decorations,' she said, walking round the room and running her fingers along the exposed stone walls, as if she might find a secret switch that would convert the room into a festive grotto. 'Do you not provide a tree, at least?' She couldn't keep the disappointment from her voice. How could you have Christmas without decorations? It was the one bit of normality she'd been counting on this year – that it would still look like Christmas, even though it felt so odd. 'I'd assumed…'

The man had crouched down by the fire, stacking kindling in the log burner. He glanced up.

'I haven't had time. Sorry.' He scratched his chin, leaving a streak of smut behind. 'I'll cut one tomorrow. I don't have spare decorations, though.'

'I'll be able to pick some up in Haven Bridge, won't I?' Tabitha asked. She smiled at the girl, remembering the glorious excess of the tree in the farmhouse, and guessing who must have decorated it. 'What do you think? Lots of lights and tinsel?'

The girl grinned and nodded. Rob lit the fire and stood up.

'We'll leave you to it. You know where we are if you need anything.'

And he led the girl away, leaving Tabitha on her own.

*

She was up early the next morning, woken by the unfamiliar silence, broken only by the occasional bleat of a sheep. She pulled open the curtains and saw what it had been too dark to appreciate last night: the Chicken House stood on the edge of a field filled with sheep, some sleeping on the grass like large white molehills, others stumbling to their feet to start grazing. She opened the window, breathing in the fresh air of the countryside, and basking in the view which was so different – delightfully different – to the estate of executive houses that appeared through every window at home. This was exactly what she remembered from childhood holidays on her grandparents' farm; exactly what she had wished for her own children's childhood. Exactly what she was now determined to give them.

She was about to close the window and get dressed when she saw Rob striding through the field, pushing a wheelbarrow containing what could only be a Christmas tree. She ran downstairs and opened the door, just as he was propping the tree up against the wall. The base of the trunk had been sharpened and fixed to a stump of wood to keep it upright.

'Hello! Is that for me? You're early.'

Rob looked at her and glanced away quickly.

'There's rain forecast,' he said. 'You need to get it in before it's wet.'

Tabitha stepped outside and wrapped her arms round the tree, trying to get a hold. The needles prickled through the thin fabric of her pyjamas.

'Can't your partner – ?' Rob began.

'No partner,' she replied, with a tight smile. 'I'm here on my own.'

'For Christmas?'

'Yes.'

Rob studied her, deep brown eyes lingering on hers, and then without a word he lifted up the tree and carried it inside.

*

After a leisurely breakfast, Tabitha drove into Haven Bridge. The farm was only a couple of miles out of town, in the village of Broadthwaite, and the journey rushed by as she admired the scenery, beautiful even in the thick of winter and with dark clouds threatening overhead. She parked near the railway station and wandered along the canal towpath into town, trying to look at everything objectively, but already won over by the charm of the colourful narrowboats, the handsome stone buildings lining the water's edge, and the well-sized children's playground. Her conviction increased with every step: this could work. This could be the right place. They could be happy here…

As if it were meant to be, the first business she saw when she crossed the bridge that led from the towpath into town was an estate agent's, and she pored over the houses in the window, mentally buying several of the characterful cottages on display whether she could afford them or not. It was the work of a moment to go inside and register her details, and walk away with a handful of property brochures to study in the Chicken House later.

The town was exactly as Tabitha remembered it from long ago visits, but now it was even better, because it was decorated for Christmas, her favourite time of the year. A huge tree stood in the market square, the shop windows held magnificent festive displays, and snatches of Christmas songs and carols drifted out as shoppers opened the doors. She was struck by a pang of regret that Joe and Lily weren't here to enjoy it with her, followed by a swift flash of hope that next year they would be exploring these shops together.

After visiting a Christmas shop – a lucky discovery that provided all the tinsel, lights and baubles even she could possibly need – she continued along the main street to explore the town further and see how well she had remembered it. A handsome building set back from the road looked familiar, and the name rang a bell: Miss Moonshine's Wonderful Emporium. Tall windows surrounded a solid black door, and in one of the windows… Tabitha had to go closer for a better look, passing under an ornate archway decorated with red and white flowers. Yes, it was as she'd thought – a vintage Singer sewing machine, the exact model her grandmother had taught her to sew on. Unable to resist, Tabitha pushed open the door and went in.

A lady stood behind the counter, stroking a tiny, fluffy dog. With fuzzy white hair, and a red velvet dress that was so long it grazed the tops of heavy Doc Marten boots, she perfectly matched the flowers outside.

'Hello, my dear, and welcome to my emporium.' The lady smiled at Tabitha. 'Take your time and have a good browse. There's something for everyone here.'

Tabitha smiled and looked round eagerly. It wasn't the sewing shop she'd anticipated, but she wasn't disappointed. Far from it: her initial glance took in numerous displays that she'd like to investigate, but there was no doubt where she had to go first, despite the bulging bags already in her hands. The back wall held a display of Christmas decorations like nothing she'd seen in the Christmas shop. These were all unique, exquisitely crafted items, and her fingers were already picking up a gorgeous group of three felted tree decorations, in the shape of a snowman, a reindeer, and a cat with a bell round its neck.

'So clever, aren't they?' Miss Moonshine had followed Tabitha over to the display. 'Handmade by a wonderfully skilled lady. These are the last ones I have left this year.'

Tabitha couldn't resist. Lily would love the reindeer, and Joe the snowman.

'I'll take these two,' she said, holding them out to Miss Moonshine. 'My children will love them.'

'Of course they will. But are you sure you want to leave poor tabby on her own? Only think how lonely she might be…'

Tabitha laughed.

'Tabby cat! That was the nickname my grandma gave me. Short for Tabitha.' She twirled the felt decoration in her hand, memories rushing in. Miss Moonshine touched her arm.

'I think the tabby cat must be meant for you, don't you?'

Tabitha smiled at this nonsense, but five minutes later, she walked away with three felt decorations tucked securely in her bag.

*

As Tabitha neared the farmhouse, she had to swerve to avoid a battered 4x4 driving down the farm track at speed. The driver, a woman in her fifties with a gaudy headscarf wrapped round her hair, thumped on her horn as she passed. Rob was standing on the gravel in front of the house, hands stuffed in his pockets and a bleak expression on his face.

'She was in a hurry,' Tabitha said, unloading her shopping from the car. Perhaps she had gone overboard with the Christmas decorations; the bags seemed to have multiplied during the journey back to the Chicken House. 'Is something the matter?'

Rob shrugged and kicked a black bin liner that lay at his feet.

'I've ruined Christmas.'

Tabitha had to laugh at the melodramatic way he announced this.

'What's happened?' She gestured at the bin liner, which seemed to be full of holes and tears. 'Is that Santa's sack? Did the presents fall out?'

She stopped laughing when Rob's bleak eyes met hers.

'Worse than that. I was storing some of the costumes for the village nativity parade. The mice have got at them. They're either full of holes, or covered in droppings. We can't use them.'

A village nativity parade! Tabitha longed to know more about that – it sounded a perfect Christmas treat – but now didn't seem the right moment to be thinking about her social diary.

'Can you buy some more? When is the parade?'

'Saturday night.' It was Thursday lunchtime now; that didn't leave much time. 'And the costumes were decades old and handmade, part of the tradition. New ones won't be the same.'

Tabitha had sympathy with that. She hated the shiny nylon fancy dress outfits she saw on sale every year.

'Could someone make more costumes? What about your wife?'

Rob's face had been bleak before; now it seemed as if his expression shut down completely.

'She died. Four years ago.' He thrust out the words like a shield, as if to repel more questions. 'But I don't need pity,' he added, before Tabitha could utter a word. 'We manage.'

Tabitha bit back the trite phrase she had been ready to use to commiserate his loss.

'Why wouldn't you manage?' she said instead. 'Single mothers do it all the time.'

And then, wondering if she had gone too far in the opposite direction from sympathy, she picked up her shopping bags and headed off to the Chicken House.

The annoying thing was, she reflected, as she pushed the door open with her shoulder and dropped her bags on the floor, that she could have helped, if only she had a sewing machine. Dressmaking was her job – or her pin-money hobby, as her ex-husband had insisted on describing it in their final years, when he had risen to managerial level and thought it beneath his status to be married to a seamstress. Tabitha loved making clothes and would have enjoyed helping, taking on more of a challenge than the shortening of trousers and dresses that occupied most of her days. The work would have distracted her from how much she was missing the children, too. But her sewing machine was at home, at least a two-hour round trip away, and besides, Rob didn't seem the sort to welcome help. That muttered 'we manage' might only have been two words, but they told a whole story.

Tabitha shrugged off any further contemplation of him, picked a playlist of Christmas songs on her phone, and sang along loudly as she started to decorate the tree, not stopping until the room was transformed into a festive grotto, with fairy lights strung across the mantelpiece and tinsel twisted along the banister rail. She found a place for all the decorations she'd bought that day, apart from the felt figures from Miss Moonshine's shop. She'd save those for when she celebrated Christmas for the second time with Joe and Lily.

She was packing the figures away again when she remembered what had drawn her to Miss Moonshine's shop in the first place. The sewing machine in the window... Perhaps she could help Rob after all, whether he wanted it or not. Spotting him pull up in the courtyard on a quad bike, she dashed out of the Chicken House and accosted him.

'Rob! I think I might have the answer. About the missing costumes for the nativity. If I can get hold of a sewing machine, I could make them for you.'

He swung his legs off the bike and stood in front of her. He was at least a foot taller than her, but she was close enough to see the genuine puzzlement on his face.

'Why would you do that?'

'Because it's Christmas. Season of goodwill to all.' She

laughed, but he still seemed sadly lacking in Christmas spirit, and didn't so much as smile back. 'I get it. You think it's none of my business. But sewing is my job. I love doing it. I can knock up a few costumes easily, and they would be better than anything you would find in the supermarket. And you'd be doing me a favour,' she added, hoping to target what seemed to be his weak spot. 'My children are with their dad for Christmas, and the novelty of freedom is quickly wearing off. Let me help. It's either sewing or gin.'

And there, at last, came a smile, and what a smile it was! Swiftly gone, but it had been there long enough to fill her with an unexpected warmth.

'Can you get a machine?' he asked. 'There isn't one here. I don't know where you'll find one.'

'I have an idea. Give me a couple of hours…'

*

Within half an hour, Tabitha was back in Miss Moonshine's shop. She burst through the door, gasping for breath; she'd run the last stretch, dreading there might have been an influx of dressmakers to Haven Bridge, and that the sewing machine might have been sold in her absence. But no: it was there in the window still, and she felt a rush of hope.

'Hello again, my dear. I didn't expect to see you again so soon.' Miss Moonshine smiled and approached Tabitha. 'Can I help you with something else?'

Tabitha leant against the shop counter as she gathered her breath. The little dog was still in its basket and inched forwards to give her a sniff. 'The sewing machine in the window – is it for sale?'

'Oh, that? It used to belong to a dear friend of mine. You'd be welcome to it, if you know how to repair it. It hasn't worked for years. Can I interest you in anything else? There are more rooms upstairs.'

'Are there any more sewing machines? Preferably ones that work?' Tabitha's heart sank as Miss Moonshine shook her head. So much for her grand plan to help Rob. Why had she mentioned it to him, before checking if the machine even worked? Now she would have to let him down, and even though she'd only known him a day she could imagine the bleak look that would return to his face and hated the thought of being the cause of it.

'Why do you need a sewing machine so desperately?' Miss Moonshine asked. 'Is there an emergency?'

'Yes! Have you heard of the Broadthwaite nativity parade? Some of the costumes haven't survived since last year. I offered to make new ones, but I'm only visiting the area while I start house-hunting and I don't have my machine with me. I hoped I could use this one.'

'Oh, I love the nativity parade. It's been going for over a hundred years, you know, and I never miss it. I played Mary for a few years, and had such fun riding the donkey.' Miss Moonshine smiled at the memory. 'How many costumes are missing?'

'Mary, three angels and a camel.' Thank goodness she'd remembered to ask Rob before she drove away. His daughter was due to play an angel, which made the situation even worse. 'I don't even have the fabric yet. I was hoping I might find something in a charity shop.'

Miss Moonshine tipped her head to one side like a bird, and studied Tabitha. Then she nodded.

'Yes,' she murmured, almost as if she were speaking to herself. 'I can see a way to make this work.' Nodding again, she walked over to an archway leading to a private area. 'Albert?' she called. 'Would you mind coming out to the shop?'

An elderly man shuffled in, wearing baggy trousers held up with braces, a woollen cardigan and slippers. A snowy white beard covered the lower half of his face. Tabitha could just make out a smile when he looked at her.

'Hello,' she said, stepping forward. 'I'm Tabitha.'

'Well would you know, I've lived nigh on eighty year and not met a Tabitha yet.' Albert took Tabitha's hand between his and shook it. 'I'm right glad to meet you. Are you joining us in the back for a brew?'

'No...' Tabitha wasn't exactly sure why she had been introduced to Albert, although she had warmed to him immediately with his twinkly eyes and smile.

'I thought you might be able to help, Albert. Tabitha needs to get hold of a sewing machine urgently, to make some new costumes for the Broadthwaite nativity parade. I thought you might let her borrow Jean's. You still have it, don't you?'

Albert nodded, but the twinkle in his eyes dimmed.

'There we are, problem solved.' Miss Moonshine clapped her hands together. 'You'll let her borrow it, won't you? I remember when Jean once played an angel in the parade. Such a pretty child.'

'That would be wonderful.' Tabitha said, as Albert nodded again. 'Now I just need the fabric. Are there any charity shops in town? I'll have to make do with whatever I can find. Some old white sheets would do at a pinch.'

'Albert, you were planning to donate some things to the charity shop, weren't you? Perhaps Tabitha could have a look through and see if any of it would be suitable for the costumes.'

Almost before Tabitha knew what was happening, it was all arranged, and Miss Moonshine had ushered her and Albert out onto the street, so they could go to Albert's house to collect the machine and inspect the clothes.

'She's very forceful, isn't she?' Tabitha said to Albert, feeling dazed. 'Please don't feel pressured into helping.'

'Oh, I don't mind,' Albert said, tying his scarf round his neck. 'She always knows what's best. I've been meaning to have a clear-out for a while, and keep putting it off.' He sighed, then lifted his walking stick and pointed up the street. 'Shall we?'

They shuffled along the street at Albert's pace, until they left the shops behind and climbed uphill to a residential road, where he stopped in front of a smart Victorian terraced house, built from stone and with a leaded bay window at the front. A flight of steps rose from the street to the front door, and Tabitha followed Albert as he made slow progress up the steps. The front door opened into a wide hall with what looked like an original tiled floor.

'This is gorgeous,' Tabitha said, as Albert led her into the living room, where the bay window gave views over Haven Bridge and across to the hills on the other side of town. 'Have you lived here long?'

'Aye, over fifty year,' Albert said. 'My Jean took one look at that view and had to live here. We thought we'd soon fill all these bedrooms with kiddies, but it wasn't to be. Still, we were happy enough here.'

Tabitha noted the past tense, and had to ask.

'So is Jean…' She didn't know how to finish the question, but Albert's tear-filled eyes answered it anyway.

'Gone these last twenty years. Cancer.' He wiped a hand across his face. 'It's a struggle to keep on top of this place now. I could get help, but I don't like the idea of strangers coming poking about. I keep thinking I should move somewhere smaller, but it would feel like I was leaving Jean behind.'

Tabitha reached out and squeezed his arm. 'Is there anything I can do, while I'm here?'

'Nay, get away, I'm supposed to be helping you out. Although,' Albert added, with a mischievous grin, 'I wouldn't say no to a brew if you can make a decent cup of tea. Kitchen's through there.'

Tabitha made the tea, her heart aching at the sight of the

solitary plate, knife and mug on the kitchen drainer, and the single chop on a plate in the family-sized fridge. When she returned to the living room with the mugs, Albert had opened one of the cupboards at the side of the fireplace and a sewing machine was sitting on the floor in the middle of the room. It was an old but top-of-the-range model as far as Tabitha could tell from a quick inspection.

'This is perfect,' she said, smiling at Albert. 'Are you sure you don't mind me borrowing it?'

'No.' The word came out slowly, as if he wasn't quite convinced. 'Will you have it long?'

'The parade is on Saturday night, so the costumes will need to be ready that morning at the latest. It will be two days at most.' She still saw some hesitation in Albert's face, and made a quick decision. 'How would you feel if I did the sewing here? I wouldn't want to get in your way.'

Albert grinned, and the anxiety faded from his face.

'It would be good to hear the sound of the machine filling the house again,' he admitted. 'But don't you have somewhere to be? Kiddies and a husband to look after?'

'Not at the moment. I have a boy and a girl, but they're on holiday with their dad and his new wife. They've gone on a Caribbean cruise for Christmas and won't be back until New Year.' It was the longest Tabitha had ever been apart from them, but she hadn't been able to say no. She'd had the children for the whole of last Christmas, as her ex-husband had pointed out. The cruise had been dangled in front of them during a weekend visit, so they'd been giddy with excitement before she'd known anything about it. She'd been played, she recognised that. It was what had finally persuaded her to make a clean break from the past, leave the marital home she hated and take control of her own life at last.

'Chicken breast for one on Christmas Day then?' Albert said. 'Join the club. Saves on the washing up, I suppose.'

They drank their tea, while Tabitha told Albert about her hopes to buy a cottage somewhere around the Haven Bridge countryside and set up a business making children's clothes. He suggested a few villages she should consider that had decent schools and a good community spirit, and mentioned a couple of craft centres that might have space for her to work. He took her more seriously than her ex-husband had ever done, despite being a stranger, and Tabitha liked him more and more.

By the time their drinks were finished, Tabitha was itching to start work, and so Albert showed her upstairs, to a spare bedroom with wall-to-wall wardrobes. He opened up the doors to reveal a kaleidoscope of outfits of assorted colours, many dating back to the sixties and seventies at a guess.

'Will anything here do?' Albert asked.

'For the costumes?' Tabitha said. 'I can't take these. They might be worth money. Some of them look vintage.'

Albert laughed.

'My Jean would be chuffed to hear you say that. She made most of them. They're probably worth nowt. In money terms, any road.'

'Are you sure?' Tabitha was already rifling through the rails. The quality of the fabrics and the stitching were amazing. Jean must have been talented with her sewing machine. Unfortunately, most of the clothes were too brightly patterned for what she was looking for, although she found a bouclé wool coat she thought could work for the camel.

'What do you think about Mary dressing in this?' she asked Albert, pulling out a pale blue silk dress. 'It's gorgeous, but probably too luxurious.'

'Beggars can't be choosers,' he replied. 'And it will be dark. Who'll be inspecting the fabric?'

It might need adjusting – Tabitha guessed it was a size sixteen – and she wondered if there was any chance she could meet the girl playing Mary to take her measurements. She would have to ask Rob, and perhaps she could ask him for any old sheets at the same time, as there was nothing here she could use for angel costumes. But then Albert opened another wardrobe door, and Tabitha gasped.

'How about this for your angels, then?' he said, with a wobble in his voice.

Tabitha inspected the single item that was hanging in the wardrobe. It was an exquisite full-length wedding dress, made of white embroidered fabric and with a matching train that fell from the shoulders like a cape. The train itself would probably be enough to make three child-sized angel costumes, but still…

'I can't take this,' Tabitha said, reverently fingering the fabric and admiring the work that had gone in to creating this. 'It's beautiful, and it must be very special to you.'

'I've no use for it now.' Albert's eyes were filling up again. 'I've been working up to taking it to a charity shop for years. My memories are all in here, and I'll never lose them,' he said, tapping his chest. 'You take it, love. Jean loved that nativity parade. We went every year. She'd be right glad to know her dress was being put to good use.'

*

It was dark by the time Tabitha returned to the Chicken House. She'd made a start on the camel coat and had brought the wedding dress home with her, so she could cut out the pieces she needed and tack them up, ready to sew on the machine tomorrow. The lights were on at the farmhouse, so she knocked on the door. Rob's daughter Jenny answered, still wearing her school uniform and with what looked like a ketchup stain on her white polo shirt. Her hair was decorated in an intricate French plait, better than anything Tabitha could manage.

She smiled when she saw Tabitha, and was immediately followed to the door by Rob.

'Good news,' Tabitha said. 'You might even say tidings of great joy.' Rob didn't return her smile. 'I've found a sewing machine and the most perfect fabric for the costumes. Do you want to see?'

She held up the bin bag Albert had given her to carry the wedding dress in.

'You'd better come in.' Rob stood back to let Tabitha enter the hall. It was a stunning entrance. It could have been gloomy with the flagged floor and wood-panelled walls, but bright paintings and lamps cheered the place up and made it cosy. Rob led the way into the kitchen, where a half-eaten meal lay on the table.

'Come on, you,' he said to Jenny, ushering her back into her chair. 'Carry on eating.'

'Sorry, I didn't mean to disturb your meal,' Tabitha said.

Rob shook his head. 'I'll grab something later. How did you find a sewing machine?'

Tabitha launched into the story of Miss Moonshine and Albert and Jean, ending with a flourish as she pulled the wedding dress out of the bag. Jenny gasped.

'Am I going to wear that?' she asked, with obvious delight.

'Not the whole thing.' Tabitha laughed. 'I'm hoping I can just use the train and leave the dress intact.' She turned to Rob. 'I wondered if I could borrow one of Jenny's dresses to use as a template while I cut out the fabric? I'll have to make something relatively loose, to suit all shapes and sizes for years to come, but it would be good to have a starting point.'

'I'll find you something.' She heard him run upstairs, and then footsteps creaked on the floor above, before he reappeared with a long-sleeved jersey dress in his hand.

'Will this do?'

'Yes, that's just what I wanted.'

Tabitha took it and started to put away the wedding dress.

'How are you going to cut it out?' Rob asked. 'Won't you need a table?'

Tabitha had thought about that. There wasn't a table in the Chicken House, only a breakfast bar, and she had reached the only conclusion possible.

'I'll do it on the floor. I'll put a sheet down to keep the fabric clean.'

'One of my sheets?'

'Oh...' Tabitha started to change tack, then realised Rob was joking. A smile softened his face, easing out the lines of anxiety that had seemed a permanent feature.

'You'd be better off using the kitchen table here.' He pointed at the large refectory table that filled the centre of the room. 'I'll clear it.'

'Are you sure? I don't want to get in the way.'

'You've saved my neck. It's the least I can do.'

Tabitha took off her coat and hung it on the back of one of the chairs while Rob cleared and wiped the table. He thudded upstairs again and came back down with a sheet, which he threw over the table.

'Best to be safe,' he said, as Tabitha laid out the dress. 'Are you sure Albert didn't mind giving this up?'

'He insisted. He said all his memories were in here.' She tapped her chest, copying Albert's gesture, and could have kicked herself when a flash of pained understanding crossed Rob's face. 'I'm sorry.'

He shook his head and turned his attention to Jenny.

'Homework time. You can use the other end of the table.'

Tabitha made a start on cutting out the costumes. She'd borrowed Jean's dressmaking scissors, and though it seemed fitting, it was still with some trepidation that she made her first cuts in the beautiful fabric. She kept her head down, concentrating on her work, but could hear Rob helping Jenny with her homework. Occasionally she glanced up to see them bent over the schoolbooks together.

'I can't believe how much I miss my children,' she said, when Jenny ran upstairs to put on her pyjamas.

'Where are they?'

'On a Caribbean cruise with their dad and his new wife.'

'Leaving you on your own for Christmas?'

'Yes. But we're celebrating Christmas when they get back, so I'm lucky. I get to have two Christmases this year.' Tabitha smiled. 'What will you do for Christmas?'

'We'll be here.'

'Are family coming round?'

'No. It will be just the two of us.' Rob sighed, and ran his hands through his hair. He glanced towards the door, but there was no sign of Jenny. 'It's complicated. My parents are with my brother in Cornwall this year. They've spent every Christmas with us since...' He stopped. 'So I told them it was Sam's turn this year.'

'And what about your wife's family?' It was a nosy question, but Tabitha couldn't resist, especially as Rob was in a talkative mood. But his face hardened, and she wished the words unsaid.

'They're not welcome.' He turned his back on Tabitha and started putting Jenny's school things away in her bag. 'They tried to take Jenny off me. Said I wouldn't be able to look after her and run this place as well. They said she'd be better off with them in suburbia. A farmer wasn't good enough for their daughter, and wasn't good enough for their granddaughter either.'

The pain in his voice was still raw. Tabitha couldn't believe that anyone could have been so cruel. She barely knew him, but she already felt she knew him enough. Seeing Rob with Jenny, watching him now as he packed her lunchbox with fruit ready for morning, she wondered how anyone could think she would be better off anywhere else but with him. But she couldn't say that. It was too intimate, even though she wasn't in any doubt it was true.

'Suburbia?' she said instead, rolling her eyes, even though he couldn't see. 'Poo to suburbia, as my darling son would say. Who wants that? I can't wait to move back out to the countryside.'

Rob glanced over his shoulder and she smiled at him. A slow, answering smile spread across his face.

'It's getting late. Do you want to stay for something to eat? It will only be soup…'

It was a surprise; the last thing she had expected. But she didn't hesitate.

'I'd love to.'

*

First thing the next morning, Tabitha was woken by a hammering on the door of the Chicken House. She staggered downstairs and found an unfamiliar girl of about twenty on her doorstep. The smart, slightly old-fashioned uniform embroidered with the name of a care agency contrasted with her short, spiky hair, black lipstick and the stud that glittered in her nose, but she wore a friendly grin that Tabitha immediately responded to.

'Hiya,' the girl said, wandering into the house. 'Rob said you wanted to see me. I'm Mary. Well, I'm Charleigh really, but I'm playing Mary in the nativity parade. You can say it, I don't look the part, do I? The nose stud is causing a few ripples, apparently, but I'm not taking it out whatever old Marjorie Twisted-Knickers says. I mean, she can go on about authenticity all she likes, but there are more fundamental problems than the stud that make me an unlikely Virgin Mary. They're lucky to have me, as I know at least three other people turned it down before I was asked. No one wanted to freeze their bits off, but the donkey swung it for me. I always wanted to be one of those kids having donkey rides on the beach, and this is the closest I'll get. Where do you want me? My shift starts in an hour, so we need to crack on.'

'Right,' Tabitha said, when Charleigh finally paused for breath. 'I'll bring your dress down. It shouldn't take an hour, but the dress will definitely need to be taken in to fit you.' She ran upstairs and came back down with the silk dress, which she had hung on one of the hangers from the wardrobe. 'What do you think?'

'I'm seriously going to wear that?' Charleigh fingered the delicate fabric, a slight flush on her cheeks. 'Is this for real? This uniform is the smartest thing I've ever worn. One of these sleeves probably cost more than everything I own.'

'Try it on while I go upstairs and get dressed,' Tabitha said. 'It will seem huge, but we'll soon sort that out.'

She gave it five minutes, then peered down the stairs to see if Charleigh was ready. She caught her in front of the oven, trying to see her reflection in the chrome surround. She flushed pink when she noticed Tabitha watching.

'You look amazing,' Tabitha said, running down the stairs. 'That colour suits you. Perhaps not with the lipstick though...'

Charleigh grinned.

'I reckon I could lose the black for one night.' She gingerly ran her hand across the fabric. 'Where did you get this from? You're too short for it, and it's got that vintage look about it, hasn't it? I couldn't see a label in it.'

'You won't have done. I met a wonderful old man yesterday, and it was made by his late wife. She once played an angel, so he thought it was fitting for us to use her dress. Stand still while I put some pins in.'

Albert had lent her Jean's pin tin, and she crawled round the floor, pinning up the hem of the dress as best as she could while Charleigh fidgeted.

'You forget that old ladies were once young girls wearing dresses like this, don't you?' Charleigh said. 'I'm going to ask some of my ladies to show me their old photos. It will make a change from talking about which of the neighbours have died.'

'Is that what you do, look after old ladies? Is it nursing care?'

'Nah, I'm not qualified for that. It's general dogsbody work I do, odd jobs around the house, cooking and cleaning. I don't mind it,' she added defensively. 'It doesn't sound much, but it lets them stay in their own home for longer.'

'It sounds a great job,' Tabitha said. A perfect job, she thought, remembering her visit to Albert yesterday. It sounded exactly what he needed. 'Are you fully booked up?'

'I was.' Charleigh let out a gusty sigh as Tabitha stood up to pin the sides of the dress. 'One of my regulars has had a stroke and been moved to a nursing home. It's ruined Christmas.'

'I can imagine. It must have been upsetting.'

'Yeah, that as well, but I was down to visit her on Christmas Day. Bank Holiday rates,' she explained, as Tabitha looked blank. 'All the other shifts are taken, so I'll be spending the day on my own.'

'Have you no family?'

'No idea. None that want me. I was brought up in care. It's fine,' she added. 'I'll have cheese on toast and a bottle of cider in front of the telly. It's only another day.'

But it wasn't another day – it was Christmas. And hearing the slight wobble in Charleigh's voice, a plan rushed in to Tabitha's head and straight out of her mouth before she could stop to think.

'Why don't you come here for Christmas lunch?' she said. 'I'm on my own this year too. I can do better than cheese on toast.'

'Really?' Charleigh stared at her. 'Do you mean it? You don't even know me. I could be a psycho.'

'You're the Virgin Mary,' Tabitha said. 'How bad can you be?' She laughed. 'I'll take my chances.'

And maybe, she thought, she could persuade Albert to take his, too…

*

It had been a hectic couple of days, but by early Saturday afternoon Tabitha had completed the outfits. Rob called to collect them only half an hour after she had snipped off the last pieces of thread and collapsed onto the sofa in an exhausted but exhilarated heap.

'What do you think?' she asked, as she brought the costumes downstairs and held them out for him to see. 'Are they good enough?'

'Good enough? They're –' He broke off, and gingerly fingered one of the angel dresses. They were Tabitha's favourites; the soft sheen of the wedding dress fabric had worked beautifully and made these costumes seem ethereal. But she had no idea from Rob's face whether he approved or not.

'Good? Bad? Ugly?' she prompted him, impatient to hear the verdict after the hours she had spent working on them. 'Will they do?'

He shook his head, and Tabitha's heart faltered. She'd been here before, thinking she'd created something special, until her ex-husband had dismissed her efforts with a look that was more cutting than the harshest words. But then Rob broke into an unexpected and delightful smile, and all thoughts of her ex vanished.

'They're extraordinary. You really made these?'

'Ah, you've rumbled me. You saw me coming home with the supermarket bags, didn't you? And I thought I'd get away with it.'

He laughed, and glanced at her, but quickly looked away again.

'I don't know what to say. Thanks. Thanks a hundred times. You've totally saved my skin. I don't know how I'll repay you for this.'

'Easy,' Tabitha said, giddy with relief that he actually did seem to like the outfits. 'Bring me another basket of logs for the fire and we'll call it quits. It's getting colder, isn't it? I hope it won't snow tonight.'

'I don't know. Some of the best parades have taken place in the snow. There's something pretty special about singing carols and drinking mulled wine while the snowflakes fall softly around us.'

Rob stopped and scratched his chin, seeming embarrassed to have shared this.

'Mulled wine?' Tabitha repeated. 'Sounds wonderful. If only I wasn't driving.'

'Then don't. There's something I can do for you. I'll be driving in with Jenny. I can give you a lift.'

'That would have been great, but I've offered to take Albert. After he donated the clothes and let me use his wife's sewing machine, it's the least I can do for him.'

'It's the least I can do for both of you. I can collect him too.'

*

A few hours later, Rob pulled up in the car park of The Fountain Arms, a popular dining pub in the centre of Broadthwaite village and conveniently next to the cricket pitch where the parade was due to start and end. This was a definite advantage of coming with Rob. The roads through the village had been closed to general traffic and most visitors were parking in a field on the outskirts. Already the streets had been claimed by pedestrians carrying lanterns and torches as they made their way to the starting point.

Rob went off to take Jenny to the head of the parade, and Tabitha and Albert made their way on to the cricket pitch, mingling with the crowd as it grew in size and noise. Albert was well wrapped up for the cold weather, with a scarf high on his chin and a hat low on his forehead, but it was impossible to miss the big grin on his face and the twinkle in his eyes.

'This is grand, isn't it?' He lifted his lantern and let it illuminate the crowd in front of them. 'We always felt this was the official start of Christmas. You'll see. It will put you right in the mood for Christmas Eve tomorrow.'

Tabitha started Christmas as soon as the calendar changed over to December, putting up the decorations and starting with the festive music, but she could see what he meant. The happiness and excitement in the air were tangible, even though it was bitterly cold and the clouds loitered overhead with the threat of snow.

'That reminds me,' she said, taking Albert's arm as the crowd jostled them forwards. 'I can't bear the idea of you being on your own on Christmas Day. Why don't you come round to me? Charleigh, who's playing the Virgin Mary, will be there too. No chicken breast for one this year. We can join forces and stretch to the whole bird.'

'Nay, you don't want an old fella like me getting in the way.'

'I do, and that's settled. I'll pick you up about eleven.'

There was no time for Albert to reply, as a trumpet fanfare sounded. The crowd turned and Tabitha found herself pushed to the edge and in the perfect place to see the head of the parade pass by on the way out to the village. It was every bit as magical as she had hoped, and she squeezed Albert's arm as tears filled her eyes. A brass band led the way, playing Christmas songs, and behind them came Charleigh, looking amazing in the blue silk dress, accessorised with bold red lipstick and the stud sparkling in her nose. She was riding a donkey, just as she'd wanted, and looking thrilled by the whole experience. She was followed by various men wearing lavish but faded costumes that were clearly some of the original set: a Joseph, a group of kings and a couple of shepherds who were each leading a live sheep. And at the rear, guarded by an adult angel and some proud parents, came the children wearing Tabitha's angel and camel outfits, accompanied by a few more shepherds with pretend sheep... Jenny caught Tabitha's eye and waved in excitement.

For the next hour, the parade wandered the streets of the village, stopping on the side roads to sing rousing renditions of favourite Christmas songs. Although it seemed that hundreds of people were out walking, there were still young and old faces pressed against windows of houses they passed, waving at the procession. The camaraderie and community spirit were exactly what Tabitha had been hoping to find in a move out to the country, although there was no point putting this village on her wish list; she'd had a quick drive through yesterday and not seen a single 'For Sale' board anywhere.

At last the procession reached the cricket pitch again, where the band led the crowd in a boisterous version of 'We Wish You a Merry Christmas'. There was a huge cheer and round of applause as an army of waiters emerged from The Fountain Arms bearing trays of mulled wine. As Tabitha reached for a glass, the snow that had threatened all evening finally began to fall, soft flakes swirling and dancing, and the children began to squeal and laugh, running round the grass trying to catch the flakes with their hands and their tongues. She wished Joe and Lily were here too, wished that next year they might all be here together. As she looked round, savouring the moment, she saw Miss Moonshine standing on the footpath on the opposite side of the road, waving.

'Miss Moonshine's here,' she said to Albert. 'I'll just go and say hello. None of this would have happened without her.'

She dashed through the crowd and crossed the road, but Miss Moonshine seemed to have vanished. She waved her torch around. She was standing in front of the gate leading to a pretty stone cottage. Had Miss Moonshine gone inside? There was no light on. She shone the torch on the front of the house, and it was only then she noticed the poster Sellotaped to the inside of the front window, too small for her to have seen while driving by: 'For sale. Please contact…'

*

The snow fell steadily through Christmas Eve, and the view from the Chicken House, across whitewashed fields and trees whose branches were laced with frozen flakes, made Tabitha excited for the day ahead, despite the absence of her children. The weather that followed on Christmas Day itself was a disappointment; a winter storm had blown up, and wind rattled the windows while rain turned the snow to sludge.

She was able to make it to Haven Bridge to pick up Albert, who looked even more like Father Christmas in a cheerful red knitted jumper, with a bow-tie peeping out at the neck.

'You're looking dapper,' Tabitha said, smiling as he invited her into the hall. 'You didn't need to make such an effort.'

'I'm dining out with two young ladies. Of course I put a bit of effort in. I don't get much chance these days.' Albert put on his anorak and picked up a carrier bag.

'You didn't need to bring anything either,' Tabitha said. 'I told you, the food is all sorted.'

'Just a little something for you and Charleigh.' He showed her the contents of the bag. Two tubs of assorted chocolates lay inside. He frowned. 'She's not one of those skinny misses who don't eat sweets, is she? I never thought.'

'I'm sure she's not. And if she is, it's all the more for us, isn't it?'

Tabitha had offered to collect Charleigh as well, but she was determined to cycle, despite the awful weather. She was waiting for them when Tabitha and Albert arrived back at the Chicken House.

'I was about to pick the lock,' she said. 'It's perishing out here. I almost came off my bike a dozen times. I might have to take you up on the lift home, if you don't mind. I don't fancy fighting back through this wind after a couple of ciders. I'm Charleigh,' she added, thrusting her hand out to Albert. 'Happy Christmas. Were you on your own too? We're like an odd little family now, aren't we?'

Tabitha didn't think she was quite old enough to be Charleigh's mother, but let it go as she unlocked the door and let her guests in to the Chicken House. She'd left the lights on so that it would be welcoming when she brought Albert back, and it was every bit as perfect as she'd hoped, with the Christmas decorations she'd bought in Haven Bridge making the place cosy and cheerful, and the smell of roasting chicken just beginning to waft around the house. All it needed now was for her to light the fire and the candles, start the Christmas music, pour the drinks and make sure they all had a better Christmas than they had expected to have.

It all went well for the first half hour. Albert's cheeks glowed pink as he moved on to his second glass of sherry. Charleigh barely stopped talking and Tabitha was thrilled to see how well they were getting on, as she planned to suggest Albert employ Charleigh to help around the house. The chicken came out of the oven looking succulent and golden, and she was about to put the potatoes in to roast when the lights went out, the oven cut off and the music stopped.

'That's not good,' Albert pointed out helpfully. 'Has the power gone?'

Tabitha flicked the kettle and tried to turn on the hob, but nothing worked.

'Perhaps it's the fuse,' she said, looking round and wondering where the fuse box might possibly be hiding. Were there any instructions in the house for what to do in an emergency? She hadn't spotted any so far.

'I told you this wind almost knocked me off my bike. It could easily have brought down the electricity lines.' Charleigh sipped at her bottle of cider, with apparent unconcern. She reached over to take another chocolate from the bowl on the table. 'Good job you brought these, Albert.'

'I suppose I should check whether the farmhouse is down too,' Tabitha said. She didn't relish the thought; she hated the idea of disturbing Rob and Jenny when they would be enjoying Christmas together. The words were hardly out of her mouth when there was a loud hammering on the door. Tabitha answered, and Rob was blown in on a gust of wind.

'Sorry for interrupting,' he said, slamming the door shut behind him. He nodded at Charleigh. 'I didn't know you were coming here as well as Albert.'

'We've joined forces for Christmas lunch,' Tabitha explained.

'But you only have two stools.'

'We have trays, and knees. There didn't seem any point us being on our own, when we could be together.'

Rob looked round the room, as if he was taking it all in. Tabitha wished he'd seen it earlier, when the lights were twinkling and the music playing, but it still looked a charming scene, with the blazing fire, candles flickering and the chocolates shimmering in their jewel-coloured wrappers in bowls on the table. He focused on Tabitha and smiled.

'What we don't have,' Charleigh said, waving her bottle at Rob in greeting, 'is electricity. Is yours on?'

'No. The power line to the whole village is down. I've reported it, but it's likely to be hours before it's fixed. I've brought you a couple more lanterns.' He nodded his head at the door.

'Food would have been more useful,' Charleigh said.

Rob groaned. 'I hadn't thought about the electric oven.' He turned to Tabitha. 'You'll have to come to the farmhouse. The Aga is still going strong.'

'We can't interrupt your Christmas. The chicken is ready. I'm sure we can manage…'

He grinned, and she remembered him brushing her off with that phrase only a few days ago. She hadn't taken no for an answer, and she could see by his determined expression that he wasn't going to either.

'Sometimes there's a better option than managing, as you showed me,' he said. 'You saved my Christmas. Let me save yours. But hurry up – I've left Jenny on her own. What can I carry?'

It was like a smaller version of the nativity procession as they paraded over to the farm: Rob in the lead bearing the roast chicken, Albert carrying the tray of potatoes, Tabitha juggling pans of vegetables and Charleigh bringing up the rear with chocolates and cider. Rob took them to the kitchen, where lanterns gave off a cosy glow and the delicious smell of Christmas dinner filled the room. Jenny was sitting with a colouring book at the kitchen table, which looked quite forlorn with only two place settings.

'We need three more places, Jenny,' Rob told her as she looked up. 'We have guests.'

'Yay!' Jenny stood up and then stopped, staring at Albert, wide-eyed. Rob caught Tabitha's eye and smiled; Jenny was clearly wondering if they had a very important guest in their midst.

The combined lunch was a triumph. There was enough food for ten, never mind the five of them, and any initial awkwardness about being relative strangers soon dissipated as they swapped Christmas stories and tapped their feet to the festive playlist on Tabitha's phone. Christmas without her children was never going to be easy, but the day was filled with more fun and laughter than she could ever have imagined.

Rob pulled out a selection of board games after they had cleared away lunch, including a couple of new ones that Jenny explained Father Christmas had delivered overnight.

'Aren't you lucky?' Tabitha said, as Jenny showed off her presents. Jenny nodded, but it was a half-hearted gesture.

'He forgot something,' she whispered. 'He didn't bring my decoration.'

'Your decoration?' Tabitha repeated. 'For your bedroom?'

'No, for the Christmas tree. Father Christmas brings me a new one every year. I couldn't find one this morning.'

Tabitha glanced at Rob. He was leaning against the sink, looking stricken. She joined him.

'I forgot,' he said in a low voice, as Charleigh continued playing with Jenny. 'Lindsay started it. She wanted to give Jenny a decoration each year so she would have a collection to put on her own tree one day. How could I have missed it?'

'Is there anything I can do to help?' Tabitha asked.

'Not unless you can sew a decoration in the next few minutes…'

Tabitha smiled. 'I can do better than that.'

She grabbed a torch and her coat, and ran through the gathering darkness back to the Chicken House. The brown paper bag from Miss Moonshine's Emporium was still sitting on the side table where she'd left it. She reached inside and pulled out two parcels, exquisitely wrapped in colourful tissue paper and with shiny ribbon curled round them. One was larger than the other, and contained two of the decorations. Tabitha could tell from the shape that the smaller one contained the cat Miss Moonshine had persuaded her to buy. Miss Moonshine must have gift-wrapped them while Tabitha continued to browse round the shop. Tabitha stuffed the small parcel in her pocket and dashed back to the farmhouse.

'Look!' she said, waving the parcel at Jenny. 'I wondered if this might have happened. I think Father Christmas dropped this down my chimney by mistake.'

The surprise and excitement on Jenny's face as she took the present and unwrapped the little tabby cat brought tears to Tabitha's eyes. She backed away, letting Rob enjoy the moment with Jenny as they admired the felt decoration. He followed her over to the shadows at the far side of the kitchen.

'I'm losing track of how many thanks I owe you,' he said. 'How will I pay you back in the two days before you leave?'

'You can carry the debt over until I move here, if you like,' Tabitha replied. 'I won't charge interest.'

'You're moving here?'

'I hope so. I put an offer in on a cottage in Broadthwaite yesterday.' She hadn't believed her luck; the owner had agreed she could view the cottage on Christmas Eve, and it had been even better than she had hoped. She'd known at once that it was the right place for her, Joe and Lily. It was half the size of the house they lived in now, but they would fill it with double the love and happiness. She couldn't wait to move there and to get to know her new neighbourhood – and maybe, just maybe, there would be a chance to get to know this lovely man in front of her better too. 'So I expect we'll see you around the village sometimes,' she said.

Rob shifted, and his fingers brushed against hers, so lightly that it could have been an accident. But it wasn't. She knew it wasn't and a spark of hope flew straight from her fingers to her heart.

'I'll look forward to it,' he said.

Kate Field writes contemporary women's fiction, mainly set in her favourite county of Lancashire, where she lives with her husband, daughter, and hyperactive cat.

Kate's debut nov*el*, *The Magic of Ramblings*, won the Romantic Novelists' Association Joan Hessayon Award for new writers.

amazon.co.uk/Kate-Field/e/B00J18F3PY/

A Raven's Gift

By Angela Wren

Thursday

It was the letter in the pristine white envelope that had brought Amy Ravencroft to the small northern town of Haven Bridge. She glanced at her watch. Plenty of time. Despite her trepidation, she kept her pace measured as she moved along the unfamiliar street. Opposite the jeweller's, she stopped to check the number. Stencilled on the glass panel above the door, in gleaming red and gold, the figures 4 and 8 glinted for a moment before the last rays of weak afternoon sun disappeared behind a thick black cloud. Amy was looking for 52. The next shop sold gifts and on the other side of it was a narrow entrance, just as had been described when she'd telephoned in response to the letter. As she stood at the pavement edge in Market Street, staring at the heavy wooden door opposite, the first few flakes of the promised snow began to fall. Amy wondered, for the millionth time, why she had come. A phrase from the letter crashed into her mind in answer.

'… in connection with a personal matter for my client…'

What personal matter, and for whom? These were questions that had been haunting her ever since she'd opened that particular envelope exactly one week earlier. She checked her coat pocket and her fingers found the second letter, which had arrived the same day. A letter in a pale blue envelope, the name and address neatly typed, and, written in flowery purple ink on the back, were the words 'Miss Moonshine's Wonderful Emporium'. But that was another matter. In fact it was a mistake. Amy had important business that needed her immediate attention.

She took the half dozen steps required to reach the traffic lights and waited for her opportunity to cross the main road. As she approached number 52 she noticed the small brass plaque beside the door confirming she'd reached the offices of Matthew and Son, Solicitors and Commissioners for Oaths. Whatever that meant! Despite her unease she just managed the beginnings of a smirk at the pomposity. Pushing the door open, Amy found herself in a narrow entrance with a flight of old wooden stairs. Her right hand on the silky smooth wood of the banister, she climbed the steep steps, each one creaking and groaning with age as she moved up them. At the top was a small landing with another heavy wooden door, painted the same dark blue as the one at street level, and a second plaque. Not that Matthew and Son needed a second plaque to announce their precise location. The only other door on the landing was labelled WC and the stairs didn't lead anywhere else. The apprehension that had dogged her all morning unravelled into nervousness at the sight of the second plaque. Her stomach flipped. She rested her shoulders against the wall to steady herself and took a couple of deep breaths. Standing straight, she lifted her hand to knock, but hesitated. Then, firmly grabbing hold of the large brass doorknob, she twisted it and walked in.

'Amy Ravencroft for an appointment with Mr James Matthew,' she announced as she closed the door behind her. The room was high-ceilinged with an old-fashioned partition dividing it. On the left were shelves full of books and two large black filing cabinets that looked as though they had been retrieved from another century. On the right was a solid wooden desk behind which sat an elderly lady with white hair. The nameplate in front of the old word processor stated she was Mrs Newsome. It appeared that Mr Matthew's attitude towards

Christmas was minimalist. The only evidence of the season was a single card at one side of the desk and a tiny Christmas tree on the windowsill.

'This way,' said Mrs Newsome. She struggled to get out of her chair, and once upright she moved slowly, hobbling the few steps from the edge of her desk to the door.

'These poor old bones don't work quite so well any more.' Her comment was accompanied by a bright smile and the twinkle of a pair of pale grey eyes as she held the door back for Amy to walk through. Amy grinned; there was something about Mrs Newsome that was reminiscent of her own mother.

In a much larger share of the floor space was a tall man, wearing a dark grey suit that was more fitting for a city broker than a solicitor in a small market town, especially one whose suite of offices looked as though they'd been modelled on a description from Dickens.

'James Matthew,' he said, hand outstretched, a welcoming smile on his face as he swept out from behind his desk. Amy took his hand and noticed the firm grip. 'Please take a seat.' He indicated an antiquated bucket chair, whose dark green leather was all scuffed and faded. 'Some tea, Mrs Newsome, if you wouldn't mind, please.'

When the door finally clicked shut, Mr Matthew smiled at Amy. 'My father's personal assistant. Should've retired nearly twenty years ago, but when I took over the work here, despite my offering a very generous retirement package, Mrs Newsome refused to give up her position.'

'Oh, so you're the son on the plaque downstairs.'

'I'm the great-grandson. We've been here in Haven Bridge since 1875. As the firm moved through the different generations of the family, no one bothered to rename it. But to business,' he said, running his hand down the silk of his pale pink tie. On the desk was a large file of papers. He flipped open the cover.

Amy waited, her shoulder bag clutched in her hands on her knee, as Mr Matthew looked at the file intently and then at her. She felt her neck warming; his stare, though momentary, was still disconcerting. She tried to distract herself from her discomfort by glancing at the shelves of law books behind him.

'Yes,' he said eventually. 'I'm acting on behalf of a long-standing client of this firm, Ms Raven, and I would like to start by properly establishing your identity. Did you–'

'But you can't.' Amy interrupted more forcibly than she'd intended. 'My name is Amy Ravencroft, not Raven. I did try to explain this to your assistant when I telephoned last week, but she insisted on giving me an appointment for today.'

Mr Matthew looked at her, his expression impassive. 'I see.'

Amy frowned. She'd expected an instant apology, or an explanation, anything but the soulless silence that now sat between them. She shook her head.

'I'm sorry, that statement didn't come out quite as I intended.' She took a breath. 'Of course I can prove who I am, but what I meant was, the person you are seeking, the Amélie Raven mentioned in your letter. I am not her.' Searching through her handbag she pulled out an envelope. 'My birth certificate, the bill for my water supply, the deeds to my house, the council tax bill. They are all in there.' She pushed the envelope across the desk.

Mr Matthew referred to the papers in his file. 'But you do live at 38 Cheviot Avenue?'

'Yes.' Amy nudged the envelope further forward.

She waited while the solicitor sifted through the papers. The bills he glanced at and placed on one side, covering them with the deeds without even unfolding the document. He fixed his attention on the birth certificate. A small rectangle of foxed and dog-eared paper, which he opened out.

'Ah, this is the short-form version,' he said, as he scanned the details. 'And I notice there's a difference of...' He glanced at a calendar on his desk. 'Five weeks and two days between your actual birth on May 27th, 1971, and the registration on July 2nd. Do you know why or how that may have happened?'

Amy's eyes widened and she stared at Mr Matthew in disbelief. 'I... um... I really haven't the least idea.' She looked away, trying to search her memory for something, anything that might provide an answer. She shrugged. 'I don't know. I wasn't even aware of the difference in dates until you mentioned it just now. And does it really matter?'

'Probably not, but to protect my client's interests, I have to question everything. Do you have the full registration details?'

'That's the only birth certificate I've ever had.'

'Well, there are two forms, this one and the full one, which contains the additional details of the mother's current and maiden name, father's name and occupation–'

'So, this is about my father,' Amy interrupted, her tone harsh and cold.

'At the moment I'm not at liberty to say,' said Mr Matthew, adopting his previous impassive look.

Amy glanced at the floor and then at the solicitor. *I suppose you would make an excellent poker player.* 'Before we go any further you need to be aware that my father abandoned us before I was born. I've never met him and, as far as I'm aware, my mother never maintained any contact with him.' Amy stared at Mr Matthew, waiting for some indication that she was right, and that this whole thing was all about her missing parent.

'I'm sorry to hear that, and I'm afraid I can't tell you anything about my client until I've established your identity without any question of doubt.'

At that moment the door opened. Mr Matthew stood and strode round his desk to collect the tray of tea from Mrs Newsome. He placed it on a table to one side of the room.

'Milk and sugar?' he asked, pouring tea into two cups.

'Just milk, please.' Amy watched as he deftly added the milk. In a moment he was back at his desk, a second wide, welcoming smile on his face, handing her a mismatched cup and saucer. *How can you do that? Inscrutable one minute and seconds later...* She let the thought drift away and looked across to his tea. His cup and saucer were also mismatched and from two completely different services. She wondered how many sets of porcelain the firm might have been through in its extensive lifetime and the thought brought the flicker of a smile to her face.

'Ms Ravencroft?'

Amy gave a little start and felt a flush on her cheeks. 'Sorry, I was just...' She grabbed her cup and saucer and sipped her tea.

Mr Matthew grinned. 'As I said, a full birth certificate would have enabled me to speed things along, but your short certificate of birth will still help. It just means I'll have to cross-check the details with the appropriate registry office before we can go any further.' He picked up the deeds to her house and ran his eyes over the contents. 'The property in Leeds, have you always lived there?'

'Yes, since I was about five years old.'

'And your address, or the place you lived, prior to that?'

Amy let out a breath. 'I was only five, Mr Matthew. The move to the house in Cheviot Avenue was a big adventure. I don't really remember much before that.' She looked towards the window, trying desperately to retrieve a memory or relevant thought. 'But there was the place with the dark green tiles,' she murmured after a moment. 'It must have been a nice place,' she turned towards him. 'I've always associated that place with chocolate.' She smiled to herself. 'Chocolate and wood panelling and a man called Mr...' She grimaced and shook her head. 'I can't recall his name, but I do remember that place as a happy one.'

When she looked up, Mr Matthew was making some notes in his file. 'But you've no recollection of where this might be?'

'No.'

'Is there anything about this particular memory that might suggest you were somewhere else in Britain, or possibly even in another country altogether?'

Amy shrugged. 'I really have no idea, and it is such a fragment. Just a picture in my mind. I doubt it could be anywhere other than Britain as I've never been abroad. Well, apart from when I went on a school exchange thing for a week when I was about fourteen.'

Mr Matthew smiled and jotted something down in his file. 'And what about your late mother's will?'

Amy frowned. *How did you know about that? Unless...* She put her tea on the edge of the desk. 'There was no will. My mother was diagnosed with multiple sclerosis when I was seventeen. At first she was able to continue to work, but eventually I became her primary carer and, while she was still able to do so, she gave me power of attorney. Some years before she died we transferred the property into my name. I was paying all the bills, anyway. Two years ago...' Amy felt the prickle of tears at the back of her eyes and swallowed hard. Focusing on the books behind Mr Matthew, she continued, 'Two years ago, when she died, there were only her personal effects to be dealt with. I didn't think I was required to do anything legal about those.' She looked at the lawyer and clutched her bag, pulling it further up her lap. 'Did I get that wrong? Is that why I'm here?'

Mr Matthew rested his pen in the centre of the file. 'I'm sure you did everything you needed to, Ms Ravencroft,' he said, his voice calm and soothing. 'If I could hang on to the deeds and the certificate of birth for a couple of days, you can take these other documents with you. I'll send the remaining items back to you by registered post when I've completed my enquiries.'

Amy took another sip of her tea. 'Is that it?'

'For the moment, yes. But I have one last question. I feel sure this won't be necessary, but I'm obliged to ask. If my further checks are not able to confirm your identity satisfactorily would you be willing to take a DNA test?'

'A DNA test!' Amy's mind was suddenly exploding with possibilities and questions.

'As I said, I'm sure everything here will be sufficient, but just in case, I would like to know if you would be willing to take the test. It doesn't necessarily mean the test will be required.'

She thought for a moment. 'I think I'd like to wait and see what you find first before I agree or not.'

'Very wise,' said Mr Matthew. 'I'll need to see you again and, as I only work for the family firm for one day a week, if you could let me know when you'll next be in Haven Bridge, then Mrs Newsome can organise all my other appointments here for the same day.'

'Thursday. That's my afternoon off from the library in Leeds, so I can come again next Thursday, straight after work.' Amy finished her tea and carefully replaced her cup in the saucer.

Mr Matthew rose and went to the door, holding it open for her. 'Thursday it is then,' he said, as she moved past him.

Amy nodded. On her way out, she approached Mrs Newsome again. 'I have to return a letter,' she said, pulling the pale blue envelope from her coat pocket and checking the name on the back. 'I was wondering if you could direct me to Miss Moonshine's Emporium, please?'

Mrs Newsome smiled. 'The other end of this street,' she said. 'Turn left as you go out, continue along and it's just before you get to The Old Green Wicket.'

*

Out on the street again, Amy wondered what to do next. She'd come today hoping to correct a mistake and to be freed from whatever obligation Mr Matthew thought he owed her. But all she had were the same questions. None of which had been answered. She stared at her feet, shoved her hands in her coat pockets and let out a sigh. In addition, she realised, there were a whole series of new questions still forming in her mind as a result of Mr Matthew's query about a DNA test. She pulled up the collar of her coat against the snow and began to walk towards the opposite end of the street. *And if Mr Matthew's client isn't my father, then who can he be?* As she meandered along the road, she realised she actually didn't know for certain whether Mr Matthew's client was her father or not. Thinking back to the conversation, she acknowledged he'd given neither a positive nor a negative reply. *In fact you gave no hint at all, did you, Mr James Matthew?*

At the bookshop, she stopped and gazed at the display in the window. She remembered the presents she still had to buy for her close colleagues at work. 'Of course,' she said to herself. 'All four of us read.' She pushed the door open, and the warm hushed atmosphere brought some calm to her jumbled conscious. By the time she'd found the shelves for novels with authors in alphabetical order, her concerns about Mr Matthew and his client had been firmly shoved to the back of her mind. Her selections made and paid for, she hurried along the street to her next destination.

Within minutes she was standing outside Miss Moonshine's Emporium, where a black, solid wooden door stood wide open, inviting her to come in. She shook her head. Why on earth should she enter? She looked along the road, festooned with Christmas lights, not yet vibrant in the fading daylight, as it was still too early in the afternoon. Around the door were more lights and seasonal motifs, all tastefully arranged.

'This is ridiculous,' she said, as she turned to walk away. 'I should've just put the letter in another envelope with a covering note and posted it back.'

'Ms Ravencroft,' came a voice from the doorway.

Startled, Amy spun around. In front of her was a small woman, fine-featured and white-haired. She wore a matching checked jacket and skirt, and a plain blouse whose colour highlighted the darker of the two hues in the check.

'It is Ms Amy Ravencroft, I think,' said the woman, advancing to meet her with her hand outstretched in greeting. 'Miss Moonshine,' she said. 'I've been waiting such a long time to meet you, my dear.'

'But… We don't…' Amy stammered as she took the woman's hand. She looked into Miss Moonshine's clear hazel eyes. What she'd been about to say vanished from her mind.

'Please come in, my dear, if only for a moment.' Miss Moonshine smiled and moved towards the doorway.

Amy shook her head again. She'd come to Haven Bridge to correct two errors. Despite the constant debate she'd had with herself on her journey from Leeds, and despite her resolve almost having failed her when she first got off the train, she had a specific task to complete. She stood resolute.

'There's been a mistake.' She reached into her pocket and pulled out the blue envelope. 'I am Amy Ravencroft, and it was my mother who was called Amélie Ravencroft. We both lived at this address in Leeds until Mum died. Now I live there alone. As far as I'm aware, neither one of us has ever been here before today. So, I'm not sure how you can have anything that might belong to, or be of interest to, either me or my late mother. That's why I'm here. To let you know you've made a mistake.' Her long rehearsed piece said, Amy nodded and offered the envelope to Miss Moonshine.

'Very well, my dear,' she said, as she retrieved her letter.

'Would you like to come in anyway? I have some lovely items that will make perfect presents.'

Amy smiled. 'I'm sure you do, Miss Moonshine, but I have a train to catch.' She turned and strode towards the station.

*

The train back to her home on the outskirts of Leeds was busy and slow. The atmosphere in the carriage was musty as wet-coated people got on and off at each of the numerous stops. Seated by the window, Amy watched as flakes of snow dashed themselves against the glass and slid down. The darkness outside, interrupted only by the yellow lights from each station, seemed all-encompassing, and her mind was in disarray. *Perhaps I should have looked for my father years ago.* She grimaced at her reflection in the window and banished the thought. *Of course not. I wouldn't even know where to start.* Another station and another pause in an uncomfortable journey. *You're not the person Mr Matthew is looking for. No, quite definitely not.* She settled herself back in her seat, her head nestled against the headrest, confident she had done the right thing. Going there, in person, on her afternoon off from her job in the library, to point out the errors was more than the right thing to do. Still, as a heavy snowflake splattered against the window and dissipated before her eyes, a tiny nagging and indistinct thought began to scratch at the furthest edge of her mind.

The lights of the city of Leeds began to encroach on the darkness and people started reaching for their briefcases, shopping bags and coats in readiness to leave. Amy remained where she was. Her connection would mean another twenty-minute wait on a cold station platform, so she remained a few minutes more in her seat while she waited for the carriage to empty.

Her connection was often late. This evening, when she consulted the information board, her train had been cancelled.

Marching straight out of the station, she got in a taxi and completed her journey in the busy early evening traffic. *At least I'm not driving.* It was a small consolation.

Sunday

After her visit to the solicitor's on Thursday, Amy had convinced herself she needed to know. She still wasn't quite sure exactly what it was she needed to know, but she persuaded herself there was something in her own, or her mother's, background that was important. Having searched through all the usual nooks and crannies in every room and found nothing, she now stood in the kitchen-cum-diner at the back of her old Victorian house, wiping the dust from a small, battered suitcase that had been in the loft for years. She hefted it onto the breakfast bar. Pale yellow rays from the winter sun were streaming through the French windows, lighting the old weeping willow at the bottom of the long narrow garden and catching at the rusting hinges of the case.

Settling herself on her favourite stool, hands on the catches, she paused for a moment. *Should I? This is all mum's old stuff. Should I really be doing this?* With a determined nod to the robin sitting on the fence outside, she clicked the case open and threw back the lid. A thick cloud of paper dust spilled into the room. Amy sneezed. Closing her eyes for a moment and breathing in the musky woodiness of aged paper and ink, she sneezed again.

'No wonder this was so heavy,' she said, starting to leaf through the piles of photos, letters, postcards and numerous bits and pieces of paper and newsprint. There seemed to be no order to anything.

Twenty minutes later and Amy had the complete contents dumped in the centre of the dining table. The suitcase she left discarded on the floor while she began to carefully sort the items. Photos to one side, letters and postcards to another, and miscellaneous pieces of paper or newsprint in a third pile at the back of the table. *Am I really going to find anything useful?*

The robin hopped up onto the patio. Head on one side, he stood there watching. Amy grinned at him but remained completely still. *I'll take you as an indication of a positive outcome.* A sound outside captured his attention and he looked away. A second later, he took flight.

Amy returned to her task and began sifting through the photos. Some were black-and-white, some colour, some faded, some with a white border, some with none. The one thing they all had in common was no order. She began picking them up at random. The seaside in summer, a wood in winter, a park and some swings, a house and… *Yellow.* She dropped the other pictures she was holding onto the table and stared at the one of the house.

'Yellow?' She turned the black-and-white photograph over, but there was nothing on the back. 'How can I possibly know those curtains in that window are yellow?' She gazed out across her garden and a snippet of long forgotten conversation flooded her mind, along with a warm feeling as she recalled being scooped up into her mother's arms.

'…look, darling, the river and the boat…' a small hand outstretched, the warm soft feel of velvet '…sunshine, mummy…' 'yellow, darling, that colour is yellow and you are my sunshine…'

A tear slid down Amy's cheek and splashed onto her hand. She pulled her thumb and forefinger across her eyes to stem the ensuing flow. *This won't help.* She placed the picture of the house on the breakfast bar. Unsure of what the memory or the image might mean, she went back to her task.

Catching sight of the back of one photo, she started turning them all over. On the back of a lot of them were dates, years and most important of all, names. One particular oblong of grubby white stood out from the rest. It was a particular date that had captured Amy's attention. September, 1970. Turning the photograph over, she looked at the image. A windswept hillside with, in the foreground, a young man in a black leather jacket astride a motorbike. Amy frowned and counted the months on the fingers of her hands.

'Are you…?' The blood drained slowly from her face. She yanked a chair out from the table and sat down. 'Have you really been here all this time?' She stared at the picture. It was some moments before she felt able to think or move. She placed this picture on the breakfast bar too. Then she rolled her shoulders back, pushed the sleeves of her jumper further up her forearms, and began to systematically sort through every other image on the table. But there was nothing. Just the one young man on that particular hillside, captured on camera at that moment on a day in September the year before she was born.

Turning her attention to the papers, letters and postcards, she read every single word. Nothing added any further detail or even a glimmer of light to any of the questions in her head. Outside, the sunlight had faded to pale moonlight, the day's hours having passed unnoticed. A house, a face, and a date were all she had.

Amy scraped her hands through her hair and cast her eyes over the morass of paper that covered the table and the floor around her. Her throat felt dry from the dust and for the first time in almost six hours, she felt hungry. The hands on the kitchen wall-clock shunted on to five past five.

'Amy Ravencroft, this will never do,' she said to herself, echoing the tone her mother used to employ to convey displeasure or disappointment. She took a step towards the sink to retrieve a roll of bin bags, but changed her mind. *Perhaps I should hang on to all of this.* She knelt on the floor and began to collect everything together to put back into the suitcase.

'Yes. I'll keep it until after my visit to Haven Bridge on Thursday.'

Thursday

The overnight snowfall had left a generous covering across the whole of the garden. The dark trunk and branches of the willow were festooned with a white veil that sparkled in the mid-morning sunshine. The clunk of the flap on the letterbox drew Amy out into the hallway. She rolled her eyes at the disarray of post that had been catapulted onto her doormat.

'Tut! The other postman. Again.' She squatted down to gather up the envelopes displaying the traditional colours of the season. 'I'll be glad when John gets back,' she muttered, hurrying back to her laptop and her research. It was only as she tossed the post on the table that she noticed a pale blue envelope, with a postmark from Haven Bridge, hidden behind a Christmas catalogue. She reached for it immediately. It had been neatly addressed, just as before, and on the back, written in the same shade of purple ink, she read 'Miss Moonshine's Wonderful Emporium'.

'What can this mean?' She tore it open. Inside was a card inviting her to visit the shop that afternoon. 'Mulled wine and Christmas treats available,' the card announced. On the back was a personal note in Miss Moonshine's distinctive script. Amy smiled to herself and decided that she would pay a proper visit to the shop. *That would be the right thing to do.* Her guilt at leaving so abruptly on her last visit had been nagging at her conscience.

*

The creaking and groaning stairs to Mr Matthew's office had not improved since Amy's last visit, and stepping into the cramped space that served as a reception area made her feel as though she was moving through some sort of time portal. The solicitor was standing at the side of his assistant's desk when Amy appeared.

'Ms Ravencroft, do go in and take a seat. Tea, Mrs Newsome, please.' Mr Matthew followed Amy into his room and took his seat at the vast desk. The file was in the same place and she wondered if it had moved at all in the last seven days. She watched as Mr Matthew ordered papers. When he looked up and smiled at her, she realised his eyes were shining and that there were little crow's feet at the sides. This time he was wearing a sharp navy blue suit with a silver grey tie. *I didn't know it was possible to have such lovely dark blue eyes. Perhaps it's the suit that's making them so noticeable today and –*

Amy sat up straight and cleared her throat. 'Mr Matthew, after my last visit… umm… I had so many questions, I thought I ought to find out a few things about my family myself. As you know, I work in a library. A colleague from the local archives section gave me some advice, which I've followed. However, I seem to be making very little progress.' She took the two photographs from her handbag and slipped them onto the desk. 'I also thought I'd look through any papers I had in the house and I found both of these in an old suitcase up in the loft.'

Mr Matthew reached across for the images. The one of the house he placed beside his own file, the one of the man he looked at carefully before examining the back.

He frowned. 'I'm assuming, from the date on the back, that you believe this might be your father. Is that correct?'

Amy looked away, trying to hide her disappointment at his response. 'I thought, perhaps stupidly, that if it was a photo of my father, you might recognise him. That was all.'

'I'm sorry, Ms Ravencroft, but I don't recognise this man at all. And if you were–'

They were interrupted by the sound of the door opening and Mrs Newsome entering with a rattling tray of crockery. Mr Matthew sprang to his feet to collect the tray from his assistant. He busied himself with the tea and returned to place a cup and saucer in front of Amy, before carrying his own round the desk and sitting down.

Amy sipped her tea. *The china hasn't improved either, I see!*

'Where was I? Yes, I'm sorry, but I can't help you identify this man.' He passed the photo back to her. 'What I can tell you is that I'm completely satisfied that you are the person I am looking for.'

'Am I? But why?'

'This is in connection with a will, and I've been instructed to hand you this letter without disclosing anything more. Once you've read the letter, I'll be happy to answer any questions.' Mr Matthew stood, came around the desk and presented her with a cream-coloured envelope. A very expensive-looking envelope. Amy gazed at it. There was nothing particularly unusual about the letter itself. It was just the name. It wasn't her name. She frowned and turned it over, as if there might be an answer there. The back was just as plain and uninformative as the front. She looked again at the name and the short sentence underneath it. It was wrong, everything was wrong. And it was in French. It was all typed in… *and who uses a typewriter these days?* Amy examined the words in detail.

'This has been typed,' she said. 'Not printed but typed.'

'Yes,' said James. 'I expect it was. We've been looking for you for over two years, Ms Ravencroft, and that letter has been in the possession of this firm for more than ten years. I'll leave you to read the letter. Please take your time.' Mr Matthew collected his tea and the file, and before Amy had chance to object or even take in what was happening, he was gone.

She placed the envelope on the edge of the desk and

considered it. *Was my father French? Is that why I know nothing of him?* She reached out to tear it open. *No, this is too –* Instead of opening the envelope, she placed her fingers on the bottom corners and squared them so that the edge of the paper sat precisely above the edge of the tooled leather inset of the desk. Grabbing her cup, she gulped down a mouthful of tea, the heat burning her tongue and throat as she swallowed.

She dropped her handbag on the floor and moved over to the window. Half of her wanted to know everything. *But this… I'm here because of a will.*

'Why now? Why deliberately deny me the opportunity of ever knowing you?' Her breathing was fast and shallow and she strode to the desk intent on destroying the letter unread. Her hands on her hips, she stood and looked at the floor, letting her anger subside. Unbuttoning her coat, she took up the envelope, slipped her thumb under the edge and opened it. Inside was a folded sheet of matching notepaper. She retrieved it, opened it out and began to read.

My dearest Amélie Corbeau,

I know this name will be unfamiliar to you, but it is your name by right of birth and heritage and if you are reading this, you will know that I have finally met my maker.

'But that is not my name,' she said, sitting down in the green chair. 'So you are French.' She looked at the picture of the man on the motorbike, studying his features to see if she could see anything of herself in his face, his eyes, the shape of his mouth and nose. The picture was more background than person and her eyes wandered across the scenery. *Is that heather?*

Amy looked at the name at the top of the letter and across to the right. Where she expected to see an address and a date, there was nothing but a blank. She let out a sigh.

I doubt very much that you will remember me, but we have met before. The first time was when you were barely a month old. The second was just before your fourth birthday, when the three of us, you, your mother and I, returned to the house in Vincellette. A house that now becomes yours. Those three weeks were a joy for me. To hear a child's happy laughter echoing through the hallways, small footsteps running up and down the stairs at all hours of the day, after so many years of silence, was such a longed-for pleasure. I cannot begin to explain or measure the happiness that you brought to me then.

As Amy reached the end of the paragraph, the tears she'd been holding back began to fall freely. One smudged the ink of the letter.

'You did know me!' For a moment, her tears were for the joy of discovery and a smile crossed her face. It was swiftly replaced by a deep frown. 'But I don't remember.' She went back over the content. 'If I was almost four, I should be able to remember.' Her hands trembled a little she read on.

I wanted your mother to stay with me so we could properly open the house again and live there as a family, but she was headstrong and fiercely independent, just like her own mother, Violette. She wanted to raise you herself and to raise you in England. We argued bitterly. I deeply regret the things we said to each other that day. The next morning she'd gone, taking you with her. Although you and I never met again, your mother always let me know how you were and what you were doing, on the condition that I never replied. It was a compromise we reached, eventually, after many weeks of trying to re-establish contact on my part. But then the letters stopped in 1976. I never knew why.

Amy looked up. '1976. Of course I would have been five then, and that was when we moved to Cheviot Avenue.' Her mother's voice played in her mind as she recalled the times she'd asked about her father. No matter how the question came or how her mother answered, there was one thing that never varied.

'… he never knew about you, darling…'

Why would you do that, Mum? Why would you lie about him? Amy ran her eyes over the first sentence in the second paragraph again and again.

'Why?' Amy shouted at the ceiling, tears streaming down her face. 'Why would you lie?'

A quiet tap on the door made her look away.

'Everything all right, dear?' Mrs Newsome appeared at her side.

Amy nodded and looked down. 'Just a little confusing,' she said, and reached into her handbag for her handkerchief.

'Would some more tea help?'

'Thank you.' Amy blew her nose and a moment later Mrs Newsome was gone, taking Amy's cup and saucer with her. Feeling a little more composed, Amy picked up the letter and began to read the final section.

So this letter, along with the house and what remain of my personal effects, both in England and in France, are yours. My most sincere wish is that you will now come to know me, your grandfather (my brother Janvier) and his wife Violette –

'Who? No this can't be right.' Amy went back over the words.

My most sincere wish is that you will now come to know me, your grandfather (my brother Janvier) and his wife Violette, who both lost their lives because of their work for the Résistance.

Janvier was shot in 1942, just after your mother was born. Violette died in the prison in Fresnes, Paris. There are letters and journals that you will also inherit. I hope that you will come to understand the difficulties we lived through during the time of the occupation and why your orphaned mother and I had to leave France in 1944. I know that I have denied you your heritage, but I hope that you will come to understand that I was acting in the best interests of the child your mother was then. This letter and my legacy are the only way that I can put right the wrong I have unwittingly done you.

Your great-aunt, Amélie

As she reached the end Mr Matthew came in, carrying a fresh cup of tea.

'This isn't from my father,' she said, standing and shaking the letter at him. 'I thought it was from my father, but instead I have this from an aunt I know nothing about.'

Mr Matthew set the cup and saucer down. 'I realise this is very confusing for you, Ms Ravencroft, but if you have read the letter, there are some things I can explain to you. Please take a seat.'

Amy needed a few moments to herself. She walked over to the window and stared down at the street below. Behind her she could hear the solicitor rustling his papers and opening and closing the drawers of his desk. She dabbed her eyes and shoved her hanky in her pocket.

'I'm sorry. This is all so overwhelming.' She took her place opposite Mr Matthew. Picking up the cup of tea, she held it in both hands and took a sip. 'The people mentioned in that letter, I've never heard of them before.'

Mr Matthew smiled. 'They are your mother's family.' From the file he produced a typed sheet and placed it in front of her. 'This is a translation of your mother's birth certificate. She was born in Auxerre in 1942 and it states that her father was Janvier Jean Corbeau and her mother was Violette.'

'But the letter says Mum was an orphan, and she told me all of her relatives were dead.' Another echo from the past slipped through her mind.

'… it's just us, darling, just us against the world…'

'That's correct,' said Mr Matthew. 'I have a copy of the family tree for you that my counterparts in France sent through. Her parents were both dead by 1944, when Madame Corbeau, your great-aunt, managed to escape to England.'

Amy blinked back yet more tears. 'And then what?'

'Madame Corbeau brought your mother up as if she were her own child. They lived in London to begin with and then came to Haven Bridge, until your mother reached the age of twenty-one. At that point, your mother moved back to London, and Madame Corbeau returned to France a few years later.'

'Why didn't I know any of this before?'

'Perhaps your mother wanted to protect you from her own difficult past,' suggested Mr Matthew. 'But what it does mean is that you are now the owner of a large property in France, which you can dispose of as you wish. There is still some paperwork to complete, and I also have to hand over these.' He presented her with a small, brown, lumpy envelope. 'Those are the keys to a safety deposit box containing family papers and journals that Madame Corbeau left in the care of my father, before she left for France. Here is the address of the bank and a letter of introduction from me, which you will need to take with you, along with proof of your own identity.'

Amy's eyes widened. 'I should be writing this down. I'll never remember it all.'

'The deeds to your house, your original certificate of birth and a copy of your full birth certificate are in here.' He handed over another envelope. 'You will probably be disappointed to learn that your father is not named on your certificate.'

Amy stroked her finger across the photo of the man on the bike. 'Of course, this man here could be anybody. A friend, a colleague or a neighbour. And I'm in exactly the same position as I was before I came here a week ago.' She forced a smile. 'I expect that will be one question I'll never be able to answer.'

Amy began to put the papers and various envelopes in her bag. As she picked up the photo of the man, she stopped. 'Mr Matthew, you said something about trying to find me. That you'd been looking for me for two years.'

'Yes?' The solicitor pushed his chair a little further out from his desk.

'Could you find my father for me?'

'I'm actually a partner in a law firm in Manchester, Ms Ravencroft, and my field is corporate law. Mergers and acquisitions mostly. As I mentioned last week, I work here in the family business for one day a week only, because we have a limited number of long-standing clients for whom we have ongoing commissions. Family lawyers do sometimes need to track down beneficiaries in wills and they do that through adverts in newspapers, on social media or, occasionally, through a private company that will search for and trace people. Matthew and Son are no longer accepting new commissions for work, I'm afraid. I can put you in touch with the private company that this firm uses when necessary, who will carry out the work for you, which will mean that you will become their client.'

'Oh!' Amy looked away and tucked the photograph into a pocket inside her bag. She tried to quell a small flutter in her stomach. 'I'll… umm… think about it. Thank you for everything you've done for me, Mr Matthew.'

'There is an advantage to you becoming someone else's client,' he said, as he moved to the door. 'It means I can ask you if you would like to have dinner with me.'

Amy felt her cheeks beginning to warm and hesitated.

'Or just a drink if you prefer,' he continued.

'Dinner would be lovely, thank you.'

Mr Matthew pulled the door open for her. 'Saturday at seven?'

Amy nodded and slipped through.

*

Hurrying along Market Street, a bright smile on her face, Amy felt her heart give a small flutter. A date! Haven't been on one of those for a while. Her euphoria carried her past the shops without her noticing, until she thought about the contents of her wardrobe. It was only then that she realised she hadn't asked where Mr Matthew would be taking her. *Mr Matthew?* By the time she reached Miss Moonshine's Emporium, her mind was a jumble of questions and worries. She stopped just outside the door to catch her breath.

'Ms Ravencroft! You've returned. Come in, it's cold. Please come in.' Miss Moonshine held open the inner glass door.

'Thank you, and I want to apologise for being so abrupt when I was here last week.'

Miss Moonshine smiled.

Inside, Amy glanced around at the various items on display. She could hear tasteful seasonal music playing in the background. As if guided by a gentle, invisible force, Amy found herself wandering through the shop. Despite the stone walls and the high ceiling, the place was warm and comforting. She removed her gloves and began to unbutton her coat. A small basket set on a table and filled with stones of many different colours caught her eye. She delved into it with her hand, feeling the coolness of the pebbles on her skin as they played through her fingers. On another table was a silver tea-set that she felt certain must be worth a lot of money. The style was art deco, she was sure. When she looked up, Miss Moonshine was standing before her, holding a tray.

'Please, take a seat,' she said, indicating the small antique table and chairs at one end of the counter. 'I always like to offer mulled wine to my customers when Christmas is so near.' She set the tray on the table between them and then lifted the silver ladle, scooped up some of the warm liquid and poured it into a small glass, which she proceeded to place in front of Amy. She picked out a slice of clementine with the spoon and added it to the glass, along with a stick of cinnamon. Amy breathed in the sweet, heady spiciness of the wine and relaxed in her chair. Warming her hands on the glass, she took a gulp. The taste and the warmth of the wine on her tongue soothed her into a contented reverie. She watched as Miss Moonshine poured herself a glass and sat down opposite.

Miss Moonshine smiled. 'Now, I have something I think may interest you,' she said, lifting an old photograph album from the counter. She placed it on the table. 'Make yourself comfortable and take a look at it while I go and feed my little dog, Napoleon. You might discover something in there that is to your advantage.'

Amy glanced at the faded, tooled leather cover. When she looked up again, Miss Moonshine had gone. She looked around. There was no one in the shop but herself. It was about an hour before her train back to Leeds, and when she looked out of the window, the sky was dark and snow was falling again. A comfortable armchair in a warm shop seemed much more inviting than time spent in a cold station. She removed her heavy winter coat and draped it over the back of her chair. She helped herself to another spoon of wine. Glancing at the album, she fingered the soft leather of the cover. Must have been expensive when it was new. She gave in to her curiosity and turned the cover. The first page contained a sepia-coloured photograph of a bride and groom. The family and the wedding guests were on the following five or six pages. Then there were photos of children – a girl and a boy at various stages of their infancy, their childhood, and finally photos of them as the adults they became.

Then there was another wedding picture. The boy from the earlier pages with a young woman. The groom was dressed in a smart suit. Amy guessed that the style was from the early forties. For this wedding there was no beautiful white dress for the bride. She wore an elegant day dress and matching jacket. In the next picture the couple had a baby and were smiling radiantly for the camera. Amy kept turning the pages. The baby, having grown into a girl about two years old, was now pictured with another woman. Amy frowned.

'What's happened to her parents?' she said to herself. She flicked back through the album to make sure she hadn't missed anything. When she looked more closely at the photograph of the couple in the forties clothing, she wondered if she might be looking at her grandparents.

'Is that who you are?' She carefully slipped one edge of the picture out from under the small black corners that held it in place and turned it over. On the back were the names, Janvier and Violette. Amy felt her heart quicken. She shook her head in disbelief. 'How can that be –?'

Carefully replacing the photo, she moved on. Another picture showed a house and garden in summer. Amy was stunned.

'But that's –' She grabbed her bag and searched for the photos she'd brought with her. She found the one of the house with the yellow curtains, placed it next to the one in the album, and compared the two.

'That's the same property. A slightly different camera angle, but it's definitely the same place.' She turned to the very back of the book and moved backwards through each page. The first four or five were blank. The sixth one contained a picture of a child on a beach in summer. Amy let out a gasp.

'That's me!' She stood and went to end of the counter. 'Miss Moonshine. Are you there?'

'Of course.'

Amy turned to find Miss Moonshine settling herself in her chair with her dog, a tiny chihuahua, on her lap.

'How did you get this album, Miss Moonshine? I'm certain it never belonged to my mum when she was alive, and yet there's a picture of me here.'

Miss Moonshine smiled and tickled the dog's ear. 'Of course you're in there, my dear. Those people are your family. It was given to me by your great-aunt. Madame Corbeau and I were great friends when she lived here, you know.' Miss Moonshine wrinkled her nose. 'Look a little further back, my dear, just a couple of pages, and you will find another photo that I think you will recognise.'

Amy put her head on one side and hesitated, unsure what to expect. She returned to her chair and settled herself with the album on her knee. Carefully turning the pages she found what she had hoped for. A photograph of a young man in a black leather jacket, sitting astride a motorbike.

'So, he is my father.'

Miss Moonshine nodded. 'Stephen Croft.'

'Wait a minute! You said Croft. Stephen Croft. My name is Ravencroft. Is that how..?'

Miss Moonshine nodded and smiled. 'When you were born, your mother changed her name to Ravencroft.'

'What happened to him?'

'I'm sorry to have to tell you that he died in a motorcycle accident a few days after that photo was taken.'

Amy looked up, lost in her thoughts. *So, you were telling the truth, Mum. He couldn't have known.*

'That's right, dear. He never knew about you.' Napoleon stretched his paws and jumped off his owner's lap into the tiny basket below.

Amy stood. 'I need to catch my train,' she said, grabbing her coat and putting it on. 'May I keep the album, please?'

'Of course, my dear. I was only keeping it safe. I knew you would come and collect it when you were ready.'

'Thank you.' Amy pulled a canvas bag from her handbag and dropped the album inside. Bending down, she patted Napoleon's head. Then she pulled on her gloves and turned to leave.

Miss Moonshine followed her to the door. 'I feel sure you will enjoy your evening with James.'

Amy turned, a puzzled look on her face. 'But how did you –?'

The old lady grinned. 'I know many things,' she said. 'And do call and see me next time you are here.'

Amy smiled and nodded. 'I will.' Looking out at the weather, she wished she had worn her boots. *Never mind, it's not that far.* She made her way carefully through the dwindling shoppers, the soft crunch of newly fallen snow underfoot. She hugged the canvas bag to her chest to protect it and quickened her pace as she realised she just wanted to get home. *There might be other photos in here that can help me understand some of the things in that old suitcase.* Her excitement at the prospect of further discoveries spurred her into a gentle trot and she arrived at the station with a couple of minutes to spare before her train pulled in.

'The bank,' she murmured. 'I'll ring and make an appointment first thing tomorrow.' She smiled to herself as she wondered what she would learn from her great-aunt's journals and letters. Her train arrived. Seated by herself at the back of the carriage, she contemplated the remarkable new turn that her hitherto ordinary life had taken.

Angela Wren is an actor and director at a theatre in Yorkshire, UK. She loves stories and reading, and writes the Jacques Forêt crime novels set in France. Her short stories vary between romance, memoir, mystery and historical. Angela has had two one-act plays recorded for local radio.

angelawren.co.uk

Make My Wish Come True

By Helena Fairfax

Chapter One

December 1912

There was the threat of snow in the clouds over Haven Bridge. Alfie climbed into his cart and drew down his cap. It was a long drive home to the farm, but he didn't have the heart to urge on his horse. Poor Molly was getting old, and so he let her have her own pace, a half-trot, half-amble, as they jolted over the cobbles. The cart was loaded with provisions. A Christmas tree – a last, impulsive purchase – was perched perilously on top. It had cost a whole two pennies of the money his dad had carefully doled out. Alfie wasn't looking forward to the trouble he'd be in, but they'd always had a tree for their parlour, every year. His mam had insisted.

Alfie kept his gaze on the street ahead. If he forced his eyes wide, the tears wouldn't come. It was a trick he'd learned the day they laid his mother to rest in the churchyard. He sat up straight, telling himself it was the cold making his eyes water.

They were approaching Miss Moonshine's Emporium. Even in the gloom he could make out the archway, covered in the most wonderful red and white flowers. Flowers in December – how his mother would have loved it!

A girl in a dark dress and worn boots was looking up at the cheerful blossoms. Her head was covered against the cold by a plaid shawl, but Alfie would know her straight-backed figure anywhere. It was Mary Collinge. She turned and passed beneath the archway, into the grounds of Miss Moonshine's.

On an impulse, Alfie drew Molly to a standstill and leapt down, throwing the reins over the ironwork railing. How strange it was. Not that long ago Mary had been just another of the half-timers dividing their day between the mill and school. She'd been a girl. The enemy. Someone to tease in the classroom. Now just the sight of her had Alfie acting in a way he would have laughed to scorn in his schooldays.

He ducked under the arch to find Mary standing in the glow of the shop window. She turned at the sound of Alfie's approach, and he could swear her cheeks turned pink beneath her shawl. Another thing that had changed. Last Christmas, Mary would have tossed her head. Alfie had been a boy. Someone to give the cold shoulder. Now she seemed quieter, more hesitant, and her reserve increased Alfie's shyness.

He took his cap off at the sight of her – another thing he would never have done before – and stepped up to stand beside her.

'What are you looking at?' These days his voice had a gruffness he had yet to grow used to.

Mary drew her hand from beneath her shawl to point at the display. A pair of mittens lay in the centre of a black plate. Their fur was a startling white; a white of dazzling pureness, gleaming against the ebony background.

'Beautiful, aren't they?' she said.

Alfie glanced from the mittens to Mary. Her face was pale and pinched, and her expression wistful. Her fingers rested on the glass. She was wearing knitted gloves whose navy wool was worn and fraying. Perhaps she saw Alfie looking, because she pulled down her hand and bundled it back under her shawl.

Alfie felt an urge to put his arm around her, to warm her, and had even made a move to do so when luckily he came to his senses. What would Mary think of him if he did something like that? Give him a right good slap, no doubt!

He hunched his shoulders against the biting air and said the first thing that came into his head. 'What use are white gloves, any road? They'll only get mucky.'

He could have kicked himself. What a stupid thing to say. After a short pause she lifted her head, flashing him a scornful look, and for an instant the old, childish Mary returned.

'What do you know about it, Alfie Thomas?' She turned sharply on her heels and made off.

Alfie felt the colour mount to his cheeks. Now to cap his awkwardness, he was blushing. He shuffled his feet, his attention drawn again to the white mittens. An idea took hold of him, surprising him with its boldness. He would buy Mary the mittens for Christmas. His spirits rose until his gaze fell on the price. Two shillings and sixpence! Who could afford that? Not him, anyway. He couldn't even earn a wage in the mill, not since Mam died. His dad needed him on the sheep farm, where he drudged day in, day out, and all for nowt.

An unusual sense of self-pity began to overwhelm him, and he could barely swallow the lump in his throat. He was about to turn and trudge back to his cart, when the door to the shop opened, letting out a beam of light and warmth. On the doorstep stood Miss Moonshine.

Alfie took a step back and eyed the old lady warily. A few years previously he'd been part of a reckless group of lads, and they'd done a foolish thing. To be exact, it was Jim Emery who'd been acting the goat, but Alfie had always regretted his part in it.

Miss Moonshine held her lamp aloft and looked at him with a kindly expression. 'So it's you, Alfie.' Her eyes twinkled. 'I've been expecting you.'

Alfie blinked. How had the shopkeeper known he was coming? He hadn't even known himself until two minutes ago.

But the old lady was gesturing him inside, and he followed, despite himself.

'Take these, dear.' Miss Moonshine handed him two biscuits from a plate on the counter. 'Run outside and give them to Molly. Then we'll have a nice cup of tea and a chat.'

Alfie took the biscuits without a word. They were still warm from the oven, and for two pins he could have stuffed them into his own mouth, but Molly still had the long walk home, and so he ran back outside and left them for her, broken into quarters, on the stone wall beside the archway.

When he returned, Miss Moonshine had a cup of tea ready for him on the counter, and another plateful of biscuits beside it. 'Tuck in, Alfie.'

Alfie didn't need asking twice. He picked up a biscuit. The dog in the corner opened an eye and began to saunter towards him.

Miss Moonshine scooped him up. 'Not you, Napoleon, you greedy dog. Ignore him, Alfie. They're all yours.' She tucked the dog firmly under her arm.

Alfie's mouth was too full to thank her. As it turned out, he had no need to speak, because Miss Moonshine launched straight into conversation.

'Now, you must be wondering why I want to talk to you. And your dad will be getting worried about you, so I won't keep you. You see, it's coming up to Christmas and I – well, the thing is, Alfie, I'm not as young as I once was.'

Alfie halted in the act of reaching for his third biscuit. He took in Miss Moonshine's bright eyes and her straight figure. She didn't appear a day older than when he'd first seen her. And when was that? He thought back, and was surprised to find he couldn't remember. Miss Moonshine seemed to have been part of Haven Bridge for ever. Napoleon poked his head out from her arm, his beady eye on the biscuits. Even her dog hadn't changed.

Alfie was about to ask the shopkeeper her age, when he remembered this wasn't a thing adults generally liked to talk about. He would have no objection to telling anyone he was sixteen, but old people were funny about it. So Alfie, who had learned the hard way that it wasn't always a good idea to say the first thing that came into his head, refrained from asking and filled his mouth with more biscuit.

Miss Moonshine began to explain exactly what it was she wanted. As she did so, Alfie forgot the biscuits and began nodding vigorously. He heard her out, and for the first time in weeks – months, even – began to smile.

*

William Thomas glanced again at the carriage clock on the mantelshelf. For the past hour he'd been feeling increasingly anxious. Alfie was well able to look out for himself. But still. The horse was old, and the cart, too. Perhaps they'd fallen in a ditch. People had been known to freeze to death on the moors in this weather. If they got stuck…

He stopped his pacing and reached for the overcoat and muffler hanging from a peg on the kitchen door. He'd just put on his boots and was about to walk the three miles to Haven Bridge to look for them, when his collie, Sally, gave a bark from her kennel in the yard. A second after Sally had heard it, he made out the sound of the horse clop-clopping down the lane.

'Easy, Sally,' Alfie called. 'It's only us.'

William, filled with relief, threw open the door. 'Where have you been, lad?' he demanded.

In an instant, he regretted his tone. Alfie's face shuttered.

The boy dropped down from the cart. 'I'd to wait an age at the wheelwright's.' He began to unharness Molly, his face turned away.

William glanced at the cart, where the iron on the repaired

wheel gleamed. Then he noticed the fir tree, balanced on top of the rest. How much had that cost? If Alfie had wanted to decorate something for Christmas, they could easily have cut a branch from one of the trees on the moors. But it had always been the same with them. Every year Ellen insisted –

He stopped, and for a moment stood motionless. The fir tree began to swim in his vision. Then Molly ambled forward, released from her harness, and Alfie was staring at him curiously.

'Here, lad,' William said, swallowing. 'I'll help you unload.' He swung the tree down from the cart in his strong grip. It was a fine tree, at least. 'Your mam would have loved this.'

Alfie nodded, without meeting his dad's eye. Then the two of them began to work in harmony, rubbing down and feeding Molly and putting away the provisions. When the first stars came out, everything was in its proper place. The tree was standing in a bucket of earth in the parlour, and they were sitting companionably by the range in the kitchen, a pot of tea and a stand pie in front of them.

After a while, William glanced up from his supper. Alfie was looking at him. What on earth was on the lad's mind? If Ellen were still here, she'd get to the bottom of it. Left alone, father and son had never been much good at talk.

The minutes ticked by on the carriage clock. Alfie closed the grate on the range, a signal they would soon be going to bed. If William didn't speak to his son now, he would miss his opportunity. He took in a breath.

'Is something bothering you, Alfie?'

Alfie gave him a swift, awkward glance and blurted out, 'I want to buy a Christmas present.'

William scratched his head. They'd never spent money on gifts at Christmas. Last Christmas he'd made a bag for Ellen out of a piece of soft leather, and a belt for Alfie.

'Was it anything in particular?'

Alfie reddened. 'A pair of mittens. For Mary Collinge. They were in Miss Moonshine's window.'

William sat back. So there was a girl involved. Now all was clear. He looked at Alfie, thinking not for the first time that his boy was turning into a handsome young man. His chest had broadened, and work with the sheep had made him strong and muscular. The flames from the fire flickered over his son's face, highlighting the narrow planes, where all trace of puppy fat had gone. Alfie had Ellen's eyes, like dark honey, and her straight brows.

And Mary was growing into a fine-looking girl. A weaver at Nutclough Mill, although he'd heard she could have left the factory and studied for a teacher, if her mam hadn't been so poorly.

There was a half-shy, half-defiant look in Alfie's eyes. William sighed. 'Where will we find the money to go buying presents, Alfie?'

'I'm not asking for money, Dad. I've got myself a job.'

William's gaze sharpened and a feeling of foreboding gripped him. He'd grown to rely on his son's help. There were a hundred and one jobs to be done about the place. Besides feeding and tending to the sheep, there was a collapsed wall to restore in the top field, and the barn roof to patch up. If Alfie left to get a job, how would he manage?

'Miss Moonshine's got Christmas parcels to deliver,' Alfie said. 'She'll pay me to do her deliveries.' He caught the look on his dad's face. 'It's just on Saturdays, Dad. And just till Christmas.' He shuffled his feet. 'If you can spare me.'

William breathed a sigh of relief. 'Just till Christmas, is it?' There were only three more Saturdays to go. 'Then I've no objections.' He stood to collect their plates and cups. 'It's getting late, lad. I'll tidy up here. You get yourself to bed.'

Alfie rose to his feet, yawning. William put a hand on his son's shoulder and gripped it, in a strong, brief grasp. 'Miss Moonshine will be glad to have you, Alfie. You're a good lad. Your mam would be proud.' He caught the look of surprise mingled with pleasure on his son's face, and the swift rush of colour to his cheeks, and he turned away, without waiting for a reply, to take the dishes to the sink.

It was hard work being both father and mother. Perhaps it was a good thing Miss Moonshine was showing an interest in the lad. Ellen had always said the old lady had a way with her, and that things often seemed to turn out right when she took a hand. As William stood at the sink, looking out at the night sky, he wondered if his wife had been right. Since Alfie had come back from speaking to Miss Moonshine, already something seemed to have shifted between the two of them.

He turned down the lamp on the mantelshelf and made his way to bed.

Chapter Two

The next Saturday, Alfie hitched Molly to the cart for another trip to Haven Bridge. It was his first day working for Miss Moonshine. The snow had made good on its threat, and a light, white blanket sparkled over the moors, as far as the eye could see. But now the clouds were gone. The day was bright and clear, and the sky a heavenly blue.

Alfie held the reins lightly, humming a cheerful tune as they clopped down to town. At last he'd be earning some money. He thought of the look on Mary's face when she unwrapped the white mittens. Then his thoughts faltered a little. How was he to get to see Mary more often? She worked all day in the mill, and he worked every hour on the farm. The only time he ever saw her these days was in chapel on a Sunday, but that was only to nod a greeting, and they were always surrounded by people.

He gazed ahead, frowning. Before his mother died, Alfie had been an optimistic soul, always sure things would turn out right. Now he knew different. Things didn't always happen the way you wanted them.

The cart jolted round a corner, and there, low on the horizon, was the Morning Star, shining silver against the blue. At least, Alfie's mother had always called it a star. When his dad, ever practical, had told them her star was in fact Venus, and a planet, his mam had just laughed.

'Planet or no planet,' she said, ruffling Alfie's hair. 'I'm still going to wish on it, whenever I see it.'

Alfie took this as a sign. He closed his eyes. 'I wish I might find a way to see more of Mary.' He opened them again, feeling a little foolish. The planet twinkled and shone, and he and Molly continued on their way into town.

Miss Moonshine's shop was bright and welcoming when Alfie pushed open the door. He stamped his feet to warm them. Napoleon, lying by the hearth, opened an eye, disgruntled at having his peace disturbed.

There was a woman standing at the counter, talking to Miss Moonshine. She turned as Alfie came in. He took off his cap. This was Miss Aiken, the new teacher at the school, now Miss Clarke had left to get married. Alfie had seen Miss Aiken several times since she'd moved to Haven Bridge, striding over the moors near their home in all weathers. Although they were neighbours, he'd kept his distance. Miss Clarke had taken a cane to him more than once, and wasn't above beating the girls. Alfie had no intention of getting to know the next teacher in a hurry.

To his surprise, Miss Aiken stepped forward in a friendly fashion, holding out a hand. 'Hello, you're Alfie Thomas, aren't you?'

She seemed much younger than Miss Clarke, and was

wearing a very fetching felt hat, trimmed with blue silk. Miss Clarke always wore purple.

The young woman's fingers pressed his. 'I've seen you helping your dad on the farm, Alfie, when I'm out on my walks. I'd wondered about bringing you both some of my mince pies. But you always seem so busy, and I don't like to intrude.'

Alfie's eyes widened. Miss Aiken didn't seem like any teacher he knew. 'Aye, miss,' he said. 'There's always work to do. But you could still bring the pies.'

The teacher laughed, her blue eyes dancing. 'Very well, I will,' she said. 'And isn't it lucky you're here? I'm helping the chapel with their Christmas nativity, and we need a shepherd. I've watched you rounding the sheep with your dog. You'd be perfect. We're having a rehearsal after chapel next Sunday. I hope you'll come along.'

Alfie's heart plummeted. This is what came of talking to teachers. He knew what taking part in the nativity would mean. He'd be up in front of everyone in chapel, all dressed up in a smock and an old tea-towel. His old mates from school would laugh their socks off. He was about to make his excuses, when Miss Moonshine cleared her throat.

'And Mary Collinge is going to be Mary,' she added quickly. 'Isn't that right, Miss Aiken? Mary is playing Mary?' She chuckled, as though this were the funniest thing, but her eyes were fixed on Alfie.

Thank goodness the old lady had spoken. Alfie had almost ruined everything. He gave Miss Aiken a nod and a smile. 'Aye, all right, miss.' Then he thought of something. He twisted his cap in his hands. 'Happen you'd best ask me dad first. He was nattered when I said I was coming to work for Miss Moonshine. He might not be able to spare me.'

To Alfie's surprise, Miss Moonshine's face lit up. 'That's a wonderful idea, Alfie! Why didn't I think of it?' She patted Miss

Aiken's hand. 'You must visit William, dear. Take him some of your pies, and some of that elderflower wine. And don't be put off if he seems grumpy. William Thomas is a big softie under that rugged, blustery exterior.'

Miss Aiken picked up her canvas bag and her umbrella. 'Well, he sounds a bit of a dragon, but I'll do my best.'

Alfie swallowed a grin.

'I look forward to seeing you next Sunday, Alfie.' Miss Aiken stepped briskly out of the shop, the door swinging closed behind her.

Alfie remembered how he'd seen Venus on his trip into town, and his wish to see more of Mary. Perhaps there was something in wishing, after all.

Miss Moonshine gave a cough. 'Now then, Alfie,' she said. 'We'd best get you to work.' She ducked under the counter and came out clutching a piece of paper. 'Here's my list. Your first call is Captain and Mrs Osborne. Their little Evie is getting a rocking horse for Christmas. I've left it out ready for you.'

Mrs Osborne often drove down to Haven Bridge in her motor car, looking very dashing. She hadn't been out much in recent weeks. Alfie had heard she'd recently had another baby – a little brother for Evie. And Mrs Osborne's sister, Miss Diamond, always had a kind word for him, despite what had once happened.

Alfie stole a look at Miss Moonshine. Four years previously the suffragettes had marched through the nearby village of Hepton. Miss Moonshine and Miss Diamond had been among the women. Alfie had been with Jim Emery when he'd thrown a rock, and a suffragette had been badly injured. It was a terrible day, one that Alfie would never forget. Although the woman had fully recovered, the memory of her, lying pale-faced at the bottom of a flight of stone steps, still haunted him. He'd never grassed on Jim, and he often wondered if Miss Diamond held him responsible.

Perhaps Miss Moonshine guessed at his thoughts. She gave him a kind smile. 'Miss Diamond is staying with the Osbornes at Christmas. She often talks of how you ran down the hill to fetch Dr Lawrence. I told her you were growing into a fine young man.'

Alfie gave a sigh of relief. Since that incident, he hadn't been sure of his reception at the Osbornes' house, even after all these years.

He helped the shopkeeper wrap up the rocking horse in a blanket to protect it from scratches, and to keep it hidden from Evie's curious eyes. As they worked together, he thought about the old lady's uncanny ability to make everything seem right. Less than a week ago he'd been standing cold and miserable outside her shop. Now he was earning money, his dad was talking to him like he was a man and not a troublesome boy and, even better, he'd be in the nativity with Mary Collinge at Christmas.

'Miss Moonshine, do you think wishes come true?' he asked on impulse.

'Alfie, I –' The old lady stilled a moment with her ball of string. A look of distress came over her. 'Alfie, what year is this?'

Alfie stared at her. 'Why, it's 1912. Don't you know?'

But Miss Moonshine didn't answer. The ball of string she was holding fell to the floor. All the blood seemed to drain from her face, and suddenly she looked very, very old

'My dear Alfie.' She brought her gaze back to his. 'My dear Alfie,' catching hold of his hand in hers, '1912 already? Don't wait for your wishes to come true, my boy. Make them come true yourself. Enjoy every minute. Enjoy this lovely Christmas, while it lasts.'

*

William was in the yard, chopping wood. The day was bitterly cold, and his breath came in great clouds of white with every heave of the axe. Despite the frosty air, he'd removed his jacket and was working in his shirt sleeves. There was a thin film of sweat on his brow. Occasionally he stopped to wipe it with the back of his hand.

From behind him came the clatter of hooves. For a second he thought it must be Alfie, home early. But Sally gave the bark she reserved for strangers. The cart that came into the yard was driven by a young woman. She was muffled up to the ears in a wool coat with fur trim and wearing a smart felt hat. She dropped the reins at the sight of him and leapt down.

'Good afternoon,' she called. 'You must be Alfie's father.'

She approached with quick strides. Her cheeks were pink with cold, and her eyes a bright blue. As blue as the winter sky above them. She came to a halt in front of him, her hand extended. Something flickered in her forthright gaze and William realised he was still brandishing his axe. He put it on the ground, wiped his hand on his trousers and reached to take hers in his grasp.

'And you're Miss Aiken. The new teacher. What's my lad been up to?' he asked gruffly.

'Why, nothing. That is, nothing bad. Just the opposite.' She hesitated a moment, considering him. 'Actually, I've come to ask if you could spare Alfie. And a lamb.'

'A lamb?' William widened his eyes. Was the girl mocking him? 'I don't have a lamb,' he said. 'It's December. Lambing isn't until spring.'

Miss Aiken looked crestfallen. 'Oh, what a shame. I asked Alfie if he'll be the shepherd in our nativity scene in chapel. And I thought the congregation would love a lamb, too.'

She looked so disappointed, William found himself saying, 'I can let you have a ewe.'

Now, what on earth made him say that? It would mean spending an afternoon cleaning the muck off the ewe and getting it fit to be seen in front of the vicar. But Miss Aiken's face lit up, as fresh as a spring morning.

'Thank you! I've a basket of mince pies in the cart. And some sparkling elderflower wine I made in the spring. I thought you and Alfie might like them.'

William still hadn't told the teacher he couldn't spare Alfie. Now he found he couldn't bring himself to say the words. She looked so vital standing there in his frosty yard, so full of spirit and enthusiasm, he couldn't help but smile. It was a rusty smile, and a bit lopsided, but the first he'd managed for anyone except Alfie since Ellen died.

'It's a while since we've had home baking,' he said.

Miss Aiken continued to look at him, her head tilted, and William understood something more was required.

'Would you like a cup of tea?'

She nodded. Then she looked at the pile of wood he'd been chopping. 'But only if I'm not disturbing you.'

William thought of the chores still waiting for him. The bales of hay to be brought in, and the meat and vegetables to prepare for his tea with Alfie.

Still, he found himself saying, 'You're not disturbing me.'

Miss Aiken gave him another of her smiles and retreated to fetch her basket of gifts from the cart. She was certainly a refreshing change from the last teacher, William thought. Miss Clarke had made the children's life a misery.

William showed Miss Aiken into the front parlour while he busied himself in the kitchen. He placed her pies on a china plate and filled a tray with cups, teapot, and a jug of milk. He had to hunt through the cupboard to find the sugar bowl and tongs. He and Alfie helped themselves with a spoon from the bag. It was a long time since they'd had a visitor. When everything was arranged, he brought the tray through to the front room.

Miss Aiken was standing beside Alfie's Christmas tree. The

winter sun was streaming through the window, lighting her profile and causing the gold stars hanging from the branches to twinkle. The porcelain angel looked down on them from the top branch, dressed in a tiny wreath fashioned by Alfie from a firethorn bush.

The teacher turned as he came in. 'Your tree is beautiful, Mr Thomas. I had no idea. Even though Miss Moonshine said you were s–' She broke off hurriedly. To his surprise, her cheeks flushed a delicate pink, and for the first time, she seemed at a loss.

He looked at her curiously. Miss Moonshine said he was s–? Shy? Stiff? He put the tray on a table, feeling clumsy.

'It's Alfie who likes to have a tree,' he explained. 'I helped him decorate it. The things were Ellen's. My wife. You might know she passed away.'

'I did know.' To his further surprise, Miss Aiken put a hand over his. Her fingers were soft on his calloused skin, and their touch was brief. 'I'm sorry,' she said. 'I can't imagine how hard things must have been.'

There was a short pause. William found he had no words to say. He picked up the teapot. Then the teacher surprised him yet again. 'I was about to say Miss Moonshine said you were soft under your tough exterior.' She was blushing again, but her eyes were on his, clear and truthful.

Now it was William's turn to redden. He cleared his throat. 'Miss Moonshine says a lot of things.' He caught Miss Aiken's eye. She was looking at him warily, as though she may have overstepped the mark, and she seemed so like a child caught out, he had yet another surprise of the day. He began to laugh. The teacher regarded him for a second or two, and then her face, too, split in a smile, and she began to laugh with him.

It was many months since the parlour had heard the sound of laughter. From the tree the angel looked down, smiling approval.

*

Alfie returned just as dark was falling. After a long day delivering packages all round Haven Bridge and into the hills, he was dreaming of a hot supper and a mug of tea.

Despite his weariness, his heart was full. The coins in his pocket clinked as he rubbed Molly down and fetched her oats. He'd earned a whole shilling at Miss Moonshine's, and when he delivered the rocking horse, Captain Osborne had given him sixpence. Miss Diamond had been there, and she'd been very friendly, telling him the Osbornes' new baby was going to be the Baby Jesus in the nativity. And now Alfie only needed to earn another shilling and he'd be able to buy the mittens. He couldn't wait to see Mary's expression when he gave them to her.

He pushed open the door to the kitchen. A wonderful aroma wafted out, of gravy and roasting potatoes. His dad was at the range, his hands wrapped in a towel against the heat, drawing a fresh-baked pie from the oven. Alfie's eyes widened and his stomach gave a loud rumble.

'Have you been baking, Dad?' he asked, astonished. The nearest his father got to cooking a meal was to hurriedly fry some liver or a bit of chicken in a pan, and boil some vegetables.

'We had a visitor, Alfie.' His dad cut the pie, putting a large slice, oozing meat and rich gravy, on each of their plates. 'The new teacher, Miss Aiken.'

Alfie said nothing. He was torn between amazement that Miss Aiken had taken the trouble to make a meal for them, and worry about the reason for her visit.

His dad lifted the lid on a pan of peas and carrots. 'Miss Aiken has asked if you'll be a shepherd in the nativity.'

Alfie waited with bated breath. His father glanced at him over his shoulder. His eyes were twinkling. 'I said I could spare you. She also asked if we had a lamb.'

'A lamb? In December?' Alfie stared at him in disbelief.

'Happen she's got a lot to learn about sheep farming.'

Now Alfie's astonishment turned to wonder. Was his father *laughing*? The sight was so unusual, he stood rooted for a couple of seconds. Then his stomach gave another rumble, and this time his father's laughter was unmistakeable.

'Best get your supper, lad. Before you faint with hunger.'

The two of them sat by the fire, and for a while there was nothing but the comfortable sound of cutlery scraping plates. Miss Aiken made an excellent pie. Alfie listened as his father explained how she'd come to ask about the nativity, about the wine and mince pies, and how she'd stayed to have a cup of tea. She'd said she'd kept William from his work, and had offered to prepare their evening meal while he finished chopping the wood.

Alfie glanced up from his plate to look round the kitchen. The range was gleaming, and the wooden table scrubbed clean. It was as though Miss Aiken had waved a magic wand.

Alfie had always missed his mam the most in the kitchen and at meal times. He thought about Miss Aiken, mixing the flour and butter in his mother's earthenware bowl, and using her rolling pin to roll out the pastry. A lump came into his throat. But Miss Aiken was a nice woman. It seemed wrong to resent her presence. And the pie was good. He'd always thought when he grew up, he'd have all the answers, but the older he got, the less simple life seemed.

Then an incredible thought came into Alfie's head. He stopped in the act of eating and gave his dad a surreptitious glance. William had finished his meal and was gazing at the fire. Alfie took the opportunity to look at him properly, trying to see him as others might see him. His father was thirty-seven, which was quite old, but he was still strong and full of vigour, and he could chop wood all day without tiring. His hair was chestnut brown, without a trace of grey, and his eyes were bright and alert. He could see a kestrel in the sky before Alfie, sometimes. Alfie supposed his dad was quite handsome.

What if his father got married again?

William must have felt his son's eyes on him. He looked up. 'Anything the matter, Alfie?'

Alfie couldn't tell him. What would he think? And so he said the first thing that came into his head. 'Did you see the planet Venus this morning, Dad?'

William smiled. 'I did. But I didn't make a wish.'

Alfie felt a little self-conscious about his own wish, but he proceeded to tell his dad how strangely Miss Moonshine had acted that morning. 'I asked her if she believed in wishes, and she asked what year it was. Then she went really quiet. She looked like she might start crying. Said we shouldn't wait for our wishes to come true. Said we should make them happen now, while there's still time.' Alfie met his dad's eyes. 'What do you think she meant?'

William frowned. 'I don't know, lad.' He thought it over for a while, and then he shrugged. 'Perhaps she just meant we should seize the day.' He stood and gathered up their empty plates. 'Seize the day,' he murmured, half to himself. 'Sometimes it's not as easy as it sounds.'

Chapter Three

On the Sunday of the nativity rehearsal, Alfie took special care over dressing for chapel. When his mother first became ill, he'd taken over the chore of doing the laundry. The drudgery of the task opened his eyes to the amount of work his mam had in keeping the family clean and fed. Now he put on his freshly laundered shirt, which he'd washed with his dad's handkerchiefs, putting a square of Dolly Blue in the water to whiten them, as his mother had shown him. His hair was washed, and his boots gleamed. Every Sunday he wore the same suit. It was an old one of his dad's, but still in good condition, if a little shiny at the elbows.

His father needed to stay behind on the farm. One of the ewes had a sore mouth and was ailing, and so Alfie went to chapel alone. It was a long walk down the hillside, and the congregation had already begun to gather when he arrived. He scanned their heads quickly and breathed a sigh of relief. There was Mary Collinge, sitting next to her mother. Miss Moonshine had said to seize the day, and he planned to seize it with all his might.

He began to make his way down the aisle, a feeling of lightness in his chest, but to his dismay a blond-haired boy stopped at Mary's pew to speak to her, and the next minute, she was making room for him to sit down. Alfie's heart plummeted into his newly shined boots. He recognised the boy. Jim Emery. The same Jim who'd thrown a rock at the suffragettes all those years ago. Ever since that day Alfie had kept his distance. Jim's curls and long lashes gave him the look of a cherub, and the girls giggled and fluttered their eyelashes whenever he was around, but Alfie knew better. Jim was trouble.

Mary's face was in profile. Her clear gaze was fixed on Jim, and she was listening as he murmured something to her.

Alfie stood uncertainly in the aisle, twisting his cap. He felt a hand tug his sleeve and looked down. Miss Aiken was in the pew next to him. Not much of her face was visible between her broad-brimmed hat and her brightly coloured scarf but her eyes twinkled. She beckoned to Alfie to sit beside her.

'I'm so glad you're here,' she whispered. 'I was worried you weren't going to come.'

Alfie was beginning to wish he hadn't. Miss Aiken glanced past him, as though seeking someone else, and he realised she must be looking for his dad. She seemed about to ask him something, but then the organist struck up for the first hymn, and the congregation rose to their feet.

The service was interminable. The vicar droned on and on. Alfie watched the winter sun filtering through the stained glass windows and wished he were out on the moors with the sheep. The woman in front was wearing an enormous hat. From time to time he craned his neck past it to see Mary's slim back next to Jim's broad one. There was no need for Jim to sit with his shoulder pressed so close to hers. A sick feeling filled Alfie's stomach. He clenched his hands on his knees, shuffling in his seat. He caught Miss Aiken looking at him and pretended to study his prayer book.

After what seemed an age, the congregation began to file out to the strains of 'O Come, O Come, Emmanuel'. Finally, Alfie would have the chance to speak to Mary. Her mother made her way past him, arm in arm with one of the women from the mill. Alfie waited for Jim to follow the rest out, but he was still sitting on the bench beside Mary. Didn't he know they were rehearsing the nativity scene?

When the last stragglers had filtered out, Alfie stood to let Miss Aiken make her way to the altar to begin the rehearsal. Jim Emery still hadn't left. A few others had stayed behind, too. On the front row sat Captain and Mrs Osborne, and between them little Evie. Mrs Osborne was holding the baby, ready for his part as Jesus.

Mary and Jim stepped out of their pew and stood in the aisle. Jim was whispering urgently to her. Alfie's boots sounded loud and coarse in the now quiet chapel. Mary turned as he approached. Did he imagine it, or did she smile at the sight of him? He must have imagined it. Jim Emery stepped forward, and her face seemed blank and pale.

Jim looked Alfie up and down, taking in his scrubbed face and his gleaming boots. 'See you've got your best bib on, Alfie Thomas. How long did it take you to wash off the sheep muck?'

Alfie felt himself turn red. He gripped his cap. 'I'm here for the nativity rehearsal.' He met Mary's eyes and looked away. 'I'm a shepherd. What are you doing here?'

'A lowly shepherd? That's about right.' Jim laughed. He put an arm round Mary's shoulder, pulling her to him. Then his eyes met Alfie's, full of taunting malice. 'I'm Joseph. Mary's husband.'

*

William was in the barn with the ailing ewe. The sores around her mouth were healing, and she'd eaten some of the hay he'd offered her. When he'd held a bottle of water to her mouth, she'd lapped at it with her coarse tongue. He was keeping her apart from the rest of the flock, but the ewe was improving. He'd used her health as an excuse not to go to chapel that morning. He was making a surprise for Alfie. A shepherd's crook. He'd had the ram's horn curing for a while, hidden away behind the bags of feed at the back of the barn. He'd been planning on giving Alfie a crook of his own to use in the lambing season, but now he had a reason to finish it earlier. His son would look grand carrying a carved crook in the chapel nativity.

William held the horn in a pair of tongs over the oil lamp, twisting and turning it in the flame. The barn became filled with the smell of heated iron, mingled with that of sheep's wool and hay. When the horn was good and hot, he carried it to his work bench and dropped it between the plates of a vice. Then he twisted it quickly with the tongs before it cooled, exaggerating the natural curl. When he was satisfied, he closed the vice shut, turning the handle with all his strength.

For several minutes he held the plates tightly clamped. Then he released them, and gave a whistle of satisfaction. The horn was pressed flat, and neatly curved into shape. Perfect. He picked it up with his fingers, tossing the still warm material from hand to hand. Now all he had to do was attach the curved ram's horn to the hazel staff, and Alfie would have his crook.

Sally barked once in the yard, and he heard the sound of a horse approaching. Alfie had walked the two miles to chapel, and he was expecting him back on foot. He went to the barn door. There was Miss Aiken again in her cart, brightening up the gloom of winter in her pale blue hat and bright scarf. Beside her sat Alfie, his face cloudy as a stormy day on the tops.

William stepped into the yard, with Sally running round his feet.

'Good afternoon, Miss Aiken.' His hands were all greasy with oil, and he didn't offer to shake hers as she jumped down.

Alfie climbed down stiffly beside her, without meeting his dad's eye. 'I'll go get changed,' he said. 'I've wasted enough time at chapel. There's the yard to clean.'

He headed for the kitchen door without another word, letting it bang shut behind him.

William met Miss Aiken's gaze, full of surprise. 'I'm sorry,' he said. 'What must you think? It's not like Alfie to be so bad-mannered, not when you've saved him the walk home. What's up with the lad?'

Miss Aiken twisted her gloved hands together. 'I should have realised. I asked young Jim Emery to play Joseph. I thought he'd be just right for it. He looks so angelic, with his curly hair and his dimples, but he spent the whole morning swaggering about and taunting Alfie. Poor Alfie. He did well not to retaliate, but if looks could actually kill, our Joseph would be lying bleeding all over the stage. Mary was nearly in tears by the end of it, and to cap it all, the Osbornes' baby cried throughout. And we haven't even brought your sheep into it yet. The whole thing is going to be a disaster.'

William could just imagine it. Another time he would have found her tale comical, but Alfie had looked too distraught for laughter. And it was Miss Aiken's first Christmas in the town and first attempt to put on a nativity. She looked on the verge of tears herself.

'Jim Emery's got the looks of an angel, all right, but he's a little devil,' he said. 'And not so little now, either. He's been caught drunk in town more than once. And that's not the worst of it, from what I gather. I hear there've been complaints from the mill girls, too.'

Miss Aiken wrung her hands. 'Oh, if only I'd known, I'd never have asked him. It's no wonder Alfie had a face like thunder.'

'I'm surprised young Jim agreed. It's not like him to hang around chapel longer than his dad makes him.' He frowned. 'But Alfie's known Jim since they were kids. That's not why he's –' William stopped. He'd been about to tell the teacher about Alfie's feelings for Mary Collinge, but perhaps it wasn't fair to go telling the lad's secrets.

The kitchen door banged open again, and Alfie stomped out. He'd changed out of his Sunday best into his fustian trousers and a jacket and woollen hat. He had a brush and bucket in his hand. The yard in front of the barn was always thick with muck in the winter, as the sheep tromped back and forth. Alfie headed to the far corner without speaking, threw down the water with a great splash and began sweeping vigorously, his back to them both.

William remembered his own feelings as a young lad, how he'd met Ellen, and afterwards how his heart either swelled with joy, like a lark rising in spring, or else plunged him into despair, and everything seemed black as moorland peat. At that age, there was never any feeling in between.

Miss Aiken looked from Alfie's unhappy figure to William. 'Would you like me to go into the kitchen and make us all a cup of tea?' she asked. 'I feel it's the least I can do.'

William's anxiety shifted a little. Miss Aiken seemed such

a good-natured, sensible young woman. Perhaps he could confide in her about Alfie's budding romance, after all.

'Aye, that would be grand,' he said.

A short while later Miss Aiken brought out a steaming mug to Alfie at his work. He had come round sufficiently to give the teacher a murmured word of thanks before carrying on with his sweeping.

As William and Miss Aiken sat with their tea – in the kitchen this time, rather than the formal parlour – William began to tell her all about how Alfie had been saving up to buy Mary a pair of mittens he'd seen in Miss Moonshine's shop.

'And then when you asked him if he'd like to play a shepherd,' he went on, 'he thought Christmas had come early. It was another chance to talk to the lass, you see.'

'I had no idea he was so sweet on her. And I ruined everything by asking young Jim Emery to be Joseph.'

William glanced out of the window. Alfie had put down his brush and was standing at the gate to the bottom field, drinking his tea. The sheep, who loved Alfie and congregated wherever he went, had trooped down from their grazing and were gently pressing their heads against the bars.

'If I could spare Alfie, he'd be able to see Mary more often.' William sighed. 'He could do some proper courting. But there's always so much to do. I don't know how I'd manage without him.'

For too long, William had been worrying about Alfie, trying to be two parents to him, trying to make up for the big hole in their lives. Now his son was growing into a man, and instead of it becoming easier to be a dad, fatherhood seemed to cause more and more anxiety with every passing year.

It felt good to be able to talk to Miss Aiken. She was a good listener, even if there was nothing she could really do.

As if reading his thoughts, Miss Aiken said, 'I wish I could help. At least let me do something to make up for this morning's disaster. Can I stay and make your supper again?'

William shook his head, embarrassed. Their provisions were running low. 'There's only a pound of sausages. Not much for a Sunday dinner. I was going to fry them up for us.'

Miss Aiken sat back in her chair. 'What would you say to a nice toad-in-the-hole, and some roast potatoes?'

William smiled. 'I'd say that sounds good. I'll ask Alfie to house your horse with Molly. Are you sure it's no trouble?'

'No trouble at all.' She stood and reached for his empty cup. 'You'll be saving me from a lonely evening supper.'

William stood, too, picking up his cap from where he'd hooked it on the chair back, ready to go back to the barn. But Miss Moonshine's words to Alfie about seizing the day had been on his mind, ever since he'd first heard them. He looked down into Miss Aiken's upturned face. 'What about on Christmas Day?' he asked. 'Will you spend it alone?'

Her eyes clouded. 'Well, I have an invitation. My brother and his wife. But they live down in Birmingham, and they have four children. I'd be imposing on them, and they only ask out of duty.'

Seize the day. William cleared his throat. 'How about coming here?' He twisted his cap in his hands. Miss Aiken's blue eyes widened. William felt his face go warm. 'I mean, we've not much, but Alfie made a plum pudding from his mam's recipe and has put it by, and I've my eye on one of the chickens. There'll be some sheep's cheese, and –'

Miss Aiken laughed. It was a merry sound. 'I'd love to spend Christmas Day with you.' She stopped, looking momentarily uncertain. 'Only won't you have to ask Alfie?'

William beamed. 'I'll ask him, lass. But if it's a question of my singed chicken, or your cooking, I know which one he'll take.'

*

Besides the toad-in-the-hole, served with crisp roast potatoes and buttered parsnips, Miss Aiken stewed some of the apples in the larder and served them as dessert, along with some sheep's cheese. William was glad to see Alfie eat ravenously. Some of the misery left his face as Miss Aiken chatted with him about the farm, and he even smiled once or twice. Under her gentle probing, the boy revealed how much he enjoyed his work with the sheep, and his days on the moors when the sun was shining. This was a revelation to William, who'd long thought his son resented being tied to the farm.

Later that evening, after Miss Aiken had gone home, William and Alfie sat together by the range. The brooding look had returned to Alfie's face.

William stood and went to the larder, returning a few minutes later with the shepherd's crook he'd hidden there. While Alfie was cleaning the yard, and Miss Aiken was in the kitchen, he'd finished assembling it in the barn.

'Here, lad,' he said. 'I made this for you.'

Alfie glanced up from his abstracted contemplation of the flames. A look of wonder slowly crossed his face. He got to his feet and took the crook in his hands. For a few seconds he turned it round and round, examining the curved horn and the hazel staff. His father had carved 'Alfred Thomas' along the length of the wood, the 'A' and the 'T' elaborate curves. There was a small ram carved beneath the horn. Alfie ran his fingers over it.

'It's beautiful, Dad.' He raised his eyes. William was surprised to see they were glistening. 'Thank you. I'll treasure it.'

'I was saving it for the lambing.' There was a sudden gruffness in William's voice. 'But then I thought you might like it now. To use for the nativity.'

Alfie nodded. He held the crook upright, resting it on the floor. 'Perhaps Miss Moonshine would like to see this. If you could make more of them, she could sell them in the shop. People come here to walk the hills. They'd pay a lot of money for a staff like this.'

William rubbed his chin. 'Aye, that's a thought, lad.'

'Aye. I'll take it to Haven Bridge next week to show her.'

The thought of Miss Moonshine seemed to cheer Alfie. Although still subdued, when he went to bed he seemed in a slightly better frame of mind than he'd been when he returned from the chapel.

Chapter Four

Alfie's mood failed to brighten much in the week that followed. The flock and the farmyard kept him busy, and his body was tired when he finally went to bed each night, but his mind was constantly revolving. Since the nativity rehearsal he'd managed to convince himself that Mary Collinge would want nothing to do with him. Why would she? He was a lowly shepherd, as Jim Emery had told him, while Jim was good-looking and sharp-witted and earned good money at the mill.

Still, despite his low spirits, Miss Moonshine's urgent words about not waiting – about making his own wishes come true – continued to play on his mind. There were still the white fur mittens, after all, and only a little more to earn and they would be his. He doubted Jim Emery would come up with a gift like that.

So the following Saturday Alfie hitched Molly up to the cart for another visit to Haven Bridge. He laid his dad's crook at his feet, ready to show it to Miss Moonshine, and set off down the hill. This week there was no Venus to wish on. Only the purple clouds and a cold wind. Alfie thrust his chin into his muffler and hunched his shoulders, the thought of buying the mittens occupying his mind.

He reached Miss Moonshine's stiff with cold, hoping the kindly shopkeeper would treat him to some tea and biscuits before he started his rounds. He dropped Molly's reins over the railing and ducked under the archway. Here he was met with the most amazing sight. Miss Moonshine had placed a Christmas tree in the shop window. It was all lit up with candles and decorated with a wild mixture of paper birds, sugared almonds, wreaths of coloured silk and glass baubles. On top was a silver star, shining brightly, although how it did so, Alfie couldn't guess. There was no candle inside it, and no electric light.

The mittens were gone from the window. For a second, Alfie's heart gave a great lurch, but then he realised Miss Moonshine must have brought them indoors to make way for the tree.

He was about to make his way inside, when to his surprise, Dr Lawrence stepped out, clutching a paper package.

'It's young Alfie, isn't it?' He reached out to shake Alfie's hand. 'Only not so young now.' He glanced at the crook. 'What a wonderful staff. I hear you're the shepherd in the nativity. And Miss Diamond's little nephew is Baby Jesus. Miss Diamond and I will be in the congregation on Christmas Eve.' His eyes twinkled. 'We look forward to seeing you, Alfie.' Then he strode off down the path in a hurry, without waiting for a reply.

The doctor always seemed to be in a hurry, but Alfie remembered his steadiness that day he'd rushed down the hill to look for him at the hospital; the day Jim Emery threw a rock and a suffragette had fallen down the stone steps in Hepton. Dr Lawrence and Miss Diamond were courting now, he'd heard, and Miss Diamond was studying to be a doctor, too. Miss Moonshine had helped her get to the university.

And Miss Moonshine was helping Alfie in a way, by giving him the wages to buy Mary's gift. She'd made Miss Diamond's wish come true. Perhaps she could still help him with his.

On this optimistic thought, Alfie stepped inside the shop.

He looked round him in astonishment. It was only a week since he'd last been, but the interior had been transformed into a Christmas bazaar. There was a table full of jars of jam, glowing red and purple, and sweet pickles, and mustard; a table piled high with packets of sweets and bonbons, all beautifully tied with gold ribbon; great towers of shimmering silk scarves and embroidered handkerchiefs. A corner was devoted to clockwork toys. A little clown played a drum while a girl in a tutu danced, and a bird popped out of a cage, whistling. Alfie would have loved a closer look, but his eyes were drawn to the display of gloves and mittens. He scanned it quickly, then stepped up to have a closer look. He began to rifle through the leather gloves and knitted mittens with one hand, the other still clutching his crook, and would have caused some to fall to the floor if Miss Moonshine hadn't appeared behind him.

'Alfie, dear, what a beautiful crook,' she exclaimed. 'Did your father make it?'

Alfie turned. Miss Moonshine was wearing a tall, green, pointed hat. From it dangled some sugar mice and a handful of gold and silver stars. But Alfie didn't have time to stare.

'Miss Moonshine, where are the white fur mittens?' he said desperately. 'The ones you had in the window last week.' He turned back to the table and began rifling again. Why hadn't he thought to ask her to put them to one side? 'I can't see them.'

'Why, Dr Lawrence has just bought them. A present for Miss Diamond, he said, and I'm sure she'll –'

But Alfie didn't wait for her to finish. With a great cry he ran for the door. 'I have to catch him,' he shouted.

Miss Moonshine opened her mouth, but Alfie rushed out and through the archway. He wasted no time with the cart. Molly was too slow. Alfie was a fast runner and had once even caught a rabbit on the moors, chasing after it.

Which way, though? He scanned Market Street up and

down. No sign of Dr Lawrence's grey suit and black hat. Then he remembered the pharmacy. The doctor generally told them his whereabouts, in case anyone needed him. Alfie pelted down the street and pushed open the door, almost knocking over a woman coming out.

'Hey, watch where you're going, Alfie.' It was one of his mother's old friends.

'Sorry, can't stop,' he panted. He called out to the man behind the counter. 'I'm looking for Dr Lawrence.'

'He'll be at the infirmary, lad.'

'Ta.' Alfie darted back out. Now he knew where Dr Lawrence was heading, the urgency to catch up with him was not as great. As he ran along Market Street, Alfie considered for the first time what he would actually say to the doctor when he found him. He would have to tell him how he'd been intending to buy the mittens for Mary Collinge, and ask Dr Lawrence if he'd sell them back to him. He began to feel all the awkwardness of starting a conversation like this, but he jogged on doggedly.

It was just past nine o'clock. Haven Bridge was beginning to fill with Saturday shoppers. A few people were staring at him curiously, and one or two called out.

'What's up, Alfie? Lost a sheep?'

Alfie realised he was still carrying his crook. In his haste to find the doctor, he'd run out of Miss Moonshine's shop still holding it. He slowed his jog to a walk. The more he thought about speaking to Dr Lawrence, the less he relished the task. And speaking to him while holding a shepherd's crook was going to look plain daft. He was now approaching the packhorse bridge. Perhaps he should return to Miss Moonshine's and leave the crook there before speaking to Dr Lawrence. But then he was supposed to be delivering parcels. Miss Moonshine might even be cross that he'd run out without explanation.

All the consequences of Alfie's impulsive behaviour began

to weigh on him. He came to a halt in the middle of the bridge and stood there, catching his breath. What a ridiculous figure he must cut. He might as well admit to himself that the mittens were gone. All his work for Miss Moonshine was for nothing, and Mary Collinge had chosen Jim Emery over him.

Alfie was so overcome with misery, it was a while before he registered the sound of voices filtering up from under the stone bridge. The packhorse bridge was a notorious place for the mill workers to do their courting. He was about to wallow in the ultimate irony of having to listen to two people in love while his own heart was breaking, when he recognised one of the voices. It was Mary.

For a couple of seconds Alfie stood rooted to the spot. Then his face flamed with embarrassment. If Mary knew he was there, she might think he was spying. He was about to try and creep away, when he heard her cry out. A male voice answered, low and angry.

Without thinking, Alfie ran down the bridge and onto the towpath. In the dark of the arch, Mary was pressed up against the wall. Jim Emery was fumbling with her shawl. Her eyes met Alfie's over his shoulder, filled with fury and shame.

'Alfie!'

As quick as a whippet, Alfie launched forward with his crook. Many a time he'd caught an escaping sheep on the moors, or lifted one from a beck, or down from whatever boulder it had climbed up to, holding the animal fast while it wriggled and heaved. He looped the curved ram's horn neatly into Jim Emery's collar and yanked.

Jim gave a choking sound and lifted his hands to his neck, tugging in vain. His cap fell to the ground. Alfie heaved the boy to one side and released him, bringing the crook back to his side. At that same moment, Mary leapt forward, her mild features blazing.

'You nasty creep, Jim Emery.' She gave the boy a push.

Off balance, Jim staggered backwards. The next minute, and with a mighty splash and a great, gulping gasp, he was in the stream, thrashing about and yelling in the icy water.

Mary turned horrified eyes on Alfie. He tried not to laugh.

'Best get him out,' he said. 'He'll catch his death in this weather.'

He reached forward with his crook again, slipping it under one of Jim's thrashing arms, and hauled him onto the bank, where the boy crouched, shivering and covered in mud, and letting forth a stream of curses. Alfie caught the gist, despite Jim's chattering teeth. Out of the corner of his eye he could see Mary was now suppressing giggles, her hand pressed to her mouth. He couldn't prevent himself. He began to laugh uncontrollably.

With a furious gesture, Jim grabbed at his cap where it was lying on the ground and rammed it onto his head. He stalked past Alfie, pushing him aside. 'And you can tell Miss Aiken she can stick her nativity,' he said. He proceeded to climb back onto the bridge, dripping water as he went.

Mary drew her shawl around her, hugging herself. The laughter in her eyes slowly vanished, and she began to look self-conscious. 'I was just walking down here, after some peace and quiet, like. Mam's been nattering all morning. And then he followed me. Ever since chapel he's been a pest.'

Alfie frowned. 'Happen a ducking will have cooled him off. But if he bothers you again, send a message to the farm.'

'Thanks, Alfie.' For a second or two they locked gazes. In the dim light beneath the bridge, Mary's clear grey eyes shone. Then she looked at the staff in Alfie's hand. 'It's a good job you had that with you,' she said. 'But why are you running round Haven Bridge with a crook?'

'Ah.' Alfie gave her an embarrassed grin. 'Well, you see, it's a long story.'

The Last Chapter

All good Christmas tales come to a happy end, and so it is with Alfie and Mary, William and Miss Aiken. After Jim Emery's watery exit, and his refusal to have anything more to do with the nativity, Alfie was promoted to Joseph. William stepped in as shepherd, carrying a freshly washed ewe across his broad shoulders. The Baby Jesus slept peacefully in Mary's arms, even when everyone sang a rousing 'Hark the Herald'. The congregation agreed afterwards it was a most affecting *tableau*.

As Dr Lawrence had promised, he and Miss Diamond were in the congregation. Miss Diamond was wearing a beautiful pair of white fur mittens. As for Mary, she wore a sparkling silver star around her neck. She'd picked out her gift herself at Miss Moonshine's shop, telling Alfie she always wished on the Morning Star when she saw it, and any road, white mittens would only get mucky.

Miss Aiken sat next to Miss Moonshine, enjoying the nativity's success, and thinking of the chicken she was going to roast and the custard to go with the plum pudding, and new friends around the table.

And Miss Moonshine? Somehow, that Christmas in 1912, the old lady didn't seem quite as happy as everyone else. The congregation sang 'While Shepherds Watched Their Flocks by Night'. When they reached the line, 'And to the earth be peace', Miss Moonshine's eyes were full of tears.

Helena Fairfax is a freelance editor and author of romantic fiction. She's addicted to reading and will read the cornflakes packet if there's nothing else to hand. Readers can keep in touch on social media, where she's the only Helena Fairfax, or subscribe to her newsletter for book news, photos of her beloved Yorkshire moors, and the occasional free stuff.

Christmas Magic

By Marie Laval

Chapter One

Two days before Christmas

'What you need, my dear, is a little bit of Christmas magic.'

Miss Moonshine's eyes were particularly sparkly that morning – as sparkly as the silvery tinsel wrapped around her neck in lieu of a scarf, the sequinned tunic tucked into her harem pants, and the beads on her babouches. On any other woman the combination would look like fancy dress gone wrong, but on the shopkeeper it looked somehow just right – although babouches were an odd choice of footwear for Yorkshire in December, when snow and ice covered the pavements and a freezing gale blew down from the moors and howled through the streets of Haven Bridge.

Tess shook her head. 'What I need is a miracle, or a large injection of cash.' And love. Most of all she needed love, but she couldn't very well say that without looking stupid, or desperate, or both. Her throat tightened and burned. She turned away to hide her tears and pretended to look at one of the many weird and wonderful items on display in Miss Moonshine's Emporium – or junk shop, as her daughter and ex-husband had unkindly called it after their one and only visit.

'Well, I think your forties-themed "Christmas Day at Olive's" is a wonderful initiative. What gave you the idea?'

'I wanted to open the café because I don't like to think of people being lonely on Christmas Day, and when I read that there was going to be a special memorial service for World War

Two veterans and their families at the local airfield, I thought I could give my event a forties twist. I know it's a bit short notice, but I need to find inspiration for the food and the décor.'

'Then you've come to the right place. Follow me, my dear.' Miss Moonshine made her way to the back room and stopped in front of an old-fashioned sewing machine, under which a cardboard box was stored. She pushed the box in Tess's direction with her babouched foot.

'I'm sure you'll find plenty of inspiration in there. Take your time and give me a shout if you need any help.' She smiled and patted Tess's hand. 'Cheer up, my dear. I'm sure things are not as bad as you think.'

Things were worse than bad, but Tess forced a smile. 'Yes... Thank you.'

As soon as Miss Moonshine had left her, she dug out a tissue from her anorak pocket and wiped her eyes. She was forever bursting into tears these days, but tears wouldn't save Olive's Temperance Bar from closing down, or bring her darling great-aunt's failing memory back, or change her daughter's mind about spending Christmas with her dad.

She was being selfish, anyway. She should have been more enthusiastic when Georgia told her that her father had invited her to spend the holiday with him and his new family in Cornwall. It was only natural Georgia should prefer a luxury lodge to the draughty terraced house Tess had bought after the divorce, and that she'd rather lounge in a spa than help out at the temperance bar.

'Dad said he's booked a posh Italian restaurant for Christmas Day just for me, and there won't be a sprout in sight. At least *he* cares that I hate sprouts. He even said he'd give me money to buy clothes, since you never do,' Georgia had snapped. 'You should be happy I get on so well with Lucinda and her kids.'

Tess had made the mistake of suggesting to her daughter that buying clothes was the least her dad could do, since he and his new partner often treated Georgia like an unpaid nanny, and that she would probably spend the holidays looking after Genghis and Hannibal, Lucinda's terrible twins. Who in their right mind named their sons after brutal and ruthless conquerors?

Georgia would have none of it. 'Dad is right,' she'd said. 'You're mean and jealous because you have a sad, boring life. No wonder, when the only thing you ever talk about is your stupid temperance bar, and the only people you ever see are grumpy Sally and your decrepit Aunt Magdalene.' Then she'd put the phone down.

Now Georgia was angry – so angry she hadn't sent Tess a card or even a text for her birthday, and Gary had left irate messages on Tess's voicemail, accusing her of trying to spoil his family holiday and ruining their daughter's life. It seemed she did everything wrong these days…

Tess sat down on the wooden floor and pulled the box closer. The delicate tapping of tiny paws came from behind her, and a dog's nose pushed against her elbow. She glanced into Napoleon's soulful brown eyes. Miss Moonshine's ancient chihuahua sank to the floor next to her with a sigh and a whimper.

'Hello, Napoleon, what a good little dog you are.' Tess stroked the dog's short brown hair, smiling at the silver tinsel tucked into his collar. Miss Moonshine usually matched her pet's outfit to her own. 'Do you think I'm going to find anything interesting in that box?'

The dog whimpered again and moved its head up and down as if to nod, and Tess couldn't help but smile. 'Let's see if you're right, then.'

The box was filled to the brim with old photos and newspapers, and metal signs showing colourful pinups with generous breasts and wasp-like waists. There were maps and postcards, copies of the *Picture Post*, as well as propaganda posters about food, the blackout or the land army. At the bottom of the box was a notebook filled with recipes.

Tess opened it and flicked through the pages, reading the faded writing. There must be dozens of recipes. Lord Woolton Pie, Steamed Pudding and Eggless Sponge, Potato Jane – whatever that was – Cheese and Potato Dumplings and Spam Hash… And so it went on. At the back of the notebook there were drinks too: ginger beer, rosehip syrup, and Christmas punch. Tess smiled. Now there was a good idea for Olive's Temperance Bar, and they didn't look too difficult to prepare.

Her phone pinged inside her bag. She put the notebook down, pulled it out and frowned as she read the text.

'Where are you? I've been waiting for ages.'

Tess glanced at the time and scrambled to her feet. Ten already! No wonder Sally was annoyed. How was that even possible? Then again, time always felt like it had stopped when she stepped into Miss Moonshine's Emporium.

She picked the box up and walked to the counter, where Miss Moonshine was arranging a display of snow globes. The shopkeeper looked up and smiled. 'Did you find what you were after, my dear?'

Tess nodded. 'There is so much in there I like. Can I buy the lot?'

'You can. I'll give you a special price. I also have vintage dresses at the back. You may want to take a look at them.' She cocked her head. 'In fact, I have just the dress for you.'

'I'll have to come back tomorrow. I'm late already.' Tess paid and made her way to the door.

'Before you go, here is a little gift to wish you a happy birthday.' Miss Moonshine put one of the snow globes on top of the box. With its little robin inside, it looked identical to a snow globe Tess had once had, and lost. Once again, tears sprang to her eyes.

She swallowed hard and forced a smile. 'Thank you very much, but how did you know it was my birthday?' And why should the woman care, when nobody else did? she finished silently.

Miss Moonshine looked puzzled. 'Didn't you mention it when you came in?' She shrugged and pointed at the globe. 'Anyway, make sure you shake it at least once a day, for good luck.'

Tess arched her brows. Since when had snow globes anything to do with luck? 'I will,' she promised, nevertheless. 'Thanks again, Miss Moonshine.'

The woman may be quirky, but at least Tess was smiling as she walked out of the shop and under the arch of white and red flowers at the front of the shop. A real smile this time.

Chapter Two

Two days before Christmas – West Yorkshire Post, *Halifax*
'You want me to do an interview on Christmas Day?' Julian glanced up from his laptop, looking in surprise at his editor-in-chief.

Derek raked his fingers through his mop of ginger hair. 'Sorry, Julian, but I need someone to cover the World War Two veterans' ceremony. It's a special event, and everybody will be there – the mayor, the local MP, even the cabinet minister who claims he loves Yorkshire but only shows up when it's election time. You're the only one in the team without kids, and you said you had nothing planned.'

Julian repressed a sigh. Derek had got that right. He had no plans except eating a supermarket turkey dinner in front of the television, drinking a couple of glasses of wine and reflecting on the mistakes he'd made, and the things he'd left too late.

He cleared his throat and nodded. 'I'll do it, of course.'

Derek looked at the paper he was holding. 'Great. There will be several veterans in attendance, including a pilot from the 306th Polish Fighter Squadron. Lezinski is coming from Bristol, where he has lived for the past six decades, and I want an interview with him for the paper.'

A buzz of excitement swept through Julian and he straightened in his chair. 'A Polish pilot? There aren't many of them left. The man must be at least ninety-five years old.'

'Ninety-eight, I was told. He lives in a nursing home but he's travelling on his own. Can you imagine taking the train at that age?' Derek pulled a face. 'It's probably the last trip he'll ever make, poor chap. I'll email you the details… and thanks, Julian. I appreciate it. I know this is hardly the kind of assignment you were used to when you were arts and culture editor for that posh paper in London.'

Julian smiled. 'Actually, meeting Lezinski will be a great opportunity. Besides, it beats the stuff I've been covering these past few weeks.'

Derek arched his bushy eyebrows in mock astonishment. 'You mean you didn't enjoy the pumpkin festival or the black pudding throwing competition?'

'The pumpkin soup gave me the runs, and I can't stand black pudding.'

'Wait until the sheep-shearing contest and the female gravy-wrestling tournament!' Derek laughed, left the paper with the details of the service on the desk and walked out before Julian could ask him if he was serious.

Knowing Derek, he probably was, but Julian couldn't complain. It had been his choice to leave the world of literary events, exhibition previews and glitzy film premières and return to Haven Bridge, where he'd spent most of his youth. He took his glasses off, dropped them on the pile of papers on his desk, and rubbed the bridge of his nose. The tragedy was that as usual he had left it too late. The only reason he'd moved back to Yorkshire was to be close to his grandmother, but by the time he'd handed in his notice, put his London house on the market and signed a rental agreement on a flat in Haven Bridge, his grandmother had suffered a fatal stroke.

Sadness washed over him once again, quickly followed by a wave of shame and self-loathing. The night his grandmother died, he'd turned his phone off to interview a pontificating literary figure and had missed the call from the care home asking him to come at once. It had been late by the time he'd listened to his voicemail, and despite setting off at once and driving too fast and without stopping, she'd passed away by the time he reached Haven Bridge.

Now he worked at the *West Yorkshire Post*, lived in a town he had left as a teenager and where he didn't know anyone any longer, and he had no idea what to do next.

He rose to his feet and made himself a coffee before returning to his desk to read the paper Derek had left there. Slowly, excitement tingled along his spine once more. Interviewing Lezinski was an incredible opportunity. He knew about the skill and heroic bravery Polish squadrons had displayed during the war, and especially during the Blitz. To meet one such man would be an honour, and would give him the chance to write a great article.

He finished the reports he'd been working on and spent the rest of the afternoon researching information about Polish squadrons in Britain during the Second World War. Next he emailed Derek's RAF contact to let him know he would be attending the memorial and to ask if he could interview Lezinski after the ceremony.

It was late afternoon and already dark when he left the office and walked across the busy square in front of the Piece Hall.

The Christmas Market was in full swing. Fairy lights twinkled on a giant tree and along the impressive building's banisters. Mouth-watering smells of roasted meat and spices hung in the air. Gangs of teenagers were hanging around – the girls dressed in fashionably ripped jeans and thin jackets open over crop tops, too cool or too young to feel the biting cold; the boys showing off their parkour skills to impress them, laughing when they missed their aim and landed on the hard concrete, when really they probably wanted to cry and howl in pain.

Giving them an amused glance, Julian dug his hands in his coat pockets and walked across the square. Had he ever tried that hard to impress a girl when he was a teenager? You bet he had – though not with his athletic prowess. It had been with his choice of reading material that he'd tried to woo Theresa Palmer. Pretty, with long red hair, freckles, and eyes as mellow as caramel, Tess had been a Saturday student volunteer at Haven Bridge library.

It had taken almost three months and the library's whole collection of Jane Austen and Brontë novels – a sure sign Julian was a romantic at heart, according to his grandmother – before he'd mustered the courage to ask if Tess would like to go out for an ice cream and a walk along the canal after her shift. She'd said yes, and as summer gave way to autumn, and hot chocolate replaced ice creams, they'd held hands as they strolled along the muddy towpath or else met at the local Temperance Bar, which Tess liked, because it was quiet and old-fashioned.

Tess Palmer… She loved reading and wanted to study English Literature at university. Julian wouldn't be surprised if she'd ended up in charge of a library or had become an English teacher.

The last time Julian had seen Tess was on her seventeenth birthday… He frowned. Actually, her birthday was that very day. How odd that he hadn't thought about her for years, but right now the images, feelings and sensations of that day were so sharp they stabbed at his chest and he had to stop to catch his breath.

At a loss for a special present to buy for her, he'd stepped into a quirky shop in Haven Bridge he'd never noticed before. The shopkeeper, a strange woman dressed like a punk rocker in tartan skirt and Doc Marten boots, had taken one look at him and pushed a snow globe into his hands. He had been about to protest that it was a boring present, but then he'd seen the robin inside the snow globe. Tess loved robins…

She'd been so happy when he'd given her the present, she'd thrown her arms around his neck and they'd kissed for the first time. A proper, grown-up kiss.

Unfortunately, after Christmas that year, Julian's father's job had taken the family to New York. He'd been excited by the adventure, but sad to leave his grandmother – and Tess – behind. When, after graduating and years working as a correspondent for a British newspaper, he'd landed a job in London, he'd been determined to visit his grandmother often, but work had got in the way and he'd only managed a few trips up north a year. And then it was too late.

On the square, a lone busker strummed his guitar and sang in a plaintive voice that he still hadn't found the love of his life. Julian sighed as he walked past. He hadn't found his either… but then, did anyone?

Chapter Three

Two days before Christmas – Olive's Temperance Bar after closing time

'I wonder why you bother opening on Christmas Day,' Sally grumbled as she hiked up her skirt to climb on a stool and Blu Tack photos of film stars from Miss Moonshine's box of treasures to the wall.

'I find it sad that people are lonely at this time of year, especially elderly people, and I want to offer a place where they can feel welcome, have a drink, a piece of cake and a bit of company.'

There was a lot more Tess wanted to say, but it was pointless. Sally wouldn't understand. She was too set in her ways. It was the same every time Tess suggested something new, whether it was letting local groups use the upstairs room, organising birthday parties or offering lattes and cappuccinos, mocktails and spritzers, or milkshakes and ice creams.

'By the way,' Sally remarked in a sour voice, stepping down from the stool, 'the crochet ladies didn't order any cake today, not even mince pies.'

'That's all right. At least we sold ten hot drinks. Then there were those two women who had tea and scones when I came back, and the gentleman who bought a bottle of Dandelion and Burdock as a Christmas present. I would say it was a successful afternoon.' It was better than the day before, when the bell above the door had only tinkled twice – when the postman walked in to bring yet more bills and junk mail, and when he walked out again.

Tess grabbed hold of the hammer, climbed on a stepladder and strung some bunting along the ceiling, securing it to the wooden shelves with drawing pins.

'Olive would never have opened on Christmas Day when she and her husband were in charge,' Sally remarked. 'They didn't have any fancy coffee machine, only a big copper kettle to make tea and hot blackcurrant drinks, and were happy selling sweets, blood tonic and ginger beer, sarsaparilla and fruit cordials.'

'And look what good it did them,' Tess muttered under her breath, recalling how run down the place had been when she'd bought it after the divorce. How Gary had laughed when she told him she was investing her savings in Haven Bridge's old

Temperance Bar. 'What next?' he'd asked. 'Are you planning to become a nun?'

Tess pictured her ex-husband's smug smile if he ever found out how badly Olive's was doing now. She clenched her fists around the hammer and drove the drawing pin deep into the shelf. She would not fail. She *could* not fail.

At least someone believed in her.

'My great-aunt Magdalene knew Olive's in its heyday – or rather Fitzwilliam's, as it was called then,' she remarked. 'She thinks a forties Christmas is a great idea.'

Sally looked at her with eyes filled with pity. 'The poor woman is ninety-five and half deaf. She probably didn't understand what you were talking about. I can't believe you want to serve Christmas punch from the forties. Next you'll want to wear fancy dress and do your hair and make-up like during the war.'

This time, Tess couldn't stop herself. 'Actually, Sally, I did think about dressing up to look the part. I'm not asking you to come and help me on Christmas Day, but I would really appreciate your support. I know I've made changes you don't like, but change is necessary to keep this place going. To put it bluntly, if I don't make a profit by the end of the year, we're closing down. Is that clear enough for you?'

The waitress paled and her smile lost its cockiness. 'Are things really that bad?'

'They are worse than bad. I have no savings left and I've run out of ideas, too. This Christmas could very well be our last, unless we have a little bit of magic.' Her voice broke as she repeated Miss Moonshine's words. She looked at the snow globe she'd left on the counter. The robin stared right back at her, its beady eyes blank.

Sally pursed her lips. 'I see. Then perhaps I'd better apply for a job at Supersave. My cousin works there and told me they're recruiting. She'll put in a good word for me, I'm sure.'

Tess opened her eyes wide in shock. 'But you've worked here all your life!' Sally had come with the fixtures and fittings, and the bottles of sarsaparilla and Dandelion and Burdock.

Sally opened the door. 'You just said Olive's is in trouble, and I have to think of myself. I'll call at Supersave to talk to my cousin on my way home.'

Chapter Four

Tess tidied the drawing pins, the scissors and the hammer away, and checked her phone, but there was no message from Georgia. She checked again after putting the chairs up, sweeping the bits of bunting and mopping the floor… still nothing. It looked like she would be spending her birthday evening alone, staring at the winking fairy lights on her tiny Christmas tree.

What if Georgia remained angry forever and Tess had lost her little girl for good? The tears she'd been holding back all afternoon started falling, and her heart ached so much it felt like a giant bruise. Georgia used to make such a big fuss of her mum's birthday. As a little girl she would decorate cards with drawings, feathers and sequins, painstakingly drawing Xs for every year of Tess's age. As she grew older she would bake a cake and buy a trinket or a book. Even since starting university in Leeds, she had never stayed more than a couple of days without calling or texting.

Tess slipped the phone into her handbag and forced a few deep breaths down. She had the forties Christmas Day to look forward to. How could she hope to make a success of it if she burst into tears every five minutes?

On an impulse she took the snow globe from the counter and tipped it upside down a few times, until the robin almost disappeared in a flurry of snowflakes. Miss Moonshine said it would bring her luck if she shook it every day. She would shake it ten times – fifty times a day, if only that was true!

She pushed the globe into her handbag, but it was too bulky and the zip broke as she pulled it. She hissed a frustrated sigh. There went her only handbag. If that was the kind of luck Miss Moonshine was thinking of, she could keep her snow globe.

Tess put her anorak on, wrapped her thick woolly scarf around her neck and locked up. Outside the biting wind burned her cheeks and brought tears to her eyes, so she pulled her scarf up over the bottom half of her face and kept her head down as she walked. She didn't look at the festive shop window displays, or the Christmas lights hanging from the lamp-posts, and tried to ignore the banter of revellers as they walked in and out of pubs and restaurants, and the children's shrieks of delight as their parents bought them a pancake or a cornet of roasted chestnuts from the stalls near the packhorse bridge. The artisan soap shop at the corner of the street blew orange and clove-scented bubbles into the cold air, and for a moment Tess was transported back to happier times, when Georgia would run around and try to catch the bubbles.

Hill View, her great-aunt's nursing home, was located in a large detached Victorian house on the edge of town, a short distance away. Still looking down, she turned into the drive… and bumped straight into a man who was walking in the opposite direction.

Tess lost her balance and fell onto a patch of snow. Her handbag flew in the air and its contents spilled on the ground.

'Oh dear, I'm so sorry. Are you all right?' The man immediately crouched down next to her.

She took a deep breath. 'I'm fine,' she replied, her words muffled by the scarf.

'Are you, really? Here, let me help you.' He slipped his hand under her elbow and pulled her to her feet. 'I am sorry,' he repeated. 'I was checking my phone and didn't see you come round the corner.'

She pulled her scarf down and forced a smile, even though her bottom hurt so much she knew she would get a nasty bruise the following day, and her dignity hurt almost as much.

'Don't worry about it. I should have been looking where I was going. I'm perfectly all right.'

The man frowned as he looked at her, then relaxed into a smile. 'Let me get your things.' He picked up her handbag and slipped her phone and purse inside, together with the recipe book, a packet of tissues and a box of painkillers.

He handed her the bag. 'Is that everything?'

She looked inside. Everything appeared to be there, except… 'My snow globe! I only got it today, for my birthday.'

'A snow globe?'

'With a little robin inside.' Feeling a bit silly, she added, 'I love robins.'

'Do you?' He gave her a searching look, as if trying to remember something. He had a kind, handsome face, and as far as she could see in the lamp-post's artificial glare, his eyes were a dark blue behind the glasses. There was something strangely familiar about him.

'Are you… Theresa – Tess, by any chance?' he asked at last.

She blinked in surprise. 'I am indeed. Do I know you?'

He smiled slowly, and suddenly she knew exactly who he was. Her heart missed a beat and her breath hitched in her throat.

'Julian. Julian Wade,' he replied. 'You probably don't remember me. It's been a long time.'

It was him, of course. Julian. The thoughtful, romantic boy she'd loved so much and who had broken her heart when he moved away.

'Julian. I remember. It's been a long time.'

'Twenty-five years.' He laughed. 'It's funny, I was just thinking about you tonight. About… you know… our Saturday outings after your library shift.'

She couldn't stop staring at him. Julian was back. He'd grown taller, and his shoulders were so much broader, although that might be due to his bulky coat. He was handsome, too. His brown hair was cut shorter than in the past and had a bit of grey at the temples. The glasses were a new addition, but they suited him.

He smiled. 'Do you still spend all your spare time reading?'

She snapped out of her trance, and shook her head. 'I don't have much spare time for reading these days.'

'Ah. That's a shame. Did you study literature at college? That's what you wanted to do, wasn't it? You wanted to write books and be a teacher or work in a library.'

She shook her head. 'I'm afraid the library Saturday job ended a few months after you left, and I didn't go to college but worked in an office as a clerk, then for my husband's plumbing business… well, ex-husband now.' Why did she feel embarrassed suddenly? It was as if she had disappointed him – and disappointed her former self, too.

'Oh. Well, that's…interesting.'

'Now I run Olive's, in town,' she added quickly, as if managing the Temperance Bar would somehow make up for the fact she had failed to achieve any of her teenage dreams.

'Olive's?' He frowned. 'Isn't that the quirky place where we used to meet sometimes?'

She smiled. 'It was about to close down for good, but it had been part of Haven Bridge's history for so long I thought it was a shame, so I bought it last year. It's fun, but it's a lot of work.' It was a money pit too, but that wasn't something Julian needed to know.

A gust of cold wind blew right through Tess's anorak, and she shuddered.

'You are freezing and I'm keeping you out in the cold,' Julian said. 'Let's find that snow globe so you can go inside the nursing home. Are you visiting anyone?'

'My great-aunt. And you?'

His smile died down and he let out a sigh. 'Sadly my grandmother passed away two weeks ago. I had some paperwork to deal with.' His voice broke a little and Tess's chest tightened.

'I'm sorry to hear that. I remember how fond of her you were.'

'She was poorly, that's why I was moving back from London, but by the time I sorted everything out, it was too late.'

He looked so sad, she reached out to touch his forearm. 'How sad… and how lovely of you to move back to look after her.' It was also very much like the boy she used to know. He always bought little gifts for his grandmother – a packet of mints, a bunch of flowers or a custard slice. It was all coming back to her now.

Julian shrugged. 'My friends and my parents thought I was crazy for giving up my job at *Our World*.'

'The newspaper? You were a journalist?'

'I still am, but these days I cover local news instead of international arts and media events. Now, where's that snow globe?' He moved away and started looking around.

'Ah. Here it is.' He picked it up and held it close to his face. 'That's cute.'

'It's very much like the one you gave me before you left for America. I kept it for years, but I lost it when I moved in with… my fiancé.' Tess had looked for that snow globe for days, searching through the boxes and bin bags filled with her stuff, until Gary grew annoyed and told her to stop fussing.

Julian smiled. 'You always did like robins, didn't you? You used to say they were little messengers of hope in the dull, grey winter. You were quite a poet in those days.'

She shrugged. 'Was I? It was a long time ago,' she said, feeling bad for sounding so dismissive, and probably disappointing him again.

'Here you are. Happy birthday, Tess.' Their fingers touched as he handed the globe over, and for one second the small sphere seemed to glow… but it was probably the reflection of the light.

'I suppose I'd better let you go or you'll miss visiting hours. It was nice to see you again, Tess. Take care.'

Her throat was too tight suddenly. She wanted to tell him to wait. Arrange a day they could meet and talk about old times, about their lives and dreams. They used to talk for hours.

She didn't. What would they talk about now anyway? They had nothing in common any more. Julian had become a journalist, and she was… well, a failed wife, a failed mother, and probably very soon the owner of a failed business.

'You too,' she said, turning away and running up the stairs of the nursing home porch.

Chapter Five

Christmas Eve – nine o'clock in the morning

'I think this style would suit you. These were called victory rolls. It was the way I used to do my hair, back in the day.' Magdalene pointed a trembling finger at the photo of a glamorous American film star on the cover of one of Miss Moonshine's magazines.

Tess smiled. 'It looks great, but my hair is far too curly.'

Magdalene patted her own short, thinning white hair. 'It'll be fine. You take a lot after me, you know, darling – your eyes, the shape of your face, and your hair too. People used to call me Gingersnap.'

'That's cute.' It was a lot cuter than what Gary used to call her – Pumpkin, when he was in a good mood; Frizzy, when he wasn't, which was often. Immediately Tess's smile vanished and sadness constricted her throat. Why was she even thinking about Gary and the way he used to make her feel?

'A long time ago, a young man told me my hair was like autumn leaves at sunset,' Magdalene added in a wistful voice.

Tess looked at her great-aunt's dreamy smile and love swelled in her heart. Magdalene had spent her life caring for others: her younger siblings when her mother died before the war, then her sister's children – Tess's mother and younger brother. Later she had also minded Tess when her parents were at work. Tess's grandmother had once hinted at Magdalene having a sweetheart during the war. Was that the young man she was thinking of now?

'You never talked about him before, Auntie. Who was he?' she asked.

'He was a very brave, very dashing young man with the clearest, bluest eyes and the kindest heart. I loved him very much... It doesn't matter now. It was a long time ago.' Magdalene's frail shoulders lifted as she sighed. 'Let's talk about your special Christmas Day at Olive's tomorrow. What are you going to wear?'

'I'm calling at Miss Moonshine's after closing time tonight to look at vintage dresses. I hope I can find one that fits me.'

'If you come back this evening, I'll show you how to do the victory rolls. You'll need curlers, combs and hairspray… and don't forget make-up too, especially red lipstick.'

Tess took her aunt's hand and gave it a slight squeeze. 'Thanks, Auntie. Are you looking forward to my forties Christmas Day?'

'I can't wait, especially now we've chosen the tipples you'll be serving. I quite fancy a cup or two of that fruit and ginger punch you're going to make, although I'd take mine with a wee bit of rum or gin if I had the choice.'

Tess drew in a mock shocked breath. 'Auntie Magdalene! I run a temperance bar. No spirits are allowed on the premises.'

'That didn't stop Bertie Runshaw – Olive's husband. If I recall correctly he did a tap dance on the bar one New Year's Eve, back in the seventies. He'd hidden a bottle of whisky under the counter and sneaked a gulp or two when people weren't looking. Olive was so angry she didn't speak to him for weeks.'

The old lady chuckled. Talking about the forties Christmas Day was bringing back memories, and hopefully being at Olive's, surrounded by memorabilia and listening to the songs of her youth, would help some more.

Tess checked her watch and picked up her handbag. She hadn't been able to mend the zip the night before and it gaped open.

'What have you got in there?' Magdalene asked. 'It looks heavy.'

Tess lifted the snow globe out of her bag. 'Miss Moonshine gave it to me yesterday. Apparently it brings good luck if you shake it, but it's not working very well. Yesterday I broke my handbag and had a nasty fall, and this morning the grocery store and the supermarket had run out of cranberry, ginger and whipping cream, so now I have to drive to the supermarket in Hepton.' And she had received yet another bill that very morning, she finished silently as she put the globe back into her bag.

Her great-aunt smiled. 'You know what they say about luck, love. It's only a matter of perspective. You only see the bad things that happened yesterday, but what about the good things? You told me you found great photos and posters at Miss Moonshine's to decorate the café... and you met up with that nice boy you used to like.'

Tess's cheeks became hot. She hadn't been able to stop thinking about Julian since the previous evening – about their walks, chatting about films and books, and holding hands. About the handsome man he had become...

'I didn't meet up with him. I literally bumped into him.'

'Maybe that was your good luck for the day. I remember talking about him to his grandmother before she passed away. Poor Elspeth... She was so looking forward to having him close by at last. She told me he was single, and was giving up a good job in London to come here and keep an eye on her. He sounded like a wonderful, caring young man. You could do a lot worse than date him.'

'Auntie, I'm not dating him.'

'You used to…'

Tess sighed. 'That was years ago. We were kids.'

'What's stopping you now?'

She shook her head. 'Someone like him would never be interested in someone like me.'

'What are you talking about? You are beautiful, brave and clever and you run your own business. And you are a fantastic mum. You raised Georgia to be a wonderful young woman. I am so proud of you.'

Tess's throat was too tight to argue that if she had been beautiful, Gary wouldn't have felt the need to be unfaithful; that if she was clever, she would have done something more than the admin for his plumbing business, and later invest all her savings in a temperance bar that was doomed to close; and if Georgia had grown into a wonderful young woman, she would certainly dispute the claim that Tess was a great mother. Once again, the rift with her daughter caused her chest to ache. She lifted a hand to her heart and let out a shaky sigh.

Magdalene cocked her head to one side. 'You know, my love, in a way you do remind me of that little robin in your snow globe,' she said. 'You are more resilient than you think. You're not scared of snowstorms and of starting again, no matter what life throws at you.'

Pointing to the globe, she added, 'Give it a shake and see what good things happen today.'

'If you insist.' Tess obediently shook the globe a few times. Snow filled the glass and the little robin peeked straight out at her from behind the flurry of flakes. How funny. It looked a lot chirpier behind the glass that morning. It was almost as if its eyes were smiling... and she was probably tired after a sleepless night worrying about her daughter and about paying her bills. She had texted Georgia at dawn to wish her a wonderful Christmas break with her dad, Lucinda and the twins, and hoped they could meet up in the New Year.

Tess slipped the globe back into her broken handbag and rose to her feet. 'I'd better go. I must dash to the supermarket, and I don't want to leave Sally alone at Olive's too long.'

'Is she still her usual moody self?'

Tess nodded. 'She's worse, I'm afraid.'

'Then perhaps it's time you hired another assistant.'

'I may have to. Sally is applying to work at Supersave.' Tess bent and pecked a kiss on Magdalene's cheek. 'I'll call later for my hairdressing lesson.'

The snow globe must be working its magic that morning, because she found all the ingredients she needed. She texted Sally that she was on her way and drove back to Haven Bridge.

A brass band was playing Christmas carols near the huge tree decorated with multicoloured fairy lights in the square, and the town centre was heaving with shoppers completing the last of their Christmas purchases. Tess parked the car, and hurried back, laden with bags, expecting to see Olive's full and Sally rushed off her feet.

But the CLOSED sign was up, the lights were off, and the door was locked. Tess gasped. What now? Puzzled, she put her shopping bags down, fished her key out of her bag and opened up.

'Sally? Where are you? What's going on?'

She only spotted the envelope on the floor as she stepped on it.

Chapter Six

Christmas Eve – seven o'clock in the evening

Miss Moonshine smiled as Tess stepped out of the fitting room.

'I knew it. This dress was made for you.'

Tess looked at her reflection in the full-length cheval mirror and smoothed the dark green, slinky fabric over her hips. The dress had a cinched waist, long sleeves fastened at the wrists with silk-covered buttons, and a pretty bow-tie at the neckline. 'I feel like a Hollywood movie star.'

'You *look* like a Hollywood movie star.'

Tess laughed. 'You're far too kind, Miss Moonshine, but thank you. And thank you for staying open for me. I know it's well past your closing time, but Olive's was busy today, and with Sally resigning I had to do everything on my own.'

'Sally resigned? I thought she would stay at Olive's until she retired.'

'It was partly my fault,' Tess explained with a shrug. 'I told her Olive's was in trouble, so she asked her cousin to help her get a position at Supersave. She was offered a job on the tills, and as she had some leave due she gave her notice this morning.'

'How will you cope without a waitress?'

At once, a feeling of anxiety and helplessness churned inside Tess's chest. Wearing a beautiful dress wouldn't help her staffing crisis. 'I'll advertise for a new waitress in the New Year. Until then, I'll have to manage.'

'What if I rang a few friends and we took it in turns to help out?'

Tess gasped. 'You would do that, on Christmas Day?'

Miss Moonshine shrugged. 'Helping one another is what Christmas is all about, isn't it? Don't worry, my dear, my friends will be there for you until you find somebody suitable. They are all very competent. Now, let's have a look at accessories. Did you say you needed combs for your hair too?'

Miss Moonshine got on the phone, and by the time Tess was ready to pay, she had organised a rota for the following day and the two weeks after that, and when Tess left the Emporium, she not only took with her the green dress, clip-on earrings and tortoiseshell combs for her hair, but the warm and wonderful feeling that she wasn't on her own any longer.

Chapter Seven

Christmas Day

'It was a very moving service,' Julian told the RAF officer as military personnel, members of the clergy, local political figures, and veterans and their relatives made their way back into the officers' mess for Christmas lunch.

The man smiled. 'We decided to have a special Christmas celebration in Yorkshire to honour the pilots who were based here during the war. There were English, American, Canadian and Polish personnel here, but Lieutenant Lezinski is the only Polish pilot who could make it. We were delighted when he accepted the invitation. He explained that he had no family to celebrate Christmas with and wanted to revisit the places of his youth.'

Julian looked at the tall man sitting very straight in his wheelchair. Dressed in a dark blue suit, with half a dozen medals pinned to his chest, Lezinski had insisted on standing up as wreaths were being laid at the base of the memorial wall and the band played hymns and national anthems.

'He is remarkable for his age. Are you sure he doesn't mind me interviewing him?'

'I asked him when I collected him from the station yesterday and he's all for it. Come with me, I'll introduce you.'

An hour later, Julian and Jan Lezinski were sitting at a table side by side in front of a plate of mince pies, drinking their second cup of coffee. During lunch Lezinski had talked about fleeing Poland as a seventeen-year-old air cadet to join the Polish army in exile, about learning to speak English, and getting used to flying English planes. 'Everything was different. We had to calculate distances in miles instead of kilometres and measure fuel in gallons instead of litres. English planes were different too. For example we had to remember to push the throttle forward to accelerate, not backwards.' He chuckled. 'There were a few hairy moments as we learnt to fly those planes, I can tell you!'

The pilot had talked about being called out up to six or seven times a day during the Battle of Britain, and being awarded a Distinguished Flying Cross for bravery, and his pale blue eyes had become misty when he recalled the names of some of the friends lost in combat.

'I believe Polish pilots were considered heroes after the Battle of Britain,' Julian remarked.

'That's right, son. We were quite the celebrities at the time. My men and I often travelled for free on the bus or the train because the conductors wouldn't take our money, and we lost count of the drinks people bought us.' Lezinski winked. 'The girls liked us too, so much so that some English servicemen would put on a fake Polish accent and pretend to be Polish pilots to chat them up.'

Julian laughed. 'Really? I didn't know that. Did you have a sweetheart when you were based here?'

Lezinski's smile faded. 'I did…' He sighed, and drank a sip of coffee. 'She was a kind and gentle soul, and very pretty too, with her fiery red hair and soft brown eyes. We met at the Astoria ballroom in Haven Bridge, and spent all my free weekends together. We used to go to the Picture House cinema and sometimes meet in a quaint little place – a temperance bar called…' He narrowed his eyes and scratched his forehead. 'Fitzwilliam's, yes, that's right. You could only drink tonic or ginger beer, or some revolting dandelion brew.'

'Dandelion and Burdock?' Julian suggested. 'I'm not too keen on it either. What happened with your young lady, if you don't mind me asking?'

Lezinski's eyes clouded over. 'It didn't work out. I was sure she shared my feelings, but obviously got it wrong. Women, hey.' He paused to drink more coffee. 'She invited me to spend Christmas with her family, so I saved my rations of sugar and chocolate for them. I even bartered my monthly ration of beer and whisky for cigarettes with American pilots because her father smoked.'

'He must have been delighted. American cigarettes were very much in demand at the time, weren't they?'

'I don't even know if he ever got to smoke them. My leave was cancelled a couple of days before Christmas and I was told I would be posted to Bristol until further notice. I panicked, and like a young fool in love rushed to Haven Bridge with my parcel of sugar, tea and coffee, my chocolate and soap, and the cigarettes. I couldn't bear the thought of not seeing my girl ever again, so I proposed there and then.'

His voice trailed off, and his hand trembled as he put his cup down. Julian knew better than to ask what had happened. The pain in the old man's eyes made the answer all too obvious.

'She said no,' Lezinski carried on. 'Didn't explain why, just that it would never work.' He shrugged. 'Perhaps I wasn't good enough for her after all, or she didn't want to commit, when chances were I would get shot down and she'd be a widow before long. Broke my heart, she did. I left for Bristol the following day and never returned to Haven Bridge or heard from her again. Never got married either.'

'I am sorry. I shouldn't have asked.' Julian swallowed the lump in his throat. He couldn't help but feel sad for the elderly man.

Lezinski shrugged. 'That's all right, son. I've had many years to get over my broken heart. Coming here has brought back a lot of memories, though, and I wouldn't mind going to Haven Bridge to see if the places I used to know are still there.' He gestured towards the wheelchair and sighed. 'Only it's not easy for me to get around these days. I asked the organisers here if anyone could drive me around, but no one's available.' He smiled. 'It's Christmas Day, of course, and folks want to stay put, but I suspect the real reason is that no one wants to take the responsibility for a very old man such as me. They're afraid I'll drop dead if I get too much excitement.'

It took about two seconds for Julian to make up his mind. 'I could take you and give you a tour of the town, if you'd like. The Astoria closed down a long time ago but the cinema is still there, and so is the temperance bar you were talking about – although it's called Olive's now.'

Lezinski's face lit up. 'Could you, really? Well, that would be very kind of you. Thank you. Will it be open today?'

Julian nodded. 'I believe they're having a special Christmas Day event.' He'd seen a poster for it when he'd called at the care home the previous day, although at the time he didn't know Tess was Olive's new landlady...

He spoke to the organisers and promised to drive Lezinski back to his hotel later that evening. Shortly afterwards, the former pilot was sitting on the passenger seat next to him, his wheelchair was folded in the boot, and they were on their way to Haven Bridge. Julian was glad to give the man a chance to recapture memories of his wartime romance, but if he was being totally honest, he was also glad of an excuse to call at Olive's and see Tess again.

Chapter Eight

Christmas Day

'Two teas, two mince pies... and two complimentary glasses of Christmas punch,' Tess said, putting the food and drinks on the table.

'Thank you, love,' one of the women answered. She took a sip of punch and let out an appreciative cry. 'This is delicious.

You must put it on the menu, and not just for special events like today.'

Tess smiled back. 'Thank you. I'm glad you like it.'

'What a wonderful idea to hold this forties Christmas party,' the other lady remarked. 'I would normally sit at home on my own today, brooding. It's lovely to come here and meet friends for a chat. And I love the music,' she added, as Bing Crosby's 'White Christmas' played in the background. 'It reminds me of the songs my mum used to listen to.'

Tess thanked them and went back behind to counter. Olive's was full, with both the downstairs and upstairs rooms packed. Customers had been pouring in all day. There were clearly more lonely people desperate for a bit of company in Haven Bridge than she had thought, and it was lucky Miss Moonshine had rounded up her friends to help. Tess would never have managed today without them. They were organised, efficient, and had come looking the part too, dressed in vintage forties dresses, with glamorous curls in their hair and bright red lipstick.

What made it even more special was that they had all brought a cake or a batch of cookies or mince pies they'd baked, to give away as a special Christmas treat.

How kind people were. Tess couldn't stop smiling. She glanced at the snow globe on the counter and looked more closely. Once again, the robin seemed to be smiling, just like her. She was imagining things, of course, but it was nice to imagine that the little bird was happy too. She took hold of the globe and shook it until it was filled with white specks. Who knows? If Miss Moonshine was right and it did bring good luck, perhaps Georgia would return her calls and texts…

The doorbell chimed. She turned round and her heart did a little flip. Julian stood in the doorway behind an elderly man in a wheelchair, and they were both staring at her in shock. Was there anything wrong with her hair or with her face? She glanced at the mirror behind the counter in case her victory rolls were askew after rushing around all morning, or else had icing or cocoa powder on her face, but everything seemed in order.

She waved them in. 'Please come in and close the door.'

'Sure. Sorry.' Julian nodded and pushed the man in the wheelchair up to the counter. His face was red with the cold, and he smelled of fresh air and citrus aftershave. His glasses steamed up at once, so he took them off, and when he looked at her his eyes were the same dark, intense indigo she remembered so well, and once again they set her pulse drumming hard and fast.

A little dizzy, she took a deep breath and gripped the side of the counter. It was as if the years were slipping away and she was that shy girl with a head filled with dreams and a heart filled with love all over again.

'I hope you won't mind me saying,' Julian said, 'but you look absolutely stunning… and this place is fantastic!'

Tess nodded, trying to keep her silly heart under control. 'Thank you, but I don't always look like this, and neither does the café.'

'I remember how dark and dingy it was in here, and how the landlady used to scowl at us if we even dared hold hands, let alone kiss.' Julian slipped his glasses back on and gestured to the man in the wheelchair. 'Tess, let me introduce you to Jan Lezinski, a former pilot who was based at the local airfield during the war. He used to come here when he was on leave and courting a local girl.'

'It was called Fitzwilliam's then,' the man said as he pushed himself out of the wheelchair, rising to his feet to bow politely in greeting. 'Delighted, miss. May I say you remind me of someone who was once very dear to me? Being here and looking at you is like stepping back in time.'

Tess gaped at him in awe. This man was no doubt almost a hundred years old, and yet he stood tall and straight, and if his face was lined and crinkled, it wasn't hard to see he had been very attractive in his youth, with clear blue eyes and high, sharp cheekbones.

The door opened again, and this time Miss Moonshine came in, with Napoleon tucked under one arm and Magdalene leaning on her cane on her other side. The little dog was dressed for the cold, with a black *chapka* and matching fake fur coat. Miss Moonshine had offered to pick Magdalene up from the nursing home in her car and drive to Olive's. At ninety-five, the walk would have proved much too strenuous for her.

Magdalene tottered in. 'Hello, sweetheart, and merry Christmas.' She glanced around and, on seeing Julian and Lezinski, her eyes widened, and the colour drained from her face.

Immediately Tess rushed to her side, slipping her arm under her elbow to support her. 'What's wrong, Auntie? Are you not feeling well?'

'Your great-aunt is absolutely fine,' Miss Moonshine declared. 'She's just had a bit of a shock, that's all.'

Tess gasped. 'What shock?' Was it too hot in the café? Were the decorations too much, or perhaps the music reminded her of people she had loved, and lost. She seemed lost in a dream and was staring at the Polish man.

Jan Lezinski stepped forward, bent in front of her and said in a low voice. 'Hello, my dear. So we meet again.'

'Jan… Are you really here, or am I hallucinating?'

Her great-aunt's voice was barely audible, and her eyes were filled with love and wonder, and sadness too.

'You're not dreaming, my sweet.' The expression on his face was soft and tender as he took her hand and lifted it to his lips.

'You two know each other?' Tess asked in a squeaky voice.

Lezinski nodded. 'Indeed we do. You look so much like

Magdalene, I should have realised you were related the minute I walked in.'

'I am old now,' Magdalene whispered, 'and my hair is no longer the colour of autumn leaves.'

Tess gasped. Lezinski was the brave and dashing young man her great-aunt had talked about!

Lezinski chuckled. 'I have grown old too, *kochanie*. I certainly could no longer jump over your garden fence to kiss you goodnight… but I never forgot you.'

Magdalene smiled. 'I never forgot you either. If only you knew how I missed you.'

She let out a shaky sigh. Miss Moonshine gestured to a free table in a corner of the room. 'I think we should sit down and enjoy a glass of Tess's special Christmas punch to celebrate your reunion.'

Tess nodded. 'Good idea.' As Magdalene, Lezinski and Miss Moonshine made their way to the table, she promised to bring drinks and cakes, and rushed back to the counter… and Julian.

'What just happened?' he asked. 'Was your great-aunt the young lady Lezinski used to court during the war?'

'It would appear so.'

'How extraordinary. Did you know he proposed and she turned him down?'

'Only because she had to look after her family, I'm sure. It's just so sad.' Tears pearled at the corners of her eyes and she blinked them back.

Julian took her hand and gave it a squeeze. 'That's one way of looking at it. You could say it's a miracle they are meeting again after all these years.'

Chapter Nine

'I cried for weeks after you left,' Magdalene told Lezinski in a shaky voice.

They had hardly touched the mince pies and the tea Tess had put in front of them, but sat holding hands, so close their heads touched. Julian bit into his small cake, but the crumbs remained stuck in his throat. They may have told him they were happy for him to write about their wartime romance and their unlikely reunion, but he still felt he was intruding.

'Then why did you let me go?' the old pilot asked.

'I had no choice. I couldn't have left my family to go to Poland with you.'

Lezinski jerked back. 'I never told you I wanted to live in Poland.'

'But you said you missed your country, your family and your friends.'

'I did, but I would have stayed in Haven Bridge if that was what you wanted – if it meant marrying you and making a life with you. Why didn't you tell me about your family, *kochonie*? All those years, all those tears, it's such a shame. We could have –'

The old lady raised a finger to his lips to silence him. 'It's too late for regrets. Let's be grateful for this chance we've been given to meet once more.'

Looking at the two elderly lovers, Julian was gripped by an uncharacteristic and embarrassing urge to cry. Time was indeed precious. Every day was a gift not to be wasted. His throat tight and his heart aching, he put his half-eaten mince pie down, excused himself, and walked to the counter, where he sat down on a bar stool.

Tess gave him a searching look. 'Would you like another coffee?' she asked. 'I would offer you something stronger, but this is a temperance bar, and unlike the former owner, I don't hide a bottle of whisky under the counter.'

He nodded. 'Coffee would be great. It seems you were right about your great-aunt sacrificing her personal happiness to care for her family.'

Tess sighed. 'I never knew she had a sweetheart. For us, she was always kind, helpful and reliable Aunt Magdalene.' She pushed a large cup of black coffee towards him, together with a pot of brown sugar lumps, and poured some fragrant gingery beverage into a glass which she handed to him. 'Here, have some of my Christmas punch, too. You look as if you need it.'

Julian drank both the punch and the coffee while Tess whizzed around, collecting dirty cups and plates, serving more food and drinks, checking on the women preparing plates of food in the kitchen and exchanging words with the eccentric old lady who was sitting with her tiny dog on her lap. It was the same shopkeeper who had sold Julian the snow globe all those years before, and funnily enough she didn't look a day older.

When Tess came back behind the counter, she put her elbows on the polished wood and rested her chin on her hands. A button of her dress had come undone, giving Julian a tantalising glimpse. She wasn't the skinny student he had been too shy to kiss any longer. She was a very attractive woman, with thick red hair he would love to run his fingers through, smooth pale skin he longed to caress, and eyes, as soft and mellow as caramel, that he could drown in. His pulse beat harder and faster. He wanted to touch her so badly he stuffed his hands inside his pockets.

'I was going to close at four, but nobody seems in any hurry to go home,' Tess remarked. 'The problem is I will soon run out of food. I'm out of mince pies, Christmas pudding and Victoria sponge, and down to the last batch of the carrot cookies Miss Moonshine's friends brought.'

Julian grimaced. 'Carrot cookies?'

'It's all part of keeping things authentic. Sugar was rationed during the war and carrots were used as natural sweeteners. They're quite tasty, actually.'

'Carrot cookies or not, this get-together was a great idea,

and not only because you helped reunite two old lovers. If it weren't for you, most of these people would probably sit at home, feeling sad and lonely, me included.' He sighed. 'All that's waiting for me at home is a frozen meal and a bottle of Merlot.'

A cloud passed over Tess's eyes, and the corners of her mouth turned down. 'It's pretty much the same for me, since my daughter is away with her father.' She looked at him, and added, 'That's my ex-husband.'

Julian glanced back at Lezinski and Magdalene, then at the little robin winking at him from his snow globe on the counter. Would he dare ask?

He took a deep breath. 'Shall we pool our frozen dinners and bottles of wine and have a joint Christmas celebration when you've finished in here?'

Tess's face lit up and her lips quirked into a smile. 'That would be wonderful.'

He felt almost faint with relief. 'I said I would drive Jan back to his hotel. It should take me about an hour.'

'I'll give you my address and you can come to my house.' She glanced at the counter, opened her eyes wide and pointed a finger at the snow globe. 'How odd... the snow globe.... It's glowing. Look!'

She was right. But there was something else, something definitely weird. The bird looked like it was smiling. Did birds smile?

'Are you sure you didn't put any alcohol in that punch?' Julian asked very slowly.

Chapter Ten

'Are you not too tired, Auntie? It's been a long day.' Tess helped her great-aunt slip her coat on. She had switched off the music and tidied everything up. Julian had left with Jan Lezinski, and

Miss Moonshine and Magdalene were now the only two people left.

Magdalene chuckled. 'Tired? I feel at least fifty years younger! Jan is coming back to Haven Bridge tomorrow and putting in a request to move into Hill View.'

Shock rendered Tess speechless. 'What?'

'He doesn't have any family in Bristol,' Magdalene explained, 'and most of his friends have sadly passed away, so it makes sense he should come and stay here. We have a lot of catching up to do and want to spend whatever time we have left together.' She squeezed Tess's hand and added, 'It was a wonderful Christmas. Thank you, my darling, for making it happen. And if I may say so, your young man, Julian, looks besotted with you.'

A bubble of happiness expanded in Tess's chest. Julian was coming to her house later. She may not want to read too much into his eagerness to spend the evening with her, but she couldn't ignore the way he had looked at her earlier, or the way he made her feel. Like Magdalene, she felt years younger tonight…

She turned to Miss Moonshine. 'Thank you for taking my great-aunt back to Hill View, and for everything you and your friends have done today.'

Miss Moonshine smiled. 'Don't mention it, my dear. We were glad to help.'

Once alone, Tess stacked the last of the crockery in the dishwasher, put all the chairs up and mopped the floor. Tiredness made her legs, her arms, her whole body ache, but her heart sang a happy song. There was only one person missing to make her day complete.

She was about to grab her bag, put her coat on and switch off the lights when there was a whistling sound behind her. She swirled round and glanced at the snow globe on the counter, and let out a disbelieving sigh. She may be tired, but not so tired as to believe that Miss Moonshine's little robin was trying to attract her attention. She lifted up the globe and gave it a shake. She may not believe it would bring her luck, but it couldn't hurt.

Suddenly, the door was yanked open and a small and thin female figure appeared in the doorway, a rucksack dangling from one shoulder.

'Thank God you're here! I went to the house but it was dark and empty, and I thought you had gone away somewhere and I would be all on my own.'

Tess let out the breath she'd been holding. 'Georgia? What happened? Are you all right?'

Her daughter dropped her rucksack to the ground and rushed into her arms. Her skin was freezing cold, her coat damp and her hair peppered with snowflakes, but Tess hugged her tightly and breathed in her sweet, fresh scent.

'I'm so happy to see you, my love,' she said as she pulled away at last, 'but why aren't you in Cornwall with your dad?'

Georgia sniffed. 'You were right all along. I heard them talking last night. The only reason they invited me to Cornwall was because they wanted a free babysitter for Genghis and Hannibal.' Tears welled into her eyes and her chin trembled, the way it had when she was a little girl. 'They were laughing and saying horrible things about you and I – I suddenly wanted to be at home with you and tell you I loved you, so I packed my stuff early this morning and left.'

'How did you manage to travel back here on Christmas Day?' Tess asked, still stunned at having her daughter there with her, and her dearest wish come true.

'By a stroke of luck, Dad's neighbours were travelling to Bradford to spend Christmas with their daughter and grandkids. I begged a lift from them and then I took a taxi to Haven Bridge. Oh, Mum… I'm sorry. I love you so much, and I was so mean to you on the phone. I didn't even wish you a happy birthday or a merry Christmas or buy you a present. Can you forgive me?'

Tess pulled her daughter into her arms again with a contented sigh. 'You being here is the most wonderful birthday and Christmas present I could ever wish for. Why didn't you call to let me know you were on your way?'

Georgia grimaced. 'The twins took my phone yesterday morning and threw it into the toilet.' She looked around and frowned. 'So what happened here today?'

Tess couldn't help but laugh. 'Nothing much, my love… only a bit of Christmas magic, and a few miracles. And talking of miracles…' She took the snow globe from the counter, and even though her daughter was looking at her as if she had lost her mind, and may very well be right, Tess pressed her lips against its cool glass and whispered a heartfelt 'Thank you' to the little robin inside.

She slipped the globe into her bag. 'Let's go home, my darling. You must be hungry, and I have to warm up our Christmas meal. We have a guest coming for tea tonight – and there won't be a sprout in sight!'

Originally from Lyon, Marie Laval now lives in the beautiful Rossendale Valley in Lancashire, and writes contemporary and historical romance with a French twist. Her bestselling romantic comedy, *Little Pink Taxi*, is published by Choc Lit, as is her latest contemporary romance *A Paris Fairy Tale*.

amazon.co.uk/Marie-Laval/e/B00A03UV3I/

The Timepiece

By Melinda Hammond

Chapter One

November 1831

Miss Moonshine's Emporium looked just as it had a year ago, the windows glowing with candles, and displaying goods as varied as a stuffed bird, a violin and a folding bootjack. John Darlington tucked the package more securely under his arm and stepped inside, out of the biting November wind. A mahogany table still stood in the centre of the floor, while around the room every table, shelf and cupboard was crowded with pieces for sale. Everything gleamed in the candlelight, inviting one to touch, to admire.

He imagined bringing a child in here, seeing his eyes widen at the colourful display, perhaps reaching out one tiny hand for the toy soldiers parading on the table. He quickly stifled the thought.

A woman appeared with a tiny dog at her heels.

'Good evening. Mr... Darlington, isn't it?'

'Aye, it is, Miss Moonshine. It has been five years, madam. Almost to the day. I am surprised you remember me.'

'I remember everyone. As does Napoleon.' She stooped to pick up the dog. 'You came in with your bride. How is she, Mr Darlington?'

John felt the familiar band tighten around his chest.

'Dead.' It came out harshly, but he could not help that. He tried again. 'She died four years ago. And the baby. My son.' He put the package down carefully on the table. 'I would like you to take this back.'

'Ah.' Miss Moonshine unwrapped it. 'The clock you bought from me. A gift for your wife.'

'Yes.'

Rosemary had seen the clock in the window and had been enchanted. It was chiming the hour as they walked in and when she turned to him, her eyes shining, he knew he must buy it for her. Whatever the cost.

Surprisingly, the price had been very reasonable, and just less than the sum he was carrying. He had bought the timepiece immediately. The money had been intended for other things, but he decided the clock was more important. The mills were recovering from the last slump, profits were up. He would be able to begin the improvements to the house next quarter day, fitting out the new nursery for their child.

Miss Moonshine touched his arm. She said gently, 'Does the clock remind you of her? Of Rosemary?'

It flashed through his mind to ask her how she knew his wife's name, but he let it go.

'Yes.' It was the reason he travelled so much now. 'I put up shelves in the parlour for her books and built in a space for the clock.' He rubbed his eyes. 'I have been back at Clough Hall barely a month and already it is too much. The constant tick, tick. The chimes. It must go.'

'Alas, Mr Darlington, I cannot offer you much. Less than you paid, in fact. The times being very hard…'

'It matters not.'

He wanted to say he would happily give the clock away, but Miss Moonshine was already opening her cash box. She held out her hand, palm up, and the coins winked in the candlelight.

'Will ten guineas be enough, sir?'

'Thank you.'

He took the money, vowing to put it into the Poor Box on Sunday.

*

Lucy stood beside her brother just inside the church door as the congregation filed out. The snow was falling and she tried not to shiver, knowing how fortunate she was to have her fur-lined redingote while most of the women who attended the service had nothing better than thick, heavy shawls to keep out the cold. The majority were poor, farmhands or mill workers and servants. There were a few wealthier patrons, but they had already hurried off to their waiting carriages.

Lucy noticed there was still someone in the church. A well-dressed gentleman in a black frockcoat. Mr John Darlington. She would not forget their first meeting some weeks ago.

Reginald had stopped the man as he was making his way out of the church.

'Good day to you, my friend. I have not seen you for some time. Have you been travelling again?'

The man had responded without a smile. 'Yes, I have been away. I spend very little time at the hall now.'

Nothing daunted by his abrupt manner, Reginald continued, 'You have not met my sister Lucy, I think. She is come from Oakham to live with me and keep house. She has been here two months and already life is more comfortable.' Reginald had chuckled at this little pleasantry, then turned to Lucy. 'Mr John Darlington, my dear. Of Clough Hall. John owns Hope Mills, just out of town.'

'Does he?'

That fact did nothing to make her feel any friendlier towards the gentleman. Lucy had heard of Hope Mills, of harsh treatment and poor conditions. However, common courtesy obliged her to shake hands with him.

To one more used to a mere touch of fingers or the weak clasp offered as a formality, his grip was surprisingly firm and warm. His dark eyes were fixed upon her, their gaze shrewd, piercing. He was a man accustomed to summing up people at a glance, she thought.

'How do you do, Miss Coates.'

'Mrs,' she had corrected him. 'Mrs Granger. I am a widow.'

Lucy had braced herself for the usual expressions of sympathy, but after a slight hesitation he merely nodded, touched his hat to her brother and walked away. She gave an uncertain laugh and Reginald raised his brows at her.

'What a – a singular man. Is he always so taciturn, brother?'

'He was not always so. He lost his wife four years ago and has withdrawn a great deal from society since then. Sunday service is possibly his only outing in Haven Bridge these days and I suspect that is only because of our friendship.'

Lucy had wondered then how her kind, mild-mannered brother could be friends with such a cold and humourless creature. In the weeks since that first meeting, she had seen him often, not only at Sunday service but also in the churchyard, which she could see from her bedroom window. His tall figure was unmistakeable, standing by his wife's grave.

Usually, he was the first to leave the church, but today he would be the last. Lucy wondered why he was loitering. Perhaps he wanted to speak privately with her brother. While Reginald continued to shake hands with each of his congregation and wish them well, she observed John Darlington.

A tall, handsome man with face and figure to attract attention. Odd, then, that he appeared to be so singularly alone. She had seen several of the gentlemen nod to him when they came in and he had returned the greeting, touching his hat to the ladies, but he had chosen to sit at a distance, away from the other mill owners. Away from everyone.

Lucy watched him now as he made his way towards the door. He paused by the Poor Box and she caught the glint of coins as he dropped them in. Not the usual pennies, but gold and silver coins. Too many to count.

'Ah, Mrs Greenwood, I am glad you could come this morning.' Reginald was talking to a pale, sickly looking woman wrapped in a faded cloak. 'How is your mother-in-law? I suppose your daughter is looking after her today.'

Mrs Greenwood worked in a local spinning mill as well as looking after her elderly mother, two children and husband. Lucy dragged her attention back to listen to her reply.

'Aye, Mother's not so good, but at her age, it's to be expected. We're managing, Reverend, thank 'ee.' She turned to the boy at her side. 'Go and wait outside, Tommy. I see your faither by t'gate.' She gave the boy a little push and watched him run outside before turning back, saying awkwardly, 'I'm reet sorry Dan don't come to church, Reverend, but since he lost his place at t'mill, he's not been isself.'

'Your husband feels the world is against him, does he? And his God.' Reginald patted her hands. 'You mustn't fret, Mrs Greenwood. Daniel will come back when he's ready, I am sure. And we will welcome him.'

Lucy glanced out through the door to where young Tommy Greenwood was waiting for his mother. He was sparking his clogs on the stone flags. Until his father cuffed him around the ear for wearing out the irons.

She held out her hand to the woman. 'I will call later, if I may, Mrs Greenwood, with a basket. Just a little something for old Mrs Greenwood, you understand,' she added quickly, knowing any hint of charity would offend. 'And I have a red flannel petticoat that I have never worn. So careless of me to buy the wrong size. Perhaps you might alter it for Agatha? It would be such a shame to throw it away.'

'Aye, I could make use of it and thank 'ee for it, too. Our Aggie has been set on in t'mill now, doffing bobbins, so we'll soon have her wage coming in, as well as our Tommy's. It all helps.' Mrs Greenwood moved off to join her husband and son, and Lucy watched them walk away along the street. There was a dejected slouch to Daniel Greenwood's shoulders. She guessed the man would be fretting, living on his wife's and children's earnings.

'Ah, John.'

She heard her brother address the final member of the congregation and turned towards them, waiting until Reginald had finished his greeting before holding out her own hand. After all, a man who put so much in the Poor Box could not be all bad.

She said, smiling, 'Will you be joining us for the Advent service next week, Mr Darlington?'

He looked a little taken aback. 'No. That is, thank you. I doubt I shall be here.'

'Surely you will not be off jauntering again so soon, John? Why, I hoped you would join us for dinner on Christmas Day.'

This was as much news to Lucy as to the gentleman, and they looked at each other, startled. They realised, at almost the same moment, that he was still holding her hand and almost jumped apart. Lucy knew she was blushing but she saw his cheeks darken, too. He muttered something incoherent, touched his hat and strode away.

Reginald shook his head. 'He is a lost soul, poor man. I wish we could do something for him. He was one of my earliest acquaintances, you know. When I first came to the parish. That was, oh, ten years ago. His father was alive then, of course, and John but one-and-twenty, but he came to me for tuition. A little Latin and Greek, philosophy and literature. He was too busy learning the family business to go to university, but he has a keen, enquiring mind and wanted to learn. He said it gave him a more open view of the world.' He sighed, frowning. 'He gave up his studies when his father died eight years since, to concentrate on building up the business. Very successfully, too, although he no longer takes much interest in it. Since his wife's sad demise, I fear he has lost interest in most things.' He looked so sad that Lucy took his arm.

'You cannot save all of mankind, you know, Reginald,' she said gently. 'Come along, let us tidy the church, and then we can go home.'

*

The snow had stopped, but thick, grey cloud still covered the sky when Lucy sallied forth later that day to visit the Greenwoods. She had raided the larder and filled her basket with food, including the remains of a ham. Reginald would not miss it. They had plenty, unlike many of the townsfolk, for whom the winter meant hardship, cold homes and higher food prices, that is, when they could find anything at the market.

It was not late, but darkness was falling by the time Lucy left the Greenwoods' little back-to-back house in Dale Street. Her basket was empty, and she should have felt satisfaction at having run her errand. Instead, she felt only a simmering anger. After what she had heard she wanted to rage at the injustice of the world, but the idea of pouring out her anger to Reginald did not appeal. He would sigh and tell her they must pray, but Lucy wanted a solution here and now. Her steps slowed. Instead of continuing to the vicarage, she turned and began to walk back along the High Street.

*

A cheerful fire burned in the parlour of Clough Hall and the red velvet curtains had been pulled across the windows, the gold fringe glowing in the lamplight. This had been John's favourite room, once, but now it was desolate. Perhaps he should go abroad again. After all, Hodgson ran the mills and Grimes, his man of business, looked after the finances. He was not needed here.

There was a soft knock upon the door.

'Mrs Granger to see you, sir.'

He hesitated, wondering for a moment if he had heard correctly.

'Send her in, Elsie.'

He rose from his chair and straightened his coat. Lucy Granger. He remembered holding her hand at the church door that morning. How small it had felt in his grasp. How small she was. A dainty little thing, barely up to his shoulder, whereas Rosemary had been a tall, golden-haired goddess. Only unlike a goddess, she had not been immortal. He shook his head and squeezed his eyes shut to clear the painful memories. When he opened them again, Lucy Granger was standing in the doorway.

Having removed her coat and bonnet in the hall, she appeared before him now in a serviceable high-necked gown of dark blue wool. It was very plain with only a small white lace frill around the neck and cuffs, and a buckled belt that accentuated her tiny waist. Her brown hair was brushed back into a sleek knot at the back of her head, but several wayward curls had escaped and framed her face, drawing attention to the large dark eyes, straight little nose and a mouth too wide for beauty.

Then he recalled how she had smiled at him that morning. Not beautiful, perhaps, but attractive. He had had to work hard not to smile back.

John cleared his throat.

'Won't you sit down, madam?' He glanced towards the side-table. 'I have sherry, or shall I ask Elsie to bring you some tea?'

'Nothing, thank you.' She waited until the maid had departed and shut the door before adding, 'And I would rather not sit down.'

He frowned. 'Then I fear we will both find that rather awkward, since I cannot sit in your presence.' He waved towards the two armchairs flanking the fireplace. 'Please, Mrs Granger.'

After a moment's hesitation she perched on the edge of one of the chairs. He resisted the urge to say, 'That's better,' and lowered himself into the empty one.

'How can I help you?'

She looked troubled and did not speak immediately.

'Is something wrong?' He sat forward. 'Is it your brother?'

'No, no. Reginald is well, thank you.' She clasped her hands together and fixed him with her dark eyes. 'How long is it since you visited Hope Mills?' That surprised him. She continued. 'I beg your pardon if you think I am speaking out of turn, but since I came here, I have heard a great deal about your mills, Mr Darlington, and nothing to the good. You have children working for you.'

'As does everyone. We start them at nine years old.'

'Some are barely eight, sir. The families have told me as much.'

'Their parents must have signed to say they are of age.'

'One only has to look at the children to know the truth!'

'Mrs Granger, that is none of your concern.'

She sat up straighter. 'These are my brother's parishioners, thus it is my concern. Indeed, it should be the concern of every Christian.'

John rose and began to pace the room. He said shortly, 'Hodgson is not breaking the law.'

'No, but he comes very close to it. I understand the children have no schooling.'

'That is ridiculous. I built the factory school myself, years before it became law.'

'But teachers have to be paid, and that reduces your profits.'

John felt his temper rising. 'I do not put profit above my workers, Mrs Granger.'

'You might not do so, but what of those who run your mills? Just how much attention do you pay to your business, Mr Darlington?'

Her words caught him on the raw. 'How dare you come here and question me!'

'Someone has to do so! Your factory manager has already turned off several workers this winter for speaking out.' She thought of the Greenwoods. She had learned only today that they all worked at Hope Mills. Daniel had been dismissed for standing up for the children. She said scornfully, 'It is ironic that the money you put in the Poor Box this morning will go directly to them.'

'Hodgson has to keep order.'

She jumped up. 'Order! The man is a tyrant. I have heard from more than one source that he beats the children. He makes them work at night, too, which they should not be doing. And your factory school is being used for storage. It is shameful!'

He glared at her. 'I think you should leave now.'

She was in no way cowed by his scowl. Instead she stepped closer, her eyes sparkling with anger. 'The workers cannot speak for fear of losing their jobs, but I can and I will. These are your people, Mr Darlington. Your father started these mills, you took them on and from what I have heard you were a good master, once. You cared. Now your mills are a disgrace.'

'Enough!'

'The workers no longer call it Hope Mills, did you know that? Now they call it Endurance Mills.'

He put up his hand. 'I do not want to hear this.'

'Well you should. Since Mrs Darlington died you have neglected your duties.'

'You will not mention my wife.'

'Why not? Do you think she would approve of your actions, or rather your lack of action in the past few years? I think rather she would be ashamed of you.'

'How dare you!

She put up her chin. 'Oh, I dare, sir, because someone has to speak out. I believe Reginald tried to talk to you, but he went about it too softly. He thinks you are still grieving for Mrs Darlington and the baby.'

'Damn you, be quiet!' He swung away from her and brought his fist down on the side table, making the decanters and glasses jump and rattle. He stood, head bowed, breathing deeply to control the pain raging inside him. With difficulty he forced out his words. 'I lost my wife and child within hours of one another. Rosemary was my world. With her I lost all my hopes for the future. How could you possibly understand that?'

John closed his eyes. For four long years he had held this inside him, accepting sympathy in silence. The pain, the agony of bereavement was a weakness he alone must endure.

He felt a soft touch on his shoulder.

'I do understand, sir,' she said quietly. 'My husband died in a carriage accident three years ago. The shock of it caused me to lose our baby. There is not a day goes by that I do not think of them, that I do not grieve, but what good will it do them if I waste the rest of my life in anguish and remorse? It is better that I am doing something to make the lives of others better.' She stepped away. 'I beg your pardon. I did not mean to distress you, but it is time someone told you what is happening in your factories. To your people.'

John did not move. He was not even aware of her leaving the room, only of the silence once she had gone. He threw himself back in his chair and dropped his head in his hands. It wasn't until Elsie knocked on the door that he realised the fire had died to a sullen glow and the room was growing cold.

'Excuse me, sir. Cook was asking if you was wanting dinner put back, you not having been up to change or owt.'

She twisted her apron in her hands. His staff were clearly alarmed at his behaviour. His 'lack of action', Lucy Granger had called it. It was the truth.

'No, no, I will come directly. Tell Cook to serve dinner as usual.'

After all, there was no one to see that he had not changed for dinner. He glanced at the shelves of books, and the space where the chiming clock had once rested. No one to care.

*

Reginald was putting on his coat when Lucy entered the vicarage. He smiled at her. 'I was about to set out in search of you. I thought you had been spirited away.'

Behind the gently teasing manner, Lucy recognised her brother's genuine concern.

'I thought I should call on – on one or two other families while I was out. I did not realise how the time had gone on.'

'Ah, I see. Well, go and warm yourself by the fire. Once I have finished evening service, we can have a quiet dinner together.'

He kissed her cheek and went out, leaving Lucy to make her way to the drawing room. She pulled a stool close to the hearth and huddled over the fire. She was filled with remorse, not for what she had told John Darlington, but for the way she had conducted herself. She had acted very badly. She should not have lost her temper. It was no way to behave towards a man she barely knew. A man who was clearly stricken with grief.

In the warm, quiet room her jangled nerves grew calmer. She could not regret her actions. He needed to know what was happening at his mills. Now, even if he did nothing about it, John Darlington could not claim ignorance.

*

John looked in vain for Mrs Granger at church the following Sunday. At the end of the service he swallowed his pride and, when everyone had left, he spoke to Reginald as he made his way towards the vestry.

'Lucy? She is gone to stay with our aunt,' Reginald told him. 'An express came Monday morning to say the poor lady was laid up with a broken leg. The household is all at sixes and sevens.'

'Oh.' John felt unaccountably put out by the news. 'And when will she be back? That is, you must be at a loss to manage without her.'

The vicar laughed. 'Oh, I do very well. I have been a bachelor long enough to learn how to enjoy my own company. I would never tell Lucy that, of course.' He chuckled. 'A very managing female, my sister.'

'I know it, to my cost.' John felt his cheeks redden. 'Did she tell you she came to see me? No, I can tell by your look that she did not. Last Sunday she came to Clough Hall and upbraided me for neglecting my duty.'

'She did? If I had known I would not have allowed her to–'

'No, no, she was right to come. She told me a few home truths. About the mills. Things I should have known if I had looked more closely into the reports Grimes sends to me. I have been a crass fool, Reginald.' He waved away the vicar's attempts to comfort him. 'Mrs Granger and I did not part on the best of terms.'

'My sister can be a little hot-headed, John. I am sorry for it if she offended you.'

'She said nothing I did not deserve.' He paused. 'I was very sharp with her. Furious. Grown men back away from me when I am in that mood, but not your sister. Stood her ground and spoke her mind. I would like–' He stopped again, then said in a rush, 'I would like her to know I do not bear her any ill will. For what she said. And I hope she will forgive me, if I was… less than polite.'

'She said nothing to me of it, so I have no doubt it is forgotten already.' Reginald clapped him on the shoulder. 'You should do the same. John. Put it out of your mind.'

'You will tell her, when you write? That I am taking measures to address the problems at Hope Mills?'

'I will indeed, my friend.'

*

It was Christmas Eve before Lucy returned to Haven Bridge. Her aunt's situation had been complicated by the discovery that her companion was stealing from her. Lucy had been obliged to turn the woman off and to find a suitable replacement.

Reginald's brief and infrequent correspondence, during her absence, had told Lucy very little and she had had no time to worry. It was only when she was in the mail coach, approaching the town, and saw the windows of Hope Mills blazing with light that she wondered if her confrontation with John Darlington had done good or harm.

'I shall find out soon enough,' she thought, as the carriage rattled onto the cobbles of the high street.

Reginald was waiting to greet her when the carriage finally came to a halt at the posting house. He kissed her cheek and held her away from him, turning her towards the lamplight.

'My poor dear, you must be exhausted. Was it a tiresome journey?'

'Not at all. We saw no snow until we reached Blackstone Edge and as you see, it has come to nothing.' They waited together until the guard threw down her portmanteau, which Reginald carried, giving his free arm to Lucy.

'And how is our aunt? Are you sure she could spare you to me?'

'She could spare me perfectly well,' replied Lucy, with a chuckle. 'I found an excellent companion for her, who has taken charge of everything. In fact, I was very much in the way.'

'I take leave to doubt that.' Reginald patted her hand. 'I am glad to have you back.'

They were about to cross the road when Lucy stopped.

'Pray go on, Reginald, I have bethought myself of something I must buy. Alone.' When he hesitated, she gave him a little push. 'Go home, my dear. I promise I shall follow in a very few minutes.'

She hurried away from him along Market Street and entered one of the shops.

'Miss Moonshine, thank goodness you are open. I need a present for my brother. We always exchange a little token on Christmas morning, but I have been away and quite forgot.' Her eyes scanned the crowded surfaces. 'Oh, that is beautiful.' She walked across the room. 'A mantel clock. I am sure it is more expensive than I wanted to pay, but Reginald could put it in his study –'

'I am afraid that is not for sale.' Miss Moonshine picked up the clock and put it into a cupboard. 'Not yet.' She turned back to Lucy, smiling. 'But I am sure we can find you something suitable for Mr Coates.'

In the end Lucy selected a pretty glass paperweight, consoling herself that it was more in keeping with the tradition of exchanging small gifts. The clock would have been an extravagance. Still, it was a lovely timepiece, she thought. It should not be languishing in a cupboard.

*

It was not until Lucy joined her brother for dinner that she had an opportunity to ask him about Hope Mills.

'You said in your letter that Mr Darlington had told you of our altercation.' She blushed at the memory. 'You wrote that he had, er, taken measures.'

'Indeed he has. Hodgson has gone and a new manager has been taken on. He seems like a good sort.'

'I hope the working conditions have improved, too,' remarked Lucy, relieved.

'Oh, no doubt of it. John has remained in Haven Bridge to oversee the business. Quite like his old self.' Reginald helped himself to more beef. 'But you can ask him all about that yourself tomorrow, when he comes to Christmas dinner.'

Chapter Two

'Oh, Reginald, no!'

He raised his brows. 'Should I not have invited him? I am sorry if you do not like the idea, but I can hardly turn him away now.'

'No, of course not.' She bit her lip. 'I am surprised he accepted, after what I said to him.'

'As to that, he told me himself he bears no resentment. Did I not say so in my letter?'

She looked at her brother in exasperation. She accepted he was absent-minded, but surely, he should have known this mattered to her. The thought gave her pause. When had John Darlington's good opinion become so important?

'I am sure he has forgotten your little disagreement,' Reginald continued. 'He asks after you whenever we meet.'

'D–does he?' The traitorous colour rushed back to her face. She gave a little shrug. 'I have no idea why that should be so. We hardly know one another.'

*

Just before setting off for church on Christmas morning, Lucy and her brother exchanged presents. Reginald declared the paperweight was just what he needed, and Lucy was delighted with an exquisite little cameo brooch set in a frame of Whitby jet. She kissed his cheek.

'Thank you, my dear. I shall pin it on my gown now and wear it to church!'

The morning service was well attended and Lucy smiled constantly as everyone took their leave, wishing her a merry Christmas as they passed. John Darlington approached, looking as solemn and austere as ever. Was he still angry with her?

'Do not forget, you are coming to dinner tonight,' Reginald reminded him when he stopped to shake hands.

'If it suits Mrs Granger.' He turned to look at her, his dark eyes sombre. 'I would like your assurance that you are happy with the arrangement?'

She gave him her hand and managed a faint smile. 'Of course, Mr Darlington. We look forward to welcoming you to our table this evening.'

There was no mistaking the relief in his face. His hand tightened around her fingers.

'Until tonight, then.'

*

John gave his greatcoat and hat to the maid and straightened his neckcloth before being shown into the drawing room.

'Ah, there you are, my friend. Welcome, welcome!'

Reginald came forward to meet him, but John's eyes were drawn to the figure standing beside the fireplace. Lucy was wearing a plain silk gown of peacock blue with modest sleeves en gigot. Her dark hair had been tamed and pulled back into a knot at the back of her head. The austerity of her appearance was relieved only by the scarlet sash tied at her waist, and a matching bow that secured her dusky curls.

'She should wear bright colours,' he thought suddenly. 'She is a creature made for light and laughter.'

'Good evening, Mr Darlington. Won't you sit down?'

Her soft voice broke into his thoughts. She was sitting on the sofa now, arranging her silk skirts about her. He took a chair opposite and dragged up a subject for conversation. Heaven knew he was out of practice at such niceties. He asked about her aunt. but only half listened to the reply, fascinated by the lamplight playing on the smooth lines of her face. The way the blue silk shimmered with every movement.

'Reginald tells me you have made changes at Hope Mills, Mr Darlington.'

It took John a moment to realise she was waiting for his answer. 'Yes. I have a new manager, but I intend to keep an eye on him this time.'

'I am glad to hear it.'

'I have reopened the factory school, too. Although,' he shifted in his chair, 'I need more teachers. I thought – I wondered – That is–' Good Lord, he was like a tongue-tied schoolboy!

'Yes, Mr Darlington?'

'I wondered if you would help me recruit them. Your brother has told me of your work in the Sunday School here. You will know better than I the qualities required.'

Lucy looked a little startled. He was about to apologise for his presumption when she smiled and said, 'I should be delighted to help you, sir. When do we start?'

'Not tonight,' put in her brother, laughing. 'Dinner is served and we will have no shop talk this evening.'

Conversation flowed freely at the table. Any restraint between himself and Lucy was forgotten. They were in agreement on most things, and where they were not, she was not afraid to argue her case with him. When he walked the short distance back to Clough Hall, shortly before midnight, John realised he could not remember when he had enjoyed an evening more, at least since he had lost Rosemary.

*

Spring in Haven Bridge brought both snow and heavy rain, but by early May there were cowslips, buttercups and primroses to brighten the landscape. Even Clough Hall looked better in the sunshine, thought Lucy, as she made her way up the short drive. When she had first seen the house in the harsh winter light it had looked as grim and forbidding as its owner.

She smiled. How wrong she had been, on both counts. The house was now basking in the May sunshine, its sandstone walls the colour of pale honey. The sturdy door was a necessity against the weather, but she knew now it opened easily to welcome friends. She was shown into the small study, where John was poring over a ledger. She waited quietly for him to finish totting up a column of figures, observing the wayward lock of black hair that fell forward across his brow, giving him a younger, more boyish look.

How had she ever thought him hard and uncaring? Over the past few months she had grown to know him very well. He was a conscientious man and hard-working too. She had encouraged him to talk about Rosemary and even accompanied him to put flowers on her grave. She had almost wept when he told her they had had barely a year together as man and wife. She was helping him to come to terms with his loss, to put it behind him and move on with his life, as he had helped her to move on, although he did not know it.

At that moment he looked up, and the smile he gave her transformed his face. Something inside Lucy jolted uncomfortably. Her heart drummed so hard against her ribs, she feared it might break out.

'Lucy!' He came around the desk to take her hand. 'Come and sit down. I am setting aside funds for a school for infants, based on Mr Owen's model at New Lanark Mills. We can build it on land I own at the edge of the town. We will take children from three years old until ten, when they will begin work in the mills. Owen advocates a regime of education not solely based on reading and writing.' He laughed as he handed her a sheaf of papers. 'In fact, he says he does not want the children "overly annoyed" with books. They will learn to read and write, naturally, as well as studying geography and history, but there will also be dancing and singing, playing outdoors whenever possible.'

'Heavens.' Lucy sat down and looked at the papers. 'This is all very commendable; almost too good to be true.'

'But it is not. Owens' school has been operating in Scotland for over a decade.'

'It is certainly revolutionary. But, John, will not your competitors think you are breeding discontent, to educate the children so?'

'No, why? If the children can find work other than the mills then good luck to them, but an educated workforce will be a boon, I am sure. The more successful the business, the higher the wages. That is my object. Well. What do you say?'

'It is an excellent plan. You know I have always been an advocate of education.'

'It is your influence that has made me see what is possible, Lucy.' He took her hands. 'Thank you, my dear. Without you I should have continued on my way to damnation, running away from my past, neglecting my responsibilities here.'

His dark eyes glowed and for one wild moment she thought he was going to kiss her. She waited, not knowing whether she was more hopeful or afraid. When he lifted her hands to his lips, first one then the other, the searing disappointment was like a blow.

She berated herself soundly. Foolish, foolish woman. How presumptuous to think she could ever be more to him than a friend. She had seen the portrait of Rosemary hanging in the parlour. A tall, blue-eyed angel with golden ringlets clustered about her head. An Amazonian goddess, John had called her. How could a dark-haired widow who barely reached his shoulder compete with such a memory?

Reluctantly she drew her hands away.

'I must be going,' she said, keeping her voice light. 'Reginald has a meeting with the churchwardens later and I promised to take notes for him. You know what a bad a memory he has.'

'Yes, of course. But you haven't yet told me why you came today. Was it just to see me?' He was smiling, his eyes gently teasing, and her heart lurched.

'No, of course not. I almost forgot. I had an errand to run and Reginald asked if I would drop by and invite you to dinner tomorrow night. He sends his apologies for not writing, but he thought, as I was passing...'

'I will join you for dinner, with pleasure. In fact,' he turned to the desk and closed the lid of his inkwell. 'I have done enough for today. I shall escort you back to the vicarage and tell him myself.'

*

'It was good of John to walk you home this afternoon,' said Reginald.

He and Lucy were in the drawing room after dinner. She had unpacked her embroidery, but although she had turned up the lamp on the small table beside her, she had set very few stitches.

'He is looking very well,' her brother continued. 'He is a changed man these past few months. Much happier.'

'I am glad of it.' Lucy stifled a sigh.

'I think it must be your influence, my dear.'

'A little, perhaps. I have merely helped him to come to terms with his loss.'

'You are very close now, I think.'

'We are good friends,' she replied quickly. 'We share many of the same views.'

'You do not think you might become more than good friends?'

She saw the speculative gleam in her brother's eyes and knew exactly what he was thinking. She had hoped for something similar herself, but pride would not allow her to admit that to Reginald. She gave a tinkling laugh.

'Good heavens, no! There is nothing like that in the wind at all. Now, look at the time. I must bid you goodnight, my dear.'

Lucy put away her embroidery and went up to her room. She would be John's friend for as long as he wanted it. But as she climbed into bed that night she knew, deep in her heart, that she wanted more than that. Much more.

'But it is not to be,' she muttered, blowing out her bedside candle. 'You must resign yourself to taking half a loaf, my girl, and be thankful for it!'

*

A bright May morning lifted Lucy's spirits, and a chance meeting with old Mrs Greenwood raised them even more. The old lady had recovered from her winter ills and was sitting in her doorway when Lucy passed on her way to market.

'I'm in fine fettle now, thank 'ee,' was her response to Lucy's enquiry. 'And a good thing, too, now little Aggie has joined her brother at t'mill. And Dan'l is back there, as well. Master took him on again. Dan'l says he looks in regular, too. Like his da, is the master. Tough, but fair.'

Lucy chatted to Mrs Greenwood for a few more moments before moving on, smiling to herself. Hope Mills was running well again and she was glad of it. John planned more changes, like the infant school, and ways to reduce the fluff in the carding room. Her smile grew. He had so much energy, and instead of expending it on endless travel, he was now using it to improve conditions for his workers. She was very pleased that he shared his ideas with her, asked her advice. If this was the best life had to offer, she would be happy with it.

Lucy's sunny spirits continued into the evening and she hummed as she pinned up her hair in readiness for dinner. She had treated herself to a new gown of sea green silk, with a straight neck and a fuller skirt in the new style. It was an extravagance, but she eased her conscience by arguing that it was the first evening gown she had purchased since joining her brother. The delicate pearl necklace and matching earrings she had inherited from her mother completed her preparations, and then she ran lightly down the stairs to the drawing room.

She walked in to find that John Darlington had already arrived. He jumped up immediately to greet her and escort her to a chair. He uttered no fulsome compliments upon her appearance, but the warm look in his eyes was enough. It brought a delicate blush to her cheek and left her at a loss for words. Thankfully, Reginald was in an expansive mood and relieved her of any necessity to speak. She was content to listen as he chatted happily with their guest.

*

John took his seat at the table with Lucy sitting opposite. The glassware sparkled and the old mahogany table was polished to a gleaming lustre. In the past he had enjoyed many dinners at the vicarage, but he thought the room had never looked better. It was Lucy's doing, he decided, glancing across at her. Not that he imagined her toiling away at the housework, but just her presence made the house brighter, warmer. More welcoming.

He wanted to remark upon it, to risk a compliment, but as he was about to speak she looked up, meeting his eyes with a shy smile in her own. His breath caught in his throat. Unfamiliar, long-forgotten feelings welled up, making him momentarily light-headed. He fought against it, forced himself to breathe, to be rational. Sensible.

He dragged his eyes back to his plate and applied himself to his meal again, although there was such a jumble of exhilarating, exciting and frightening thoughts going through his brain that he barely noticed what he was eating.

At last the dinner was finished and the plates were cleared away. Lucy was preparing to rise from the table when Reginald stopped her with a gesture.

'I am glad you could come tonight, John,' he said, as Lucy settled back into her seat. 'You see, I have some news.' Reginald looked from one to the other, unable to hide his smile. 'I have been offered a new ministry. In Somerset.'

'Somerset!' Lucy's astonishment was obvious. Clearly her brother had given her no hint of this. 'How – how long have you known?' she asked.

'A week.' He reached out and caught her hand. 'Forgive me, my dear, but I was not sure quite how to tell you.'

Lucy's face was as white as the table linen. 'When do you take up your new post?'

'July. But my replacement here has already been chosen. We must quit the vicarage at the end of the month.'

'Barely four weeks, then.'

'Yes. It is an exciting prospect, a country parish near Glastonbury. The climate, I understand, is very mild there.' He beamed. 'More sunshine and less rain than Haven Bridge.'

Lucy looked stricken and John's heart went out to her. She dabbed her mouth with her napkin and managed a small, tight smile.

'How, how exciting. If you will excuse me.'

She left the room, closing the door quietly behind her.

'This is a surprise, Reginald.' John sat back in his chair. 'Your sister had no suspicion of it?'

'No. I have been trying to find the right time to break the news. Yesterday I decided that a small dinner would be the very thing. With you, our closest friend.'

The vicar was smiling at him, and as he accepted a glass of port, John had a sudden, blinding insight.

He thinks I will propose to Lucy! That she will stay here as my wife.

His hand shook as he sipped his wine. It was a dizzying prospect. In other circumstances. In another life…

He responded mechanically to his host's conversation. Inwardly he raged at the presumption, but at the same time he acknowledged that there was nothing he would like better than to marry Lucy. He was comfortable with her. She understood him. But there was Rosemary, his dead wife. His golden goddess.

The rich, sweet port tasted of ashes.

Chapter Three

Alone in the drawing room, Lucy could not be still. She paced the floor, clasping and unclasping her hands. Somerset! It had been a wrench to leave Oakham and her husband's family, but she had relished the challenge and had grown to love her life here in Yorkshire. She told herself she would make a new life with Reginald in his new parish. There would be work to do, other, different challenges. She stopped suddenly, forcing herself to face the truth.

'I do not want to go,' she whispered to the empty room. 'I do not want to leave Haven Bridge. I do not want to leave him.'

As if conjured by her thoughts, John Darlington came in.

'Your brother has gone to fetch something from his study,' he said, closing the door behind him. 'He will join us presently.'

She nodded, too wretched to speak. She gestured to a chair, but she did not sit down, so neither could he.

'Lucy.'

He came closer and in a panic she turned away, saying quickly, 'Reginald expects you to propose. I am very angry with him for putting you in this position, John. Pray be easy, I do not expect–'

She froze when he put his hands on her shoulders.

'Well you should expect it,' he said roughly. 'You have been my saviour, Lucy. You showed me what I needed to do. You have been there to help and advise with all my plans. No one would make a better wife.' He sighed, his breath warm on the back of her neck. 'I want you, Lucy. I do not know how I will go on without you, but–'

'But Rosemary still holds your heart,' she finished for him. She stepped away, out of reach, watching his reflection in the mirror above the fire. 'I know how much you loved her, John. How much she still means to you.'

'You are too good, too kind.' He put a hand up and rubbed his eyes. 'I could not ask you to take second place to her. You deserve better than that. You deserve a husband who values you and loves you wholeheartedly, not a man who cannot forget his first love.'

Lucy closed her eyes. It would be futile to argue, if he did not love her. She turned, summoning up a smile.

'Your honesty does you credit, John. And you are right. I should abhor taking second place to any woman. Especially a goddess.'

She spoke lightly and was relieved he did not appear to notice the hurt and pain she was suffering, although he regarded her for a long, long moment. She was obliged to hold her head up and keep her smile pinned in place.

'Thank you. If only–'

'No.' She stopped him. 'Let us not dwell upon it. I wonder what is keeping Reginald? We are such old friends that I hope you will forgive me if I retire and leave you to wait for him alone. It has been a very busy day, and if we are to quit this place within the month, I have a lot to do tomorrow.'

'Yes of course. I, too, should be going.' He came closer and fixed his black eyes upon her. 'You do understand, don't you? You are not angry with me?'

'Angry? Heavens no! I am looking forward to the challenges of a new parish. And one in the south, too, away from the smoke and grime of a mill town, where it is so difficult to keep everything clean.'

It was a petty comment but John did not appear to notice.

'Indeed,' was all he said.

A nod, a brief handshake, and he was gone.

*

The next two weeks flew by in a whirl of activity. Lucy was far too busy to dwell upon her own unhappiness but it was there, a weight upon her spirits. She told herself it would pass. She would learn to be happy again. After all, she had done so before.

She did not see John, even at church. He sent a short note to Reginald explaining that the mill was particularly busy and he could not spare the time. Lucy could not be sorry for it, although she still looked for him at every service.

As her final week in Haven Bridge drew nearer, she decided she must give John something to mark their friendship. She scoured the shops in the town looking for a suitable token, but nothing caught her attention. In desperation she went back to Miss Moonshine. There were no new goods sold at the Emporium, but she hoped to find something he might like. Something he might even treasure.

It was a gloriously sunny day and the shop was cool. Miss

Moonshine's little dog ran up to sniff at Lucy's skirts and she bent to pat him.

'Ah. Mrs Granger, what can I do for you today?'

Lucy straightened. 'I need a gift. For a gentleman, but not my brother,' she added, blushing slightly.

Miss Moonshine's bird-bright eyes gleamed. 'Well, take your time to look about you, my dear. Everything you see here is for sale.' She scooped up her little dog and continued with a chuckle, 'Except Napoleon, of course.'

Lucy moved slowly around the shop. Clough Hall was very well appointed. John had no need of paintings or mirrors for the wall, and even the inkstand on his desk was more valuable than any piece on offer here. Disheartened, she turned back towards the door and was about to leave when she noticed the assortment of items on a side table.

'Oh, the mantel clock!'

She moved closer and reached out to touch the walnut case. The polished burr veneer was silky smooth beneath her fingers. She remembered sitting in the parlour at Clough Hall with John, discussing his plans for the factory school and improvements to Hope Mills. How often had they been so engrossed, they had quite forgotten the time?

'It would be quite perfect for that room,' she murmured to herself.

'It is French. A triple-chime clock from the last century,' Miss Moonshine told her. 'Quite a rarity in these parts.'

Lucy's hopes fell. 'It will be expensive, then.'

'Not at all. I can let you have it for five guineas.' When Lucy stared, she spread her hands. 'I have had no interest in it. I cannot afford to keep stock I cannot sell.'

Lucy was tempted to remind her that she herself had wanted to buy it for Reginald at Christmastime, but she refrained. Five guineas was a great deal of money; more than she had intended paying for John's present, but she could just afford it. She turned to Miss Moonshine and smiled.

'I will take it!

*

Lucy's spirits sang as she walked to Clough Hall the next morning. Reginald had business in Manchester and would not be home until the following morning, and she could not deny that the thought of seeing John alone made her heart give a little kick of excitement. If he was at the mills then she would leave the clock for him, with a note. She would not want him to think she had brought it merely as an excuse to see him.

However, notes were unnecessary. Elsie told her the master was at home and showed her into the parlour to wait for him. With mounting excitement, she unwrapped the clock and placed it gently on a little table. She released the catch so its gentle ticking could dispel the silence. Then she heard John's firm step, and she turned towards the door.

'Lucy!'

John's pleasure at seeing her was unfeigned. Lucy felt suddenly shy and she hurried into speech.

'I wanted to see you, just once more before we left for Somerset. To bring you this.' She stepped aside and gestured to the table. 'It is a small something. To remember me.'

His smile disappeared and he stared at the clock. 'How could you?'

'I know,' she said. 'It was not dagger cheap, but I thought it would look very well in this room. If not on the mantel, then in that little space on the shelf.'

'Take it away.'

'I beg your pardon?' John was glaring at her and she stammered. 'I – I don't understand.'

His scorching gaze shifted from her to the clock. 'I do not want that – that thing in my house.'

'But, why? You have no timepiece in here. I thought it quite perfect–'

'Of course it is perfect!' he roared. 'I bought it for Rosemary. I made the shelf up there to hold it.'

Lucy gripped her hands together, trying to steady herself. She felt as if she had walked off the edge of cliff.

She whispered, 'Oh John, I am so sorry.'

'And so you should be.' His voice was hard as cold steel and the words cut into her. 'I sold it. I could not bear to have it in the house any longer, reminding me of my loss.'

'You s–sold it to Miss Moonshine?' Lucy swallowed. 'She did not say. She could not have known.'

He gave a savage laugh. 'Of course she knew! Damn the woman. How dare she sell it to you?' He turned suddenly and gripped her shoulders. 'And how dare you bring it here, raking up old memories, bringing back all the pain.'

Lucy tore herself free. 'John, I did not know! Do you think I would have bought it if I had known it would upset you?'

'No, you came here hoping to buy your way into my life. Thinking you could use the timepiece to bribe me into forgetting Rosemary and marrying you–'

He stopped as she brought her hand up in a stinging slap.

'That is not true and you know it,' she cried, her own anger rising. 'I do not want you to forget your wife. I would never ask that of you. Oh, you are impossible. You are so eaten up with self-pity that you cannot see anything else.'

'Get out. And take that damned thing with you!'

'I am leaving,' she threw at him. 'As for the clock, you may do with it what you wish.' She turned to leave, fighting back the tears that threatened to choke her, but when she reached the door she stopped. 'I would never ask you to forget your wife,' she repeated. 'But I would have you forget the pain of losing her and remember the happy times you spent together.' She glanced back at him. 'If Rosemary loved you then that is what she would want.'

He was staring at her, such a look of fury on his face that she did not wait for any further tirade. She fled.

*

Lucy reached the vicarage and went directly to her room. She was thankful Reginald was not at home. If he had seen her distress he would have demanded an explanation. But what could she tell him? She would not admit to anyone that she had lost her heart to John Darlington and that she was crying not only for her own unhappiness, but for his, too.

Such violent grief could not last forever and finally she fell asleep, waking towards evening with a sense of profound depression. She dragged herself from her bed and washed her face and hands with the water from the jug. It was still warm, and she supposed Dora, the maid, must have come in while she was sleeping. It would soon be dinnertime, and common sense told her she must eat something. Tomorrow there would be more packing to do.

With a sigh she walked to the window. From here she could see the church that had been her brother's responsibility for the past decade, and around it the churchyard, with its grey headstones and the occasional sculpted angel. A movement caught her eye and she felt the sickening swoop of her stomach when she saw John Darlington. He was standing at his wife's grave, hat in hand. There was a splash of yellow at the base of the headstone where he had placed a bunch of fresh spring flowers.

As if aware of her gaze he turned and looked up at her window. Immediately she stepped back, but too late. He had seen her and was making his way towards the vicarage.

*

John moved restlessly about the drawing room. The maid had gone to tell Lucy he was here but would she see him? He heard the door open and he turned, half-expecting to see the maid with a message that the mistress was not at home to visitors. Instead he saw Lucy. Still in the cotton gown she had worn that morning, her face pale, eyes downcast. She would not look at him.

'I came to apologise,' he began. 'I had no right to speak to you as I did.'

'No.'

He waited. The silence became insupportable and he spoke again. 'I bought the clock for Rosemary when she was carrying our child. It was a shock, to see it in the parlour this morning.'

'It brought back the pain of your loss.' She nodded. 'I understand that.'

'No, that's not it.' He straightened his back. Time for the truth, whatever it cost him. 'I decided last year that I had spent long enough mourning Rosemary, but I had not recognised how difficult it would be to stop. I thought disposing of the clock would help.' Still she did not speak. 'Then you came to Haven Bridge and showed me I was not going about it the right way. I had been running away from the pain, not dealing with it. Any more than I had dealt with my responsibilities at Hope Mills.'

He looked across the room. Lucy remained with her head bowed but she had not walked out and she had not told him to leave. That was something.

He continued. 'The night I came to dinner, when we were alone in the drawing room. I was not quite honest with you. I let you believe I would not marry you because I–' He stopped and took a breath. 'Because I was still too much in love with

Rosemary. That is not quite the truth. I love you. I have been in love with you for some time. Months, possibly, but I was frightened. Frightened that if I married you, I might lose you, as I had lost her.'

She looked at him then, her gaze so intense he could not meet it. He turned and walked to the fireplace.

'I have been fighting with myself every day since, going over the arguments, trying to convince myself I should let you leave without telling you my true feelings. The day you brought the clock back into the house I had decided I was wrong. That I should put it to the touch, ask you to be my wife. Then you were there, with the timepiece.' He put his hand on the mantelshelf, as if to steady himself, and stared down into the empty hearth. 'It brought it all back. What had happened to Rosemary. What might happen if I married you. If you carried my child.' He swallowed. 'You know the anguish of losing those most dear to you. I told myself you would not wish to risk that again. But it was more than that. I was being much more selfish. I am terrified of killing you, as I had killed Rosemary.'

There. He had said it. He gave a long sigh, feeling the weight of it lifted from his shoulders.

'It does not excuse what I said to you,' he went on. 'I was rude and boorish and I do not expect you to forgive me. I just wanted – needed – to explain.'

The silence was so absolute, he wondered if she had left the room. Then he heard the whisper of her skirts as she came up and put her arms about him. He felt her cheek pressed against his back and for a long time it was enough. He closed his eyes and put his hands over hers where they rested over his heart.

At last she slipped around him and it was her head that was resting on his heart. He held her lightly, hardly daring to breathe.

'No one can foretell the future, John. No one can guarantee

a long and happy marriage, or a happy life, for that matter. We can only do our best.'

'I have been such a fool, Lucy.'

'Yes, but a very dear one.'

His heart leapt. He said carefully, 'Then tell me what I should do now.'

She placed her hands on his chest and looked up at him. 'You should ask me to marry you. Let me decide.' A shy smile lurked in her eyes. 'It is my life to risk, after all. And my happiness that is at stake, as much as yours.'

He could resist no longer. He lowered his head and kissed her, gently, as if afraid she might break. When he would have broken away, she gave a little sob and threw her arms around his neck, drawing him down for another kiss, this time a long, passionate embrace that left them both shaking.

He said unsteadily, 'Do I take it, then, that you will marry me, Mrs Granger?'

She smiled up at him mistily. 'Oh yes, Mr Darlington. Yes, indeed I will marry you!'

With something between a growl and a roar he swooped on her again, dragging her close for another long, lingering kiss, breaking apart only when Dora came in.

'Cook says dinner is ready, ma'am – Oh!'

The maid broke off in confusion and Lucy took pity on her, saying with a laugh in her voice,

'It is quite all right, Dora, Mr Darlington and I are engaged to be married. Now, go and lay another place at dinner, there's a good girl.'

When they were alone again she glanced up at John. 'I am correct, am I not?' she asked, her eyes twinkling. 'We are going to be married?'

'I think we have no choice, madam, after a kiss like that.' He drew her towards an armchair, where he sat down and pulled her onto his knee. 'I will obtain a licence, then we can be married by your brother before he leaves for Somerset. What do you say? Will that please you?'

'Very much.'

He kissed her again and she snuggled close, until the church clock struck the hour and she looked up. 'What have you done with the timepiece?'

'It is where you left it, on the table.'

'I think it belongs at Clough Hall, John. If you can bear it.'

'I think so too, only–'

She touched his cheek. 'Only what?'

'Can you be happy with it in the house? It was Rosemary's clock. Will it not remind you of her?'

'Yes it will, but that will not upset me.' She cupped his face with her hands. 'I do not want you to forget Rosemary, John. She was part of your life. Part of what has made you the man I love. I do not begrudge Rosemary your past,' she said, drawing his mouth down towards hers. 'As long as I can have your future, whatever that may bring.'

Melinda Hammond is a West Country girl who spent thirty happy years in the Yorkshire Pennines. In 2018 she decided to realise a lifelong ambition to live by the sea and now writes her award-winning romantic historical adventures from her new home in the Scottish Highlands. She also writes as Sarah Mallory for Harlequin Mills & Boon.

melindahammond.com

Miss Moonshine's Advent Calendar

By Jacqui Cooper

It was early December and the streets of Haven Bridge were growing increasingly busy with Christmas shoppers. Eleanor dodged and apologised on the narrow pavements as she headed for Miss Moonshine's Emporium, a shop she had noticed several times since moving to the Yorkshire village three months ago, but not yet visited.

Inside, the shop was a haven of peace from the bustle of the streets. Scented candles and soft music filled the air. An elderly woman, her silver hair pulled back severely and wearing a heavy plaid shawl, was assisting a customer in choosing some candles. She glanced over at Eleanor and smiled a welcome. Miss Moonshine, presumably. From a basket by a radiator, a tiny chihuahua huffed his complaint at the cold air Eleanor had brought in with her.

Eleanor's sole purpose today was to buy a Christmas card, so, refusing to be distracted by the many wonderful displays, she made her way directly to the card rack.

A child of about ten, presumably the daughter of the candle buyer, was fiddling with the cards when she suddenly squealed. 'Mummy, Mummy. Can I have this?'

'No,' said the woman automatically. Then, 'What is it?'

'An Advent calendar.'

'You already have one.'

'But this one is so pretty!'

Eleanor glanced at the calendar in the child's hand. And did a double take. She edged closer.

The child, seeing her interest, narrowed her eyes and clutched her prize close. 'Ple-e-ease, Mummy?'

'You don't need another one. Can I see the lemongrass again?' the woman asked Miss Moonshine. 'It's not a typically Christmassy scent, but I do love it.'

'But I want it,' wailed her daughter.

'Katie, I said "no". Put it back.'

The girl stuffed the calendar untidily back onto the rack and Eleanor immediately snatched it up. And stared. The calendar itself was nothing special, certainly without the chocolate and trinkets and whatnots of modern Advent calendars. It depicted a Christmassy scene of a house, candles in the windows, a holly wreath on the door, carol singers gathered around a tree on the snow-covered lawn.

It was Eleanor's house. Her new house. She was sure of it.

There was the exact same curved driveway lined with white painted stones leading to a red front door. On the calendar house a Victorian lamp-post shone over the carol singers but apart from that, it was identical to the house Eleanor had left not twenty minutes before.

She glanced at Miss Moonshine, desperate to ask how this could be. Thankfully the candle woman had made her choice and was completing her purchase. Twitching with impatience, Eleanor waited till they were gone then approached the counter.

'Excuse me? This calendar...'

'Yes?' Miss Moonshine put her glasses on. 'Ah, yes. Amber House. Pretty, isn't it?'

'It's my house.'

'Is it?' Miss Moonshine didn't seem surprised. 'Then you

must be the famous author. Welcome to Haven Bridge, my dear. You're so much younger and prettier than I expected.'

'Er... thank you,' said Eleanor, pushing her glasses up her nose. She supposed she could accept the young, but felt pretty was an exaggeration. 'But how on earth did my house end up on a calendar?'

'Oh, it's quite simple,' said Miss Moonshine. 'Margery, who used to own your house, had a calendar made every year. One of my suppliers did it for her. Did you know you can put pictures on anything these days? I have a cushion with a very lifelike image of my dog. Isn't that right, Napoleon?' She addressed the chihuahua, who twitched an ear and no more. 'Between you and me, you can barely tell the difference between the cushion and the real thing,' whispered Miss Moonshine. 'I've almost sat on him twice. Anyway, Margery's children all live abroad, and she liked to send them a calendar every Christmas. Apparently it was a great family joke.' Miss Moonshine's frown suggested she didn't quite see the joke. 'At least it used to amuse Margery no end.'

'Are there any more of the calendars?' Eleanor could not say why the idea disturbed her.

'This is the only one,' said Miss Moonshine. 'I found it at the back of the storeroom just this morning. Would you like it? I can give you a reduction, since today is already the first of December.'

Eleanor had no need of an Advent calendar. Indeed had never owned such a thing. She looked at it again. The house looked so warm and inviting, as if someone inside was just about to throw that red door open and welcome the revellers inside.

Actually, with its welcoming glow, it looked less and less like her house by the minute. Yet somehow she couldn't bear to put the calendar down.

'I'll take it,' she said, though she had no idea what she was going to do with it.

'Excellent.' Miss Moonshine slipped it into a bag. 'Anything else I can help you with? Gifts? Tree decorations?'

Eleanor had as much need for those items as she did for the calendar. 'No thank you,' she said, completely forgetting about the card.

She walked home in the grey December dusk. Her house was on the edge of town, surrounded by farmland. When she turned into her driveway, the building loomed. The same three-storey Victorian house with gabled roof and red door as on the calendar. But there the similarities ended. Eleanor's house had no Christmas tree on the lawn, no warm glow from the windows, no festive wreath on the door. A second glance did reveal the Victorian lamp-post by the front door. Now Eleanor remembered the estate agent pointing it out as a security light. But she hadn't used it once in the three months she'd been here. Indeed, had no idea how to turn it on.

An overwhelming feeling of sadness washed over her. The calendar house looked so festive and bright and friendly. While her house looked... glum.

She was unlocking the door when a noise drew her attention. There, crouching in a corner of the porch, was a cat. For such a scrawny, bedraggled-looking creature it had a great deal of attitude as it mewed impatiently for Eleanor to open the door.

'Shoo,' she said softly. 'Go home, cat.'

The door was only open a crack. No way could the cat get in. But it did.

'No!' Eleanor shot after it.

She chased it through the sitting room and the dining room before it came to a halt in the kitchen. It glanced at the fridge, then blinked its green eyes at Eleanor.

Eleanor could see the little cat was in a rather sorry state.

Thin and scrawny, its fur so sodden she couldn't even determine what colour it was.

'OK,' said Eleanor, melting. 'I'll find you something to eat. Just this once. Then you have to promise to go home.' Taking the cat's silence as agreement, she opened a tin of tuna and tipped it onto a plate. The cat gobbled it as if it was the first meal it had had for a week. Eleanor opened another. Half of this tin was consumed too, before the cat began washing its face and the sound of soft purring filled the otherwise silent kitchen.

'Don't get too comfortable,' Eleanor warned it. 'You can't stay.' This time the cat seemed to agree, because it trotted to the door.

When Eleanor opened it, the cat shot out, leaving tiny paw prints in the frosty grass before disappearing into the bushes without a backward glance.

Eleanor closed the door. The tuna had been for her tea. Resigned, she had beans on toast.

Sitting at the table eating her solitary meal, she looked around the kitchen. Throughout her childhood she had dreamed of owning a house just like this. The runaway success of her first novel had allowed her to turn that dream into reality just past her thirtieth birthday. She had first seen Amber House on a sunny July day and fallen head over heels. Everywhere she looked she had seen potential, and yet, somehow, since moving in she had done nothing to make the house her own.

At first she'd assumed that after she had lived here for a while, inspiration would simply come to her. That hadn't happened. But then she wasn't much of a shopper.

And then she remembered. Today she had bought something. She fished the Advent calendar out of her bag.

Holding it up, Eleanor was once more filled with a sense of longing. The calendar house was so warm and inviting. After

Christmas she vowed to do more to make Amber House a home. Definitely. After Christmas.

Since today was the first of December, she opened the little window on the calendar and found… a grey cat sitting by a roaring fire.

She remembered the speed at which the stray had run off and felt a tiny stab of rejection – which was silly, considering she didn't even want a cat.

Propping the calendar above the cold, empty fireplace, she settled at her computer and soon lost herself in her writing.

*

Next morning Eleanor heard a scratching at the door. When she opened it, the cat was on the mat along with three tiny kittens. While Eleanor looked on in consternation, the mother cat carried the kittens inside one by one and deposited them behind the settee. Then she entwined herself around Eleanor's ankles, purring madly, as if she was the cleverest cat in the world. As Eleanor obediently took some leftover chicken from the freezer and blasted it in the microwave, she rather thought she might be.

'You can't live here,' she told the cat. 'Someone will be looking for you.' Even as she said this, Eleanor had her doubts. The cat was so thin. Chances were she was a stray.

'I don't know anything about cats,' she continued desperately. 'I don't want a cat. I mean it. I have no idea how to look after you or your kittens.'

Even while she was talking, Eleanor lifted a soft throw off the arm of the settee and placed it gently around the kittens. Immediately the mother cat curled around them and began to give them a good wash. Something caught Eleanor's eye, a bag tucked down between the arm of the settee and the wall which had been hidden by the throw. A knitting bag, with colourful, half-used balls of wool and some knitting needles.

That she hadn't spotted it before was a sad reflection on her housekeeping skills. She put it on the table out of the way.

After her own breakfast she grabbed her coat and went out to visit Miss Moonshine, reasoning that as the old lady had a dog, she probably knew a vet who would hopefully be able to tell her who the cat belonged to. When she arrived, the only person in the shop was a dark-haired man in his thirties working on a fanciful Christmas tree which looked as if it was made out of bubbles and light.

He gave Eleanor a friendly nod and yelled, 'Miss Moonshine. You have a customer.'

'I certainly do know an excellent vet,' said Miss Moonshine, when she emerged from the back shop and Eleanor explained her problem. 'My Napoleon would not go to anyone else, isn't that right, Napoleon?' The dog ignored her. 'I'm sure if the cat is microchipped he will know who she belongs to. The problem is, he's really busy at the moment. The other vet in the practice has gone home to Australia for an extended Christmas holiday, so our vet is having to spend much of his working day on the farms. The surgery is only open for emergencies and your cat doesn't sound like an emergency.'

'She's not my cat,' said Eleanor. 'What do you think I should do?'

'I'll give him a ring, shall I?' Miss Moonshine picked up the phone and talked for a few minutes. 'Yes, it's just as I feared. You can take the cat into the surgery and the nurse can check for a microchip, but you can hardly separate her from the kittens to do that, can you? The receptionist says she'll have the vet pop by your house when he has a spare moment. Assuming you're not going to throw her and the kittens out?' She regarded Eleanor with bright, questioning eyes.

Eleanor thought of how thin the cat was, of the three tiny balls of fluff, their eyes barely open.

'No, of course not–'

'Then you will need supplies,' said Miss Moonshine firmly. 'Food. A litter tray. Somewhere for them to sleep.'

'Oh. Right. Where do I get those?'

'Excuse me?' The workman came over, shoving his screwdriver into the back pocket of his jeans. He had rather an engaging smile, Eleanor noticed. 'I might be able to help you with that. My mother's cat died in the summer. She meant to donate everything to the animal shelter but never got around to it. You're welcome to whatever you need. She might even have taken the cat–'

Eleanor perked up.

'–but she's in Tenerife. I can bring the stuff round this afternoon, if you like. You'll still have to buy food though.'

Eleanor was not used to spontaneous generosity from strangers, certainly not such good-looking ones. She was unsure how to react. 'Well that's very kind of you, Mr…'

'This is Dylan,' said Miss Moonshine. 'Dylan, this is the lady from Amber House.'

'Ah. The famous author. Nice to meet you.'

Did everyone know who she was? 'I'm Eleanor,' said Eleanor, blushing.

'It's a very good thing that you met Dylan today,' said Miss Moonshine. 'He's a very handy man to know.'

'He is? Why?'

'Because he's an actual handyman. Dylan, give Eleanor your card,' instructed Miss Moonshine. 'There's nothing he doesn't know about… stuff,' she told Eleanor as he obliged. 'Especially stuff that goes wrong. Like my Christmas decoration here.'

Grinning, Dylan flicked a switch. 'You do know it wasn't plugged in?'

'No?' Miss Moonshine was unabashed. 'How could that have happened?'

'I know Amber House,' said Dylan. 'I did some work for Margery. I'll bring the cat supplies round this afternoon. The pet shop is down by the river. You can get cat food there.'

'Thank you.'

Eleanor found the pet shop and explained her predicament to the woman behind the counter.

'I'll put a card in the window, if you like,' she offered. 'But I haven't heard of any lost cats. It's late in the year for kittens, too. Poor little mite is lucky you took her in.'

Eleanor would have explained that she hadn't had much say in the matter, but she had already spoken to more people today than she normally did in a week and she was exhausted. 'Thank you.' She left her number.

Dylan arrived around four just as it was getting dark, bringing the scent of pine and outdoors. He refused her invitation to come in.

'Best not if you don't want to be hoovering up pine needles for days. I've been cutting Christmas trees,' he explained, shaking a shower of needles from his sleeve.

'Well thank you, again.' She took the bundle, which included a fireguard. She looked at him questioningly.

He laughed. 'You're going to need it soon. Trust me.'

With a wave he drove off, and belatedly Eleanor wondered if she should have offered him payment. She really was hopeless at the sort of interaction other people took for granted.

That night, after she'd fed the cat and settled the little family in the new bed, she remembered her Advent calendar. Holding it up, she looked at yesterday's picture of a grey cat, snug by the fire. Clean and dry, Eleanor's visitor had revealed itself to be a silver tabby.

The calendar cat was sitting by a warm fire. Eleanor looked at her own empty fireplace. She had no idea how to light a real fire, other than having a vague notion that chimneys had to be swept regularly. Lighting a fire was not something she would ever risk.

Inside day number two she found a candle. 'Very Christmassy,' she told the cat and sat down at her computer to work.

*

The next day when she woke the house was freezing. A quick check told her that neither the heating nor the lights were working, although the nearest neighbours' house had lights, which suggested hers was the only one affected. The fuse box was in the basement. She found a torch in a kitchen drawer but the batteries were low. It provided enough light for her to inch her way downstairs. Before it died it revealed a stub of a candle and box of matches on top of the fuse box.

An image of the Advent calendar leapt to mind. Coincidence, Eleanor told herself, striking a match.

Two minutes studying the fuse box forced her to admit she had no idea what she was looking for.

Back upstairs she found Dylan's business card and dialled.

'I'm sorry to bother you at this time of the morning.'

'Eleanor?'

He recognised her voice. Why did that give her a warm glow? 'Yes.'

'Are the cats OK?'

'Yes, yes of course.' Not strictly true. The mother cat was glaring at her, tail lashing as if doubting the wisdom of her move.

'What can I do for you?'

She told him.

'I'll be there in twenty minutes.'

He was as good as his word. Eleanor barely had time to splash some icy water on her face, run a comb through her long hair and get dressed, before his pickup truck pulled up outside.

Blessedly, he was carrying two cups of coffee. 'I thought this might be welcome,' he said.

'I could kiss you!' Eleanor immediately grew flustered. 'I mean… I mean… I don't mean… of course I wouldn't… ever…'

He laughed. 'I had no idea what you take, so I just got black,' he said.

Gratefully she warmed her hands on the cup. 'Thanks. I'm sorry to be such a nuisance, getting you out so early.' Away from a wife and family?

'No worries. I was looking for an excuse to avoid my morning run.'

That was no answer. Though why Eleanor was even interested she had no idea. In a gorgeous, muscled man wearing – be still my heart – a tool belt?

'It's a couple of fuses,' he confirmed after just a few minutes. 'Easily fixed.' He even showed her how to fix them should the need arise again.

'Thank you.' Eleanor hesitated. He'd brought coffee. Should she offer him another? Was that the polite thing to do or would she be keeping him?

'How's the cat?' Dylan asked. 'Happier now the heating is back on, I'm sure.'

She showed him the kittens behind the settee. They were utterly perfect. Eleanor's heart filled every time she looked at them.

'I'd say they are about three or four weeks old,' said Dylan, speaking softly. 'You'll have your hands full in a week or so.'

'I will?' The mewling kittens looked so helpless and innocent.

'They'll be into everything.'

Eleanor didn't like the sound of that.

Dylan rubbed his hands together against the still cold air. 'It'll warm up soon, but you should have lit the fire. There's no need to ever be cold in a house like this.'

'I wasn't sure about the chimney,' she admitted.

'It's been swept,' said Dylan. 'Margery had me do it in case it took a while for the house to sell. She reckoned a nice log fire might make all the difference. In fact, hang on….'

Before she could stop him he nipped outside and returned with an armful of logs which he dumped into a basket. 'As I suspected, there were still some in the shed. Here, I'll show you.'

He began to arrange kindling and logs in the fireplace. 'There. You can light it any time you want to feel extra cosy.'

Eleanor was touched by his kindness and confused by his friendliness. 'Thank you.'

As he straightened up he nodded to the neat stacks of folded curtains which had graced the dining room table since she'd moved in. They had been included in the price of the house and the previous owner had generously sent them out to be cleaned, even leaving them neatly labelled with the rooms where they belonged. 'I could give you a hand hanging your curtains if you like. That would make the place more cosy too.'

'I don't have any ladders,' she mumbled, embarrassed that he clearly thought her house looked cold and spartan.

'I do. I could bring them round tomorrow?'

Why was he being so nice? Suddenly it clicked. Dylan was a handyman. He was simply looking for work. 'Well, if that's not too much trouble…'

'Of course it isn't.' They were now standing by the front door and he opened it. The sky was still a murky grey. Dylan reached to the left of the door and flicked a switch. Outside, the old lamp-post lit up. 'Anything to brighten a winter's day, eh?' he said. 'See you tomorrow.'

Eleanor watched him get into his van and drive off. The lamp-post cast a warm glow over the steps and a circle of lawn. She had lived here three months and not once noticed that light switch. Leaving the light on, she closed the door.

Normally Eleanor had no trouble losing herself in her writing, but today she kept getting distracted by thoughts of a Victorian lamp-post and a Christmas tree on a lawn.

She had never owned a Christmas tree. Oh, the foster homes she'd been raised in all had them, of course, and she had always been invited to help decorate them. But that kindly meant offer had only served to make Eleanor feel even more of an outsider. She'd had no connection to the baubles she hung on the tree, hadn't understood the in-jokes or shared the reminiscences of her foster family as they unwrapped a decoration with a special meaning.

It was no one's fault that each Christmas tree only reminded Eleanor that next year would bring a different tree, a different family.

But now she had a house of her own, perhaps she could start her own story. The garden centre had trees and she had noticed some gorgeous decorations in Miss Moonshine's – No! Her budding excitement vanished as quickly as it started. Decorating a tree all alone? Were those really the memories she wanted to bring out, year after year?

Christmas trees were for families. They were not for the likes of her.

That night, remembering the cat and the candle, she approached her Advent calendar with a sense of trepidation. And found a Christmas tree.

*

Next day, Eleanor suddenly remembered she still hadn't bought a card for Tom. Not knowing when Dylan would arrive, she nipped out to the shops first thing.

'Eleanor! How lovely to see you again.' Miss Moonshine was dusting a display of beautiful handmade toys. 'What can I do for you?'

'Just a Christmas card, thank you.' But Eleanor lingered over the toys. Tom's children, her niece and nephew, would be really excited about Christmas by now. That sturdy wooden truck would be perfect for three-year-old Toby and five-year-old Kim would adore that colourful rag doll.

No. Surely a contribution to their financial future made more sense? But still, the rag doll's button eyes drew her, triggering a memory of a Christmas morning when she wasn't much older than Kim was now. Father Christmas had left a doll under the tree for Eleanor. All Christmas Day she had clutched that doll, thrilled to own something so beautiful.

The doll had been lost in one of the many moves.

She saw a little knitted teddy bear at the back of the shelf which reminded her of the bag of wool she had found stuffed down the side of the settee. One of her foster mothers had taught her how to knit and she had loved the thrill of creating something from a tangle of nothing. That pleasure and skill had somehow been lost too.

Tom and Mhairi's baby was due any day now, though. Should she knit something for the baby? She had the wool. No. Quickly she dismissed the idea. It wasn't as if she would play much of a part in any of their lives, after all.

Abandoning the toys, she selected a card.

'That's a lovely choice,' said Miss Moonshine, slipping it into a bag.

'It's for my brother and his family.'

'Will you be seeing them over Christmas?'

'No.' That sounded abrupt so she added a mumbled, 'Very busy,' without going into detail as to who was busy.

Outside in the crisp cold air, she was passing a baker's shop when a swinging door released the scent of mince pies. Pulled into the shop, she bought a box, reasoning that she should have something to offer Dylan later. Then, as she passed the greengrocer's, she had to step around a stack of Christmas trees crowding the pavement. They were huge, but there, right at the front, was a tiny tree no more than three feet tall, proudly set in a pot decorated with a bright red ribbon. A beginner's tree. Impulsively she bought that too.

When she got home, Dylan was waiting in his van.

Immediately Eleanor became flustered. 'I am so sorry–'

He waved her apologies away and took the tree from her. 'It's my fault for not saying when I would be here.'

The moment Eleanor opened the door, the cat came to investigate. Two of the kittens tumbled after her. Dylan put the tree on the table and gently picked them up and returned them to the basket.

'They're going to be underfoot more and more from now on,' he said. 'Maybe you should put them in the kitchen while we're working?'

Eleanor did as he suggested while Dylan brought the ladders in. She had assumed he would hang the curtains on his own, but to her surprise he seemed to expect her to care about what they looked like and constantly sought her opinion.

'They're curtains,' she said finally, bewildered. 'Surely as long as they cover the windows, they're doing their job?'

Dylan thought that was funny until he realised she was serious. 'Don't let my mother ever hear you say that,' he said. 'Or my ex-wife.'

So, he was divorced. He looked at her as if he expected her to say something, but she had no idea what, so she busied herself shaking out the next curtain.

They worked busily all afternoon, ending up in Eleanor's office. On the desk were several advance copies of her latest book.

Quickly she moved them aside, worried he would think she had left them there on purpose for him to see.

'May I?' Dylan picked up one of the books and leafed through it. The author photo on the jacket, a professional headshot her publisher had insisted on for book two, held his attention.

The photographer had caught Eleanor on a good day. That was the only explanation she knew for the bright-eyed, clear-skinned, smiling face staring out from the photo.

'It's been photoshopped,' she joked. 'They made me take my glasses off, too. It looks nothing like me.'

'No?' Dylan smiled as he handed the book back. 'I'll come clean and confess that I've never read any of your books. But I'll make sure Santa brings me one.'

Eleanor had piles of author copies. Should she offer him one? Or was he just being polite? As usual, she did nothing and the moment passed.

When the final curtain was hung, Dylan folded the ladders.

'Would you like some coffee?' she asked shyly.

'That would be great.'

They sat in the kitchen drinking coffee and eating mince pies, laughing as the kittens attacked Dylan's shoe laces.

When he finally rose to go, Eleanor remembered that she hadn't paid him.

He waved her money away. 'Call it a housewarming gift,' he said, giving her that smile again.

'But–'

Dylan was adamant. 'I offered to do it, remember?'

By this time they were standing at the front door. When Dylan opened it, the mother cat slipped outside.

'Looks like you're babysitting,' he grinned.

'I don't think Holly is really an indoor cat,' said Eleanor.

He laughed.

'What?'

'You named the cat?'

'So?' She was defensive.

'Nothing.' He was still laughing as he drove away.

That night when Eleanor opened the calendar she was not surprised to find a ball of wool stuck with a pair of knitting needles. To be honest, she was becoming resigned to the way the calendar seemed to reflect the goings on in her life.

But as she went to find the knitting bag, she began to wonder; reflect or predict? Although it was cheating, she opened the next door too, the sixth of December. Inside was a donkey.

No way. Laughing at her own foolishness, Eleanor picked up the knitting bag and began to sort through the wool.

Holly had returned at tea time and immediately came over to investigate, followed by all three kittens, who were getting steadier on their feet with every passing minute. They chased the wool around the room and when Eleanor made some little pompoms to hang on her tree, they chased those too, until they collapsed exhausted.

There was a storm getting up outside. Eleanor closed the curtains with a little buzz of satisfaction. She was home and she was warm and cosy. Impulsively she struck a match and lit the fire Dylan had laid the day before. She smiled as she carefully placed the fireguard to keep the kittens safe. He'd thought of everything.

Next she made herself a cup of tea and had another mince pie. The pastry was nice, but the filling was a little too sweet for her taste. Could she try and make her own? Opening her laptop she searched online for a recipe and in a what-the-heck moment also looked for a knitting pattern for a teddy bear.

As the storm raged outside, Eleanor picked up the knitting needles. Before casting on, she glanced at the calendar.

A donkey. She chuckled, reckoning she was safe enough.

*

Next morning Eleanor had barely finished breakfast when a knock on the door heralded the vet's arrival.

'I was in the neighbourhood. A horse with colic,' he explained. 'That was some storm last night.'

'It was,' Eleanor agreed as she showed him Holly and the kittens, hovering nervously while he examined them.

'Well, mum isn't chipped,' he said. 'You say she doesn't like being indoors, but she's too comfortable in here to be a farm cat. I'd think she's probably a stray who attached herself to one of the holiday cottages. She'd have been well fed through the summer, but come winter she's had to fend for herself. She's lucky she found you. It'll be at least another month before the kittens can leave their mother. I could call the animal shelter–'

'No,' said Eleanor quickly. 'They can stay. Until after Christmas.'

'Until after Christmas,' the vet agreed, smiling. 'Actually, while I'm here, could I ask a favour?'

'Of course?'

'The storm last night did some damage to one of your neighbours' property,' he said. 'His stable lost its roof and Kasper is homeless. I wondered if he could use yours until Dylan can fix it?'

There was so much in that sentence that made no sense to Eleanor. Who was Kasper? Dylan fixed roofs too? 'I have a stable?'

'And a paddock,' said the vet. 'Margery's kids had a pony when they were little.'

Eleanor knew about the paddock, of course. But calling the wooden structure at the bottom of the field a stable seemed a bit of a stretch. She'd had it earmarked for gardening tools. 'And Kasper is…?' she asked, though she had the feeling she already knew.

'A donkey.'

Eleanor felt she was bowing to the inevitable. 'I don't mind. But I don't know anything about donkeys.'

'That's OK,' said the vet cheerfully. 'According to Miss Moonshine you didn't know anything about cats and you're doing a grand job. But Fred – that's Fred Tomlinson, your neighbour – will sort out the stable and he'll continue to look after Kasper as normal. You won't even know he's there.'

'Then yes, of course,' she said doubtfully. The vet left. Eleanor looked narrow-eyed at her calendar.

A donkey.

Fred Tomlinson arrived shortly in a battered Land Rover loaded with straw and hay and some water buckets. He waved to Eleanor then drove off, returning on foot half an hour later, leading a little brown donkey.

'This is right good of you,' said Fred, when Eleanor came out to greet them. 'I can't thank you enough. Kasper here's a retired seaside donkey. He does the local nativity play every year. He likes his comfort and was discombobulated to lose his roof last night. He'll be no trouble.'

'It's fine,' said Eleanor as Kasper gently nudged her pocket.

Fred laughed. 'I'll check on him regularly. You don't need to do anything. But if you have any spare carrots, he'll not refuse.'

After Fred left, Eleanor went into the house and returned with a carrot. Kasper was waiting by the gate and took her tentative offering with gentle grace.

That afternoon, while she was writing, Fred returned with a hamper from his smallholding, including honey from his own bees, home-made jam and cheese. Also a large, freshly cut fir tree. 'Just a little thank you,' he told her.

Eleanor was delighted with the food but was at a loss as to what to do with the tree. She had managed to decorate the tiny one using old costume jewellery and the woollen pom-poms she had made. Now the tree had pride of place on the windowsill, well out of reach of the kittens. But this monster would dominate any room indoors.

She remembered the outdoor tree on her advent calendar. Could she put this one on the lawn? Dylan might help– No! He was probably busy. Especially now, with a stable to reroof.

Did that mean he would be passing her lane…?

Eleanor stopped that train of thought immediately. Dylan's activities were no concern of hers. None at all.

That night when she opened the calendar she was actually a little nervous. But all she found inside was a cartoon drawing of a smiley Rudolph. Whew! Nothing to worry about there.

Next day, she was out feeding the last of her carrots to Kasper when Dylan drove along the lane. She stared in fascination at the fake reindeer horns and red nose attached to the front of his van. Had they been there before?

He stopped to say hello and before she knew it she'd invited him to join her for a coffee break later.

His brilliant smile made her tummy flutter just a little too much. 'Thanks. I'll be there.'

When he returned at eleven she had the kettle on. 'Fred told me about the tree,' he said, blowing on his hands to warm them. 'How about I rig it up in the garden? I'm sure I have some lights left over from the summer fete that would look good on it.'

'Oh, I couldn't ask–'

His eyes twinkled. 'You didn't.'

Shyly Eleanor offered him some of her home-made mince pies. 'My first attempt,' she admitted.

'These are great,' he said. 'You're a natural.'

To Eleanor's surprise she had really enjoyed the whole process of making pastry. And she liked seeing someone enjoy her efforts even more.

'How is the writing going?' asked Dylan. 'It can't be easy with so many interruptions.'

Actually it was going really well. She had already written

Kasper into a scene. And she knew old Fred would, heavily disguised, also play a role.

'The kittens keep having to be rescued,' she told him. 'But it stops me sitting at the computer till my feet get numb.'

'What are the kittens called?' he teased.

'Why would I name them when I'm not keeping them?' But Eleanor couldn't meet his eye.

Dylan waited.

'Dancer, Prancer and Vixen,' she said sheepishly.

He laughed. 'You do realise how silly you'll feel calling them home in the middle of the summer?'

'They won't be here in the summer,' she reminded him.

His smile widened. 'Right.'

The next few days passed in a blur. Dylan returned and erected the tree in the garden and they had a grand lighting session. Standing beside it, Eleanor looked back at the house. It looked so much better with curtains in every window. It was silly, but she thought the house looked happier.

Thankfully the calendar held no new shocks for her. One day she found a picture of a holly leaf and she cut some greenery in the garden to adorn the mantelpiece. Another day it was a poinsettia, and the next time she was in the village she bought one of the vibrant red plants.

A picture of some choirboys led her to the church on Sunday, where she was roped into making mince pies for the carol concert. There she also picked up an invitation to the annual nativity play and could hardly refuse since Kasper had a starring role.

In mid-December she got a card from Tom and remembered she hadn't posted hers. In it he announced the baby was late and he and Mhairi were on tenterhooks.

She put the card on the mantelpiece, feeling guilty. It would have taken a few days to get here. The baby might even have arrived by now. She would call him later. She would.

Dylan had taken to dropping in every day and she always put the kettle on at eleven, trying not to watch for him as he strolled down the lane.

Taking more breaks was actually good for her. Living alone and working at home was such a solitary job. She spent far too much time in her own company. These days, though, as well as Dylan calling in, Fred often stuck his head round the door on his way to or from checking on Kasper. And Holly was either at the window wanting out, or at the door wanting in. And then there were the kittens, tumbling and squabbling and getting into trouble.

Dylan arrived, bringing the usual chill of frost and the smell of sawdust. As he closed the door the draught sent her card tumbling to the floor. He picked it up and put it carefully back in place. 'Who's Tom?' he asked casually.

'My brother.'

Was that relief on his face? 'I didn't know you had family.'

'I don't,' said Eleanor. 'I mean, not really.' That obviously needed an explanation. 'I… I grew up in care. I didn't even know I had a brother until a year ago. Our parents gave me up and kept Tom.'

Dylan couldn't hide his shock. 'Why?'

The million-dollar question. 'I have no idea,' she admitted, a shrug hiding the deep cut of rejection. 'Tom didn't know about me either. He only found out after his… our mother died and he was going through some papers. He contacted me a year ago.'

Dylan was clearly at a loss. 'That must have been incredible. To believe you are all on your own, then find out you have family.'

Eleanor nodded because it was easier than telling the truth. That as a child she'd concocted all sorts of fanciful stories about why her poor mother might have been forced to give her up. To learn that she had chosen to keep one baby but abandoned the other had been devastating.

'Was your mother very young when she had you?' asked Dylan, full of sympathy.

'Yes.' She and Tom had at least been able to establish that. But she hadn't been that much older when she'd fallen pregnant with Tom. This time though, she had married their father, who died when Tom was ten. 'It seems my grandparents were dead set against her marrying her sweetheart. But when she got pregnant a second time, we think they bowed to the inevitable. Who knows?' Certainly not Eleanor. Or Tom.

'Will you see your family at Christmas?'

It seemed petty to keep saying they weren't her family, but a family couldn't just be handed to you on a plate. A family was history and memories and love and connection. She and Tom had none of those things, despite his efforts.

'Mhairi, Tom's wife, is expecting a baby any day now. Her third.' She should call. She really should.

Dylan was silent. Eleanor refused to look at him but she could feel him watching her as she carried her cup to the sink.

'Eleanor –'

'Well, I suppose I should get back to work,' she said brightly.

For a horrible moment she thought he was going to push it, to say something trite, but luckily he took the hint. Or more likely, he couldn't wait to get away from the woman who was so unlovable she had been given away like an old coat.

She waited until she heard the door close behind him before she allowed the stupid, stupid tears to fall.

*

That night the Advent calendar revealed a row of Christmas cards strung on a wall. Eleanor quirked an eyebrow at her solitary card and went to bed.

But next morning when she came downstairs there was a card on the mat from Fred and Kasper, which made her smile. And when she went shopping the greengrocer also gave her a card. Even though Eleanor knew she probably wrote them to all her customers, she was touched.

When she popped into Miss Moonshine's, to buy a box of cards to reciprocate, the old lady also had a card for her, a delicate watercolour by a local artist, picturing a canal boat with a border collie on deck, wearing a Santa hat.

'The artist's name is Laura. She does them especially for me,' Miss Moonshine said proudly.

At home the postman had been and Eleanor found even more cards on the mat. From her agent and publisher. Her publisher had forwarded some from her growing band of fans, too. Others had been hand delivered by the neighbours. There were more than enough to hang up.

She put the shopping away. Fed the cat. Took a carrot out to Kasper. Made some chocolate brownies. All the while, she kept thinking about calling Tom and all the while she just kept putting it off. Until she opened the calendar and found three little stockings hanging on a mantelpiece. Did this mean the baby had arrived? Before she could talk herself out of it, she picked up the phone.

'Oh. It's you.' Tom sounded disappointed and immediately apologised. 'Sorry, Ellie. I was expecting the insurance company. Wait – you don't know! Baby Nicolas arrived safe and sound last night!'

Eleanor was delighted and told him so. 'But why were you expecting the insurance company?'

Tom sighed. 'We've had a disaster. We took the kids to see Father Christmas yesterday. Kim had been sneakily eating the decorations off the tree and was covered in chocolate, so I sent her upstairs to wash her hands. She left the tap running and the plug in the sink. While we were out, Mhairi went into labour. We only had time to drop the kids off at a friend's house and rush to the hospital. Anyway, by the time I got home last night the kitchen ceiling had come down and the bathroom and stair carpet are sodden. No way can I bring Mhairi and the baby home to this. We can go to her mum and dad in Cornwall, but it's some drive at this time of year, never mind travelling with a new baby and a load of Christmas presents. And the kids are worried Santa won't know where to find them if we're so far away.'

Eleanor could feel his despair. Her heart was pounding. The words were in her mouth, but still something held her back. Tom would sort it out. The insurance company would put them up in a hotel.

At Christmas? Who was she kidding? Even if they had a room, what would they do with a baby and two young children in a hotel on Christmas morning?

She glanced at the calendar, at the three little stockings and took a deep breath. 'You could come here.'

'What?'

'I have room,' she said. 'Come here. Stay for Christmas. All of you.'

'Are you sure?' Tom whooped. 'Thanks, Ellie. Wait till I tell Mhairi. She's done nothing but cry and worry. Kids, we're going to Auntie Eleanor's for Christmas! Yes, Santa will definitely find us there but to be sure, we'll leave a note.'

When Eleanor put the phone down her heart was racing. What on earth had she done?

*

Next morning Eleanor hurried to Miss Moonshine's, where she had noticed a display of beautiful, hand-embroidered Christmas stockings. Her heart sank when she saw the shelf was empty, but Miss Moonshine saved the day by remembering she still had a few in the back of the shop. 'A few' turned out to be exactly three.

Eleanor clutched them. 'My family are coming for Christmas,' she said. The words sounded so natural, but they were so very not.

'That's nice,' said Miss Moonshine.

'My sister-in-law has just had a baby.'

Miss Moonshine beamed. 'Then that teddy bear you're knitting will come in handy.'

Eleanor frowned. 'How do you know I'm knitting a teddy bear?'

'Er… you bought some ribbon the other day. Didn't you say that was for a teddy bear?'

Had she? She supposed she must have.

Next stop was the supermarket. Eleanor chose her usual small trolley then returned it for a monster one. She was struggling to release it when she heard a familiar voice.

'You must have a healthy appetite.'

She turned to see Dylan, jacket zipped, scarf fastened, his breath frosty white in the morning air.

'Tom and Mhairi and the kids are coming. With the new baby. For Christmas.' She could hear the slight edge of hysteria in her voice.

So could he, apparently. 'Do you need a hand?'

'Oh, yes please.' She almost wept with relief. 'I have absolutely no idea what to buy. Except it must be a lot.' She eyed all the other harassed shoppers struggling to control overloaded trolleys.

'Coffee first,' instructed Dylan, guiding her gently in the direction of the café. 'We should start with a list.'

He sat Eleanor at a table and fished a notepad and a stub of pencil out of the pocket of his plaid shirt. While Christmas music played he went off to get their drinks, and Eleanor stared helplessly at the notepad. For her, Christmas day usually involved a ready meal, a bottle of good wine and a new book. She had never cooked a Christmas dinner in her life.

When Dylan returned and saw the blank page, he took the notebook from her and licked the end of the pencil. 'Right. I'm assuming turkey and all the trimmings?'

She nodded, having already established with Tom that no one was vegetarian.

'There should still be time to order a turkey from the butcher. And of course you'll need food for tonight and tomorrow, too. What about a bottle of champagne to wet the baby's head?'

Eleanor nodded, grateful for any and all suggestions. With the list completed, they set off bravely into the crowded shop. They worked from the list, but neither was averse to some impulse buying. Eleanor added a table runner to the trolley. Dylan added crackers. She also chose some nice festive table mats, for a moment picturing her dining room beautifully decorated with greenery and candles. The warm glow this image brought lasted all of ten seconds before the panic returned.

'Relax,' said Dylan. 'Look.' He picked up a magazine which promised a 'Christmas Dinner Countdown with recipes and timings'.

'When will I get time to read it?'

'Good point,' he conceded. 'Listen, I could come round and help you cook. If you like. I mean, I don't mind.'

Relief flooded through her once more. 'Oh, please. Please do.' Then she remembered he was talking about Christmas dinner. 'But what about your own family?'

He smiled as he helped her load the shopping into her car. 'I'll be going to my sister's, but they prefer to eat in the evening, so it's no problem.'

Eleanor smiled back and discovered she was really looking forward to Christmas.

Tom and family arrived in the afternoon, the kids racing around in a flurry of excitement and yelling and shushing from their parents. Mhairi looked tired but radiant as she showed off baby Nicolas.

Tom brought their bags in. 'This is a great house,' he said, and Eleanor felt guilty that she hadn't invited them before.

The promise of kittens caused much excitement, and when the children heard she had a donkey too, they almost passed out with delight.

'Can we ride him? Can we feed him? Ple-e-ease, Auntie Eleanor?'

'They'll never want to leave,' laughed Tom.

The house was filled with noise and laughter and movement. While Tom and Mhairi settled their new addition, Eleanor, under Holly's watchful eye, introduced the children to the kittens, explaining how gentle they had to be, that the kittens were still babies.

'But they can walk,' said Kim. 'Not like Nicolas.' It was clear to Eleanor that the hype around having a new baby brother was not living up to expectations.

'Maybe Nicolas will be climbing the curtains by next Christmas,' she said, rescuing Prancer for the umpteenth time, and the two children rolled on the floor giggling.

Kim and Toby had brought their own Advent calendars with them and were not impressed by Eleanor's calendar. Before going to bed that night Eleanor opened tomorrow's door and found a sledge. So she wasn't surprised to be woken next morning by excited squeals and shrieks.

'It's snowing!'

Over breakfast Kim and Toby begged to go sledging.

Mhairi wasn't up to it, of course, and Tom had to drive home and somehow smuggle the kids' Christmas presents back to the house, so Eleanor bravely offered to take them.

She immediately phoned Dylan. 'Where can I buy sledges?' she whispered.

'Nowhere,' he said cheerfully. 'You need to buy them before the snow starts or they'll all be sold out. But don't worry. I'm sure I have some in the garage. I'm not working today. I can bring them round if you like, and show you where the local kids sledge.'

'How did it go last night?' he asked when he arrived.

'Good,' she said happily. 'Tom and I did the cooking. We had fish fingers. And the ice cream and jelly went down well, so thanks for the suggestion.'

And afterwards, Eleanor had sat at the fire, finishing her knitting, as she listened contentedly to the sounds of a full-to-bursting house settling down for the evening.

Eleanor had never been sledging in her life. It was so much fun and she laughed more than was decent. All four of them were cold and wet but happy when they arrived home. Mhairi had made warming soup, but Dylan couldn't stay.

'Thanks again for the sledges,' said Eleanor, positioning herself to avoid the knowing looks Mhairi kept throwing her way. 'I am now officially the best aunt in the world.'

'No problem,' said Dylan warmly. 'I had fun.'

It was Christmas Eve. By late afternoon the children were at fever pitch when they suddenly remembered that in the excitement of waking up to snow, they hadn't opened their calendars for today. That occupied them for all of ten seconds and the chocolate did nothing to calm them down. Eleanor opened hers too. Mistletoe.

Mhairi grinned suggestively. 'Pity Dylan's not here.'

Eleanor told herself her cheeks were red from the sledging. She was certainly not blushing.

Everyone was delighted when, late afternoon, a group of carol singers arrived. As they gathered on the front lawn beside the tree, a living enactment of her Advent calendar, Eleanor couldn't help thinking how much her life had changed since that first visit to Miss Moonshine's shop.

The children's Advent calendars finished today, but Eleanor's had one more door for Christmas Day. The bright red front door. With the carol singers belting out 'Ding Dong Merrily', she couldn't wait to see what was behind it.

When the carols were over, she invited everyone in for mince pies and a warming drink. So many of these people she recognised now – Dylan, Miss Moonshine, Fred, the vet. Everyone she knew from the village and many more. Soon she and Tom were busy serving up the Christmas goodies she had bought and the mince pies she had made. It was truly wonderful to have her house so full of friends.

'You look as if you are having a good time,' said Mhairi.

'I am,' she admitted.

Mhairi winked. 'That Dylan might be nice to catch under the mistletoe.'

Eleanor flushed, not denying it. 'Except we don't have any.'

'Ah, but we do. That funny Miss Moonshine person has a basketful. She's pinning it up everywhere.'

Baby Nicolas, who had been placed in a Moses basket in the corner, let out a squawk and Mhairi jumped up. 'My master's voice.' She paused. 'I mean it. That handyman of yours is quite a catch. You'd be mad to let him get away.'

As Mhairi picked the baby up amidst collective oohs and ahhs, Eleanor looked around for Dylan. And saw him under the mistletoe kissing the woman from the pet shop.

She stood, frozen, as it struck her that she knew almost nothing about Dylan. She knew he was a handyman, that he had a mother, a sister and an ex-wife, but that was it. She certainly knew nothing about any romantic attachments.

That peck on the cheek, innocent though it was, drove that home.

Dylan wasn't her handyman. Any more than any of this was hers. The family, the friends, even the donkey and the cats would all disperse after Christmas. The lights would come down and the magic of her Advent calendar would be over. It would be just her. On her own, the way she always had been.

The sense of impending loss hit so hard she couldn't breathe.

She had been stupid. And weak. She had wanted all of this so much that she had let her guard down.

All at once she had to get out. The chatter, the laugher, the heat, the over-excited children were all too much. Eleanor grabbed her jacket and a carrot from the kitchen and slipped out into the cold and silent night. Fresh snow had fallen and she felt it crunch underfoot. The velvety night sky was lit by a thousand stars. Kim could stop worrying; Santa would have no trouble finding his way tonight.

Standing under the ghostly, snow-covered trees, she glanced back at the house. Every window was lit. She could hear someone singing. Miss Moonshine washed dishes at the kitchen window. Despite her mood, Eleanor smiled, marvelling at the old lady's energy.

After a moment she turned and continued to the stable.

'Hi Kasper.' She stroked the donkey's ears as she fed him the carrot. 'I did it again,' she said softly. 'I fell for the dream. The only difference is, this time I'm not moving on. This time I have to stay and watch everyone else leave.'

'What do you mean?' She hadn't heard Dylan approach and she jumped. 'Aren't you enjoying the party?' he asked.

How could she explain she had been enjoying it too much?

'I didn't want old Kasper here to miss out,' she said. But there was a catch in her voice. Immediately Dylan enclosed her in his arms. It felt so good to be held. He was so warm, smelled so familiar. Eleanor allowed herself to relax into his embrace for one, glorious second before she pushed away. 'Shouldn't you be with Laura under the mistletoe?'

Dylan looked at her. 'What's this all about, Eleanor?' he said softly. 'I've known Laura since we were kids. There has never been anything between us. I kissed Miss Moonshine too, and your sister-in-law.'

'I know,' mumbled Eleanor, hating herself. 'I'm sorry. Ignore me. I'm just feeling out of sorts.'

'At Christmas?'

'It's never been a good time for me,' she admitted.

'Tell me.'

She didn't want to. She really didn't. But somehow it all came pouring out. 'Everyone tries so hard at Christmas. It's easy to get swept up in the magic. You let yourself feel happy. You think that this time it will be different. And then you come home one day and your bags are packed and since no one ever explains anything to a child, you never know why.'

Dylan listened keenly but he said nothing.

'I fell for it,' she whispered. 'Every time. I so very much wanted to belong that I fell for it again and again. I let myself be happy…'

Until she just couldn't do it anymore. She had retreated inside herself. Put up her walls and kept them strong. Tom couldn't knock them down, though he had tried. The kids had chipped away at them too, so she'd had to distance herself from them. This past month had chipped away still more.

But come January the emptiness would descend again and this time it would be so much worse.

'You plan to go back to how it was before?' asked Dylan. 'Just you and your empty house?'

'It's not like I have a choice.'

'Of course you have a choice. Will you stop speaking to Fred when Kasper goes home? Not visit Tom and Mhairi or have the kids to stay? Stop shopping at Miss Moonshine's?'

'No, but–'

'Will you stop having tea breaks with me?'

There it was. The one that would hurt the most. 'You won't be here once the stable is finished.'

'The stable has been finished for days, Eleanor,' he said softly. 'I'm just finding work to do, a reason to come out here.'

She looked at him in confusion. 'What? Why?'

He grinned. 'Well it's not Kasper or Fred that brings me here every day.' He turned serious. 'There are people who love you, Eleanor. And people who like you, and animals that need you. I've been talking to Tom. He's as bewildered as you are by your mother's behaviour. But he knows he can torture himself about what else they hid from him or he can get on with his life, making a future for his family. His whole family. But you keep pushing him away. Who else are you pushing away, Eleanor? Because I'm not going anywhere.'

He smiled his crooked smile and held up a sprig of mistletoe. 'I'm staying right here.'

'In the stable?' She managed a watery smile.

'By your side. Tomorrow and as long as you'll have me.'

'But not tonight?'

His smile was the devil's own. 'Much as I might want to, there's too much going on tonight. But I'll see you tomorrow. And I warn you, I'm bringing the mistletoe.'

Eleanor returned to the house on cloud nine. People were beginning to leave, uttering Merry Christmases as they pulled on hats and scarfs and gloves. Miss Moonshine gave Eleanor a knowing look.

'Come for lunch tomorrow,' said Eleanor impulsively.

'Thank you, but I have plans,' said Miss Moonshine. She

hugged Eleanor. 'May this be the best Christmas ever. You deserve it, my dear.'

After everyone had finally gone and the door was closed, Eleanor made a confession. 'I gave the last carrot to Kasper.'

'Then Rudolph will have to settle for sprouts,' said Tom. 'Would you like to help put the kids to bed? For once they're anxious to go to sleep.'

'I'd love that,' said Eleanor

'That Dylan seems a steady sort,' said Tom, his eyes full of questions.

'Mmmm.' Eleanor was non-committal, but she couldn't stop smiling.

Once the children were asleep and Tom and Mhairi had filled their stockings and set out their gifts under the tree, they too went to bed, knowing they faced a disturbed night with the baby as well as an early start.

Eleanor locked up. She peeked through the curtains at the lamp-post and the tree. She checked the fireguard. Made sure the turkey was protected from the cats. Her teddy bear was finished and wrapped, along with the doll and a wooden train set from Miss Moonshine's.

She approached the fireplace and picked up her calendar. Drawing a deep breath, she opened the red front door.

A man and a woman stood in the doorway. He had an arm around her shoulders and she was showing a tiny baby to the carol singers on the lawn.

It wasn't Tom and Mhairi or even Mary and Joseph. The man had a plaid shirt and jeans. The woman wore glasses and the baby had a pink headband.

Eleanor and Dylan and…?

She had no idea. But the house knew. The house would look after her and guide her. No. Not the house.

Her forever home.

Living on the edge of the Yorkshire moors, Jacqui Cooper doesn't have to look far for inspiration for her writing. Her short stories regularly appear in popular women's magazines, including *Woman's Weekly*, *The People's Friend* and *Take a Break*. Writing has always been her dream and she is thrilled to now be able to do it full time.

ABOUT THE AUTHORS

Christmas at Miss Moonshine's Emporium is an anthology put together by a group of romantic novelists and short story writers from Yorkshire and Lancashire in the north of England. The group meet regularly in the little town of Hebden Bridge, and this location, lying as it does on the moors near the border between the two counties, led to the group name Authors on the Edge, and to the inspiration behind this collection.

Many mince pies were consumed by these authors in the making of this anthology.

Top: Mary Jayne Baker, Sophie Claire, Jacqui Cooper
Middle: Helena Fairfax, Kate Field, Melinda Hammond
Bottom: Marie Laval, Helen Pollard, Angela Wren

More by the Authors on the Edge...

Miss Moonshine's Emporium of Happy Endings

Sometimes what you need is right there waiting for you...

Miss Moonshine's Wonderful Emporium has stood in the pretty Yorkshire town of Haven Bridge for as long as anyone can remember. With her ever-changing stock, Miss Moonshine has a rare gift for providing exactly what her customers need: a fire opal necklace that provides a glimpse of a different life; a novel whose phantom doodler casts a spell over the reader; a music box whose song links love affairs across the generations.

One thing is for certain: after visiting Miss Moonshine's quirky shop, life is never the same again...

* * * * *

Thank you so much for reading *Christmas at Miss Moonshine's Emporium.* We hope you enjoyed our collection of stories. If you did, please consider telling your friends or posting a short review on Amazon or Goodreads. Word of mouth is an author's best friend, and much appreciated!

Merry Christmas!

Printed in Great Britain
by Amazon